Nicholas
Monsarrat

❖

THIS IS
THE SCHOOLROOM

Deus est mortali juvare mortalem,
Et haec ad aeternam gloriam via.

**HOUSE OF
STRATUS**

Nicholas Monsarrat was born in Liverpool in 1910, the son of a distinguished surgeon. He was educated at Winchester, then at Trinity College, Cambridge, where he studied law. He gave up law to earn a meagre living as a freelance journalist while he began writing novels. His first novel to receive significant attention was *This is the Schoolroom* (1939). It is a largely autobiographical 'coming of age' novel dealing with the end of college life, the 'Hungry Thirties', and the Spanish Civil War.

During World War Two he served in the Royal Navy in corvettes in the North Atlantic. These experiences were used in his best-known novel, *The Cruel Sea* (1951) and made into a film starring Jack Hawkins.

In 1946, he became a director of the UK Information Service, first in Johannesburg, then in Ottawa. Other well-known novels include *The Kapillan of Malta*, *The Tribe That Lost Its Head*, and its sequel, *Richer Than All His Tribe*, and *The Story of Esther Costello*.

He died in August 1979 as he was writing the second part of his intended three-volume novel on seafaring life from Napoleonic times to the present, *The Master Mariner*.

To LEWIS CLIVE
The Ebro River, August 1938

AUTHOR'S NOTES

1. Such 'history' as is included in this book may be judged by some to be tendentious to a degree. This is no accident: it is indeed natural and inevitable, partiality in one form or another being a major product of the Schoolroom.

2. Any reference to anarchism, communism, socialism, liberalism, conservatism, atheism, christian-socialism, christianity, jewry, fascism, mammon and unrighteousness must be understood as personal interpretations, on the part of the various characters, of these several creeds. They are no more official declarations of policy than the Living Skeleton or the Bearded Lady are official specimens of the human being. But as a footnote to this disclaimer it may be added that I have never seen anything inherently vicious in being *plus royaliste que le roi*.

Part One
Play
PAGE 1

Part Two
Politics
PAGE 103

Part Three
Personal
PAGE 345

Part Four
Tendency to a Design
PAGE 427

PART ONE

❖

Play

CHAPTER ONE

I remember, I remember ...

❖

I was unusually drunk the night my father died.

That was the autumn term of 1935, and I remember coming out of the Pitt Club into Jesus Lane with Charles Terrington and Archie van Tyler and some others – we'd all been to Newmarket, and Alastair had had three winners off the reel, and to celebrate we'd had one of those lovely pointless dinners that go on and on and infuriate the waiters till they start to mutter and fidget with the lights. (Not that they could do much about it, though, because Archie was so stinking rich he could have sold the place up between hiccoughs and put them out in the street. I suppose that was true of me too.) Cambridge seemed swell that night, and it wasn't only alcohol interpreting – even moderate work was about six months ahead of me, I'd just finished being gated for a week, I'd made money at the races, Alison had written that she was going to take a flat not in London but just down the road at Newmarket. (We'd only just started, we were still in the thick of it, still fighting to get at each other. When we touched each other we would flare up like the first discoverers of lust.)

3

Outside it was raining a thin drizzle, but that didn't seem to matter because the street lamps looked so grand, all blurry, and I've always loved the rain in my hair – you don't feel it at first and then suddenly it comes through and your whole scalp tingles and goes cold. I stood enjoying it, and then there was a noise which I thought was Archie paying the bill (he couldn't add, and he loved an argument anyway), but it was somebody else shouting for me to come back. I didn't think I could manage the steps again, so I waited to make sure.

A voice behind, in the hall, called out: "Marcus."

That was certainly me, so I said "Yes" but not too loudly, because the whole thing might blow over and I'd be saved the trouble.

There ensued one of those shifting slurring conversations that you can join in anywhere, without listening.

"Marcus. Marco. Are you there?"

"Yes."

"Marco."

"I'm here. What is it?"

"The man wants you."

I thought this over. Then: "No he doesn't. He can't do."

"The man wants you, Marcus."

"No man wants me. I'm fixed with Alison. Everyone knows that."

"There's a message for you."

"Men don't want me. It's Charles he wants. Try Charles."

That got a laugh from the others, because it was fairly true: Charles did like chaps: he used to tour the Cathedral cities, pretending it was architecture.

"I swear there's a message. You've got to come back."

Then the porter came down and touched me on the arm, and said: "Mr Hendrycks."

That was so pointless that it made me angry.

4

"You know damned well I'm Mr Hendrycks. What *is* this? Why don't people trust me tonight?"

But he only smiled. He was about fifty: he'd been dealing with drunks and difficulties for thirty years: he was probably sick of it, but he knew exactly what to do.

"I'm sorry, sir. The light's a little difficult out here … It's your porters' lodge on the telephone, sir."

"Did they say what?"

"No, sir." He turned to go in again, rather cleverly, not leaving me any choice. "I'll tell them you're coming, sir."

It looked as though I'd have to go in after all. "What's the time?" I said. "What do they want me for now?"

"Ten." That was Charles out in the road, looking up and trying to identify some stars. "Which is Orion, Marco? There's nothing that looks like a belt here."

"I wouldn't know. Venus is the only one I can tell. It's the one you take girls out to see during parties in August. It's a good star. It's the best there is. What does the porters' lodge want me for at ten o'clock?"

"Probably Murray wants you to have coffee with him."

That got another laugh (extraordinary how easily we laughed in those days): Murray was my tutor, and it was fairly clear that I couldn't have managed him at that moment. I couldn't really have managed anything: if the whole Senate wanted me – if it was God and the Vice-Chancellor arm-in-arm – they'd have had to wait till I'd got a good grip, about three hours later.

I went up the steps, cursing. Archie was wandering about the hall trying to find a better gown than the one he had brought in. He said: "Marcus, the man wants you."

"I know."

"Telephone for Mr Hendrycks, please."

"Coming."

I got stuck going into the box, but they straightened it out nicely and shut the door with me inside. Say what you like, those porters were clever at that sort of thing. They had to be.

A very tinny voice said: "Is that Mr Hendrycks?"

"Yes. What's the matter?"

"There's a telegram for you, sir. I thought I'd better try to reach you."

"Oh," I said, surprised. Vaguely I had been expecting some kind of official trimming. "Thanks. Will you read it out?"

"Very good, sir." I heard, faintly, the envelope tearing, and then he started to read: " 'Marcus Hendrycks, Trinity College, Cambridge.' "

I said: "All right, I know that part," but of course by that time he'd finished. The little box was very hot and stank a bit: I shifted about, wanting him to hurry up so that I could get out.

But he didn't read any more: instead he said in quite a different voice: "I'm afraid it's bad news, sir."

I jumped, hurting my elbow. "What? Who's it from? Is it signed 'Alison'? Is it from a Miss Erroll?"

"No, sir. It's signed 'Armstrong'. It's about your father."

"Oh." There was a solicitor called Armstrong. I didn't know any others. "What's he want?"

Archie was knocking on the window of the box, making faces that he was tired of waiting. I signalled to him to keep quiet.

"I'd better read it out, sir. I'm very sorry." He put his voice into quotes, and read: " 'Much regret father died this evening. Suggest you come down tomorrow. Armstrong.' ... That's all, sir."

I said "Oh" again. I couldn't deal properly with the news at all. Dinner had got there first.

"Are you all right, sir?"

"Me? Yes, fine."

But even at the impact I was struck by the singular unfairness of my being drunk when the news came through. There was no earthly reason why it should have happened just at that moment: it wasn't as if I was liquored up every hour of the day and night, because that was no longer true. There were lots of times, sober times, when I might have been told about him, and could have reacted properly and been sorry. As it was, I couldn't manage anything except a stagger and one of the sillier sorts of grin.

Of course we'd hated each other ever since the divorce, but still it meant a lot one way and another, even apart from the money which I was just about ready for. (Everything seemed to cost double, that last year at Cambridge. And of course there were the first two years' bills beginning to come in, too.)

I hung up. Archie was still hammering on the box, automatically, hardly knowing I was there; when I opened the door I nearly knocked him over. He said: "Why do you always take so long? You'll see the girl tomorrow. Give yourself a rest."

We went out into the street together. There was a ring of people waiting under the lamp: Rhys-Evans was trying to crack a whip and not making a sound.

"What was it?" said Charles to me. "Was it Murray?"

"No," I said. "My father's dead."

There was a silence, and then the whip cracked suddenly, so that we all laughed; and then there was silence again.

I couldn't tell whether anyone was embarrassed or not: the rain in my eyes made their faces blurred, gave everything a sort of up-and-down halo, as if the light were leaking and splashing out of them. I couldn't even tell whether everyone had heard me, because there were people passing and damned cars going past being revved at least two gears too low, the way people used to drive them. So I said again: "My father's dead."

"Did you like him?" asked Charles.

"No."

"Oh, well then ..."

That was inclined to annoy me, of course, his taking it like that and being offhand about it: it wasn't a thing that happened every day, and if I couldn't be properly sorry at least the others could give it some attention. So I sat down on one of the steps and began to be fairly rude to him.

Presently he cut in: "I'm not a pansy." He was tough, about six feet, fair hair, boxer's chest with great slabs of muscles on it: you could see his triceps flexing under his coat-sleeves. "Don't call me a pansy," he repeated, swaying towards me and then back again. "You should look out what you call a chap. I'm a — "

He explained what he was, shortly: he repeated it over and over again, getting louder and louder, till a man across the road in the shadows shouted: "We can tell that. Why don't you shut up?"

Charles wanted to go over and fight him, but he'd got into a fit of blinking and couldn't see properly. Instead, he sat down beside me on the step and said:

"Marcus, go and cut that chap's guts out for me."

"Sorry," I said, "I wouldn't know what to do with them when I'd got them. Can't you stop blinking?"

"I like it." He was growing a bit sad: he'd been drinking gin, which has a lowering stage very hard to get past. "I don't know what he wanted to be rude to me for: I only said – "

He took up his little chorus again, so insistently that we all had to join in. It went rather well to the *William Tell* overture, rendered as one of those fake operatic quartets where everyone plays his own hand and you can plough any furrow you like as long as you're in at the finish ...

Round about us windows began to bang upwards; a policeman on the corner looked away, pretending not to hear; a couple of tarts started to chi-ike us and then shut up suddenly. Alastair said "Progs!" and backed into the Pitt again: two top hats appeared suddenly under the nearest lamp, surging round Rhys-Evans: and the rest of us followed Alastair, making less noise but still rather a lot.

They didn't seem very glad to see us inside: they said they were just shutting the place up; they shuffled chairs and clicked lights to prove it. Archie gave a man several pounds, but it didn't make any difference: he just took them, and then looked grimmer than ever. It was clear that we had to move on somewhere, and equally clear that we didn't want to break up the party by going back into college. (Charles, Alastair and I were Trinity, Archie was Magdalene, Rhys-Evans Caius, Peter Tresham and another rather vague man Trinity Hall. It would have meant the total wreckage of the evening.) But Rhys-Evans had rooms in Jesus Lane, and a venal landlord with a squint: so when he came back from his interview with the proctor we said: "We're playing poker, on you."

He said "All right." He looked a bit depressed: that was the fifth time that term that he'd been pounced on for not wearing a gown, and probably he'd be gated as well as fined.

Actually his landlord was inclined to waver at the sight of Rhys-Evans standing on the doorstep with six near-drunks and wanting to bring them all in: we probably did look an uninhibited lot and I dare say his squint didn't help either to tone us down or make us look a smaller party. We had to have a whip-round then and there, at five shillings each, and hand the pool over to him before he'd consent to the inrush; and even then he muttered and looked up and down the road as if he were letting in a gang of safe blowers. And of course Archie, who was inclined when feeling whimsical to wipe his nose on ten-pound notes and then throw them on the fire, kicked up the most awful fuss about paying and said five bob was iniquitous and how about a reduction for quantity. But old Munnings just looked him up and down with both eyes one after the other, and said: "Mr van Tyler, this is my living, just the same as widows and orphans are your dad's."

After that Archie kept quiet. And of course, in common with the rest of us, he hoped to get his five bob back on the first hand.

For undergraduates I suppose we played fairly high poker: half a crown ante, and a five-quid limit on the rises. It was all right for me because I always held the cards anyway, and had the kind of transparent expression which people mistake for extreme guile and stake up accordingly. It was all right for the others, too, because they had bank balances to suit. Only the Trinity Hall man, a rubbery little chap with a big rowing reputation, seemed a weak spot – he was indeed so prudent about staking and so downcast over his losses that he must have been well out of his class financially. I think that by and by we all noticed this, and it made those of us who could react feel rather uncomfortable.

I remember it was about one o'clock that the fight started. I'd missed about three hands in succession, thinking about a time somewhere near my seventeenth birthday, before my father was divorced, when he'd taken a villa at Antibes for the summer and the whole family had settled down to enjoy themselves. The parents even shared a room, which they never did at home. My sister was in love with Max Brennan then, and as he had come out to be with her she wasn't much in evidence except at mealtimes; but father and mother and I used to go on grand expeditions together, by car inland or sometimes hiring a little sailing-boat and going down the coast. I got very brown and fit – and of course there was Christine that year, the first love affair of mine that left a true sensual imprint: I could recall its quality minutely even at that moment, a flowing impression of laughter always shared and kisses never withheld, of the sweetness and secrecy of love which had to be hidden from the adult world, of whispering to our moonlight shadows on the sand, of hands clasping for the first time, the physical reality of countless daydreams, countless images of desire. She was a little older than I was, fresh and delicately eager and cunning in her enjoyment.

At that point I decided to stop remembering and go back to the game, because, though the memory of Christine didn't hurt, yet it consorted very badly with the thick atmosphere of that smoky little room, the spilt liquor, the stacks of ivory chips, the circle of flushed or noisy or heavy-breathing players. I poured a drink and swallowed half of it quickly, so that I could stop being aware of and disliking my surroundings; then I gave my attention to the game, which, as it happened, had suddenly become interesting.

They must have had a round of jackpots without anyone opening, because there was a good deal of money in the pool, about two pounds. Archie had just opened and made it five shillings to play: two other people came in – Stephenson the rowing man and Peter Tresham. Alastair was meant to be dealing, but showed signs of falling asleep. So I took the cards from him and prepared to dish them out.

"How many, Archie?"

"I'll stand."

There was no expression in his voice at all. I winked at him.

"I believe you," I said. "Cards, Peter?"

"Three, please, Marcus."

"You'll need them."

Stephenson took one, and looked quite happy about it.

When the betting opened Archie checked – i.e. did not bet but reserved the right to come in later. I imagined that he had a poor hand and wanted to get the strength of the others. Peter bid five shillings, fairly confidently, and Stephenson raised him to fifteen. That sounded promising, as Peter was looking pleased with his cards, and Stephenson, who had become increasingly cautious as the evening went on, probably held something good. But now came a surprise, because Archie, who I thought must have opened on a pair of Jacks and would be scared out, suddenly woke up and raised them another pound.

Trying to read the hand as I would have done if I'd been in on it, I calculated that Peter had improved to three of a kind, that Stephenson had two good pairs or possibly a full house, and that Archie was bluffing. (He might even not have looked at his cards: vodka sometimes took him that way.) At any rate it was thirty-five shillings to find out, and Peter, who was already five pounds down on the evening, wavered. He looked at his cards, and then turned to me.

"Is he lying, Marcus?"

Archie cut in, fairly roughly. "Play your own hand, Peter. Marco isn't in on this round."

That convinced me that he was bluffing: he wasn't usually anxious, and didn't mind talking. But Peter's nerve didn't last out: he shook his head, said: "I think he's got something," and threw in.

That left Stephenson, who I thought would be scared away too; and Archie thought so as well, because he stretched out his hand to collect the pool. But Stephenson didn't throw in: he stared across at Archie, made up his stake to thirty-five shillings, and said with a bit of a break in his voice: "Raise you three pounds."

It was the right bet, of course, because by now there was six quid in the pool: but it still came as a bit of a shock. I remember that moment quite well, and the quick increase of tension that it brought, as if someone had suddenly switched on a searchlight which filled every corner of the odd landladyish room with its aspidistra and baize cloth and the smoke and heat of the game. All of us were affected by it: Rhys-Evans looked up quickly, and delayed putting on another record; Charles laughed and leant forward, elbows on the table; Peter said "I'm glad I'm out of this," and pushed his forfeited chips further into the pool. Only the two chief actors confronted each other without moving. Archie looked bored with the whole thing, and I suddenly felt rather sorry for Stephenson – I could see by his eyes that he was as nervous as hell, I realized that he literally could not afford to lose so much on one hand, and I know that Archie was drunk, didn't give a damn for losing, and would probably get away with the swag by sheer weight of money.

As he made no comment, Stephenson repeated: "Raise you three pounds."

Archie leant forward, as if taking an interest for the first time in something hardly worth his attention. "Put it in," he said. It was an offensive remark in any case, and the tone he used didn't improve it.

Stephenson flushed. "I haven't got enough chips. I'll owe it." He was too worked up, and too keen on winning, to quarrel with Archie: he wanted nothing to go wrong, he wanted the hand over and done with and the pool pushed across to him.

Archie laughed. He really was in a rough mood. "Think you're going to get it back in a minute? Got some good cards? Well, so have I." He frowned viciously. "I'll equalize," he threw in a handful of chips without counting them, "and I'll raise you another five."

For us, this was real betting, and it made a corresponding sensation: the five of us who were not playing the hand

13

closed in on the centre as if it might slip away before we had fully taken it in. But the effect on Stephenson was pitiful: I was sitting just opposite him and I saw him start, and shiver, and then lick his lips as if he'd been caught red-handed in something which would cost him his neck. He certainly was in a poor position: he knew he had good cards, and yet an extra five pounds was far more than he could afford. And if he raised again Archie would see him for certain, simply out of curiosity: and by now he was probably convinced that Archie had not been bluffing when he took no extra cards and had picked up a first-class hand. And yet, if he threw in now he would lose all his stake, nearly five pounds, besides what was in the pool … Finally he looked at his cards again, and they seemed to cheer him up, because he put his head back immediately and said: "I'll see you."

Everyone looked at Archie, who seemed to be in no hurry to show. First he frowned, then he peered at his cards, then he leant over and examined the full house from every angle he could. In fact he behaved maddeningly. Finally he sat back with an iniquitous grin, and said: "Not good enough."

And began to rake the pile of chips towards him.

Stephenson flushed. "What have you got?" he said uncertainly. "For God's sake stop playing the fool and show your hand."

Archie put down three nines very slowly, one after another.

"Well?" asked Stephenson.

Archie put down a Jack. He was behaving lousily: however much he'd had to drink, he must have known the torture that the other man was going through. Presently, still smiling, he put down a fourth nine, and said: "That'll be eight quid."

I think Stephenson would have been able to take it reasonably well, in spite of the shock, if Archie had behaved like a normal person instead of playing with him; but the cat-and-mouse manoeuvre was too much for him, and as it was he nearly broke down altogether. Probably he couldn't believe his eyes at first, or take in the significance of the four nines; and then he gave a horrible sort of gasp and flopped back in his chair like a woman trying not to faint. Presently he looked down at the cards again, and then at the huge pile of chips opposite Archie, greedily, as if he wondered what would happen if he snatched the lot and made for the door. I felt extremely sorry for him and livid with Archie for playing on his nerves like that.

But there was more to come; for after a moment Archie asked, with a faint sneer: "Have you eight pounds on you?"

There was a pause. Then: "No. No, I haven't. I'll write you a cheque." He fumbled in his breast pocket. "I don't usually carry that much money about with me. And I owe for my chips as well."

"Why not leave it till the end of the game?" remarked Peter helpfully. "You'll probably get some of it back."

Stephenson looked up at him mildly, without expression of any sort: I could see that his mind was far away, thinking of his overdraft or his bills or his parents who couldn't afford things on this scale …

"I'm afraid I'll have to go now," he said at length. "That hand has about cleaned me out."

"Oh – sorry."

He began to write a cheque, but stopped as Archie muttered something under his breath.

"What did you say?"

"I said," Archie told him truculently, "that it's not my fault if I win a hand."

"Nobody said it was."

"Then don't whine about paying."

I told Archie to shut up. I knew the mood he was in, and the extraordinarily crude sort of remark he'd be making in a minute. But Stephenson himself cut in: "Let him say it if it amuses him. I don't mind." He turned back to writing the cheque.

His coolness caught Archie on the raw, and he shouted out: "If you can't stand the stakes, don't come in. Rushing off in the middle of the game like this – it's too damned childish."

Without saying anything Stephenson passed the cheque over. Archie took it between his finger and thumb as if it smelt, looked at the figures, and drawled out: "I suppose this is all right?"

Silence. I think most of us frowned, wondering why Archie was being so fantastically offensive. Then Stephenson said very quietly: "Just because you've more money than you know what to do with, just because you stink of it, that doesn't give you the right to sneer at me."

"It gives me the only real right there is." At that moment, full of alcohol, he probably believed that. He stared across at Stephenson, and then he made a remark which the more I thought of it the bloodier it sounded. He said: "The van Tylers hate poor people."

That was pretty thick even for Archie (who having about a million quid in his current account naturally came out with some stingers in the way of insults now and then). No one in the room was within a hundred miles of being on his side: and the fact that the two of them started fighting a moment later came as the only possible relief.

As a scrap it was a good murder, since Stephenson was in reasonable training and immensely strong in the arms and shoulders, while Archie was soft with drink and a lot of other things, and probably hadn't made a prolonged physical effort since sitting through his Confirmation. At all events Stephenson certainly took his eight pounds' worth. They wrestled for a matter of seconds, overturning chairs and pulling the cloth and all the chips off the table: then Stephenson got in a short arm body-blow that doubled Archie up, and followed it with a hook under his ear that knocked him senseless. As he was toppling over, Stephenson threw in one more jab and split his eyebrow open right to the bone. That appeared to complete the sequence: Archie lay on the hearthrug pouring blood in a flow surprisingly regular, Stephenson gathered up his gown and left without a word, sucking his knuckles, and the rest of us burst into a roar of laughter which the entrance of old Munnings and his wife, both in furry dressing-gowns, brought to an ecstatic climax. That was just the way things were meant to happen: unexpectedly, colourfully, and before anyone who might have been so inclined could have said 'Jack Robinson'.

But after a bit we had to face the realities of the situation, because Munnings was standing there as black as thunder, and Archie showed no signs of stirring and indeed looked cheaper every minute. Mrs Munnings of course ran true to type, flopping on her knees beside the body, trying to stop the blood with a feminine sort of handkerchief, and gabbling protests over her shoulder at the ring of assassins round about. Her dressing-gown gaped everywhere, but we all tried not to look. Not that any of it was particularly rewarding.

"Oh the poor young gentleman!" she began wildly. "Whatever's been happening? We want no fighting in this house. And Mr van Tyler wouldn't hurt a fly, either. Just look at it all over the carpet! Munnings, run down and fetch some hot water and a towel."

"What, one of *our* towels? No bloody fear." He really was in a towering rage. "Them as spills the blood ought to mop it up. We don't run a private slaughterhouse for you young bastards here."

"Get on with you and don't argue." She pushed her hair back and bent over Archie. Munnings swore again, but for all his rage he was under her thumb, as always, and presently he turned and went out. I dare say also that he had started to add the thing up and work out what his cut would be.

There was silence in the room after he'd left, Mrs Munnings doing her best with the handkerchief and the rest of us lounging about feeling defeated: for all we knew, Archie was dead and we were in God's own tangle. I was reading Law, too, and knew all about manslaughter and contributory negligence and accessories-before-the-fact (I mean, I knew there *were* such words), and though I was rather too hazy to work out the details I could see that the evening might have something more than the usual hangover. One could even start to make up the headlines: UNDERGRADUATE DEATH FALL SENSATION MYSTERY – Mrs Munnings cut in on a promising soliloquy: "You ought to be ashamed of yourselves, standing round and letting a thing like this happen. You'd all be up in the courts if I had my way. Which of you did it?"

"It was suicide," said Charles heavily. "We couldn't stop him."

"Suicide!" She dropped Archie's head plonk on to the carpet, whereupon he woke up and said: "Hey! Careful with that."

"Are you better now, sir?" asked Mrs Munnings.

"No," said Archie, and closed his eyes. I don't know why: he must have had a superb view.

After that we stopped taking the thing seriously and began to guy everything. Rhys-Evans dug up *Pavane pour une Infante défunte* and put it on the gramophone: Peter Tresham and Alastair started a cross-talk in which every third sentence was "The van Tylers hate poor people." Soon the phrase began to sound funny instead of merely sickening. Of course we were all extremely relieved that Archie still had the breath of life in him.

Presently Munnings came in with a bowl of water and some towels. He was a good deal behind the times, starting straight away with: "It's criminal, that's what it is. Just look at that wound. And what about my licence?"

"It's all right," I said. "He's alive, and it's only a little cut."

He began to get in a rage again, but I said "Listen" in an oily sort of voice and drew him to one side. Then I counted out ten pounds, and said: "I'm sorry about the carpet. You'd better get it cleaned."

I had calculated that it would be easier to take his breath away at the beginning than to start haggling over the price of wounds, and I was right: he set to and helped his wife to clean up the mess, without saying another word. Archie woke up, felt his forehead, and with admirable calmness remarked: "I think this ought to be stitched."

He had sobered up completely. We all gathered round and looked at the cut: it had stopped bleeding, but it certainly gaped a bit, especially when he shut his eye.

"He better go to Addenbrookes," said Charles. "I'll call a taxi."

"Better by car," Peter cut in. "Otherwise it'll be in all the papers. Who's got a car handy?"

Alastair's was in a garage not far away. It would be dangerous knocking them up at that time of night, but we told him to risk it and he went off. Peter said good night and went with him, on his way to climb into Trinity Hall; Charles and I supported Archie to the door and stood waiting. It was a cold night, but clear and moonlit; while we were hanging about in the doorway staring at the trees and the sky Rhys-Evans came up from the cellar with a bottle of champagne, which we took from him saying it might be useful later on but not at that moment;

whereupon he went up to bed, somewhat confused and that much the poorer.

Presently the car came round, piloted by Alastair looking conspiratorial in a dark muffler. Earlier on I wouldn't have said he was fit to drive, but the fight had sobered us all up and he was probably quite trustworthy. In addition to starting to bleed again, Archie had gone vague and was muttering and asking to be told what had happened; we even had difficulty in getting him into the car, because he turned nasty on the doorstep and accused us of kidnapping and a lot more besides, but finally we stowed him away in the back seat, with Charles lying across his chest and me dabbing at his eyebrow with the cloth for wiping the windscreen. (The champagne was also very carefully cherished, wrapped in a rug on the floor.) On the way to the hospital Archie was sick: Alastair said it was a good sign, but I couldn't see the connection myself. At all events we delivered him over to an unimpressed night porter and then sped away, in the best foundling-on-the-doorstep tradition. He could sleep the night there, and by morning would be able to make up his own story – he had had years of practice, and in any case could have bought himself out of a situation a hundredfold more delicate. Without a doubt, money was specifically invented to grace and grease such slipways as these.

I don't know why I can recall the details of that night so minutely: I suppose because it was the last night of Cambridge, or of my life either, that was consistent with the manner of my upbringing. Not that I'd been poker-playing and swilling vodka and mopping blood for twenty-one years on end: but up to that very night things had been secure and settled for me – I was, without effort or hesitation on my part, one of the young company which went from public school to University, and then to a year abroad, to the Bar or to some smooth money-spinning job in the City, at the same leisurely pace which had ruled the years of childhood. I was following that track because it was the one wholly natural to my world, because any other sort of track, any elaboration or omission (save a detour via one of the services), was unacceptable in that it made for embarrassment at nearly every turn – and particularly so in the holidays, when young men, if they were to visit and ornament the great houses of England, must be of this mould and no other ... It needed neither sustained work nor specific merit, but only a bank account and perhaps good manners. No crisis, no sense of sharpening reality could affect it: it was, and would remain, one of the rules, like Carlsbad Plums from Fortnums, le Roith's cigarettes, women's birthday presents from Aspreys, and ties from Hilditch & Key in Jermyn Street ...

But though I was unaware of it then, and indeed did not realize it fully for some weeks, for me the tradition and manner died that night. The fabric of existence, till then smooth and handsome and unquestioned, began to crumble and give way: it was as if my father had in his own person held it together, and his body's dissolution had laid bare a fissure which widened and spread before it could be brought under control. Nor could there be any compromise over the process: for one was either one of the favourite children, the *jeunesse dorée* and *adorée*, or one was relegated to that vast outer throng, that anonymous bank of seaweed which never came to the surface. To be *déclassé* was to vanish without trace, there being, to the official eye, only one class – first, reserved, and paid for in advance.

Can it be otherwise? Since clothes and transport cost money, since nearly every engagement involves, in one form or another, paying as you go in, what is to be done with poor So-and-so, who is down to his last flyer and cannot afford a clean dress-waistcoat? It is 'quaint' at the

21

beginning, but it cannot go on being quaint: complimentary tickets and shared taxies may patch up the cracks for a time, but it is inevitable that So-and-so's company should in course of time become either an embarrassment or an expensive luxury – he is chary of the second bottle of champagne, public familiarity with his wife's wardrobe earns it contempt in every restaurant in the West End of London, and the fact that they cannot return even the most modest form of hospitality is a trenchant debit in the social budget. Besides, sooner or later So-and-so will be wanting to borrow money, which is a different thing altogether ... It was said of Sheridan that one could not take off one's hat to him in the street without its costing fifty pounds, and that to stop to speak to him meant a certain loan of a hundred: news of such a financial hazard travels fast and widely, and reduces one's social circle to a literal nodding acquaintanceship. When poverty comes in at the door, love not only flies out of the window but bolts the shutters on the outside.

After delivering Archie f.o.b. the hospital we found ourselves at a loose end, and ripe for any sort of excursion: the fight and the short car ride had woken the three of us up, to the extent of being quite unable to bring the evening to a finish. Of course we were in a thorough mess if anyone in authority noticed us: but it was too late for any proctors to be about, and the only chance was a don tacking home from dinner who might guess that the car was an undergraduate one. And at that hour his perceptive faculties would be unlikely to include such discernment ... We drove around for some time in an aimless fashion, and then Alastair stopped the car in Trumpington Street and began to rummage about round his feet.

"It's cold," he complained, "and I can't find my hat."

"I don't wonder." That was Charles, stretched out on the back seat and speaking with a die-away air, like a blasé god. "It may be under any one of a dozen beds in this city."

We talked a good deal of slush in that mode, imputing to each other excesses which belonged to the realm of athletics rather than of sex; but for the most part it didn't mean a thing, it was all bark and no dog. I should imagine that sexual experience was the exception rather than the rule for the majority of undergraduates, however indignantly they might deny such a reflection on their unchastity; for the public school spirit died profoundly hard, and one of its tenets – the one-woman, wait-until-marriage rule – often did not die at all. The word 'clean' was of course the operative one: in fact, it was a word which was drilled into the adolescent until he or she came to think that only certain parts of the body *were* clean, and that there was a section of the person which bore an irremediable stigma and was shameful in any context … At all events, undergraduates of my day, who for the most part did but reflect the adult prejudices of the powers-that-be, in their turn subscribed to and buttressed the fervent ideals of the sexually unambitious.

I say 'for the most part', but naturally there were irregular spots, grateful oases, groups of friends who had evolved a common taste and were by no means to be numbered with the chaste herd: and if one attached oneself to such a clique, any irregularity lost its significance – one was insulated from criticism or the impact of other influences, and behaviour of a marked unorthodoxy became easy and natural. Thus it might be said that Archie and myself and Peter Tresham had developed well apart from our contemporaries; and there must of course have been many others similarly placed, having their own coterie of friends to whom very little came amiss … But there again one could not generalize, because we in our turn had friends who were impervious to the dread infection, who had not caught the habit, who simply went without and only guessed at what they were missing.

Alastair did not find his hat: I dare say he had never had one in the first place. But stopping the car recalled to us that our next objective had still to be decided: the dashboard clock showed half past two, and even allowing for the fallibility of dashboard clocks, time was running against us, and the evening's anticlimax was near unless we gave it some fresh injection of energy. And for energy we could hardly rely on Charles, who had his feet up on the back seat under a rug and was patently unsure whether he had had too much or too little to drink. I turned round to him.

"Are you all right, Charles? Would you rather toss the evening and just go home now?"

"My dear Marcus," he answered drowsily, "it's too late in the day to consider whether I'm all right or not. *Jacta alea est* – and I must lie here and await results. But as a footnote to this, I may say that I could no more climb into college now than I could lift myself off the ground by shortening my braces ... Drive on!"

"Where to?"

"Sir, I am but the poor passenger." And he closed his eyes again and drifted away from us.

"Well, the world's ours," said Alastair at length. "All except my hat, that is." He pondered, lying back and fiddling with the window-raising mechanism. "The Communist headquarters opened today," he went on idly. " 'Workers, you have nothing to lose but your chains.' ... We could go and break it up."

"It'll be locked and barred."

"We could tear posters, and chalk up rough answers."

"Not very exciting."

"It's not meant to be exciting – it's a civilizing mission." His head lolled sideways and he frowned at me "Marcus, you're not getting soft-hearted about that Bolshie crew, are you? Believe me, it doesn't pay. All they want is a thick ear apiece."

"I'm in no state to give them that."

"All the same, you must see – " he began, and launched into a grumbling dissertation on something or other, to which I didn't listen. He was inclined to be a bore when he talked about Socialists: he seemed to have some kind of grudge against them – I don't know why. They'd have had to go a long way before catching up with *his* bankroll.

There was a General Election due in about a month, and political Cambridge was just beginning to wake up and start its campaigning. I took no interest in politics and knew virtually nothing about the election, beyond supposing – as all my friends did – that the National Government was the only possible one for the country, and that the sooner they were safe for another five years, the better for everyone. They seemed to have done us pretty well over the last stretch, especially after the muck-up the Labour people had left us in, in 1931, and there really seemed no earthly reason for replacing them, even had there been anybody to replace them with, which I didn't imagine there was.

Of course Alastair had been right, in a way: even if one didn't pay any attention to politics or listen to speeches, one had a natural resentment against Communists, who were simply too tough to live in the same country with normal people ... Hunger-marches, May Day processions, slogan-shouting, wall-chalking, 'clashes' with the police and with the opposite coloured shirts – they were all new, all quite un-British, and an infernal nuisance into the bargain. I recalled especially an occasion, a few months before, when I had been watching the Jubilee procession from an office down near Whitehall: opposite us there was a building half completed, with its various floors open to the outer air and its scaffolding crowded with spectators cheering the troops and waiting for the royal carriages to go by. Suddenly one of us – we were a party of about eight – drew attention to a man who was for some reason climbing up the scaffolding from the side away from the main street: he kept looking round to see if he was observed, he dodged from floor to floor and girder to girder, he was trailing behind him a long red banner ... Finally, just as the King was due to pass, he reached the roof, fastened his banner to the topmost cornice, and then stole away again: I saw him slip off into the crowd and disappear, while the banner fluttered outwards, a dark splash of red against the gayer streamers and flags. It bore the hammer and sickle, and the words 'TWENTY-FIVE YEARS OF HUNGER AND WAR' in scrawling gold letters ... I remember how shocked we all were at its intrusion: we looked at the banner as if it were an indecent caricature, and the girl next to me said: "That chap ought to be shot," in as angry a tone as I'd ever heard her use. And of course I agreed: quite apart from its inappositeness, the thing was such damn bad manners, with the King and Queen passing by only a few yards away on their Jubilee drive.

Alastair droned onwards with his lecture, while I looked back on my memory of that occasion and drew what seemed the obvious conclusion: if that were modern politics, then only someone with a social grouch or a permanent urge towards mischief-making would want to join in. And as far as I was concerned, what was it all about? Couldn't political action be safely left in the hands of the real experts? I didn't know much about the mechanics of the thing, but presumably the Government during its recent term had had the greatest good of the greatest number at heart: they had done their best for everyone and if they couldn't provide work they provided the dole – exactly how much I didn't know, but enough to live on anyway. Perhaps even too much: for one certainly heard odd stories of what the unemployed did spend it on – going to cinemas and football matches, throwing it away on horses, even actually marrying and setting up house on it …

Of course one couldn't help feeling a certain amount of sympathy with them, but that didn't alter the fact that sentiment was for the most part quite out of place in a matter of that sort. My father always said that half of them had never done an honest day's work in their lives and wouldn't work now even if they were given the chance – I remember him once talking to me about it, lying on the beach at Cap Martin, and getting absolutely black with rage because that very day the Government had climbed down and restored some pay cuts or children's allowances or something. It was the sort of thing he took seriously; and I suppose that, being a magistrate, he saw a lot of those fellows and knew the proper way to deal with them. (That was the day we drove over to Eden Roc casino, and he lost sixteen thousand francs in half an hour. That made him angrier still.) There were always a good many unemployed in the nearest big town at home: one would see them hanging about round the pubs or the labour exchange, lounging hands-in-pockets, looking shiftless and no good to anyone at all. One became, in time, resentful of their presence – everyone knew that there were unemployed, and there was no need to advertise the fact, day in and day out, in the main street itself …

Nor was it really any use trying to help them – they only sneered at you and threw it in your face, raving about charity or some such nonsense; and even if they were given decent houses to live in they soon had them as filthy, inside and out, as the slums they had left. Having regard to which, it was probably better to let things work out their own way, and not try to interfere or take any short cuts … In any case, one had one's own life to fashion and make sure of first: one could count on precious little help from outsiders if one neglected this and went chasing off on some idealistic pathway, or led a crusade against God-knows-what which would finish up God-knew-where. Charity began at home – that had been firmly fixed in my mind ever since I was a kid: basically speaking, I didn't give a damn how all those people lived, and so far I hadn't met anyone, barring a few cranks and agitators, who gave a damn either.

I emerged from my vague political daydream to hear Alastair saying, with extreme emphasis: "And *that's* why you shouldn't miss a chance of doing these chaps down, whenever you can. See, Marco?"

"Yes, Alastair," I answered dutifully. "It's been a lovely explanation and I'm miles better for it. And now have you any suggestions about what we do tonight?"

He looked at me suspiciously. "I suppose you haven't been listening to a word of it."

"*I* have," broke in Charles unexpectedly. "It was sterling sense from beginning to end." He heaved himself up and looked about him – at the car windows steamed over with heat, at the long tail of street lamps ahead, at the glimpse of black sky and grass verge, already rimed with frost, on the roadside. The night was cold and clear and windless. "It looks just the sort of evening we want," he went on. "Turn the car, Alastair, and get on to the Newmarket road."

Alastair started the engine: it spluttered once, and then recovered to its normal three-and-a-half-litre roar. "Where are we going?" he asked reasonably. "There'll be very little racing at Newmarket before daylight."

"I have now assumed command of this carload," Charles answered him. "If all you two can do is argue politics till three o'clock in the morning, it's time that a realist took over the reins." Then he sat back. "I am now going to sleep again for half an hour: when you get through Newmarket, bear right on the Bury St Edmunds road. After six miles, wake me up."

Alastair and I looked at each other. "I suppose it's all right," he began doubtfully. "Or is he just talking in his sleep?"

"This road's as good as any other," I answered. "And if we're finishing up near Bury, you can take me the odd twenty miles and drop me at Nine Beeches in the morning."

"You can't go straight home without saying anything." We were moving swiftly towards the outskirts of the town, flicking past the long railings of Maid's Causeway: Alastair steadied the Bentley at the hilltop, where the police car usually lurked. "They'll kick up no end of a fuss here," he went on. "You'll have to come back with us, and then get an *exeat* in the ordinary way."

"Too much trouble, especially when I'm so near home." I considered the matter, in the light of what I knew of my tutor's prejudices and convictions. "I'll write to Murray, or telephone him in the morning, and say – oh, stress of the moment – rushed away uncontrollably in the hope of seeing Father alive."

Alastair laughed, "You'll be sent down one of these days on account of those uncontrollable rushes." Momentarily he glanced behind him at the couched and huddled figure on the back seat. "Good old Charles – I wonder if he knows what we're going to do."

Presently it transpired that we were going ghost-hunting.

Charles, being in Army Class, rarely handled books and had no occasion to read them, but apparently he had been reading one that day and it had made a profound impression on him. It had been called *Famous Ghosts of England and Wales* – so he told us as we passed the July Course stands at Newmarket and swung on to the straight stretch of road that cuts the Heath in two; and what had especially taken his imagination, among a long tally of lesser horrors, was a highly spiced account of 'The Ghost of Lanehanger Hall' – a putatively haunted manor house not far from Bury St Edmunds. For here, more than three hundred years before, the third baronet had in a drunken fury strangled his mistress, subsequently throwing her body, together with those of her stillborn child and freshly raped maidservant, into the moat below; and it was said, not unreasonably, that their ghostly forms were often to be seen swimming round and round in the pitch black water, clutching at the steep walls and crying out to be rescued ... It was a pretty story, not without its moral for this politely squeamish generation which accepts the fact that one may be mulcted of crippling damages for so much as trying to kiss a young woman in a railway carriage; and we endorsed Charles' choice of entertainment, though with no great confidence in its running according to the rumoured programme.

It happened also that I knew the house, which was not far from our own, and found pleasant the idea of revisiting it.

If we had been fairly drunk by midnight we were certainly fairly sober by half past three, when we arrived at the village we wanted. (Those were the days for quick sobering-up: a bout of fresh air, a few regretful hiccoughs, and there you were – roaring to be off again. I suppose the tissues of the brain were then more adept at knitting themselves up. Or perhaps we simply thought ourselves into being drunk, and drifted out again on a tide of absent-mindedness.) Since it was only twenty miles from home, the layout of the village was known to me: and after wasting a certain amount of time staring up at an open window which we thought might enshrine a young woman undressing, but which we presently made out to be a light left on over the staircase of the Public Library, we made for the side road bordering the estate. The main gate I knew well – a huge wrought-iron affair flanked by pillars and laughing stone lions with their paws at the ready: that certainly could not be stormed, even discounting the lodge which lay just beyond it. But I had an idea that there would be another gate, off the main road and more scalable: and presently the car came level with it, bumping over the rutted car track, and Alastair drew into the side and switched off his engine. We got out. It was good to stretch after the drive, to stamp on the hard turf, to look about us at the belt of trees backed by a neat and coldly glowing half moon, to mark the stretching fields which sloped away from us, the small hummocks like waves tossed up and static in their elevation, and the bands of mist which lay heavy or drifted close to the ground, luminous under the moonlight, seeming ready to ensnare all travellers' footsteps and choke their movement. It was a setting exactly suited to zero hour; it was soft on the eye and hard on the nerves.

Alastair busied himself arranging a rug over the radiator. Then he glanced up at the wall, measuring it with his eye. "I don't think we'll get over that in a hurry: there's no foothold."

I walked over to the gates, and found them appreciably lower than the main ones: neither was there any lodge behind but simply a gravel pathway which wound out of sight between two lines of beech trees. I rattled the bars. They only rattled.

"It's padlocked," I called out to them. "But it's climbable. Do we go on?"

"Sure," answered Charles. He walked over, took up a swaggering stance, and stuck out his chin in the contemporary political manner. "To these gates we oppose the force of our heroic will and irrevocable destiny. Addis Ababa or bust!"

Addis Ababa or bust ... How meaningless such a phrase is now, and how real, how charged with significance it was at that date. The Abyssinian war had then been going on for about ten days, and even the least politically minded undergraduate, preoccupied with cars or horses or gambling, or with more recondite strata of Litterae Humaniores, could not escape, in a greater or less degree, the impact of it upon his consciousness. For its public manifestations were inescapable – the newspaper posters were all either ADOWA BOMBED or WOMEN AND CHILDREN IN MASS-SLAUGHTER or sanctions: NEW MOVE AT GENEVA, and all the available wall-space seemed to have MIND BRITAIN'S BUSINESS chalked up on it – the Fascist boys' contribution to the current of history. For a long time I had been pretty vague about the whole thing; but then the novelty of its development had caught my imagination and latterly I had been reading a fair amount of the enormous mass of stuff that was being written about it.

Whatever the ulterior significance of the projected struggle – whether a domestic unrest which must be distracted or an economic need for expansion which would not be denied – it was clear that Italy was determined on war as the solution: in fact she was spoiling for a fight, had chosen her opponent any number of years ago, and was prepared to break (it had been calculated) nine separate treaties and pacts in order to have her way. And on the appointed day, League or no League, Mussolini had marched in with horse, foot, and a good thick wedge of native soldiery in the vanguard.

It hardly seemed our affair, except for the single item that the source of the Blue Nile at Lake Tsana would eventually come under Italian control and might conceivably be diverted in some way from the Sudan and Egypt (or held in check by barrages – or even poisoned, as one hard-up leader writer suggested): but over this, I imagined, we could do a deal later, and thus I couldn't understand the indignant flurry which was being raised about something which we ourselves had done countless times, and with genuine self-satisfaction, in the past. But a flurry there was: Italy had forthwith been condemned by the League Council for resorting to war in defiance of Article So-and-so; and the League, gathering weight in the most inexplicable way, contrived to gain for Italy an almost universal unpopularity – the phrase 'Soon she will not have an ally left to betray' earning a wide currency. In addition to the embargo on arms and ammunition some kind of financial boycott had been fixed up; and the real League enthusiasts, not hitherto recognizable as a body of opinion, appeared to be hoping for much more – hoping indeed for a complete trade embargo enforced against Italy by the whole world.

It seemed a funny sort of thing for us to be mixed up in, and funnier still that the Conservatives were endorsing it; and yet, in spite of its oddity, it had its own underlying attraction. One couldn't help feeling that perhaps some kind of stand ought to be made; one couldn't help feeling that, whatever the provocation, the war was a base and cruel exploit, that Italy was playing the bully from an impregnable position, that the blessing of civilization and the fine flower of Western culture were purveyable in some less determined fashion ... One wondered whether Mussolini had a conscience, and if it worked at such moments as these, when he gave the word to unloose a steel slaughter on a people virtually unarmed and impotent to strike back. I remember the day war was declared, and how impossible it seemed that at that very hour killing was going on; and I recall particularly listening in to the wireless news that night, or a few days afterwards, and being moved by the manner in which the thing was handled. There was one moment especially good, one touch of near-genius which stayed in the memory ... The day had been a brutal one – fighting, bombing, slaughtering: the announcer had recited a tale of Italian aggression and bloodshed which sickened the imagination: we heard of mud villages bombed, of children heaped and tossed into death, of humanity crucified on this stinking altar. And then, in a quiet voice, unexpectedly: 'On October the 4th, nearly seven hundred years ago, there died an Italian, St Francis of Assisi, who would greet everyone he met with the words: "My dear brother, God give thee peace." That is the end of the Second News.'

That was all – not even a rebuke, but simply Humanity's comment, a modern Still Small Voice.

Of course we never saw a ghost or heard anything more other-worldly than an owl haunting a beech tree; but it was a good rag, and an occasion of some enchantment as well, and it left its mark on my memory as the last wholly carefree excursion I was to be granted for a very long time ... From that spiked gate, over which we climbed with infinite difficulty and stifled laughter, the country sloped gently downwards – a spacious parkland intersected by white wooden fencing, broken by great oaks and chestnuts, swathed now in a knee-high ground mist which parted before us as if our passage could melt the very ether itself.

It was odd to walk down that slope, to pierce the forward darkness and be conscious, at the same time, of its closing in behind us, to feel rather than see, looming out of the mist, a succession of fresh objects – a shed whose sloping roof gleamed with early dew, another long fence stretching away into blank infinity, a tree throwing in our path a black shadow round which we skirted instinctively. There were cows here and there, staid and reflective in the moonlight, eyeing us and then turning away in accented boredom: once two ponies, sniffing us downwind, trotted up to examine their visitors and then followed us delicately, snuffling and whinnying with excitement, to the confines of their paddock – to watch them coming towards us out of the white mist, indefinite blacknesses at first and then taking shape and resolving into reality, induced a vague uneasiness, like some supernatural conjuring trick before which the whole adult world was reduced to the ecstasy and terror of little children …

We went on. Soon our feet crunched on gravel: we made out greenhouses, walls laced by cherry trees, dark shrubberies, a summerhouse full of cobwebs and piled deck chairs, a terraced rock garden in which there gleamed here and there white stones and clumps of dwarf chrysanthemums. It was the beginning of civilization, the sharpening of danger, the lurking-place of watchdogs and wakeful outdoor servants … We came to another clear patch, a smooth lawn on which the dew outlined our footmarks: and then suddenly the great house rose up out of the darkness, confronting us as the solid nucleus of our quest.

We stood stock-still, gazing up at the most noble outline. It was a huge place, four storeys high, built round three sides of a courtyard which must have been fifty yards across: we could make out every detail of that courtyard, one side of it shadowy, the other clear-cut in the slanting moonlight: parts of it were neatly grassed over, with four paths leading up to a fountain in the centre, and at the top a great tier of steps flanked by pillars with fluted capitals. The noise of that fountain's playing came to us clearly across the courtyard; it leapt in the moonlight, it glittered and splashed, rejoicing to be the only living thing in all the stillness; and its central figure, a slim boy holding aloft a torch, seemed to reign over the surrounding dusk like a princeling come to judgment ... But it was the house itself which truly claimed the attention, with its aloofness, its silence, its mystery; from its façade the countless black eyes of its windows gaped and stared, not at us but sightlessly into the void of night.

We stood there without a word, content to come under the spell of its distant splendour.

"It's good," said Alastair after a long while. "It's *genuine*. Look at the design of it – perfect. And that fountain, playing, playing, just as it's done for centuries." This was a new Alastair, already transformed by the building's pervasive alchemy. "There's no one living there, is there, Marcus?"

"Only caretakers, I think. The family haven't opened it up for years. We knew them when I was a kid: there was a rather sweet daughter, who used to come over and play with me and Tania at Nine Beeches: and I've been to tea here often, though I don't remember any of it. That must be about fifteen years ago now. They went broke just after the War. I think the daughter died about the same time – that influenza epidemic."

We walked forward a few yards, to a low wall which guarded the steep drop to the moat. Directly in front of us was the stone bridge which now took the place of the drawbridge: it was gated and cunningly spiked – so cunningly that it could not be surmounted: it seemed that our advance was barred, that we would never gain the courtyard or approach closely the little fountain boy. Thus checked, we turned aside and leaning on the wall looked straight down to the moat below: there was a drop of twenty feet, and at the bottom a stretch of pitch black oily water overhung by trailing ferns and low bushes: protected from the night breeze, its surface was smooth and unbroken, and the moon's track glittered on it in a wide and scarcely wavering line. One had the impression of danger – danger and something else besides, something shameful and beastly: it was too shadowed, too clearly lying in wait, and the occasional plop! of a rising fish (descendant of some ancient foul feeder on a murdered body?) seemed to carry this idea to its horrible conclusion. Beside me I could feel Charles shivering: he was the only one who had read the ghost story, and I was glad I hadn't done so – this was a case where mastery of detail did not ensure a quiet mind …

"This is one of the nastiest corners I've ever struck," he whispered presently. "Do you see the wall of the house ? – it's a sheer drop straight into the moat, it must be about fifty feet. And look at the sides of it – black and slimy, without a handhold anywhere. You'd have as much chance of climbing out of there as a frog down a well. And look!" his hand closed on my arm in a tight grip. "There's a window set right high up, all by itself. That must be *the* window, the one they were all thrown out of."

But it was the moon's effect which was the most startling. It was the only light in all that blackness: it hung above our heads, and its reflection in the water – *was* it only a reflection, could it not have been a body, or something floating helplessly on that tideless pool? I stared at it in fascination, imagining that it moved: and when a fish broke its surface, and the widening ripples made it tremble and change shape, I was ready to swear that we were witnessing something outside the boundaries of human agency.

Presently, feeling the need for movement, we made a tour of three sides of the building, following the edge of the moat as far as we could; but nothing new came to light, and by and by we went back to our old position by the bridge, and settled down to watch. It was clear that we could not wait long: the time was now half past four, and already the sky was growing pale towards the east, already the whole form and depth of the house were emerging out of the darkness: if we were not to be discovered we would soon have to retreat. But the moment was good: a mixture of novelty and discomfort and some kind of fulfilment. I looked about me now, and felt, suddenly, supremely content to be there with my friends: everything about that moment was *right* – the superb house proclaiming its outline, the fading sky, the dew-crusted lawns, the variety of sound – fish rising, trickle and splash of fountain, owl behind us in the orchard, far-off whistle of train – which wove their pattern and laid their spell. Even the moat seemed to have lost its menace, and to have become no more than a guardian for the towering walls beyond, a guardian whom one could admire and need not challenge.

But of course we *were* there to look for ghosts … The side glance at death recalled my father to me, and the house recalled the many times I had visited there, and the little girl who had so often come to play with me and my sister Tania. (I'd be seeing Tania tomorrow – today, rather.) Had that little dead seven-year-old – her name, I recollected now, had been Geraldine – had Geraldine been my first love? I searched my memory, scanning the childish years. Certainly I could remember holding her hand stickily while we watched some conjuring tricks; and tying her bow for her in the middle of a game of tick; and showing her my ferret and my new pony and my own private patch of garden with the wild strawberries that sometimes turned from green to white but never from white to red: so perhaps it was true that we had loved each other dearly ... That was where my father came in: he would give the three of us pickaback rides all round the rose garden: Tania and Geraldine he would swing up on to his shoulder as if they were featherweight dolls, but when it came to my turn he would always pretend to groan with the effort, and say: "I can't lift you, you great piece of beef." However, I always got my ride in the end – hanging on to his hair, jogging up and down pretending to lash my steed, and (as a special favour) being tipped bodily into the privet hedge at the end of the circuit. At which Bridges the head gardener would protest, righteous in his indignation: "That 'edge, sor," he would say, "that 'edge is a delicate plant. Master Marcus don't do it no good." And my father would answer: "I'm sorry, Bridges: that's the very last time it happens," and then turn to me and say: "There, I told you you were a piece of beef. Come on, Geraldine, it's your turn. *Up* with you ..."

That was how I would like to have remembered him always: before the muddle and misery of Taormina, before my mother divorced him and died within the year, before the county cut him dead and the whisky bottles started to pile up and pile up in the corner of the stable yard. So very long ago now.

We beat a retreat just after five: it was getting altogether too light for safety, and we were cold to the bone and very stiff. Back in the car, we settled down to a couple of hours of cramped sleep: towards eight I got out, leaving Alastair to the whole front seat and Charles snoring under a rug in the back, and walked to the end of the lane to look at the sun. It was a superb day, cloudless, fresh, gradually warming: the dew on the trees and at the lane's edge glittered from a million tiny facets, the birds poured out their welcome in a dazzling variety of song, continually prompted by cock-crows from every point of the compass. My first day as head of the family, my first day as heir – the omens seemed about as favourable as they could be. I returned light-hearted, and thumped on the back of the car.

"Time to get up," I called. "It's no good pretending to be asleep, because it isn't possible."

Alastair tumbled out, yawning and stretching. I ranged about on the grass verge, picked a poppy, stuck it in the radiator. From within the car came heartrending groans as Charles tried to face the morning.

"Marcus!" Alastair suddenly woke up. "The champagne … Good lord, I'd forgotten all about it." He opened the rear door, and Charles fell into the road. "Sorry, Charles. But there's some champagne – that'll cure you."

"Nothing will cure me." Charles unwound his cocoon of rug and staggered to his feet. "I've got a mouth like the roof of a railway station, the most grotesque pins-and-needles, and a head – " he gave it, up. "But the fact that during the course of the last two hours I have finished every drop of champagne gives me peculiar pleasure."

"No!" Alastair's voice was tragic. "Oh no …" He darted into the car, emerging with the unopened bottle. "Fool," he said. "I really believed you for a moment."

The noise of that cork was really the most admirable sound I had ever heard: it beat the birds into a cocked hat … Alastair poured out three glasses, and handed them round: I held up mine between my face and the sun, from where it winked at me with its clear golden eye, and bowed its thanks for release. *Moriturus te saluto* …

"What's the toast?" asked Charles. Even he had cheered up. Alastair looked across at me. "We ought to drink to Marco's future," he said. "It's going to be a new era, I imagine. By the way, are things going to be any different? – I mean, will you be broke or anything?"

"Good lord, no."

"Hardly worth drinking to, then." But he smiled, and raised his glass. "To Mr Hendrycks, upon his attainment to the adult world."

"Hear, hear," from Charles.

"I think I'll drink that too." I said. "Here's luck."

It was one of the best glasses of champagne I'd ever drunk. It was also one of the last.

Not more than half an hour later, with myself at the wheel, we rolled to a standstill before the shabby gateway and the long drive curling out of sight: surveying them, I wondered if it were only my imagination which made the place seem derelict. Surely the lodge should have been painted before it got in that state … I jumped out, and smiled at them.

"Thanks for the night," I said. "It's been a whole lot of fun." Alastair moved across to the driving seat, and Charles joined him in front.

"Will you be back tonight?"

"I doubt it."

"Well, see you later." Alastair flicked the car into gear. "And cheer up, Marcus: come back soon, and we'll have a lot more champagne."

"Do you want to back Turtledove?" asked Charles. "It's running again today."

"All right," I said. "Put five – no, ten quid on for me."

"Plutocrat …" They both smiled, and waved: the car drew away, whining smoothly through its gears, raising little puffs of dust which hardly hung at all before settling. At the first corner Alastair did a particularly neat change from top to second. Then they were out of sight behind the wall – my wall.

I faced the long drive, and the sun just mounting behind Wood-End spinney.

CHAPTER TWO

'Mon petit fils qui n'as encor rien vu,
A ce matin, ton père te salue:
Viens-t-en, viens voir ce monde bien pourvu
D'onneurs et biens qui sont de grant value.'

FONTAINE

❖

Dobson, the lodge keeper, came running out as I swung the creaking gates open. He was in his shirtsleeves, collarless, with two days' greying stubble on his chin: he seemed much older than I remembered, the skin of his neck crinkled and loose, the few wisps of hair plastered flat across his bald head. In some odd way he no longer looked like a countryman at all …

"Why, Mr Marcus!" But it was the same old voice, the same good-humoured touch-the-forelock deference. "I saw a gentleman get out of the car, but I didn't think it was you. You've changed a bit, haven't you, sir? And grown, too."

I laughed as I shook his hand. "Well, let's hope it's a change for the better. How long is it since I've been here?"

"Best part of four year, sir." He nodded, completing some private reckoning. "That's what it is – four year by Christmas. Mrs Dobson will be main glad to see you. We often talk of the old days, when you and Miss Tania and – yer mum and dad were all together."

He looked at me anxiously, afraid of having said too much. "They were good days," I answered lightly. "And how's Mrs Dobson? Keeping well?"

"Mustn't grumble sir." But his face had clouded over again. "Of course we've got eight now, and she don't get about like she used to. Would you come in and see her for a moment, sir?"

"Of course. I'd like to."

He led me up the little path, and through a slit of a hallway where five round-eyed and not over-clean children were playing: and suddenly, from being glad to be back and in good form generally, I was almost on the instant taken with the most profound dislike of my surroundings. For the little dark boxlike house was immensely depressing, after the freshness and fragrance of the morning: the walls looked damp, the wallpaper was flaking off here and there in ugly torn strips, the whole place smelt of cooking and dry rot and a long succession of washdays. I looked about me in some dismay: the lodge I remembered had been neat and clean, the curtains fresh chintz, the children not snivelling and sitting sullen on the floor but crawling all over the garden like pink-and-white slugs. This horrible shrunk little place didn't exactly accord with Dobson's thirty years of service.

Nor was his wife any more reassuring. She lay propped up on a tumbled bed, with a baby lying in the crook of one arm, a baby (as I guessed) but lately snatched away from an intimate breakfast and resenting the fact with a feeble wailing. I saw that she wasn't plump and jolly any more, but quite colourless, like very fine sand: her face had a sunken pallor such as one sees in 'coloured supplement' lithographs of the Crucifixion. Her hair was in curlers, screws of rag dotted here and there as if they had settled of their own accord: she wore round her shoulders a grubby Shetland shawl which my mother had given her on her marriage. The bedroom also was indescribably untidy and ill-cared-for, the two other beds unmade, the deal dressing-table a mess of cooking utensils and soiled napkins and dirty crockery and cheap 'souvenirs' and tangled furry hair-combings …

I gave her a smile as I shook hands.

"How are you, Mrs Dobson?"

"Mustn't grumble, sir. It's a treat to see *you*." And her face actually did light up for a moment, and lose its horribly nondescript air. "How you've grown, too."

"Four years is a long time." I was sitting on the bed, trying not to kick the chamber-pot which menaced my feet: Dobson was out in the passage, where I could hear him shushing the children. I suppose most of them had forgotten who I was. "I understand that's the eighth," I said, indicating the baby which was now sucking a safety-pin and staring at me with mild pale-blue eyes. "I must congratulate you – *and* Dobson."

"Thank you, sir." The old dimple that I remembered came and went, like the very ghost of good humour. "We were wondering where to put the stitch – if you'll excuse such an idea."

I laughed with her. "Well, you haven't changed much, Mrs Dobson. Do you remember when Dobson was teaching me to ride a bicycle, and I'd come running in here every half hour for a bread-and-treacle sandwich? Gosh, they were good too."

"We used to say you was reg'lar brought up on bread-and-treacle, Master Marcus – Mr Marcus, sir." But she was looking about her rather helplessly. "Could I make you a cup of tea now? I'm sure the kettle's – you look worn out, you really do."

I laughed again. "I must have got up too early … No, I won't have tea, thank you very much – I'll come down later in the day, shall I?" I looked at my watch. "I'm afraid I ought to be getting up to the house."

She laid her hand on my arm, in that motherly fashion in which she used to comb my hair before I went up the drive again, or wash the scratches from my knees.

"I'm real sorry about your dad – about the master, sir," she said gently. There were tears in her eyes, tears which shamed my own indifference, and the baby gave a single tiny wail as if to endorse her distress. "He was good and kind to us all, right up to the end."

"Yes," I said, not knowing how to answer.

"If I could just say something …" Her voice tailed off, and she looked away as if afraid of meeting my eye: I thought at first that she wanted to add further condolences, to express her sympathy more fully, but then her real reluctance – her terror even – brought me up sharply: there was something here, and there were things about the house, which I didn't at all understand.

I said: "Why, what is it?"

"It's just – " after hesitation, the words came out with a rush, "you'll not forget Dobson's been here nearly thirty years, will you, Mr Marcus? Your dad – the master was good to us – he did all he could, that we do know. And we'll work all hours, both of us, if you keep us on, sir. I've had some of the washing, and Dobson's been helping in the garden too. You see we're willing, if you'll just give us a chance, Mr Marcus."

For a moment I thought her mind was wandering: what she was saying didn't make sense at all – the laundry was always sent to Bury, and why Dobson should be expected to help on the estate when there were nine other outdoor servants was beyond me. But of course she had been ill – was still ill: she had been worrying, she had got hold of some idea that there were bound to be changes, and had magnified it out of all semblance to the truth.

I smiled at her, and touched her hand as gently as I could. "I can tell you straight away," I said, "that if there are any changes at Nine Beeches, you and Dobson will be the last to go. After thirty years? – and *you* were ten years up at the house, weren't you? And suppose I wanted another bread-and-treacle sandwich, what on earth would I do? There's no treacle in *our* larder – I've looked. So just forget all about it. And now I must go."

I got up, awkwardly now, for I was appalled to see that she was crying, without stress or movement – the tears were coursing down her cheeks in a silent unhurried procession. They splashed on to the baby's forehead, and it looked up in a surprised way, already failing to understand the older generation.

She was trying to speak – something like "God bless you" – as I backed out and walked through into the garden.

Dobson was there, leaning against the railings, cleaning a rake. For some reason I felt very angry, not with him but with the fact that Mrs Dobson was crying, that she looked so ill, that the house was so drear and smelt so stale: something seemed to be badly out of joint, and I hadn't been there long enough to place my finger on it.

"What about that wallpaper?" I asked straight away, as I joined him. "And the damp in the passage. What's the agent been thinking of?"

Dobson shook his head.

"We don't see much of him nowadays, sir."

"Well, you're going to see a lot more, then."

"Do you mean, sir, that – that we'll be staying on here?"

"Of course you will," I looked at him closely, trying to understand what was at the back of his mind. "Why shouldn't you stay on?"

But he was smiling now, all the timidity and hesitation gone. "I knew you wouldn't forget us, sir."

I gave it up. Probably they had both had a worrying time with the last kid. Also I was tired, and wanted a bath and shave and breakfast.

"Well, that's that," I said. "Now I must get up to the house."

"Very good, sir." He paused. "You'll find changes up there, sir ... If there's anything I can do – I've been working on the garden, as the wife told you – "

This was verging on the nonsensical again – more than I could cope with, without coffee and grilled kidneys and coarse cut marmalade to sustain me. I patted him on the shoulder.

"That's fine," I answered. "The best thing you can do is to stop worrying and cheer Mrs Dobson up. And if you're on the lookout for a godfather for the latest – "

"Would you, sir? That 'ld please her fine."

"That's settled, then ... "

I glanced up the long drive, curling away past the edge of the wood where I got my first pheasant and first left-and-right – a brace of woodcock. The drive needed weeding, and trimming at the edges ... "And now for a long walk."

At any rate Beach, who opened the front door, hadn't altered a scrap: he was as fat, as bulb-nosed, as fruity of complexion and ambassadorial of manner as he had ever been. He had entered our service the night I was born, and as his first official task brought my father and Dr Maddison a congratulatory brandy-and-soda at half past four in the morning: nothing came amiss to him on that night, nor at any time thereafter. Between the ages of five and seven I used to overdraw my pocket money through him, until Tania, who had not thought of coming to a like arrangement, caught us going over our accounts in the pantry and made the fact public at a particularly high-class tea-party of my mother's. The practice was then discontinued, to my own prolonged financial embarrassment.

"Well, Beach?" I said as his portentous gaze took in my presence. "You're looking better than ever."

"Thank you, Mr Marcus. It's good to see you again." His manner was professionally subdued, as befitted the occasion, but the kindly indulgence in his eye recalled half a dozen forgotten difficulties and hazards which he had smoothed out for me. "We were not expecting you so early. Have you breakfasted, sir?"

"No, Beach, I haven't. And I've been dreaming of those grilled kidneys of Mrs Beach's all the way up the drive."

"I will see if they are available, sir. We may be limited to eggs and bacon, Miss Tania not being partial to breakfast in any form."

"She's still in bed, I suppose. How's Mrs Beach?"

"In excellent health, sir, thank you."

"Good. Well, I'll have a bath first, I think."

Two dogs leapt up at me as Beach took my overcoat – Don, the old Irish wolfhound, now so grey about the chops that another winter would probably finish him off, and a liver spaniel of Tania's that each of us in turn had tried to train as a gundog. No one, however, could break him of the habit of barking joyfully whenever a gun went off and thereafter retrieving, with particular diligence, each spent cartridge as it was ejected. Tania had kept him because she liked his eyes.

I patted and fondled them until they were less excited, and then looked about me. All the curtains were drawn – naturally, I supposed, though from the outside it had looked as though one wing of the house was completely shut up: but for some reason the furniture was still dust-sheeted, and there seemed to be less of it. And surely there was something else.

"Why, where are the pictures?" I asked in surprise. The hall had always had a ring of portraits round it, a notable array of intent faces which included two Hendrycks by Reynolds and a Leland (my mother's family) by Gainsborough at his most imposing ... I looked at Beach again, inquiringly, as he turned away from the coat cupboard.

"Why, Mr Marcus ..." His hand had gone to his chin in deep perplexity: his eyes as they dwelt on mine were distressed, for the first time within my memory. "I – I thought you would have known. They were – disposed of, a matter of two years ago."

"What – sold? Whatever for?"

"That I couldn't say, sir. I understand they went to a London firm to be valued."

"Look here, what *is* this?" The absurd gap in my knowledge, which every fresh discovery only seemed to make wider, was becoming almost embarrassing. "The house from the outside looks like a shabby sort of hotel, all the portraits have disappeared, and half the furniture as well, and the lodge hasn't been vetted for repairs for about three years. Is everyone out of their senses? What has my father ...?"

After a pause, a moment of grim silence, Beach said:

"If I may offer you my sympathy, sir ... We were all sorry to see him go. We couldn't wish for a more considerate master."

"Thank you, Beach. But ..." I looked about me again, while the dogs panted and watched every movement I made; "what does it all mean?"

"I can only say, sir ..." His hesitation was so out of character that I stared at him in astonishment. "Perhaps Miss Tania ... If you will excuse me, sir."

He had begun to back away on the word "Perhaps"; and the service door swung shut behind him almost before I had taken in the fact of his departure. Frustrated, I shrugged my shoulders and went upstairs to bathe. The riddle would keep for another hour, anyway. And then ...

And then, almost without a conscious effort of my will, I had left the breakfast table and was making my way towards the bleak astringent bedroom where my father had slept for fifteen years and now lay in that sleep which was no longer Death's counterfeit. Pushing open the door was like entering, as a child, some dark attic which one *knew* was the haunt of unnamable terrors. Indeed, so unreasoning and so strong was this reluctance that it was some moments before I could bring myself to complete the task and to look towards the draped and burdened bed ... I had never seen a dead man before: but he lay exactly as I had pictured him in my mind – calm, significant, terrible for a brief instant, and then tremendously saddening. If only we had got on better, if only I had made proper use of our scant years of companionship ... His face was smoother and more gentle than I had seen it at any time during the last ten years: he really *did* look at peace, all harshness, all overlay of lines and crosscut wrinkles wiped away by the only true alchemy: the pride of the jutting nose and brow contrasted with the crossed humility of the hands to form a picture essentially complete and irrevocable.

Presently I turned aside and walked to the window: stationed there, I had within my view a whole panorama of the garden and the lower pastures, slanting away until they merged with the covert which hounds always drew first when they met at Nine Beeches. As within the room, so with the outside world – autumn had stretched out and taken its toll: the sere leaves lay thick, and were joined by others, fluttering down like wounded birds or buoyed along by a chance breeze till they found in their turn a more distant, more final resting-place. The day had already belied its earlier promise, a drizzle of rain now fluting the window-panes and pattering on the ivy which framed them: I knew exactly what the lawns and pathways would feel like underfoot, I could call to mind, even after a four years' interval, every badly drained slope, all the dank places and shadowed corners where rain dripped from overhanging branches a full two hours after each shower was ended. My own small patch of garden (probably long since overgrown or requisitioned for something else) lay out of sight near the orchard: but *there* was the sunk garden and the sundial (chipped grey stone, and a cautionary '*Non semper erit aestas*' in formal lettering round the pedestal), *there* was the swing whose brave sweep could reduce Geraldine to tears of anguish, and *there* the cinder path, flanked by rhododendrons, where my father and I used to walk every evening after dinner, when I had demolished a half glass of port and was busy on the mildest of cigarettes ...

And if those days could be recalled? The rain pattered, the darkened room made itself felt as the formal setting of death: and standing there surveying that scene in which had been set so much of my childhood and adolescence, and then turning again to the stilled figure on the bed as the author and focus of those small years, I tried to determine how strongly I felt about his passing, and how much it was to be centred on the debit side of my account.

If it had happened four years before, when I worshipped him, then such a question would have been inconceivable: if Taormina and the divorce had been wiped out, then I could hardly have borne to enter the room, then I would have wept as Tania perhaps was weeping now – Tania who had never wavered in her faith and had chosen to remain with him even when Mother was still alive. But it had *not* happened then: the four years had unwound their brutal history and taken toll of the past: and too much had been said and done and thought for us ever to approach the old relationship again. Taormina would have smashed a love or a friendship a hundred times stronger than ours; and even now I could not think of that September without a pang of misery.

It had been a month after the family holiday at Antibes, the holiday which had been so perfect: almost as soon as we got back to England he had said to me: "We're not making the most of your vac. Let's go on our travels again – let's go to Sicily."

I agreed with him, not caring much either way: I had said goodbye, probably for ever, to Christine a few days before, and the knowledge that she was on her way to America and that my first real love affair was at an end made it a matter of indifference how I spent the odd three weeks before school. So Sicily it was – and pain it was, and misery and astonishment: for, whether by accident or no, he had been joined out there by a girl, Viola Rattray, whom my mother and all of us knew quite well, and they had settled down in a suite on the floor below mine, as if such were the most natural thing in the world.

I suppose he was a little mad, or driven to an insanity of desire by her slimness and availability: but I wasn't able to appraise the thing except in terms of infinite horror. From the moment when he had said, with the worried friendly smile which it seemed Iscariot might have worn: "Mark, old man, I've got something to tell you," and then introduced her to me on the cream-and-red hotel terrace, there was too much for a seventeen-year-old to cope with, there were too many strands to the rope: the idea that he had only been pretending all through the Antibes holiday, that he had been burning to get away from us all, that he had now only brought me out as a cloak … And of course, more overwhelming than anything else, the knowledge, each night, that below me the two of them lay together – I was fresh from Christine's shy passion, I knew exactly what they did – and he was my father, he was forty-five and greying at the temples, he had been with my mother, on the same terms, only a week before ...

Taormina ... that lovely poisoned place: those sunsets which turned the water to purple and emerald and turquoise, and my brain to a cage of distress: those solitary anguished walks to which I was driven, up among the hills of Linguaglossa within sight of Etna, or along the coast to Santa Teresa di Riva, tiny village spread like a red-and-yellow canvas against the foothills and the toy seascape of the Mediterranean ... Of course I went back to London, in spite of his pleading, as soon as I could: and the whole thing came out, since they had been seen together by friends of ours; and then there was the muck-raking of the divorce, and my mother's refusal to see me afterwards because I would not give evidence (how could I, even though I hated him so?), and my last meeting with him, when he arranged to give me an allowance and we bid each other goodbye finally, and he said, in a beaten voice that remained with me for years afterwards: "Viola's gone too – she couldn't stand the racket. You may understand some day, Marcus, to what hell one can be driven by a woman – and then be left there."

Only Tania stayed with him. I saw her occasionally when she came up to London: but my mother I never saw again till she lay dying, a year later, and my father I met now for the first time since that goodbye. I knew from Tania that his health had been broken, I heard about the whisky and the senseless drinking bouts and the wall of outraged propriety behind which the County and all his friends barricaded themselves; but I hadn't been able, in all those years, to approach him again or return to the house –

Taormina had done something to me, and it had lasted until now.

And was it lasting beyond the grave? I turned once more and looked at his dead body, striving to assess my reactions to it on a basis of reason instead of sentiment. 'To understand all is to forgive all': and though I could not understand the manner in which he had (as I supposed) made use of me, and the startling hiatus in his judgment which had led him to think that I would stay on at Taormina with the two of them, yet I could appreciate the forces – of boredom, of vanity, of lust – which made him take what was offered without adding the cost or concerning himself with the feelings of others. Viola had been there, and my mother in England: she was twenty-three to my mother's forty-one: she was clearly a 'conquest', when he might have thought that the time for such affairs was already behind him: his physique, his looks, his virility were such that this was probably his last chance of having youth and softness and beauty at his command. To snatch at a vanishing loveliness, to bask in this Indian summer before its course was run and its promise denied for the last time – these were things I had never encountered, these might be of overwhelming moment even for the very strongest. Most people, of course, stuck in their groove: but was there, for most people, a like temptation and a like ease of fulfilment? One could be wonderfully virtuous when virtue was a necessity, when nobody asked you to step out of line because nobody thought you were worth bidding for ...

But only a short time ago the figure on the bed had had strength and mature good looks and a charm which shone out of him like a lantern at dusk. I had been under its spell nearly all my life: it was the same for everyone he met, and it must have been astonishingly difficult for him to resist its natural consequences. And if that meant anything at all, it meant that he was not to be classed and judged with the common run of humanity, which stayed in its rut because it would freeze to death outside. There was a bigger scale than that against which to measure him, and he had been a candidate for it all his life; and if I only said this now that I saw him dead and mourned his passing, that was my fault and my added sorrow.

And as this thought struck me, and I approached a reconciliation with his memory, the door opened softly and my sister Tania entered the room.

She nodded as soon as she saw me, and crossed the room without saying anything, glancing sideways as she passed the bed with a more natural air of greeting than I could have managed. She was a good-looking edition of me – a rare and lovely edition, indeed: we had the same crest of black hair and the same clear skin which kept its sunburn from year to year, but her mouth and the studious lines of her forehead gave her face an entirely novel significance, a veritable transformation of quality, so that it left the ranks of the commonplace pleasant and attained those of the individually lovely. Indeed, she could attract attention in any surroundings: let her enter a room or step on to a dance floor, and there was never any doubt that she had arrived. She was slim and long-waisted and very square as to the shoulders: if she had had lovers I could not name one of them, if she had any ideas on marriage or a career I could not have hazarded what they were: in fact, I realized suddenly as she crossed towards me in her plain black dress and bare legs, our encounters during the last few years had been so limited and so superficial that I really knew nothing about the grown-up Tania at all, except her taste in wine (which ran to white Burgundy) and the fact that she always stopped and talked to pavement artists, no matter how inferior their wares.

"Hallo, Marcus dear." She kissed me very sweetly, putting her arms round my neck and smiling into my eyes. "I am glad you've come so quickly … You do look tired. Out with the boys, as usual?"

"Something of the sort." I looked at her closely, wondering how much the last few days had meant to her. She and my father had been very close together, but that might be due only to the fact that he leant on her strength and depended on her for everything.

"Yes, I *have* been crying," she said after a moment. She looked back at the bed. "You won't be able to understand it, Marco, but – for me he hadn't changed a bit. Even when he was hopelessly drunk, I could still see the same man there all the time."

If only from the way she pronounced the word 'drunk', I could tell that this was true: for she gave it, not the usual feminine accentuation which conjures up a vision of a dirty saloon full of unbuttoned men wallowing in spilt whisky, but a sort of loving caress, as if 'drunk' meant to her only a puzzled child who needed her help, a situation which called for understanding instead of blame.

"Drink was as bad as ever, was it?" I asked. We were still watching the bed, and holding each other like children.

"That's why he's there, I'm afraid. It was some kind of stroke, but Dr Maddison said it was due to – to that."

I sighed. "Oh well – the last few years must have been pretty hellish."

She nodded. "Yes, they were." And then she added, in the same gentle voice: "But you were all right, weren't you? We gave you everything you wanted … That's true, isn't it?"

"How – how do you mean?" I stammered slightly, taken aback by her phrasing. "How do you mean, 'we gave you everything'? I don't understand."

"Haven't you noticed anything about the house – about *everything* at Nine Beeches?"

"Well, the pictures have gone, and the outside of the house is – " An appalling thought struck me. "Good God, Tania, do you mean …?"

She smiled wistfully, and kissed my cheek again. "Poor Marcus," she answered, "you *are* out of it, aren't you?" Then she slipped out of my arms and sat on the window seat, drawing her knees up until her chin could rest on them: crouching there, she looked a picture of resignation and despair, and when I said: "Please tell me everything," and she began to speak, her words fell from her like Niobe's tears which nothing could arrest and nothing made dry again.

I must understand (she said) that no one was to blame for what had occurred: it was just bad luck, it might have happened to any other set of people at any time, it was, least of all, the dead man's fault … After the divorce he had been driven by idleness and lack of any other preoccupation to speculate, increasingly heavily, on the stock exchange: things had gone right at first, and then quickly wrong, until there had come a day when he had had to sell nearly the whole of his remaining capital to square up for some tin-mining shares which he had bought on margin. (I could myself remember reading of that resounding crash, and wondering how many people had been caught.) The estate swallowed up most of his income: drinking complicated the issue at every turn: he had begun to lose his grip, to plunge deeper without telling her or anyone else, and to keep pace with the whirlpool by selling a field here and there. Soon it was not fields only, but everything which made life tolerable for him – horses, cars, pictures, whatever furniture was of value: half the house had been closed down, the paddocks and meadows let as grazing, the shooting handed over to a syndicate: finally, nearly all the servants were dismissed, and they had settled down to a virtual siege …

"The servants that stayed have been angels," she said softly, hugging her knees and staring out across the waste of rain. "Beach and Mrs Beach run the whole house, with a girl who comes up from the village twice a week. Bridges left, but Allen – do you remember him? the little under-gardener with the stammer – does the best he can, and Dobson and his wife have been helping in countless ways. It's due to those five that we're still here: and none of them has been paid full wages for goodness knows how long. Mrs Dobson has been terribly ill, too, but they wouldn't leave or try to get another job: they just hung on and said they'd stand by Daddy and me as long as we wanted."

I had been trying hard not to interrupt, but this was too much.

"But why didn't you tell me?" I cried in misery. "Do you think I wouldn't have tried to help? And why and how in God's name have I been allowed over seven hundred a year, when everyone else has been practically starving?"

She lifted her head for the first time, and looked across at me with a faint and gentle smile. Then she nodded imperceptibly towards the bed.

"That was his idea," she answered, her voice hardly above a whisper. "He set it aside, he wanted you to have a good time while you could." She raised her voice slightly, as if wishing to explain this to me beyond any trace of doubt. "He used to say that if there was any way he could make up to you for Taormina he would find that way and follow it. Cambridge would only be once, one tiny part of your lifetime: the rest might be hell, but he wanted that part to be good." Her head came round again. "It has been good, hasn't it?"

I looked at her, aghast. "Tania, you're like another person. You're – you're hundreds of years old ... You don't hate me, do you? I could never have guessed this."

"Hate you? Of course not – you mustn't think that. I'm just tired, I suppose … Anyway, he did what he wanted, and he kept it all from you. Darling Daddy – he wasn't so bad, you know, Marcus. And losing Mummy did break him up." She stretched her arms out above her head: the recital had left her face pale and exhausted. "Now he's gone, I think that everything will collapse. Armstrong will tell you this afternoon, anyway, and you'll be seeing Morrison about the estate details as well." Her head drooped again. "Then the place will be sold, you are going to get a job, and I am going to marry Demetriades."

"Christ Almighty!" I jumped up as if I had been stabbed under the heart. "Tania, you're mad – you can't mean it. That bloody Greek – why, he's older than Daddy."

She did not look up: she only answered evenly: "That bloody Greek lent us fifteen thousand pounds when we hadn't a dog's chance of not going bankrupt."

"So that's why …"

"No, it isn't."

"Oh, Tania, listen to me." I dropped on my knees beside her: she began to fondle my hair without looking up. "You can guess what I feel like, knowing that all the time I've been tossing money down the sink, you two have been going through hell to keep it like that. But don't give up now, don't throw everything away." I took her hand and pressed it to my mouth. "What if the house does go? There are other places. And there's sure to be some money left, even if it's only a few hundreds: we'll make a new life together, we'll start again, and be as close as we used to. You can't marry Demetriades – it's too filthy an idea altogether. What can he give you – "

"*What can he give me?*" She flamed out suddenly, throwing off my hand and tensing herself like an animal attacked. "You ask me that, when you've had it yourself for the last four years … Money, that's what he can give me:

security, and rest, and being able to walk about freely without meeting stares and sneers, or being openly presented, in the street, with grubby bills that have haunted me for months past ... What can he give me? If you hadn't been playing at life for twenty-one years you wouldn't ask that question: if you'd been here, instead of loafing up at Cambridge, if you'd watched this place, and my father, and everything I loved, rotting away like ..."

Her voice broke suddenly, her head dropped in her hands: pitiful sobs shook her whole body, so that when she looked up once and tried to say: "I'm sorry, Marcus," the words were strangled and washed away by tears.

I could not resent anything she had said, for it was all horribly true: I *had* been loafing at Cambridge, and it was her misery which had kept me there. But Demetriades ... He was an immensely rich Greek whom we had met at Cannes, that same holiday: he had paid some attention to Tania, sending her hothouse flowers from his villa, driving over to invite her, in a thick Levantine accent, to the Casino or the Jockey Club: we had been able to laugh at him then, because Tania had been so preoccupied with Max Brennan all that holiday, and he with her, that they had hardly been aware of Demetriades except as a thickening shadow which occasionally crossed their path or obtruded itself too early in the morning to be circumvented.

"My God!" I said suddenly, thoughtlessly. "If only you had married Max, straight after Antibes."

She said: "Shut up, Marco," in a taut voice which told me the whole story ... She had refused him then, first because of the Divorce, then because she was in mourning for Mummy, and finally because she would not leave my father. Max had gone round the world, and then married Margaret Rackham as soon as he landed in England – about three years previously. I had gone to the wedding, but had not seen them since: they lived down in Gloucestershire, and had one child. It should have been Tania's, and clearly she knew it should have been, and remembered the fact now with longing and the most bitter regret. But Demetriades …

Tania and I had never in our lives quarrelled for more than ten minutes at a time: and the rule held good in this case, for presently she dried her eyes and apologized for everything she had said or implied – an apology which I neither needed nor deserved. Her story had made me feel more shocked and ashamed than I had ever been before, and the worst part of it was that I knew that I should go on being so, far into the future. Of course, in a way it wasn't fair: they should never have put me in so false a position or left me ignorant that I had any alternatives save to stay up at Cambridge and spread six weeks' work over three years; but such a feeling of resentment was merely petty beside the fact of their generosity, and it did not stay with me for more than a moment. What did stay with me was a conviction of horror at what they had done, a blinding gratitude towards both of them, and the fiercest of resolves to do something in return.

And that something must be done quickly, for the afternoon brought a succession of incidents which drove home, as with hammer-blows, the actuality behind Tania's recital. First I saw Morrison the agent, who was smooth – rather too smooth – in his account of savings effected at this, that, and the other point, of the struggle he had had to keep things going, of the confidence my father had reposed in him, right up to the end … The surface of it was all right: but I could not help seeing, underneath, a keen little Scotsman whose wages had not been docked, who lived in a trim cottage in perfect repair while Dobson pigged it down at the lodge in damp, and neglected flooring, and flayed wallpaper, and who was now lobbying softly for a job which he must have known the place could not support … In fact, I saw in him my own reflection, save that he had been able to watch all the time the decaying fabric of his surroundings.

There was nothing much I could say to him, beyond commending his industry and expressing the hope that we would be able to keep him on; there followed a telephone call to my tutor, who was duly sympathetic and gave me four days' leave of absence, and a painful interview with a stockman who had been in my father's employ thirteen years and had been dismissed six months earlier. He wanted his job back, on any terms … And then, after tea, Armstrong the solicitor called: and in my father's study, with its heavy oak desk and gun cases and Badminton Library, he swiftly threw aside the gentilities and introduced hard fact in distilled, carefully phrased portions.

I liked him: he was meek and unassuming, he was clearly good at his job, and he treated me with a deference which, viewed in any light, was a complete reversal of our mutual deserts. Black-suited, spectacled, nearly bald, with no eyebrows and really enormous white ears, he sat deep in an armchair which came close to swallowing him whole, with an open dispatch-case on his knees vomiting forth a mass of papers – papers which set out in the clearest terms the true disaster which was now breaking over the house.

"In the first place," he began, after swallowing visibly, in a high hesitating voice, "I should like to offer you my sincere sympathy in your bereavement. I may say that, for my part, I have lost a valued friend of many years' standing. I am deeply sorry, for those two reasons."

I said: "Thank you," and played with the blotter on my father's desk.

"And now," he continued, in a far less uncertain tone, "now for the position." He brought the tips of his fingers together. "You are probably aware that I enjoyed your father's confidence for a great many years, and that the entire conduct of his affairs was in my hands – indeed, the Nine Beeches estate has been the concern of my firm for three generations. I need not disguise the fact that his circumstances have been a source of great anxiety to me, particularly during the last two years. I was, of course, at all times acting under instruction ..." He paused, and looked across at me between his parted hands.

"I'm sure," I said, "that you have done everything you can to help. I know that he had the greatest confidence in you."

"Thank you ... The relationship of solicitor to client is in some sense a peculiar one, involving as it does both the giving of advice and the acceptance of instructions: it is by no means certain that – " He coughed. "But I must not dwell on that aspect, absorbing and intricate though it is. His position, as I say, was a matter of increasing concern to me. I understood from him that you were in some ignorance as to the true state of affairs?"

"That is so," I answered. (The professional turn of phrase was infectious.) "I had no idea that he was in any difficulty at all – in fact, my sister only told me of it when I arrived this morning. His idea was that – that I should not be worried about things but just enjoy myself up at Cambridge."

The neat fingertips came together again. "As to the wisdom of that course I cannot venture an opinion ... But at all events he made you a substantial, even a generous allowance."

"Yes."

"An allowance which you exceeded from time to time, and which he thereupon made good to your bank."

"Yes." There was nothing in his tone to make me feel ashamed, but already I was – horribly.

"I have the relevant figures here." He produced from his dispatch-case a clipped bundle of cheques and a file of letters, among which I could distinguish my own grey Trinity notepaper. "On March 25th of last year – your first year at Cambridge – he sent a cheque to cover the amount of your overdraft, a matter of some seventy pounds. In November of the same year he again forwarded a cheque to your bank, this time for one hundred and fifty pounds. A substantial amount ... I understand that you had enjoyed an extended holiday on the Continent?"

"Yes, in Germany ... You do understand, don't you, that I had no idea he was short of money?"

"Quite." For a moment his eyes sought mine, as if to gauge my sincerity: then they dropped to the bundle of cheques again. He cleared his throat. "There were no further payments until this summer, the end of your second year at Cambridge, when a cheque for two hundred and fifty pounds – more than the amount of your quarterly allowance – was forwarded to you in response to your request."

I said nothing. It wasn't much good explaining where the money had gone – chartering the 6-metre at Burnham, squaring up after that fantastic day at Ascot, the Stockholm trip with Ingrid and Lucia. It had seemed so grand then, and was so second-rate when considered in these surroundings: it wasn't fair to rob me like this, to turn memories sour and daydreams into sordid little futilities.

But Armstrong was speaking again: "By my reckoning," he said evenly, "you have, in two years, received sums amounting to four hundred and seventy pounds, over and above your agreed allowance of seven hundred pounds a year. That means that your father allowed you a sum in excess of nine hundred each year, at a time when his own financial embarrassment was acute."

Once more I made no answer.

He put the papers away again in their neat compartment.

"I will not disguise from you," he went on, "that this was a course which I opposed from the outset. And that for two reasons. I did not think it fair to keep you in ignorance of the facts, when a word of explanation might have resulted in your curtailing your expenses to a – er – to some degree. Furthermore, the payment to you of nearly nineteen hundred pounds in two years accelerated in no small measure the general decay of his affairs and particularly of the Nine Beeches estate."

"If I had known," I answered as earnestly as I could, "I wouldn't have stayed at Cambridge. I would have been here, trying to help him."

"Quite so." He nodded. "That was a point which I myself put to him. But he seemed unable, or unwilling, to see it in that light: as he expressed it, he wanted you to have a good time as long as you could. He also had some idea – the – er – Taormina affair: he felt himself under some sort of obligation … However, that is neither here nor there."

"Taormina *was* a shock," I agreed, to help out his embarrassment. "But it didn't need that sort of sacrifice on his part. It was squared up by my leaving home and living by myself in London."

"A regrettable affair altogether." He dived into the dispatch-case again. "And now if we can go over the exact situation together."

"I suppose it's pretty hopeless."

He looked over his spectacles at me. "That is not a term which has any professional significance, but I fear it may prove substantially correct. The bulk of your father's income, apart from investments and inherited stock, was derived from a life interest in his brother's – your uncle Joseph Hendryck's – estate. That interest, of course, ceases with his death. And with regard to the details of the past four years …"

And then he started, lying bare the whole tragic progress in page after page of figures and relay after relay of facts: so much lost on this and that transaction, so much overdraft at the bank, so much due to creditors, so much stock left, so much expectation of future dividends. For each development and each fresh phase he would produce a sheaf of closely typed pages: so that soon I began to hate those two thin hands of his which went on and on delving into the miserable past and bringing out yet another misfortune, yet another pitiful blunder. This was the second time that day I had to sit helpless and listen to an account of disaster; and this frigid documented version was immeasurably the worst. And what my father had suffered in the process …

Presently Armstrong broke off. "This must be a distressing experience for you," he said, an unexpected humanity in his voice. "I can assure you that it is not easy for me, either. But" – he raised a finger to emphasize his point – "I must make it clear that the conduct of your father's stock-exchange activities was *not* in our hands – in fact, very far from it. It was my painful burden to have to see him selling out good stocks, of trustee standard but unfortunately not safeguarded in any way, without knowing what he was reinvesting in. The Sunamina Tin Mine failure was but one incident in a profoundly ill-advised and ill-managed series of ventures, during which – I will say it quite frankly – his associates and ultimate despoilers were by no means men of professional standing, or indeed of any marked commercial honesty." He paused and blew out his cheeks: for him this was harsh speaking. "All his recent transactions were speculation in its purest –

or rather its most impure form: and as such they were bound, sooner or later, to defeat themselves."

"He must have changed tremendously," I murmured, half to myself. The recital, and the frigid brutality of the figures, had left me spiritless. "And my God! all that time I was … Nineteen hundred quid which he simply hadn't got …"

"You mustn't reproach yourself too hardly." Thank heaven the dispatch-case was momentarily shut. "A certain amount of extravagance is excusable, and you could not know the real price which was being paid. But I fear you will find things very different in the future."

"Oh, I don't mind economizing. Not after this."

"It will be economy of a basic order. I think it unlikely that you can remain in residence at Cambridge."

I stared. "But I've only got two more terms to run. And what about taking my degree?"

He spread his hands in a gesture of resignation. "Most unfortunate, I agree: but a matter of plain necessity under these circumstances. By the way, I hope you have not contracted a further large amount of debt during the course of the past two or three months?"

"Well …" I said.

He fingered his chin. "If it should be more than twenty pounds – "

"Good God!" I interrupted involuntarily. "That isn't very much margin, is it?"

"Er – you think it will be more?"

"I don't know." I was too depressed to bring it out. Taking London and Cambridge together, I supposed I owed about three hundred pounds. "But I can start cutting down straight away," I went on. "I'll sub-let the flat, and we'll just carry on here as best we can. After all, we can practically live on the place."

He shook his head: for the first time I noticed a sign of weariness in his manner. "I am afraid you still do not realize the extent to which your father committed himself. There is a mortgage on the whole Nine Beeches estate for approximately eighteen thousand pounds."

I suddenly felt sick.

"The mortgagees are clients of ours," he went on, "and will not press you unduly – of that I am sure. But if, as is probable, the estate is declared insolvent, it is difficult to see how you can keep up interest payments amounting to nearly nine hundred pounds a year."

I swallowed. Even Tania had known nothing of this. "But the eighteen thousand – has that gone too?"

Armstrong inclined his head. "Sunamina. The mortgage was in fact arranged for that purpose. But the matter is not entirely hopeless." He fumbled in the dispatch-case once more, and held up a single sheet of paper. "I have had a communication from a Mr Demetriades – "

"No!" I said suddenly.

"I beg your pardon?"

"Whatever he offers, I won't accept it."

Taken aback, Armstrong let the paper fall to his knee. "But this is most surprising … He has lent your father large sums in the past – a matter of friendship, as I understood it. He now offers to take over the whole mortgage, and to defer pressing for interest until you, or the estate generally, can support the charge." He looked across at me. "You object to such an arrangement?"

"Yes."

"May I ask – ?"

"He wants to marry my sister."

Armstrong, getting the implication clearly enough, flushed. Avoiding my eye, he answered: "That of course puts a different complexion on the matter, one in which your personal feelings – I do not think we need pursue the question further at this stage." He locked his dispatch-case finally, and rose. "I believe I have told you enough, Mr Hendrycks, to indicate the general position. Under your father's will you and I are appointed joint executors, and the transaction of legal business is left in my hands. We need come to no decision of any sort until the will is proved and the estate assessed in detail."

"How long does that take?"

"Six months – possibly less."

"And, roughly speaking, there'll be nothing left – in fact, a debit balance?"

"I fear that is so." He preceded me into the hall, preparing to take his leave. "I can hold out no hope that there will be sufficient either for you or Miss Tania to live on. I wish I could give you any other assurance, but I cannot. Good day to you."

That, however, was not the end of the day by any means; for Armstrong's car had hardly cleared the drive before another one appeared, bearing a solid phalanx of creditors, among whom were numbered the farrier, the general-provision merchant, and the local wine-people. This interview also was immensely depressing, for these people had obviously called to attack, to put in a hard claim before the storm finally broke: they faced me across the breadth of the desk, four men in black suits each armed with his statement of account, and stared at me as if by so staring they could outwit some contemplated trickery on my part. Of course I was able to stall them by saying that all debts must now be handled through the solicitors: but the suspicion on their faces and the sly questions and hints they dropped were an atrocious reminder of the dark world I was now entering.

When they had gone I looked round the room in which I had received them, my father's room, and could find no comfort in its stillness and solid masculinity: for the outside world was no longer at arm's length, but was closing in, and this room and the whole house with it would soon be submerged in that swiftly flowing tide. The desk, the smaller escritoire, the safe, all were loaded with papers which tomorrow I must sift and dispose of: there was the furniture to sell, there would be interminable business with Armstrong, there was the funeral, and the mountain of debt at Cambridge, and going down degreeless, and Beach and Dobson, and Demetriades who wanted Tania and would get her ... I slumped into an armchair and put my hand over my eyes. For the moment I was defeated.

Perhaps it was as well that I had so much to do: for with such a background the appalling crudities of the burial service could make little impression. Indeed, it seemed the most natural thing in the world that, in the midst of this intense and never-ending disturbance, my father should be lowered deep into the ground, that the little party should shiver in the icy wind, that earth should patter and thud on his coffin, that Tania should hide her face in my shoulder ...

But then I knew that I had to get away from it. I wanted a respite. And I wanted to see Alison, in London.

I took no lengthy farewell of Nine Beeches: that was something I had done four years ago, and since then, it seemed, the place had lost its power to move me. I walked with Tania a little way into the garden, and then across the damp lawn fringed by bare trees that I would not see in leaf again: we paused, arm-in-arm, as we reached its margin, and stood looking up at the outline of the house. By agreement we talked no more of her marriage: it was something that she had settled in her mind, after long thought, and though during the past two days I had pleaded with her at least to postpone it, I could not really be sure that the preceding four years did not warrant a surrender of this sort. Two days had been enough to reduce me to despair; and I had known nothing of the longer struggle, I had not been miserably short of money or gone in fear of what the next day would bring. She had the right to choose a cure for that circumstance, without a third person putting difficulties in her way ... She was to go to Paris almost immediately, and be married within a month.

"I won't see you for a long time, Marcus," she said presently, breaking in on my thoughts. "You've decided finally about – about the mortgage, haven't you?"

"Yes," I said, as gently as I could. I wanted to avoid any reflection on her own choice. "I'll go my own way – to begin with, at least: I'll find a job, and live in London, and see how it works out." I looked up at the house again: by my side the dogs themselves dispirited, sniffed at the grass without interest or enthusiasm. The old wolfhound was to be destroyed, and the spaniel given to Morrison. "In any case, I'll never come back here."

"Nor I."

I shivered suddenly. "I envy you having a winter out of England ... I must be thinking of going, my darling."

"I know. It's sad."

We moved across the lawn, the dogs padding after us: the touch of her hand on my arm tightened momentarily, as if she sought thereby to delay my going. Close under the house, dwarfed by its mass and the shuttered silence of its rough walls, she said suddenly: "Don't forget I'm still on the earth, Marco. You don't like the idea now, but later, if things are too difficult, if you can't hold out ..."

"I will bear in mind my rich sister." I smiled at her, against the sense of my words: she knew that I hated their implication. "I'll be making my own fortune one of these days – you just wait."

"I'll wait as long as you like."

Together we entered the house for the last time, our footfalls on the stone passageway seeming quickly lost in its rigid silence. Now there remained only a few more farewells.

CHAPTER THREE

Reason has moons, but moons not hers
Lie mirror'd on her sea,
Confounding her astronomers,
But O! delighting me.

RALPH HODGSON

❖

Afterwards Alison lay still, as if cut down by my body, smoking lazily our shared cigarette, and murmured: "I got your note … I'm so sorry, Marcus."

They were the first words that either of us had spoken. Words just weren't things that we used at that stage, because we were never in doubt as to each other's readiness and availability: I had come there to be comforted, a fact of which we had both been immediately aware, and speech needed only to make a late entry, like a murmured afterthought to which the speaker himself hardly listened. We knew our real currency, and were in no danger of thus debasing it.

"Thanks, darling," I answered. "The last two days have been pretty deadly. I'm broke, as well."

"Oh, darling …" But she hadn't taken it in at all: at such moments her attention was always elusive and impermanent, liable to slide away on its own moonbeams; she was sensuously drugged into waywardness.

I rolled over on my elbow and looked down at her. It was hardly the moment to appraise her with any sort of eagerness, but even the slaked eye could find delight in her milky skin and grey-green eyes slanting upwards at the corners, and the masses of auburn hair spread fanwise over the pillow. I kissed her still-flushed cheek, and said: "No, I mean really broke. He died bankrupt."

Even that word didn't penetrate. She must have been swept far away …

"Poor Marcus, how dreadful!" she murmured huskily. "I'll make it up to you."

"Well, you can't at the moment."

"What'll you bet?"

I laughed. "You always were a trier, weren't you?"

Presently she asked: "Did you say bankrupt, or did I dream it?" She was playing with the hair on my forearm, and frowning to herself. "What will it mean? That won't spoil the Newmarket idea, will it? I couldn't bear that."

I shook my head. "The Newmarket flat is about as remote as the moon. I won't even be able to stay up at Cambridge any longer."

She woke up at that, instantly conscious of my words and of me lying by her side: she sprang into life, crouching her superb body over mine like a vivid canopy protecting a child from harm.

"Marcus, it can't be as bad as that. Is it really true? No money at all?"

"No money at all. In fact, the estate may be several thousands in the red, and I'm overdrawn myself. Nine Beeches will have to go – oh, you don't know what that is do you? It's the family house, but it ain't any longer. And as for me …"

"You're fine," she answered quickly. She drooped and caressed and kissed me, all in one movement. "You're all right. Don't believe anybody else. Is there anything I can do for you?"

"Not quite yet … I'm *not* all right, Alison – by the way, you've got the loveliest legs I've ever seen – I'm very far from all right. I've got nothing to live on, no job, and no degree – "

She put her hand over my mouth. "Don't think of it now, darling. It's too sorrowful. Think of being with me instead."

"And that's another thing," I was suddenly immensely depressed by it all, so that her cheerfulness was almost an irritant.

"What do you mean?"

"Dearest, I can't afford it. I can't afford to take you about or give you nice things. I've NO MONEY."

"We'll think of a way."

"Now you're being so feminine that I could strangle you."

"Please strangle me."

I looked at her steadily. "Alison, what I've been saying *does* mean something, you know." I tried to make her understand with one sentence. "I can't afford a mistress any longer."

For a flickering second her eyes sought mine: I saw doubt in them, and a realization of circumstance. Then her lips curved to a huge wide smile, and she brought her face very close to mine.

"It's no good, Marco," she said gently. "I *like* being called your mistress." Quickly lapsing into childishness, she pretended to knock on the pillow. "Knock, knock, Mistress here. Can I come in?"

"Nought out of ten for biology," I said. "But I see the idea."

We abandoned words once again. I was never very much in favour of them, in any case.

But we couldn't abandon them for very long – or rather, I couldn't: the past two days were too fresh in my memory, the facts too real, the menace too close to be ignored. It was perfection to lie there in a sunken dream of satisfaction, to listen to one's slowing heartbeats and the rise-and-fall of nearby breathing, to savour the best cigarette of all; but to this perfection I had, in logic, no sort of right. Even as I lay there I was playing at reality and cheating the facts: for they demanded immediate action, they ordered me to be in Cambridge clearing up my affairs or out on the streets looking for a job: they could not conceivably be stretched to cover this bed and this cushioned room and this submergence of reason in sensuality. I tried to make Alison understand this, a little later, after she had pattered off to the kitchen and returned with an immense brandy highball chunking with ice blocks: after I had peered out into the afternoon dusk and seen the mist gaining ground along the wet Chelsea street: after she had said: "Sweet, can we go to a theatre? Can we see *Tovarich?*"

I sighed, not too plaintively: just a medium sigh. "Dear Miss Erroll," I answered, "to speak roughly to you at this moment would be an act of peculiar ingratitude. But my theatre-going days are over, for the time being: even if I had the money, which I haven't, I should hang on to it."

She took the glass out of my hand, and sipped at it. The ice clinked and rattled. Then she looked at me over the rim, and said: "I'll stake you. I've got two pounds."

I shook my head. "Oh, it would be all right for tonight, I know. But I must look ahead: it's no good just going on at the old rate, and then suddenly waking up to the fact that I haven't a cent left."

"But, darling Marco, *I'll* take us to the theatre."

"You can't afford it either, can you?"

Alison had about three hundred a year of her own, but made no attempt to do much more than dress on it. I'd met her just after getting back from Stockholm, at a Bloomsbury party where nothing mattered; we'd had one dance together, and that was that. Roughly speaking, I paid for the flat.

As she didn't answer, I said: "It's going to be different for you too, darling. I won't be able to contribute on the same scale – or any scale at all, probably."

She pulled a face. "I'll give this place up and come and live at Hill Street, then. Marcus, this is so dreary. Don't be serious all of a sudden. Do it more slowly – tighten up tomorrow. You seem to have put on about ten years since I saw you last."

I sat down on the bed, and took over the highball. The inside of the glass was misted with her warm breath.

"I don't suppose," I said presently, "that I can keep Hill Street on – it'll be right out of my class. And the sort of place that I'm going to live in won't appeal to you."

She was lying down again, playing with the light switch which hung at the end of its long cable. She clicked it on, and her whole body glowed, a warm rosy-golden length: then off again, so that only her pale outline in the dusk could be seen, merging with the lighter sheets. I watched fascinated, sinking into fantasy once more, losing contact with the hard world I had summoned up.

"What sort of place?" she murmured.

"Oh, I don't know. An attic somewhere, or some dreary boarding-house. It depends if I get a job soon, and what sort of one it is."

"I know one you could get straight away."

"So do I." I downed the rest of the drink at a gulp: the spirit hit the back of my throat like a fiery cross summoning the clans to action. "Are we thinking of the same job?"

"We are now, anyway …" But she held me off for a moment. "And then we'll go to a theatre?"

"Yes, darling."

"And have a lovely supper at Quag's?"

"Yes, darling."

"Hot lobster?"

"Yes, darling."

"And you'll stay the night here?"

"Yes, yes, yes … That's all I'll answer, just at present."

"How funny," she said softly. "I was just going to stop talking."

The palpable insanity of that evening, which cost rather over eight pounds, occurred to me at various times during its course, but never too strongly to break through the bright surface of its exhilaration. For it was so exactly to my taste, it was the best possible evening as I understood it: the play, witty and incisive and for me faintly nostalgic, had tonic properties, so that, sitting in the stalls watching Cedric Hardwicke's polished self-possession, and the glowing Leontovich, I could convince myself that any other kind of evening would have been too dreary and too quick a descent to the new level; and later, demolishing the promised *Homard Thermidor* and dancing to 'Let's Begin' in the brilliant noisy cellar that was Quaglino's grill, I was forced to agree with Alison that we had both needed cheering up and that this was the only way to do it. And indeed, clasping her loosely (we excluded sex from our dancing) and laughing together for sheer pleasure in the warm gaiety, the packed uproar, the swinging music which wove its pattern over the room, it was impossible to believe that this was something which I must give up, that it must be rationed down to zero, that I actually could not stay in this world. There must be some way …

Next morning, of course, was different. Towards ten Alison dragged herself out of bed and went hunting for something eatable in the kitchen, while I lay entwined in tumbled sheets and fingered yesterday's shave and began to realize what a godforsaken fool I'd been. Eight pounds had been flicked away into the night, when I owed three hundred and had about forty in the bank: time and money had been wasted in a retreat from reality, reality which grew in imminence and menace the more it was denied. It was as if my father had never died in distress, as if that story which had fallen gently from Tania's lips was still unuttered: it was as if I had turned my back on truth and would continue cheating … I frowned blackly, under conviction of shortcoming: lying there in picturesque tumult and some exhaustion, I determined that this day would see a basic change of habit.

Alison came in, with a not very crowded tray. She wore my dressing-gown and one pink-feathered mule: her tangled hair and violet-shadowed eyes gave a swift picture of desire fulfilled, a thumbnail of temporary sufficiency. But her vitality did not seem in doubt even at that moment.

"Coffee," she said brightly. "And hot-buttered-toast and honey. And me again." She put the tray down on an edge of eiderdown. "Aren't I wonderful, darling?"

"Yes, darling. But I'm not sure that I am. Do you realize what we did last night?"

Pouring out coffee, she glanced up for a moment, with a smile.

"Sure …"

"No – I mean the damned silly way we behaved."

"Coffee, darling."

"Thanks." I balanced the cup on my stomach, and began to stir it. "This is all very well, you know, but it's pretty far from the facts. And last night ..." I waved one arm in sudden excitement: the coffee slopped over and splashed my chest. "I've got to *economize*, and we go off and supper ourselves solid and dance and drink till three. What sort of a way is that to behave?"

She bit into her toast, looking across at me thoughtfully.

"Darling, don't depress," she said finally. "We had this last night, didn't we? It's no good just going *on* about it: that doesn't help a bit. Eat some toast and be normal."

Then we began to quarrel.

I could understand how boring she must have found my droning on about poverty and economizing, but I did think that she'd be a bit more sensible about it that morning. She had always been so quick at picking up any other idea, and just because she disliked this one I didn't see why she couldn't help me to face it. Particularly as it was going to affect her as well ... At all events we had a rousing scrap, which ended in her saying that she hadn't any use for me if I was going to gloom all over the flat, and my answering "Very well" and clearing out in a rage shortly before eleven. For once I saw my way clearly, and I wasn't going to be turned from it ... Lugging my suitcase down Cheyne Walk, and wondering where on earth the nearest bus stop was, I found myself saying with extreme conviction: "If that's the way she feels about it, then that lets me out."

It was a mood which did not last long; the cold morning air, and the fact that I had to wait half an hour at Liverpool Street for a Cambridge train, militated against any prolonged outburst of temper. For Alison hadn't changed, and I *did* need her: it wasn't her I was quarrelling with, it was my own position; and I could understand what an unsatisfactory escort I must have seemed and how poorly my behaviour of that morning must have compared with the sort of companionship she had come to expect from me: going down from Cambridge, and debts and bankruptcies and little garrets, hardly accorded with her reasonable expectation, remembering how from our first meeting I had signed any cheque, and bought any dress or ticket, and generally given her *Cartier blanche* ... And suppose she got the idea into her head that a broke Marcus was hardly worth her attention, suppose she preferred to cut loose and start somewhere else – I tried to ring her up at the last moment, but the number was engaged, and in the end I had to run for my train without getting through.

That meant a wretched journey down, the very worst start to what I had to face at Cambridge.

Murray, my tutor, seemed somehow to be coloured with my own ineffectiveness. He expressed his sympathy in suitable terms, and his regret that I would have to go down straight away; but as regarded practical help he did not advance beyond the vaguest expressions of goodwill.

"You are most unfortunately placed, Mr Hendrycks," he said at length, after we had disposed of the details of my actual leaving. He paced the small confines of the window embrasure, his thin hands clasped behind his back, his head bent on his chest. He was tall and slight and bald, with a good presence (for a don) and a normally pitched voice: I used to dine with him once or twice each term (he had been up with my father), when we talked shooting and travel and undergraduate scandal. I don't suppose he thought much of me, since I did no work and was always being fined and gated and generally threatened with extinction: and even if he had taken in the full details about my finances, which he clearly had not, it wouldn't have given him any notable shock. He had his own vacuum, to which such realities hardly penetrated.

Being far better aware than he how unfortunately placed I was, I made no answer.

"Most unfortunately." He stopped suddenly in his tracks, and peered at me from the edge of the carpet. "The failure to take a degree is liable to weigh heavily with any prospective employer. It is unlikely that the Appointments Board can do anything in such a case."

I made the usual joke about the disappointments Board. It was coolly received: in fact, not received at all. Murray resumed his pacing.

"You have no work in view?" he asked presently.

"No, sir."

"Or any inclination? I should say," he smiled dryly, "any personal inclination towards some definite sphere. Of your inclination towards work itself I am well informed."

"I'm afraid," I said frankly, "that I have been pretty lazy at times."

He stopped again, for another quick peer in my direction.

"You have been consistently idle for the last twelve months," he said smoothly. "You did some small amount of work your first year, and obtained a second in the Intermediate. You passed the first part of the Tripos with the lowest feasible number of marks. And this year – but you would hardly think it fair for me to review the amount of work you have done this term. And I would hardly think it possible."

Hell! I thought. Is this the time to produce cracks like that?

"I've no actual job in view, sir," I answered, "nor any clear idea of what I want to do. I know one or two people up in London who might be useful: I'll be seeing them as soon as I go down." (It had just occurred to me that Uncle Octavian, about the only friendly relative I had, might be able to do something for me.) "I really wanted to try writing or journalism." I looked at him as he paced off again. "I suppose you wouldn't advise that?"

"For ordinary newspaper work," the answer came pat, as from a scholarly slot-machine, "that is, for reporting, you are now too old. Newspapers enlist their reporting staff at the age of seventeen or thereabouts. But journalism generally offers a wide field, and I should judge that you have the requisite fund of – shall we say, independence and cynicism, to attain to success there. But starting is a slow business. Have you friends or acquaintances in the literary world?"

"No, none."

"Or any experience of writing?"

"I've had a certain amount in the *Granta*."

He stopped again, and smiled. "Yes, I seem to remember various outbursts of exuberance over the initials 'MLH.' The *Granta* has been a training ground for many distinguished men of letters. But even so, I fear that you will find writing as a profession a matter of initial difficulty and possibly prolonged hardship. Nor can I remember a report from your supervisor which indicated any marked facility of expression in the presentation of more serious work."

"One can't exactly let oneself go over Roman Law, sir. Things like *tutela* or the manumission of slaves don't call for sparkling writing, do they?"

Disliking even this small amount of opposition, he peered at me again, his brows flexed.

"They call," he answered fairly stiffly, "for clarity of expression, which is itself a primary postulate in any branch of writing. And though of course one must guard against too high a degree of specialization – you remember the definition of a specialist? 'A man who learns more and more about less and less, until finally he knows everything about nothing.'" He chuckled reminiscently. "Rather good, don't you think?"

"It has always been considered so." It was clear that he could do nothing to help me, and was simply enjoying the occasion as a relief from boredom. I felt entitled to resent the fact.

He affected not to have heard my answer.

"Writing …" he murmured. "Well, well … There is great scope for enterprise there. I can only wish you luck if you do decide to enter the field." He looked out of the window towards the clock on Chapel Tower. "Four o'clock already. You'll stay to tea?"

I rose. "I'm afraid I can't, thank you very much, sir. I've got a great deal to do."

"I expect you have. An unfortunate business altogether …" At the door he said: "Come and see me before you go."

There was no one in my rooms, so I went across to Alastair's in Neville's Court, in search of more inspiring company. I suppose it was unreasonable to have expected much help from Murray, having regard to the way I had behaved during the past two years and the sort of undergraduate I had been; but I did think he might have put in a word for me with the Appointments Board, degreeless though I was, or at least got me one or two introductions to editors or journalists in London. That was something he could have done without loss of dignity or sacrifice of principle. And, knowing how I was placed, he really needn't have emphasized how slack I'd been and how ill I deserved of the university: I wanted cheering up, not lecturing and showing to the door …

The Neville's Court rooms were full of what at first appeared to be dead bodies, but which presently resolved themselves into Charles, Alastair and Peter Tresham sprawling half asleep in attitudes which traversed the limits of abandon and approached those of dissolution. It was clear that they were recovering from some physical effort which had left them devitalized.

"You boys look drunk," I said, as I switched on some more lights. The figure of Archie, curled up in a distant chair with a bandage round his head, sprang into prominence.

Peter opened one eye. "Oh, that was ages ago. We're all right now. See you later ..." His head flopped down again, and he sighed his way back to sleep.

Next it was Charles who woke up suddenly, stared at me and said: "Congratulations."

It was the one word in the English language which I would have laid any odds against hearing.

"Thanks," I answered. "Why?"

"Turtledove."

"Hallo, Marcus," said Alastair from the sofa. He rolled over and looked at me. "We've missed you. How you've grown."

"Turtledove?" I stared at Charles uncomprehendingly. Then I got it. "Good God, did it win? What was the price?"

"A hundred to eight," said Alastair. "You get a hundred and twenty-five quid. Very nice too. Mine's a brandy and ginger-ale."

"Hallo, Marcus," said Archie suddenly, at the top of his voice. "Notice me, Marcus – I've been an invalid."

"How's the eye?" I asked vaguely.

"Fine. I've had three stitches and – Aren't you interested?"

"I'm still thinking about winning all that money."

Charles wandered across to the sideboard and splashed some soda water into a glass. "I suppose you owe most of it?"

"To my bookmaker? No – only about thirty pounds, so I'm ninety-five up." I was suddenly immensely pleased with life. "Think of that, now – ninety-five quid dropped in my lap."

"It'll keep you in cigars till the end of term."

"What did it win by?"

Alastair laughed. "A neck, in about the roughest race ever seen. Objection to the real winner upheld, and the race awarded to Turtledove. You've nothing much to be proud of."

I smiled in answer. "I'm proud of ninety-five quid," I said. "In fact, I doubt if I've ever been prouder of anything in my life."

Then I told them about my father.

A full hour later Archie was still lying in a haze of astonishment, repeating: "Hell! It can't be true …" over and over again. The others weren't much less stricken, either.

"But a job, a regular daily job – that's the sickening thing about it." Alastair's voice still reflected his supreme amazement, and he was nursing his brandy and ginger-ale as if *he* were in danger of being stripped of his possessions as well. "One might get used to having very little money, though I wouldn't bet on it; but to settle down to go to an office every day …"

"Don't harp on it," I said. "I feel raw enough already."

"But an office …" Alastair simply couldn't get past the word. "No more spare time, no more getting up after lunch or playing poker for sixteen hours at a stretch: no more spending the day in the open air, miles from anywhere, if you feel like it. It's – it's *immoral!*"

"If you boys think you're cheering me up," I put in mildly, "then you've got a funny way of going about it."

"Hell!" came Archie's slow chorus from the chair by the window. "I still can't take it in."

"And anyway," I said, "I probably won't be in an office. It'll be something like freelance journalism, I should think." I had been drinking with fair concentration for the past hour, and was beginning to feel less like a bath running out than hitherto. "I'll get used to it. And I can always take up betting professionally, you know: a hundred and twenty-five quid in one day is – is far too hard to work out, but it would add up to a fair sum at the end of the year."

"What's it all about, anyway?" Charles sounded faintly aggrieved. "Marcus can work: he's got a perfectly good brain."

"Steady!" I said. "You're going to the other extreme now."

"Of course you're clever. You read Law, don't you? You can understand – " he looked round at Alastair's bookshelves, "well, just look at the size of those books." He picked up the biggest. "I'm only trying to qualify for the poor bloody infantry, but I know tough reading when I see it." He flipped a few pages, and then suddenly bent and stared. "I mean, listen to this – this is the sort of thing Marcus can understand … 'Where any person or persons' (he read) 'shall be seized of any hereditaments to the use confidence or trust of any other person or persons or of any body politic, such person persons or bodies politic that have any such use confidence or trust in fee simple, fee tail, for term of years or for life, or otherwise, shall from henceforward stand and be seized, deemed, and adjudged in lawful seisin estate and possession of and in such hereditaments of and in such like estates as they have in the use confidence or trust.' Now I contend," he said, in the abashed silence which followed, "that anyone who can make sense of that isn't going to have much trouble earning his living when he goes down."

There was general laughter, in which I joined. This was better, this was more like a proper finish …

" 'Fee tail'," murmured Archie to himself. "What a sweet name: it sounds like a furry little animal with a frightfully expensive skin."

The boys were now settling my future with competence and finality.

"After all, even if he doesn't get a job straight away," said Alastair, "he can live on his relatives for some time. Have you any relatives, Marco? Can you live on them?"

"No, I don't like them."

He laughed. "When you're broke? Nobody dislikes anyone as much as that, do they?"

"Anyway they don't like me. And most of them aren't in London, but spread over Bucks and Berks. I'd rather be broke, and have London to myself."

"Grand," said Peter. "It gives you a free hand with the debs."

"Debs!" Charles gave one of those snorts which splay drink all over the carpet. "My God, you're welcome to them. I took a real deb out once – "

"My dear Charles," I said, "what were you doing with a girl?"

"My mother wanted to do her a favour … Anyway, I called round for her – I'd better not tell you her name, Marco, because her parents are rolling and you might want to marry them – her, I mean. Her mother saw us off, and said, 'Be careful of little Patty, won't you?' Mind you, little Patty was the real thing, white gauzy dress, no chest, stuffed-egg expression, and a kind of Maypole wreath in her hair – and I really was *frightfully* careful: didn't even take her arm, sat in one corner of the taxi, and talked about the Royal family."

"As if you'd have known what to do, anyway."

"Oh, I belong to a library … Well, we had dinner at the Savoy, and I said 'No cocktail' very firmly and poured her out exactly half a glass of claret. Then I looked away for about two seconds, because she really was *abysmally* depressing, acres and acres of Pond's Two Creams laid on with a fireman's shovel – and when I turned round again she just wasn't there – she was under the table, tight as a tick. Half a glass of claret … Of course I was booed all the way down the restaurant as I went out – one old chap called me a young puppy – as if *I'd* made the mess. And her mother naturally swore that I'd doped the drink: and I had to interview the father and be glared at across a big mahogany desk. Even my mother said the evening wasn't quite what she'd planned … Debs? – give me something hardboiled above the forty line."

We all laughed: standing there, looking injured, he had really made the recital pretty amusing.

Then: "Hell, I must go to hall," said Peter suddenly. He stood up, and looked across at me. "When do you leave, Marco?"

"Tomorrow afternoon." And how sad that sounded.

"Don't slip off without seeing me, will you?"

"How about poker?" asked Charles when he had gone.

"Can't afford," I said. I glanced at Archie. "Mr van Tyler, you haven't given us much of your attention. What's on your mind?"

"My dear Marcus," he heaved himself up in his chair, fingering the bandage across his forehead, "what else but you? I still can't think of anything except extravagant leisure where you're concerned." He made a hopeless gesture. "How do you start? What's the strength of it? I feel I want to take it all apart and watch it tick. Broke? It's just a word … How much money *have* you got?"

"Well – none."

"No, really how much?"

I laughed at his puzzled expression. "I took a long time to wake up too … With this win over Turtledove, I'll have about a hundred and fifty pounds. I owe approximately twice as much, so *that* earth is pretty well stopped. I've got a car to sell, a good stack of books, a pair of guns – lots of things like that: I've got one rich uncle who might or might not contribute: and I've the chance that my father's estate might just turn out on the right side – that depends on the valuation of shares and things." I spread out my hands. "So altogether, as I said, I have just about – nothing."

There was a long silence after I finished speaking: Alastair was slowly sipping his drink, Charles staring at me without a word, Archie sunk in thought behind his cupped hands. I really hadn't meant to go into such detail, since it might embarrass them and certainly did nothing to raise my spirits: but Archie's straightforward question and obvious interest had sufficed to overcome this reluctance. And, indeed, it was the first time that I myself had faced the actual query of how much money I had in the world – hitherto I had simply cited the word 'broke' as a cushion against the full facts …

Presently: "How much will you take for the car?" asked Charles.

I shook my head. "You don't want a car. And before this becomes embarrassing, I may as well say that I am *not* going to palm off my surplus possessions on any of my friends."

"We'll see about that," said Alastair briskly. "And personally, whether I'm a friend of yours or not, I've always had an eye on those guns and I'm in the market for them."

Now that was perfectly true, for they were a lovely pair given me by my father, and Alastair had often used them and *did* think a lot of them. But once this sort of thing started … I shook my head again.

"It's good of both of you, but it'll be more satisfactory if I don't do any private selling." And before they could object: "So that's that," I went on. "I'm now going across to telephone Alison: come round to my rooms in twenty minutes and I'll brew you something to stunt your growth. All my liquor has to be finished up tonight."

"It's no good being obstinate, Marco," said Archie. "We're going to do a lot of talking about money before the night's out."

I smiled, and said: "Telephone – see you later."

"Remember me to Alison," called Alastair as I was going out.

"I can't. It would take too long." I paused in the doorway and looked back at him. "That's rather funny, if you work it out."

"It would be simply uproarious," he answered, "if it meant anything at all. Goodbye."

Great Court in the dusk of that evening was the perfect microcosm of the gentler Cambridge life. That air of mystery and quietness which overhangs any centre of learning was plain to feel – and plain to see, for everything aided the eye: everything about that square of grey stone, turned here and there to yellow by the lamplight, broken by the orange rectangles of curtained windows, added to the sum of its intense and embracing peace. Even the tall fountain in the centre, restless and chattering, was no agent of disturbance: rather did it seem to knit the darkness together, so that the flow of night sounds – the chiming bells, the distant traffic, the calls of figure to figure across the court, the slurring footsteps on the cobblestones – were welded by the splash and play of water into a single continuous entity. The fountain did not break the peace, it only bound it together into a more shapely and more enduring pattern: midway between the still twilight and the human stirring beneath, it preserved unbroken that invisible chain whose compass was loveliness and whose links antiquity.

The moving pattern of figures formed and fell apart and formed again as I crossed the court; and they too were the very fabric and essence of the past two years, so that before I was halfway over I had the impression of having cut a cross-section, of which these various figures were the revealed specimens of Cambridge life – top-hatted porters bearing messages from staircase to staircase, freshmen going to first hall, people in muddy football clothes drifting in through Great Gate, a kitchen porter with a loaded tray on his head, two slow arm-in-arm walkers – dons in studious colloquy – their heads bent as they paced the grass, an occasional hurrying figure, bearing cap and gown, in swift flight to a supervision class. I myself was included – by a "Good evening, Mr Hendrycks" from one of the college servants, by a sudden "Hallo, Marcus!" from a half opened window near the gateway ... This was the Cambridge I knew well, the part which no one could escape; and it was leaving and regretting this aspect of community which already weighed heavily, and would soon bear down upon me with the full significance of its finality.

The telephone call was a wretched one: I could hardly be cheerful, under the circumstances, and Alison herself seemed to be still displaying that feminine unawareness which had occasioned our quarrel that morning. Of course we made it up, with a rush of endearments which might well have led to some kind of prosecution: but that was as far as the thing went – she did not sound ready to give me any more help, she still hardly knew what I was talking about.

"I'm coming down tomorrow," I told her presently. "Will you be there?"

"Of course, darling. Can we go away for the weekend?"

"Well …" Between us the wires hummed, reproaching my hesitation.

"London's so dreary, Marco. Let's go to that pub in the New Forest."

"Dearest, I won't have a car. I'm going to sell it up here."

"Oh dear," she said, "that's going to make a bit of difference, isn't it? Can't you really keep it on?"

"You know I can't."

"Don't snap, darling … I'm so *bored*."

"Cheer up. I'll be there about six. We'll have a lovely evening together."

"It's not much fun when you've no money, is it?"

"But, Alison, I'm the same man. We still like being together, we're still a success."

She sighed. "Of course, darling. It's just that … Oh well, we can go to a flick, can't we?"

"If you like, yes." Not that we could: but it would be easier to tell her when we were face to face.

The time-signal went.

"That's three minutes," I said. "I must ring off. Goodbye, darling."

"What's the hurry? Stay and talk to me. I'm all alone."

"Honestly I can't afford it, darling. See you tomorrow."

She had started "But, Marcus," in an aggrieved voice as I hung up. It was a shame to have to do it – the contrast with our usual twenty-minute session was absolutely ludicrous: but trunk calls were one of the first things to be rationed, under the new regime which beset me.

I went across to the Hawks' to have one single drink and pay my bill at the bar, and then walked slowly to my rooms on H staircase. 'H 3 Great Court' – what a lot that simple designation had meant to me during the past year, and how much I was going to miss the blend of salon, saloon, and stamping ground which I had made of it. Entering it now,

I was struck more strongly than ever by its essential suitability to life as I had lived it so far: grossly untidy though it might be, its exact fitness for purpose could never be questioned.

That untidiness was something that no gyp could ever have cured, but I had in any case saved Rowlands the trouble of going on strike by explaining at the outset that that was how I liked it, and he needn't bother any more ... It was larger than most rooms in College, and the furniture I had taken over from a third-year man with a pretty sense of comfort – the couch was in the grand tradition of voluptuous resilience, the five armchairs promised their loyal support under every conceivable circumstance. Cream walls and a set of six Rowlandson cartoons completed the formal setting. But for the rest ...

Things placed here and there, things dropped about in odd corners, things sprinkled in piles and heaps, scattered, strewn, broadcast; things left about or tidied away (indistinguishable); things seemingly divorced from human control, lying, not where they had been put, but where they had chosen to take up a position. The eye went from one to the other, on a strange criss-cross journey alight with novelty: from the sideboard loaded with bottles to the empty glasses on the writing desk; from the cigarettes on the small table to the matchbox on the hearthrug; from the jumbled novels and law books in the bookcase to the club fixture cards on top of it and the bridge markers stuffed in between. On and on, round and round, from this side to that: from golf clubs to decanter, from wireless to gun case; slipping past a few odd poker chips, skirting a derelict evening tie, dodging round scarves, orange-squeezers, photographs of the Backs, of women in bathing costumes, of men in trances. The gramophone (with a gown over it) stood by itself in one corner, but the trail of records led all over the room like a pathway of large mournful confetti;

the squash racquet was in the fender, the press belonging to it hanging from a hook on the picture-rail. A glance at the coats behind the door would have had to travel to the window seat to find a hat to wear with them: and even then it was a mighty queer hat.

And somehow, I thought as I surveyed the familiar turmoil, all this had to be cleared up, the marketable things disposed of, the rest given away: somehow the room had to be gutted, between now and the next afternoon.

Rowlands, my gyp – a little downcast man with red-rimmed eyes and a voice which seemed to spell 'whisky' in phonetics – came out of the bedroom where he had been turning down the bed.

"I've got news for you, Rowlands," I said straight away. "I'm afraid I'm going down, tomorrow."

"I know, sir." The hoarse tone was barely above a whisper. He cleared his throat. "Lord Mackinnon told me, sir – he was in here a moment ago. I'm right sorry about it, sir, and there's a good few of us will say the same."

"Thank you, Rowlands." The idea seemed an unlikely one, but I wasn't a discussion I felt like being drawn into. "Somehow," I went on, "I've got to get this place straightened up, and everything sorted out. Can you give me a hand later on?"

"Of course, sir. I'm waiting at third hall, but right after that I'll come across. I suppose," he hesitated, blinked at me, cleared his throat again. "I suppose you'll be selling a bit here and there?"

I nodded. "Everything possible, yes. Have you got your eye on something?"

Scratching his chin, he looked towards the sideboard. I followed his eyes.

"Alcohol?" I asked. "You can naturally finish up whatever's left."

"That's very kind of you, sir. But – it's that beer-mug: I've always had a fancy for it."

I smiled to myself. The mug was a favourite, of porcelain, with a hinged top and '*Rats-Keller, Dresden a.d. Elbe*' in flowery blue lettering round it; I had meant to keep it. But Rowlands had had a lot to put up with …

"You can have that as a leaving present," I told him. "But take care of it, because it's rather a good one." I cut short his thanks. "My dear Rowlands, gypping for me merits a far more spectacular reward … You'd better go now: you might call in at Lord Mackinnon's rooms and remind him that he was coming round for a drink."

"Very good, sir. And it's very kind of you, Mr Hendrycks: I really didn't mean – "

"I know damned well you didn't. That's quite all right."

"I'll be back in an hour, sir." As he was passing through the outer doorway into the court he called: "Here's his lordship now, sir."

A moment later Alastair came in, looking vaguely shifty. "Hey," I said, "you boys were meant to be coming here for a drink. Are my friends cutting me already?"

"Yes," he said. "No, of course not … Listen, Marco." He coughed, while I stared at him: an embarrassed Alastair was a positive collector's piece. "Listen, and don't go up in the air. We – the boys want to float you."

"I know they do," I answered. "It's damned good of you, but the thing's been voted on already. It's not possible."

"This is something different." He waved his hand vaguely in the direction of his own rooms. "We've just been talking about it. The others are coming over in a minute."

"But you've been detailed for the rough work?" I smiled at him. "What's it all about, Alastair?"

"We want to lend you some money," He brought it out very quickly. "We've got it all fixed. Peter a hundred, me and Charles two hundred each, and Archie five. A thousand in all. Set you up for a bit." He was beginning to mumble. "You must have something, mustn't you? Don't refuse, Marco. You know we can afford it. And we can't just let you go without a cent … May I have a drink after that?" he asked in his normal voice. "I don't feel too strong on my feet."

"Help yourself." I sat down in an armchair, afraid to answer him or even to think of the idea: it had somehow caught me on the raw, coming on top of so many other things: I wanted to cry or shout with laughter. "Peter?" I queried, trying to be casual. "I thought he went off to dinner."

"Charles broke his way into Trinity Hall to ask him …" He turned away from the sideboard, holding his drink and looking much brighter. "Does that mean you agree?"

"It does not." I faced him squarely at last. "You know how grateful I am to you, but don't you see it wouldn't work: sponging on my friends for the rest of my life wouldn't solve anything."

"But you'd stay alive until you got a job," he answered frowningly. "That's all we want to do, Marcus: keep you afloat till you can do it yourself."

I shook my head. "It makes it too easy: that's why I can't accept. I've put off being serious for twenty-one years, and unless I start straight away I'm liable just to drift back again into being supported by other people. You do see that, don't you?"

"No, I don't."

The door opened, and Archie and Charles came in. The latter looked inquiringly at Alastair.

"I take it that it's all settled?" he said casually. "If so, we needn't talk about it any more."

"It isn't anything like settled," Alastair answered. "Marco's got some crazy idea – here, *you* talk to him."

Rowlands left towards midnight, hugging the beer-mug: and with everything else settled and labelled and disposed of, I set to work on the last task of all – clearing out the writing desk and destroying the past year's accumulation of papers. It was a depressing job, exactly suited to my mood: the interview with Charles and the others had left me dispirited, and the mountain of work which Rowlands and I had got through since had completed the process and rounded it off with something like exhaustion. I hadn't been able to take the money, attractive though the idea was, but in face of their united protests – their sheer bad temper, even – I had compromised over selling my things: the guns, the car, and some odd furniture had gone, after a lengthy wrangle over prices – another loophole for their generosity: Archie had bought the remaining two dozen of claret which Uncle Octavian had given me earlier in the year – a *Leoville Poyferré* of 1928 from which I took a heartrending farewell; and, unexpectedly, Julian Wingate looked in, heard the news, and took the Rowlandson pictures, a much-prized steel engraving of Anthea Lorensen's which I had not yet had framed, and such of my gramophone records as were not, to his mind, arrant slush.

(I liked Julian a lot: he was so different from other undergraduates who advertised their brains by not washing or by out-of-the-way clothes: one could find nothing self-conscious in his nature, greatly talented though he was; and though of course he was tremendously highbrow and far out of my depth – meeting dons on their own level, already doing a fair amount of book reviewing, writing poetry which various weeklies seemed to think worth printing – yet he adopted no pose nor ever made me feel that he was talking down to me. He knew rather a lot about the *Côte d'Or* wines – our initial point of contact: none of my other friends had much use for him, and Alastair loathed his guts because he was vaguely Socialistic and could argue Alastair to a raging standstill.)

The desk yielded such a variety of trash that I presently gave up examining the contents with any real attention, and tore up whole tracts of paper with no more than a casual glance at its bearing. Once or twice I held something in my hand for a moment longer, perhaps an invitation which had worked out well or a telegram in code which I could decipher and laugh at: here and there a letter brought back pictures and associations to me – of twenty-first birthday parties, of meals on balconies in the sun or on night-lit terraces bordering some water's edge, of scenes and people glimpsed in Berlin or La Baule or Wengen (deep crusty snow on the Kleine Scheidegg), or relationships once vital and now turning to dust and grey-black ash. These things I could not let go without a faint sentimental re-creation ...

I poked up the fire and turned to yet another pigeon-hole, which yielded a bundle of Proctorial summonses at 6s 8d a time, a distressing number of old tote tickets, a photo of the 6-metre smoking up Southampton Water, and a virgin copy of the Sale of Goods Act. Then more letters: some of Alison's which I would keep; then Ingrid's and Kay's and Elaine Herrick's, all done up in packets – I didn't want them any longer; then the single one from Helga Sangstrom, saying that it was no good at present but might become so later. Well, it would never become so now: Swedish actresses – even minor ones – needed a good deal more upkeep than I could manage. Besides, Alison had intervened ... And whatever the praise or blame or burden of conscience, it was all over now: that sort of careless irresponsibility had dried up and vanished, within the space of a few days, and something very different had now to be put in its place. Looking round the strangely ordered room, glancing at the bare walls, turning over the last few dusty sheets of paper, I felt the whole tide of my affairs to be at the very lowest ebb: tomorrow, straight away, it must be taken in hand and the flow set in motion, if I were not to stagnate or remain flaccid or myself evaporate altogether. This moment was the division of time: at this point one either gathered oneself for the spring or sank to rest without ever leaving the shadows.

Some time after half past one Alastair walked in, with a cheque for three hundred and sixty pounds – the combined sum for which they had bought the various things I had to sell. After I had thanked him we drank the last of the *Bisquit Dubouché*, sitting deep and slack in our armchairs, savouring morosely the wide hand-filling brandy glasses, and hardly talking at all.

I was very fond of Alastair. And of all the others too.

PART TWO

❖

Politics

CHAPTER FOUR

Why, how now, Rosalind, dismayed with a
frown of contrary fortune? Have I not oft heard
thee say that high minds were discovered in
fortune's contempt, and heroical seen in the
depth of extremities?

THOMAS LODGE

❖

Always, when the gong sounded, the whole crazy building
became alive, like a cinema at the cry 'Fire!' or a nudist
colony disturbed by a whistle over the hedge. Even from
two floors above the dining room I could distinguish the
elements of that liveliness as I wallowed in an expensive
depth of water, inhaling the fumes of someone else's bath-
salts and wondering what it would be like to slit a vein and
bleed to death.

The gong was the first gong, which meant a quarter of
an hour to dinnertime: but the amount of movement it set
in train would have flattered an emergency fire-call. Doors
banged, feet pattered in the many corridors: the stairs
creaked as though they were made of wickerwork, plaster
fell in substantial flakes from the hall ceiling ... If I had
been particularly hungry I should have headed the rush

myself instead of dawdling: but the water was hot, the scent of pink lilac eminently soothing, and weighing this against the imagined odours (or were they quite imagined?) of vegetable soup and boiled cod, there did not seem more than one answer to the question. Let the other inhabitants wait for me: or rather, let them scurry on ahead, wolfing the longest bones and the juiciest bits of gristle: I had no great appetite, and there were too many feet scaling the trough already.

That Bayswater boarding-house had been my headquarters from the day I came down from Cambridge till now, which was November the thirteenth – the eve of the General Election: thus there was behind me a period of three weeks which could only be described as a slow fluttering down into hell … It is said of the Abbé Sieyès that when someone asked him what he had done during the Reign of Terror he replied simply "*J'ai vécu*"; and the blend of misery and triumph in the words seemed particularly applicable to my own case – I was doing nothing save contriving to live through a period at once novel, uncertain, and supremely uncomfortable.

That very day might have been taken as a sample of the past few weeks. I had had my fifth interview for a job during the morning: I had lunched with Uncle Octavian at his club: I had called round for tea at Alison's flat, only to find her on the point of going out: and I had added up my total assets for the tenth time, discovering them, as usual, to be just on the wrong side of one hundred and fifty pounds. And now here I was, back in this fearful boarding-house which was for the moment all I could afford: with its smells and its genteel discomfort and its crowd of hearty young men and dispirited old women: with its rocklike complacency and triumphant cheapness … There was nothing between now and the next day of frustration and boredom save a long-spun-out meal which I did not want, a pint of beer at the local, and a look-in at an East End Boy's Club with Cummings the schoolmaster; and already I was regretting the latter promise – that sort of thing was far out of my beat, though I was myself gradually qualifying for the same kind of charitable supervision.

Running some more hot water in defiance of the 'economy' notices which here and there splashed the wall, I recalled with a kind of retrospective embarrassment the morning's interview. It had been one of Mr Armstrong's introductions, to a firm of general exporters in the City: I had been kept waiting nearly half an hour in a room full of staring office boys and typists who patted their glinting hair and talked with gum-baring gentility; at the end of that time I was received by a pompous fool of a senior partner, smooth and solemn as a clothier's dummy, who in his repetition of such phrases as 'the uncertain state of business' and 'the rationalization of our personnel', and his expressed eagerness to file my name and keep in touch with me, might have been all the non-employing, non-helpful businessmen in the City of London rolled into one. I had been able to smile as I stood there, for I knew the course of the interview by heart; but later, going down into Cheapside and meeting the wet pavements, the grey sunless street, the unheeding anonymity of the crowd which jostled and disputed my progress, I felt the onset of such a depression as not all the preceding weeks' rebuffs had been able to bring. With a past so tantalizing and a future so deadly, this town seemed to have nothing to offer me; apparently I must tramp the streets till my hundred and fifty pounds was exhausted in weekly driblets, and thereafter either sponge on whatever friends were to hand or devise some unspectacular but final exit.

Then lunch with Uncle Octavian at the Aquascutum – that inscrutable bolt-hole of peers and princes of the Church, in which, conscious for the first time in my life of a rumpled shirt and wet suede shoes, I felt suddenly quite devoid both of courage and of merit. Even the porter's glance, as he said: "I will inform his lordship" and bade me wait, seemed unreasonably critical: it was quite certain that he disbelieved my story of a lunch appointment, that he was only sending word to Lord Edmondsbury for form's sake, that privately he was preparing to have me slung out as a tramp ... That was what the past three weeks had done to my self-confidence, and they were the speediest dissolvent I had ever known.

"Hallo, young Marcus! What about a glass of sherry?" was Uncle Octavian's greeting as presently I found him in the domed, slightly musty smoking room which seemed, to my present mood, to be peopled not by near-horizontal club members but by one vast critical faculty which could peer into my passbook and analyse my unemployability. I had not seen him for some considerable time, but that distinguished presence ('the noblest façade in any European capital', as a lobby correspondent had once written) was unaltered; and for all his seventy years I could see, in the portentous brow and chin, in the laughter and fierceness of the eyes, in the fine white hair, something much more tangible than an echo of my father's vital good looks. Technically he was not my uncle but a distant cousin of my grandfather's generation: too restless for House of Lords politics, too impatient for a diplomatic career, his public life had been limited to the chairmanship of one or two innocuous Royal Commissions, to the writing (as a young man) of a monograph on the conjectural age of the Beaker stone circles at Avebury, to his famous quarrel with Edward VIIth at Newmarket (this was a family classic, retailed in half a dozen diaries and daybooks), and to a yearly speech in the House of Lords wherein he expounded a plea for Free Trade none the less urgent for its reasoned impeccability of phrase and what my father called its purely Cobdenite peroration.

He had been one of the admired figures of my childhood, with his tremendous wardrobe, his coach-and-six at Richmond, his habit of tipping with sovereigns instead of pound notes, his quaint angular writing on postcards from Bucharest or Warsaw or Florence. And now, as I shook his hand and took the deep chair beside him I felt suddenly comforted: he was so solid a personality, and I knew so well all his mannerisms – summed up perhaps in the look of bland inquiry with which he would have greeted an impertinent servant, an attempt at murder, an earthquake, or a streetwalker in the Burlington Arcade; so familiar and enduring did the whole of him look and sound that the past seemed to come tumbling back like a penitent child, to sustain and surround me and draw me back to normality.

"Not looking up to much, young fellow," he said, when the sherry had been ordered from a footman unusually deferent. "What do you weigh nowadays?"

"About twelve stone," I answered. "Of course I haven't had much exercise lately."

"Pity ..." He looked round the room, and then catching my eye indicated with a wave of the hand his arrayed contemporaries – somnolent behind newspapers, drinking with tremulous concentration, labouring to rise on legs spindly in Episcopalian gaiters or stricken with some mortal storm of senility. He leant towards me, charmingly confidential. "One might hazard," he said in a stage whisper, "that you are not alone in that shortcoming ... I have a notion to change my club: these people are all far too old for me."

I laughed. "I don't think you'll ever find one to suit you in that respect."

He looked pleased, but made an effort to disguise it. "To that I must advance Sheridan's retort in the Commons: 'The right honourable gentleman is indebted to his memory for his jests, and to his imagination for his facts.' " He nodded to himself. "A trifle brusque, perhaps. Ah, here's our sherry."

Presently, over cold grouse pie and a salad at the lunch table, he talked about my father.

"I was sorry that I could not attend the funeral," he said. He gestured. "Urgent affairs. It was impossible for me to get away: otherwise I would not have hesitated." And as I looked at him, in some doubt: "Divorce in our family may be rare, but it does not carry with it the necessity of social ostracism. I was extremely fond of your father, and it was my view that all this – this disintegration could have been avoided."

"But how could Mother ignore what happened? It was so blatant."

He nodded. "I agree … Waiter," he leant to one side, "a little more wine for Mr Hendrycks. But even so," he turned back to me, "there is no doubt that they enjoyed nearly twenty years of married happiness and that there was no necessity – no real compulsion – to put a term to such an arrangement. But your mother, of course, would listen to no one – not even to me."

He said the last words with such bland confidence that one could not find fault with them on any score.

I fingered the stem of my wine-glass. "She had her own strict rules," I answered slowly. "She wasn't likely to break them herself, and saw no reason why he should do so." Then I paused, wanting to bring the conversation round to a more real topic: it was good to be sitting there, in that lofty pillared room full of celebrities, eating cold grouse with this distinguished, this really superb old man, but outside was my world, to which I would have to return within the hour, and if possible I must be better equipped upon my re-entrance. "I hadn't been back to Nine Beeches for four years," I continued. "You know he died bankrupt?"

Uncle Octavian nodded slowly once or twice, trying to assimilate the blunt word, avoiding the necessity of reacting strongly to it.

"Armstrong told me something of the sort," he answered presently. He consulted the menu with negligent attention. "How about a savoury? Scotch Woodcock? – they do it quite tolerably here." When he had given the order: "Nine Beeches will have to go, I suppose," he went on. "It would be a great deal too big for you in any case, though were I a richer man I would certainly make some effort to keep it in the family."

Oh lord, I thought, is that the line he's going to take? How very unlike him! … I pondered his last words, wondering what was behind them, wondering if he were informing me as smoothly as possible that he could do nothing for me: I had always thought of him as a man rich enough to do anything he wanted at the most leisurely pace, but perhaps that was no longer true. And immediately this thought struck me, I realized how impossible it was to introduce the idea of his helping me: perhaps later I might write to him to ask for some introductions, but not now, not over lunch at the Aquascutum where no one was ever in any doubt of his solvency, or could stomach the sheer vulgarity of soliciting employment. I backed away from the idea as though it were suddenly chalked with a plague-cross; and when Uncle Octavian asked what my plans were, I only answered vaguely: "Oh, I'll be getting a job fairly soon. But I'm all right for the moment."

Better that than to have later to listen to a refusal, however charmingly phrased. And I *would* be getting a job soon, and things were not yet so desperate that I must go cap in hand to my only tolerable relative. Especially after a lunch of such particular nobility.

Presently, at the coffee stage, there came a diversion – a small sprightly gentleman in the neatest pearl-grey suit imaginable, who stopped at our table on his way out and pecked forward at my uncle like a blackbird before a worm-cast on the lawn.

"My Dear Edmondsbury!" he exclaimed. "I thought you were a hundred leagues away. Surely you are not going to grace our city during November?"

"Ha, Crisp!" Uncle Octavian surveyed him in some amusement. "You're so infernally tidy I didn't recognize you. The last time we met – "

Mr Crisp waved his hand airily. "What one wears on the shores of the Black Sea is hardly evidence. May I sit down?" He looked at me interrogatively.

"My young nephew, Marcus Hendrycks ... You knew Adrian, of course?"

"Indeed yes." And as he shook hands (his was tiny, like a bird's claw enclosed in velvet): "May I offer my condolences, sir? Your father and I, though never intimates and not recently met, shared a great many pleasant memories."

"Crisp and I," said my uncle, when I had mumbled something and we had settled down again, "have made quite a habit of encountering each other in remote parts of Europe."

"As a traveller I fear I am by no means to be numbered among your company," Mr Crisp's face, which was smoothly pink and shining, puckered suddenly to a frown. "Not a hundred miles from the next table a most lamentable brand of cigar is being smoked," he said in mild reproof. "Let us either enter into competition or adjourn elsewhere."

"Or both." My uncle offered his cigar case, and we both possessed ourselves of outsize Laranagas. "Waiter, if you have a bill I shall be glad to sign it."

Back in the smoking room the talk abandoned personalities and drifted into current politics, while I sat and smoked in some contentment, and considered the odd turn which the lunch party had taken. For I had entered the double doors of the Aquascutum with the full intention of laying my case before Uncle Octavian and making sure of his help in one form or another; and already I had given up the idea as being out of the question, and was treating the occasion exactly as I would have done in the old days – as a mild treat extended to me by a man with whom I always got on extremely well. And besides, it might be true that he could not afford to do anything for me: his estate was, of course, entailed for the next heir, and his own extensive mode of life could hardly have been run at a profit.

I looked across at him and little Mr Crisp as they drew smoothly at their cigars or cupped their brandy glasses in jealous cherishing fingers; and suddenly I warmed to them, as being two of the sort of people that I admired and would like to grow into myself. They seemed to be cast in the exact mould – the George Moore-ish, 'Celibate Lives' tradition: *bons viveurs* of dry intelligence and fitting appreciation, who attached importance to fine books, good wine, and leisurely exactitude of address, and who saw to it that such things met with their support and co-operation. For all the stuff which Cummings the schoolmaster had been talking lately – about what he called, with a certain insolence, 'the cost of their upkeep' – the world would be immeasurably poorer without their leadership.

Mr Crisp was talking, as were most people round us, about the morrow's election.

"A big majority for the Government is essential," he said, his little pointed chin stuck outwards in a minute Napoleonic flourish. "Unless it is made clear to these fellows that Baldwin and the Foreign Office are backed by the whole country, our policy abroad will come to nothing."

'These fellows', apparently, were the Italians.

"I quite agree," said my uncle. "An election at such a time is a national necessity. As you know," he settled back in his chair, "I do not take a great deal of interest in Party politics, but at dinner the other night the PM was most emphatic on that point. And even the smallest Socialist gain, he said, would be misinterpreted abroad."

"Isn't that why they're staging an election now?" I asked, feeling rather brave.

"*Staging?*" Uncle Octavian's eyebrows shot up in an alarming fashion.

I repeated something which Cummings had said the day before.

"Isn't it true," I asked, "that they're having the election a full year earlier than they need, simply to make capital out of this Sanctions business? If you put it like that – that there'll be a war unless the country presents a united front – you can naturally stampede people into voting for you. And that makes you safe for another five years, whether anything comes of the war idea or not."

"Nonsense!" said my uncle, without heat. "You've been talking to one of those Socialist fellows. You will find them habitually misinformed."

"My dear young man," this was Mr Crisp, far more pained at my suggestion, "I beg you to disabuse yourself of such an idea. There is no warrant for it – no conceivable warrant at all. To make Party capital out of the present crisis would be obnoxious to the whole Cabinet, as well as to the rank and file of Conservatives." His distress seemed to grow, as the full implication of what I had said penetrated deeper. "Upon my word," he cried, "I trust you are not serious in making such a charge."

"I don't know anything about it," I answered, in full retreat. "I just happen to know that that is what the Socialist people are saying. But it certainly doesn't seem very likely."

"A vexatious insinuation." And his suspicions were far from allayed: to the very end of our encounter he kept shooting brisk little glances in my direction, as if daring me to pursue my preposterous advance. Even Uncle Octavian seemed susceptible to the general discomfort, for when we parted and he urged me to keep him informed of my progress, he added, with his hand on my shoulder: "Don't worry about politics, young Marcus: just stick to the task in hand."

That had sent me along to Alison in a curious mood, not of rebellion but of independence. Lunch itself had been far from my expectation, owing to the attack of shyness in the middle: I now felt more than ever that I was on my own and that, subject neither to supervision nor the prospect of rescue, I must fight the thing out for myself. And that being so, did it matter a damn what I said or how much I shocked funny little amateurs like Crisp, who from one point of view had about as much contact with reality as a cod in an aquarium? And furthermore, though I had hedged on that General Election question, it had seemed to me that Cummings' theory had a certain logic behind it: we had talked a good deal during the last few weeks, and though most of his ideas were frankly repellent, yet their cumulative effect had been one of disturbance. It was not that I was being converted to Socialism, or anything drastic like that, but simply that I was being shown, and discovering for myself, a far more uneven world than I had yet visualized – one in which the National Government, though possibly an admirable thing for the country as a whole, had some queer chinks through which privilege slipped and the draught of poverty followed ... Supposedly the monarchy was the best system, or it would not have lasted so long; but whether it was being honestly worked to the best advantage, and whether there really was room for the current complacency, was another matter. And what was most difficult of all to solve was the problem of how to reconcile this criticism, however tentatively made, with the instinctive pleasure which had been induced by that luxury lunch and by watching my uncle moving sedately among his contemporaries, in a *milieu* unchallengeable, incapable of improvement, and essentially enduring.

Very puzzling, I thought, as I left the Mall and set a brisker pace up Constitution Hill: very puzzling, and not really germane to the more personal dilemma, which was that I was still broke, still jobless, and that the only conceivable solution had been voluntarily sacrificed, almost on a point of etiquette. That made it Marcus Hendrycks against the world; that meant that I had to do the thing off my own bat.

"Advice?" Uncle Octavian had said at one stage during lunch when we were speculating on the future, "advice? I won't give you any advice – there's far too much of it nowadays, and not enough personal exploration. An old Frenchman – Fontenelle, I think – once said: '*Si je tenais toutes les vérités dans mes mains, je me donnerais bien de garde de l'ouvrir aux hommes*' ..." The stilted FO French had come out with Mosaic authority. "I've lived seventy years, I have not spent them ill, I have amassed a store of information on a variety of subjects; but it is by no means certain that such information is applicable to circumstances other than my own, or that it would be acceptable if I proffered it. You must live, Marcus, on the solid nourishment of experience – not on intravenous injections of precept."

That was all right as far as it went, and vastly preferable to any avuncular assumption of authority; but I felt myself to be somewhere between the two – on the lines of 'Who so loveth instruction loveth knowledge: but he that hateth reproof is brutish'. No, that was wrong, that made me as brutish as General de Bono ... Perhaps after all I would not have had the occasion take any other course.

I had not seen Alison for a week, since she had been busy flat-hunting and had just moved into a little box of a place at the back of Knightsbridge; and to find, when I arrived there, that she was on the doorstep waiting to pick up a passing taxi, was a further agent of depression. And though I persuaded her, under protest, to come upstairs again, she would not stay – she was annoyed at the interruption, she was too restless to settle down, she was not Alison at all ...

She said "No" too, for the first time.

"Why ever not?" I asked. "God, I've slept alone for a week!"

"No time," she answered briefly. She flipped her cigarette ash into the grate. "I can't keep these people waiting."

"Who are they?"

"No one you know. Darling, I must go."

"Well, let me stay till you come back."

"It'll be no good, anyway."

"Why not?"

"Curse."

"Oh ..." I had an idea she was lying, an idea which depressed me beyond measure: already we were miles away from the stage of a few weeks before. "All right, then ... Darling, you're not angry with me, are you?"

She stood up. "Why should I be?"

"I don't know … It's hell being broke … What about dinner tomorrow?"

"Where?"

I had meant dinner at her flat, but perhaps it didn't sound too good. "Oh, a Lyons or something. Best I can do."

She frowned. "As a matter of fact I'm not sure – I half promised a woman – I'll ring you up." She started to cross to the door, drawing on her gloves, fiddling with the gardenia at her throat: I had the sudden conviction that she was counting me out, that she would be meeting another man within a few minutes, that probably she would bring him back here …

I sat quite still in my armchair and said: "Alison, you're being bloody."

"I'm not."

"I can't help it if I'm broke."

"Sweetheart, don't whine. You're so – so *wet* nowadays. Everything's so different …" She looked at the clock. "Out!" she exclaimed suddenly. "I can't spare another minute."

I got up. "All right. What about tomorrow?" (A few weeks earlier she would have been made to break her date: I wouldn't have asked questions, but just told her what to do: and she would have enjoyed the process.)

From out on the landing she said: "I've told you, I'll ring up. Do come on, Marcus – these people will be livid."

"Is it another man?"

"It's a lot of people … Get that taxi for me."

And that was all. I suppose, I thought as I sloped up Knightsbridge, that I *was* rather wet nowadays. Taking it all in all, I couldn't afford to be anything else.

Now, heaving myself out of the tepid bath and padding along to my room to change into flannels and a rough-coat, I saw quite clearly that the Alison affair was going wrong and was almost past repair already. For that teatime meeting had only been a reflection of the last three weeks' encounters, an extension indeed of that first meeting after my father's death, when I had tried to face reality and, surrendering, had been lured back to the earlier plane of romantic illusion. Alison had been quick to note that I had lost my grip; and that uncertainty was making me give a very poor performance as a lover, quite apart from the fact that to be penniless was to be a bore, for a variety of reasons. And I had other things to do, things which must be grappled with ...

I brushed my hair, which needed washing, in the indifferently silvered mirror.

There again, that 'grappling with circumstances' idea brought its own problems and its own infusion of cowardice and sloth. For try as I would, I still could not really shake off the feeling that the whole thing was a very trivial affair, and that something would happen which would set me in place again with not much more effort than a snap of the fingers. Surely I could play for a little longer, for much longer, for ever ... And it was more than a question of making an effort, of settling down and taking one's place in society: it was a question as to whether one bothered to fit in at all, or ever developed a sense of duty with regard to one's own life. A lot of money meant that one could play expensive hell all over Europe: with none at all one drifted to the status of vaguely romantic beachcomber. They were pathways of a precisely equal merit, they led you to the same conclusion: and if from a certain point of view one could be rated above the other, what did that matter? – did it make a ha'p'porth of difference how far you were left behind, when Death scooped the whole collection without regard to the placings? In the final analysis, it didn't matter ten cents whether you wore your old school tie round your neck or your navel.

It was in this mood of profound ineptitude that I went down two flights of stairs to the dining room.

The dining room, like the rest of the house and many of the inhabitants, was large, lofty, and decayed: tables for two and four people were ranged round it, with a larger central one, standing in a conspicuous draught, for the younger members. (When you were young you didn't need anything so eccentric as privacy.) At this latter I took my place, after saying good evening five times with a sort of bloodless cordiality and smiling twice – at Cummings and Dr Barrow, who shared one of the smaller tables reasonably near the fire. My companions were a number of young men, only two of whom I had so far managed to get focused: the lean Stokes, who worked in an insurance office, and a man called Jack something-or-other who throughout the meal drew wireless circuits on the tablecloth with a thumb only averagely clean.

Of course this was no ordinary guest house (if you ever made that mistake you went out on your ear): it was a Happy Family whose constituent parts were now grouped round about me, awaiting the fish with ravenous decorum. Nearest the fire was Miss Glasshouse, tremendously ladylike in brown velvet, tremendously hung with bangles and loops and ruchings: then the two mousy little girls, Miss Hope and Miss Crutchwell, both engaged, both only waiting the word to go out to India to join the men they loved: then the table shared by the two chartered accountants who hated each other – Mr Graves with a beard and no tie, Mr Leggett who fidgeted with his hair and read out aloud from the newspaper: then Colonel Pearson, who never spoke to his wife but had a special bottle of chutney all to himself: then Cummings and Dr

Barrow, the only people who had shown any signs of friendliness: then an anonymous widow, startlingly made-up and *decolletée* to a menacing degree, about whom everyone else whispered and complained; and then, coming full circle again, the crux of the establishment, the lodestar, the queen bee (in loose analogy) – Miss Fleming the proprietress.

She was as respectable as Miss Glasshouse, which was saying a good deal: thin, scanty-haired, with a searching nose, dressed now in black lace and a gauze neck-container. At our first meeting, she had impressed on me two facts: first, that she was the daughter of old Colonel Fleming; and secondly, that she ran the house simply as a hobby, simply to employ her wonderful vitality. Her friends all laughed at her, she had said, for taking so much trouble: but she would certainly be at a loss if she ever gave it up (an ingenious statement which covered nearly everything). At any rate she ruled: she had collected more than a dozen people and bound them to her with hooks of macaroni and chocolate blancmange. She had collected me, as with a flick of the wrist, via an advertisement in the *Telegraph*.

As I sat down she said reprovingly: "Good evening, Mr Hendrycks. I'm afraid you've missed the soup."

"Frankly, Miss Fleming, you can take the soup and stick it in your ear." That was the right answer: Archie van Tyler would have snapped it out like a favourite garter. But aloud I said brightly: "Have I? Oh, what a pity. I think I must have fallen asleep in my bath."

"How very dangerous!" remarked Miss Glasshouse. "How very, very dangerous!" There were other murmurs, and the widow caught my eye and smiled, bathing me in a Niagara of teeth. Perhaps, if Alison continued to give me such a rough time I would come around to that …

By the sideboard the strange maid Mona, in trouble with the soup-plates, started muttering to herself the reiterative burden being something to do with one pair of hands. Miss Fleming turned to frown at her, a stage frown carrying no hint of reproof: Mona was mad – or odd, anyway: but she had been there such a long time, like the linoleum upstairs, and servants were hard to come by, even for a guest establishment of such blinding merit.

Dr Barrow and Cummings were both reading – by mutual agreement they dispensed with the formalities; the old doctor, thin and dried up, his nose deep in the book, gesturing with a fork to an unseen audience, might have sat for a Hogarthian 'Portrait of a Scholar'. I had struck up a strange sort of friendship with him: he was approximately three times my age, retired from practice for many years, and engaged on some immense book – a co-ordination of science and philosophy which he himself agreed would never be finished: here, however, was no dry-as-dust pedant, but an individual, widely experienced, and entertaining human being. Opposite him Cummings, almost as deeply immersed in the *Daily Worker*, supplied the contrast between reason and emotion: he was about forty-five, thin and lank as to body, with the hard lines of disillusionment (or perhaps even of want) in his face, and a tossing lock of hair like a never-surrendering banner. He was a Council schoolmaster and a Socialist, which I didn't think those people were allowed to be: but apparently no one made any objection as long as the fact did not obtrude upon his official duties. A little time ago I would have called him a dangerous man in a dangerous position: now I wasn't so sure, if only because he interested me enormously and had an answer for everything.

Miss Fleming carved the fish. It was wet and loosely knit and rather brown in parts: it still retained a frisky tail and one unavoidable eye: all the same, it constituted a 'Fish Course', and what more could one ask, in a household which would not have recognized *Sole Bonne Femme* if it had been titled in Neon lights? For Miss Fleming kept what she described as a Good Table (as though one could strip off the veneer and cram it into one's mouth); and in practice this meant that the quality could go hang as long as the illusion of liberality was maintained. Clearly she was content to shop in the cheapest market and chance the result: thus the dreary succession of soup, fish, meat, pudding, and cheese worked itself out nightly, sounding swell, tasting horrid, and having as much nourishment value as a string of beads.

No one spoke to me. I really didn't see why they should. And it was amusing to listen to the general run of conversation – Leggett with his vocabulary about ninety-under-proof, little Miss Crutchwell talking about India and love in what one could only describe as a coy shout, the brisk young fellows on either side of me discussing their favourite film actresses with an air of proprietorship which, in any other context, would have been grossly suggestive. And furthermore, whenever anyone verged on a political topic or referred, even indirectly, to the next day's election, the whole room seemed suddenly to get up on its toes, with that air of suspended apprehension commonly displayed by a roomful of strangers when a puppy is introduced thereto. For the previous evening there had been a resounding scene, following a political argument between Cummings and the rest of the room, headed by Miss Glasshouse: the latter was CONSERVATIVE, in her usual tremendous fashion, and when she had come out with some shattering crack about Russian Gold, and Cummings had pointed out, quite reasonably and gently, that she was personally a fool and politically a lunatic, there had developed such an exchange of views and counterviews that the whole meal had been disorganized and Mona (possibly as a demonstration of working-class solidarity) had tendered notice at the top of her not inconsiderable voice between the sweet course and the silver-papered cheese.

Of course everyone had later apologized to everyone else, Cummings with a sardonic politeness which might have been mistaken for humility; but obviously the scene had left its mark on the collective memory, and it was not going to be repeated for want of a little common discretion.

Dr Barrow laughed suddenly, drawing back from his book and pinching up his face so that it looked more thin and dried up than ever. He was grey and untidy as usual: when he laughed it was like an old man making, with difficulty, a joke of death.

Miss Fleming exchanged meaning glances with as many people as possible, including a tentative flick of the eyebrows at me: I suppose she deemed it prudent to build up a backing of responsible opinion, a wedge of orthodoxy, in case anything funny happened. She had, I already knew, very clear ideas on what was funny and what was not: Dr Barrow, of course, was hardly funny yet, but she could not forget the half dozen occasions when other people had overstepped this borderline – the woman who sold the chairs out of her room, the clergyman who had had such odd ideas about the duties of the servants, the Indian student who practised RITES in the bathroom. And now (I could see her thinking) here was Dr Barrow laughing to himself in the middle of a meal – nothing special really, but (taken with his continued friendship with Cummings and the fact that he and I had been discovered singing 'Malbrouck s'en va-t-en guerre' in the front hall two nights previously) something of a pointer ... She leant forward and asked sweetly: "An amusing book, doctor?"

"Monumentally stupid." He had a hard dry voice, to match his body. "I would as soon turn Hindu as entrust my destiny to Bergson. Just listen to this." He looked across at

Miss Fleming, paused for a moment, and then said: "No, I won't bore you with it."

"Stick to Hegel," said Cummings without looking up from his newspaper. "An idealist philosophy in search of certain invariable laws of transformation and development: the world interpreted as a complex of processes instead of mere things: the dynamic conception of reality – that's the proper stature of philosophy. You waste your time reading that modern nonsense."

"Then I apologize," said Dr Barrow mildly. "A complex of processes? – possibly, possibly. And all culminating in the pure broad stream of Marxist dialectics?"

"Naturally. The river winding slowly to the sea."

"Sententious, and far from conclusive." The doctor surveyed the fish on his plate as if it were a problem of metaphysics. "There is no limit to the number of tributaries: there is more than one major ocean. The history of human thought did not come to a dead stop with Karl Marx."

The dreadful name rang through the room, like a hammertap on a sheet of iron. Miss Glasshouse's eyes darted their indignation, the young man on my right said "Bolshie swine" into his glass: even Colonel Pearson, who was hardly susceptible to outside atmosphere, fiddled with the top of his chutney-bottle and almost spoke to his wife.

"Hush!" said Cummings, *sotto voce*. "Let us keep the discussion anonymous."

I would like to have joined in, but that would have meant shouting; and anyway the idea of me paddling my toes in philosophy came almost within the realm of clowning.

"We can't all be highbrow, you know." This, after a pause, from Leggett, in his hearty voice which should have compelled attention but somehow alienated it. "How about the simple things of life, eh?" And he winked at Miss

Fleming; but receiving in return a severe glance (no one winked) he essayed an alibi by rubbing his eye and blinking up at the light.

As the fish plates were cleared away the young man Stokes, who disparaged Miss Fleming's Good Table by looking blue and half starved, addressed me suddenly.

"How's work?" he asked. "Any luck?"

"Well," I answered, conscious that a lot of people were listening, "nothing's absolutely settled yet. But I had quite a promising interview this morning."

"Good." He crumbled his bread, searching for an enlargement of this comment and finding none. "Good," he said again. "There's nothing like a settled job of work."

"I suppose you've been in your firm a good long time?"

"Eight years," he answered. His eyes gleamed suddenly. "We're all due for a rise at the New Year, unless they welsh on us."

Presently there was a stir, and some fierce whispering, from the sideboard; Mona's voice rose, in scandalized reproof: "Take your thumb out of the gravy!"

To say that everyone present affected not to hear would be a laughable understatement. There was something like an inrush of oblivion: heads bent low, conversations started like spring-guns: forks, pieces of bread, salt-cellars – all were fingered and clinked and rolled to and fro in an ecstasy of preoccupation. Miss Fleming, her eyes fixed burningly on the middle-distance, seemed to be resolving some life-or-death conundrum: Miss Hope ejaculated "Ceylon will be nice" out of the blue, as if Ceylon were the next course: only Cummings turned round in his chair, stared fixedly at Mona for some moments, and then gave me a wink of such muscular totality that it might well have dislocated his jaw. Since Miss Fleming was directly regarding me, I affected not to notice it ...

But all the meals so far had been on the same plane, somewhere between farce, pantomime, and social drama; and though at the end of three weeks I still found the mixture entertaining, I could foresee a time when this household would rout the most broad-based sense of humour and attain to its true category of bore. That indeed was another reason why I liked listening to Cummings: he was the very best antidote to the deadweight of gentility which overlay the house like a blanket of mist.

I listened to him a good deal more that night: I had promised to accompany him to the East End boys' club where he presided twice a week, and as he insisted on walking the whole length of the Whitechapel Road in quest, as he said, of fresh air (the atmosphere, a compound of fog, fried fish, and acetylene flares, was about as fresh as a herring-drifter's bilges), we found time for quite a prolonged session of our usual brand of disjointed argument.

"You won't have to stay long," he told me, as we made our way along the wet pavements thronged with late shoppers, and tired dragging children, and hawkers thrusting celery or handfuls of lemons crosswise into the passing crowd, as if in hope of their offerings being caught up by the human cogs. "I've got to speak later on at the local hall – eve of poll meeting, though we're safe enough down here. So that exquisite suit and public school sniffiness of yours won't have to endure the lower classes for more than an hour at the outside."

I laughed, turning towards him, watching the thin lined face half hidden behind the turned-up collar of a greasy raincoat. Trust Cummings never to surrender an ounce of his prejudices.

"The suit may be exquisite," I answered, "but it's got to last me the next five years or so, and I don't suppose I'll be very proud of it by then. And as for the public school outlook – well, if you knew the sort of upbringing I've had, you'd think it pretty marvellous that I was *coming* to this place at all, much less looking as if I enjoyed it."

Cummings shook his head. "I'm going to wake you up," he declared, "if it takes a year's work." He avoided, skilfully, a pram full of vegetables, from the middle of which a negro child peered out, knuckling its eyes with wet pale-yellow fingers. "You're quite intelligent enough to understand the Socialist idea," he went on, as we converged again. "You only want to stop being pig-headed and settle down to study it properly."

"I haven't time," I answered. "I've got to earn a living somehow."

He turned towards me. "I suppose what you told Stokes about your good interview this morning was pure eyewash."

"Of course. But I wasn't going to have my failures slapped down on the dinner table for everyone to see."

We passed a street corner, where a Fascist was addressing a small tough crowd. The posters said: 'KEEP OUT THE REDS' – 'A VOTE FOR FASCISM IS A VOTE FOR FREEDOM' – 'MOSLEY OR REVOLUTION' ... As we went by I caught the words 'The usual campaign of lies, the usual Jewish twisting, the usual sweat-shop tactics', roared out in a thick raucous voice which echoed against the garish cinema-front opposite.

Cummings snarled: "Bloody buffoons ... They just come down here to kick up trouble, and trade on bad feeling."

"I can't say I've much affection for the Jews."

"Why not? You're thinking of the word 'Jew' simply as a label as the *Daily Mail* uses the word 'Red' – to express an idea which you're meant to dislike by instinct. They're human beings, you know, behind the epithets ... Jews in the mass are no better and no worse than any other collection of humans: you'll find the same proportion of crooks and liars, the same leavening of saints."

"Then why do people hate them?"

"Because they've been taught to. And they can be taught not to, just as easily."

I shrugged my shoulders, trying to get my chin below my coat collar. It was bitterly cold, and the damp rising from the street put me in mind of a plague-swamp.

"Well, that's your job," I said. "You've got the chance to catch them young."

"And what a job! ..." There was such extraordinary bitterness in his voice that I turned to him in astonishment.

"Good lord, I thought you were keen on it."

He dug his hands deep in his raincoat pockets. "So I am, in a way. And if I could do what I want, and teach those kids what I really believe, it would be the finest job on earth." For a moment he paused. "But you see," he went on, in a harder voice, "we're so hedged about, we're so dictated to, we have to hand out such oceans of slush with such minute veins of truth running through it ... And the history we have to teach ..." The breath whistled out through his teeth as though he were in physical pain. "Do you remember the fuss in Parliament about that child's essay, last summer?"

I nodded. "Yes, I think I did read about it. It seemed to me to be a most ludicrous fuss about nothing at all."

"In point of fact it could hardly have been more important." He cleared his throat. "Here you have a child who's never been out of England in her life, who knows nothing of foreigners except that Frenchmen are naughty and Germans fat and Spaniards lazy, whose entire life has probably been bounded by one single street and half a dozen relatives; and she sits down and licks her nib and solemnly writes" – he mimicked a child's voice with startling cruelty, " 'England is only a small country, but it is the finest in the world.' ... And when it's quite reasonably pointed out (*a*) that this may not be true, and (*b*) that someone has been teaching the child that precise brand of nationalist complacency that's pushing the world down the drain at this very moment, why then" – he took a deep breath – "you bring the whole Tory Party down like a ton of bricks, you have a resounding shindy in Parliament, and you have nearly every newspaper in the country screaming its head off about sloppy internationalism and Moscow propaganda and God-knows-what besides. It's heartbreaking: here you have the best idea that's struck the world so far, and you're not allowed even to hint at it for fear that these kids might not grow up into good little patriots."

I frowned, in complete bewilderment: all this was so much nonsense to me.

"But what's wrong with patriotism? Everyone has a right to be proud of their country – there's nothing stupid or wicked in that. And what did you mean by 'the best idea that's struck the world so far'?"

Cummings laughed suddenly, as if at the release of some inner tension. "My dear Hendrycks," he said, his hand on my arm, "we have about thirty yards further to go: I could not dispose of that topic in under two miles. But I'll say this, to give you a preliminary twinge of indigestion. If patriotism meant being proud of your country without jealousy of your neighbours, then no one could say anything against it; it's perfectly natural to think well of your own hills and valleys, to love your own people's writing and music and art, to praise famous men who deserve it. But that isn't patriotism as the modern State understands and teaches it. Patriotism to them means that England is right on every single occasion, no matter what trickery or evasion she practises, and that if she chooses to bite off enormous tracts of land, and dispossess whole nations of people, and stake claims for goldmines and oilfields and mineral rights which are nothing more or less than insolent theft, then every Briton must join in and back her up, on pain of being labelled a coward or a traitor." We were standing now in an ill-lighted porch, leading through to a bare stone passage full of movement and youthful laughter: Cummings stared at me, holding my eyes with his own slate-grey troubled glance. "And when you have that spirit cherished and fostered not only by England but by every country in the world, so that each child is taught that to die for such an idea is its highest duty, can you wonder that we are never free of wars and, unless they are taught something different, we never will be. Love of country is right and admirable: but blind patriotism, which can be fooled and abused for purposes of sheer international brigandage, is the most dangerous sham that the world has ever seen." He came out of his trance, and laughed again. "End of Part One," he said lightly. "Let's go and amuse the next batch of cannon-fodder."

"But ..." I hesitated, unwilling to break off so sharply: he had given me an idea which had never before come my way, and I was far too confused by its implications to dismiss it as carelessly as he had done. "But what's to be put in its place?" I asked in a tone of perplexity which must have sounded excessively foolish. "If you do away with national consciousness and – and competition, what have you got left?"

He was already moving down the passage, unbuttoning his coat, preparing to meet an advancing wave of urchins in shorts and gym shoes.

"The world-state," he threw over his shoulder. "The logical outcome of improved communications and expanding resources. Keep your local customs if you like, but do away with the scrapping and snarling – there's plenty of everything to go round, if you'll only agree to share it. So *do* share it – pool everything on a world-basis and share it out by a system of exchange. It's a problem first of common sense and then of the mechanics of distribution. That's all – it's as simple as two-and-two, only the fools can't see it and the knaves won't." He turned away again. "Hallo, Ginger!" he said in a voice entirely transformed. "Hallo, Ted! ... To start with, let's have a bit less noise."

I can't say that I paid much attention to my surroundings in that club, or to the odd activities in which I presently found myself taking part. I was there for an hour, and found time to drink a cup of tea, to take part in four incomprehensible round-games, and to spar with a much larger young man who, stripped to the braces, came at me like a whirlwind and hit me hard in the throat; but I was thinking all the time of what Cummings had said, and wondering if his views, which seemed at a first glance to have their own particular logic, could possibly be valid. Naturally, I myself had been brought up to believe in the invincible superiority of my own country and people – that sort of thing was never questioned, tied up as it was with the Church and the Conservative Party and one's own self-esteem; and if I had never interested myself in things like the Junior Imperial League, that was only because it seemed to be doing very well as it was, without the dubious support I could give it.

Of course, now and again while reading history at school one could not help feeling a little suspicious of the fact that England had never been in the wrong on any occasion, that she had never lost a single battle (except Bannockburn, when the damned unsporting Scots actually dug pits and covered them with brushwood), that God had always been on her side and would continue to show this conspicuous good taste ... And I could remember meeting, one night in a café bar on the Bordeaux water front, a young student just through his *Baccalauréat*, who had never heard of Crecy, Agincourt, or Poitiers, but who recited, over a carafe of *blanc*, a list of seven battles in the same war in which the English, he had been taught, were flogged right off the map of France ... Needless to say, I had not heard of any of them and thought he was pulling my leg; but if that were history as taught to the young all over the world, then no wonder the nations were never at peace and pursued with spiritual fervour their eternally just quarrels.

But of course, I told myself as I answered a chorus of good nights and shouldered my way out of the gaslit draughty building, of course that was all rot: Socialists always took a sock at the Empire because Russia wanted to weaken it from the inside, and if one fell for that sort of specious nonsense one was simply doing Lenin's (or was it Stalin's?) work for him. And England *was* a damned good place to live in, and worth fighting for, whatever Cummings might say.

He had wanted me to come with him to his meeting, but I was already sick of those surroundings – the East End must be a hell of a place to spend one's life in – and I went back to Bayswater instead. Perhaps also I'd really had enough of Cummings for one night ... As it happened, I met Dr Barrow on the steps of the local pub, and we went through the swing doors together in search of a nightcap.

The saloon of the Chester Arms was full – fuller than usual which was saying a good deal: whatever the reason, whether pre-election excitement or a home race meeting or the curling fog outside, it had certainly brought the boys in at full strength ... The room was large, shiny, boisterous: there seemed to be no wall-space that was not occupied by mirrors or advertisements or notices couched in a heavily jocular vein; there appeared to be no single inch of floor or bench that had not its full burden of noisy humanity.

Glasses clattered, beer-handles dipped and sprang back, the inverted spirit bottles bubbled reassuringly: plenty for all, that was the watchword – plenty for all, and a good half hour to closing time ... A small boy, who should have been in bed far earlier in the evening, collected empty glasses on a froth-swamped tray; and behind the bar two decorative young women laboured, filling up, swabbing down, and all the time keeping at bay with glinting efficiency the three large gentlemen who had, somewhere, had a run of luck.

There was variety, indeed, in everything – clothes, faces, voices, drinks, desires: the jumble of mankind was here, taking its ease, loosening its grip on reality; a beery face neighboured a thoughtful one, a chauffeur's peaked cap contrasted with the dusty undress of a foreman-ganger. The windows were steamed over like a laundry on a winter's day, the smoke of tobacco drifted round the lamps and hung in smudges, shadowing the ceiling; and above it all a hand-written notice – 'Keep your temper: no one else wants it' – held place of honour over the dartboard, setting the tone, limiting the pace, and reassuring the timid.

It was into this press of humanity that we presently contrived to insinuate ourselves: gaining a step here, creeping past the jutting headland of a shoulder, swinging round always, like a compass-needle towards the magnetic field of the bar. The old doctor, whom one might have supposed to be entirely out of his element, confounded expectation by the self-possessed cunning with which he made progress and the genial smile which sat oddly on his lined dried-up features, like a robin perched on a windowsill at high summer. He also greeted amiably as raffish a series of acquaintances as I had seen outside of Cruikshanks' cartoons ... Installed at last against a cramped section of counter, we waited patiently until such time as the more determined of the blondes should win through to our service: at length, with a final "You're too smart, you are," aimed at some luckless amorist further down the bar, she turned towards us with a smile.

"Good evening, Ellie," I said. "Or is it Dorothy? – I'm never quite sure."

"It's Dorothy this time, Mr Henry – you ought to remember, you know. Where have you been hiding yourself this last week?"

"Epsom Common. I'm the Mystery Man in the papers."

"They say he's got a beard … Bit of a crowd, isn't there?"

"Yes. What's the celebration?"

She shrugged elaborately – a crib (as I judged it) from la Dietrich. "I dunno. Election, maybe."

"You going to vote?"

"No fear," she answered with huge scorn. "They're all alike, they only want to diddle you. Like a lot of others I could name" – she glanced severely down the counter. "You'd think they'd bought the earth, some of them."

"It's a wicked world … Ted all right?"

"So-so."

"When's the wedding?"

"That's asking."

"Your thirst for knowledge," broke in Dr Barrow in his stateliest manner, "cannot equal my need of alcohol. May we not cut the formalities – or at least postpone them to a less critical moment?"

"Why, it's the doctor." Dorothy leant over the bar and beamed at him. "I didn't see you. How's the cold?"

"Better, thank you."

"That's good. You want to keep wrapped up, this end of the year. What'll you have?"

"Two half cans," I said. "Bitter."

She drew them expertly, filling the tankards brim-full by little squeezings of the beer handle. The liquid was cool, unusually clear, and no viler to the taste than the general run of synthetic swipes: savouring it, one could sympathize with the despairing slogan of another election-time – 'Food is up – sixpence a pint' … Content, with one elbow on the bar, I turned to survey the room; but my view was curtailed to negligible proportions by a quartet of thin bleached men discussing the furniture trade, and a little rat-faced chap in a greenish bowler who, clearly, would not be allowed much more grace in the matter of expletives. Perhaps he would last out till closing time, perhaps he wouldn't, and that was all you could say about it.

I turned back to Dr Barrow, who was staring fixedly into his quarter-empty tankard.

"What have you been doing with *your* evening?" I asked. "Or did you stay in and confuse Leggett with polysyllabics?"

He looked up at me, with that twinkle in his eye so oddly at variance with the rest of his makeup.

"If it will set your mind at rest," he answered gravely, "I have been reading a paper on Femoral Embolectomy to an audience of eleven university professors, three of whom were more or less convulsed with amusement throughout. I excused myself from subsequent discussion, fearing to be stripped of such few pretences to authority as still remain to me … And you? – did you go down with Cummings?"

"Yes. It was rather fun, though I was lured into a boxing exhibition and nearly had my neck laid open. You know," I went on, tapping the edge of my tankard, "I can't make out whether that man talks sound sense or absolute balderdash."

"In what connection?"

"Oh, patriotism and Empire-building, this time. But nearly everything he says cuts across what I've been taught, and what my parents and all my friends used to take for granted. I'd like to know which side is right – though I'm pretty sure, really."

"That you are?"

"Well – yes."

"All the same, it is an admirable exercise to re-examine one's premises from time to time, on the supposition that the growth of experience may reveal some flaw or misconception. And it is an exercise, indeed, to which the young men and women of your generation are far more addicted than was the general habit in my day."

"What about patriotism, for instance?" I asked. "*Is* it true that England has grabbed off more than her share, and that one shouldn't really be proud of her on that account?"

He gestured with his hand. "That illustrates precisely what I have just been saying. Fifty years ago, any young man who asked such a question or propounded such a view would have earned public contempt and, possibly, private reprisals of some social or financial kind. A 'Little Englander' we would have called him – a supposedly trenchant epithet from which no one who expressed even the mildest criticism of our colonizing methods was safe."

"But what were those methods like? Were they so brutal?"

"Of that one can hardly speak in general terms," he answered judiciously. "But our habit of staking a claim in a country – South Africa, for example – and then casting our eyes outside its boundaries, and deciding that we liked the view, and thereupon working up an agitation which culminated in our taking possession of that coveted section as a so-called defence measure – such a habit would hardly have commended itself to people who were preoccupied with justice instead of commercial ambition."

"But our colonies," I said, "we do good there, we develop them, we spread civilization."

"True, true. But one may confess to a certain suspicion of a civilizing crusade the ultimate result of which is our own resounding financial benefit. Does that answer you?"

"I don't know." Temporarily I had given up: that day had dealt me too many jolts already. "It's all too confusing at the moment."

He laughed gently. "That at least is an advance on a blank denial. What is important is that you should not retreat from the subject: examine it at your leisure, and form your own opinion. And as a corollary to that, don't swallow wholesale what Cummings tells you; and don't, on the other hand, dismiss it as a pack of nonsense just because it is labelled 'Socialism' or 'Anti-Imperialism' or plain treason. Give all these things your own labels – you are quite intelligent enough to collate the facts and deduce the truth from them."

"But it's against everything I've been taught so far," I said, half to myself.

He shook his head vigorously. "The least valid of all objections. If you had been brought up in different surroundings or in a lower stratum of society, you might be now equipped with facts and opinions directly opposed to your present ones. Education is not intended to fit you out with a static fund of knowledge: and *your* education especially should give you the faculty of criticizing and determining the genuine from the base. And now," he said, with a change of tone which would in any other man have made me suspect his sincerity, "this round is on me – if that is the current phrase. The same again?"

Round us the clamour and urgency, which my preoccupation had driven into abeyance, surged up again: the four furniture men were no longer there, but their place had been taken by a trio of fat men with black overcoats and blue necks, who were counting out wads of banknotes carelessly, as one might run through a pack of cards to see if the Joker were included. Snatches of their conversation came to me, Cockneyfied, assertive, alarmingly technical: "Neaow, you c'ld get plenty of six-to-four right up to the off. Isn't that right, Barney boy? – plenty of six-to-four?"

"Gawd, you should 'a' seen the stuff come back on the blower. And that bloody runner got caught in the crowd and there was me, ladling the stuff out at three points over the market."

" 'Oo's doing tic-tac?' I said. 'Morry,' 'e said. 'Well, tell Morry,' I said, 'to take a look at 'is mucking code and not poke around as if 'e was playing slap-and-tickle.' "

And all the time the shuffling and checking and exchange of notes went on. One might have called it astuteness coming into its own. They at least weren't exercised overmuch about the next meal – though one of them appeared to be still having trouble with the previous one.

As I sipped my new drink: "Haven't you ever been interested in politics?" I asked the doctor. "You've lived through such a hell of a time – the War, suffragettes, and everything. Didn't you feel you wanted to join in?"

"I did not," he answered with decision. Under the lamp his thin grey hair seemed to take on a new lustre: the old face a few yards from mine had an animate significance that was ageless. "I did not," he repeated. "I am one of those people whose activity has been confined to what is vulgarly known as getting on with the job. I was in practice for thirty-five years; and it was always enough for me that I was alleviating suffering, occasionally saving life, and certainly doing work which was necessary under any system and in any context."

"But if a different system would have given you less work …" I hesitated.

He smiled, as it seemed with a sudden increase of interest.

"The first pricking of intelligence," he remarked ironically. "I must confess that that thought *did* strike me, and that even as a medical student I resented having to patch up human material, human wreckage, whose distress was directly attributable to ruthless social neglect. With a lower-class practice and a Free Hospital appointment, poverty gave me seventy per cent of my work, poverty which many people then, as now, held to be avoidable. But there was still strong in me the conviction that changing the system was not my concern: I was the doctor, not the economic diagnostician: my task was plainly indicated to me, and I had neither time nor vigour left for anything else."

"And now," I said, "now that you're not in practice any longer?"

"I shall be seventy-two next March," he answered simply. "I am writing the book of which I have told you, I give an occasional lecture or write a technical review, I am in correspondence with a variety of people, on subjects," he smiled, "whose abstruseness is almost their sole recommendation. Not for me the political arena; not now. When you are seventy-two – " but he did not finish the sentence.

Presently a light went out, and then another: the first signs of approaching dissolution … As though at the prick of a needle, the whole place leapt into a quadrupled energy: drinks disappeared in cavernous swallowings, coins were slammed down on the bar as though force could enhance their value; and last orders rolled against the counter like a great breaking wave. A few more minutes, an increasing twilight: the door swung on its brass hinges, once, twice, a dozen times, a breath of night air swirled through the room and sent the smoke chasing up to the ceiling: then the last "Time, gentlemen, please" – distinguishable from the mere warning signals by an anguish of finality in the 'please' – fell on the company. The facts could no longer be baulked: closing-time, that nightly robbery of freedom like the echo of some unimaginable disaster, was upon us at last.

We emerged into the street, buttoning up our overcoats instinctively. The session had been a pleasant one, but now we talked no more: there was a kind of stricken silence between us, as though the transition from close confinement to the great width of the pavement had taken away our self-possession. Not until we were at the gate, with the three gaunt trees which marked the house gleaming fitfully in the lamplight, like rusty weapons, was this curious spell broken.

"Are you any nearer to finding work?" the doctor asked suddenly.

"No," I said. "The present system doesn't seem to need my co-operation."

"I sympathize with you. It is a dilemma which I never had to face, nor indeed any of my contemporaries."

And in the bleak yellow-tiled hall, where his neat boots rang in contrast to my own lush rubber soles: "You are going through a difficult period, I know. And the discontented, the unhappy, and the dispossessed are the most lively recruiting material for all forms of extremism, not only political but in the realm of personal violence – even," his pale eyes flickered up at mine, "self-violence. If you can treat your own case objectively, this period may be of primal value to you."

"And if I can't?" For a brief moment I was again dejected, again powerless to fight the ineluctable battle. "If the only thing I can think of is not being able to get a job, and having a hundred and fifty quid between me and the bread line? How do I proceed then?"

"You proceed to bed," he answered, "and next morning you regret even such a temporary lapse into infirmity. Good night."

"Good night," I said. "I wonder what makes you such a fountain of common sense."

"Seventy-two years. But no one expects you to catch up in less than a third of that time."

CHAPTER FIVE

You talk when you cease to be at peace with your thoughts.

KAHLIL GIBRAN, *The Prophet*

❖

One night after the election, when I went up to my own room to fetch a pipe, Cummings' door was open, and seeing him sitting at his desk, surrounded by pamphlets and a mound of envelopes, typing away with bent back and hair falling over his forehead, I went in.

"Can't you give that a rest?" I asked. "The election's over now, you know."

"That means the next one's started." He looked up, his pale face still frowning with concentration. "Sit on the bed: I'll be through in a minute. Anything in the paper?"

"Just jubilation over your defeat." I sat back, leaning my head against the bedrail, and looked round the mean little room, with its two cane chairs and cracked yellow washbasin, and the long fiery line of books which cleaved the whole length of one wall. "And it looks as though Kingsford-Smith is done for: they can't find any trace of his plane, though they've had half the Air Force out."

"Waste of money," he grumbled, his hand poised over the typewriter as though some letter or other had vanished entirely. "Every single person in this country ought to be decently housed and fed: then we can see about records and Atlantic flights. But until that's done, anything else is criminal extravagance."

"I suppose so."

"You damned well know so." He wrenched the completed sheet out of his typewriter with a sound like tearing oilcloth. "It's the labour of the mass of the people which makes all these things possible – not only things like aeroplanes and liners and racing cars, but every sort of fantastic luxury. The masses work, so that a few people at the top can cram themselves with food and live in huge houses and deck out their women like Christmas trees."

"But that's how the machine keeps going," I said frowningly. "There's a demand for these things, and so it gives employment."

"It gives employment," he mimicked, with a bitter sneer. "That's something you've been taught to say, isn't it? If anybody like me shoots off their mouth about the injustice of the system, if it's suggested that building Jerusalem in England's green and pleasant land shouldn't include ten people swilling champagne while ten thousand have to crawl for skim-milk, you say, 'Oh, but it gives employment.'"

"I didn't say it in that futile way," I told him angrily. "And it's perfectly true that building cars and making dresses *does* give work and provide wages."

"Sorry," he answered, with that quick smile which always managed to retrieve my ill-humour. "But it's a parrot cry, all the same, and it misses the point for two reasons. One is that most of that employment is parasitic: it diverts capital which should be invested in more necessary production – foodstuffs, cheap houses, all the sort of things that don't pay so well: and it diverts and misdirects the labour market in the same way. It pays wages, of course – but why should the general human welfare be a by-product of luxury? Why should eighty per cent of the population be graciously allowed to remain at a subsistence level, while the other twenty corner what the workers produce and keep it for themselves?"

I frowned again. "That's so ridiculous. You talk as if everyone was starving."

"So they are ..." He got up, sweeping aside papers and booklets, and began to stride about the room. He looked very thin, though that was hardly conclusive. "You know that many of your fellow countrymen do not get enough to eat, don't you? But if you can contrive to forget that, because it's hidden away in South Wales and up in Durham and Northumberland, then consider how the rest live, the people who have enough to eat but not much besides. Have you considered the sort of people they're turned into? – the miserably stunted and confined lives they lead? They know nothing of good music, good books and pictures, good plays: all they can afford is TRASH," he brought the word out with a sweep of the hand, "and not much of that either ... You can say that they're happy because they don't know what they're missing, but that is dishonest. And cowardly, and cruel." His eyes burned, as if he saw in me an image of that unworthiness. "It means that you're deliberately denying to your fellow creatures the right to any beauty or significance in their lives, that you are ready to keep them in ignorance of the fact that life can be any better than a period of drudgery and animal struggle, just because you want more than your fair share of culture and luxury for yourself."

I shrugged my shoulders, feeling that he was being unfair to me but unable to put my finger on it.

"You exaggerate," I told him at length. "You always exaggerate. Things aren't as bad as that. And people *don't* have such bad lives."

But he wouldn't take up the challenge: he seemed to have withdrawn within himself: he only said, in a subdued voice: "All you see is London, the spit-and-polish end of England. Go north, or go to Monmouthshire: take a look at one of those villages built on an old slag-heap, where people pass their whole lives, and watch their children growing up, in a stench which you couldn't endure for ten minutes: where a man has thirty bob a week to keep a wife and two children, where everything is in pawn and the only covering you have at night in midwinter is a filthy worn blanket and a few old newspapers: where the plaster's flaking off the walls and showing up nests of lice in the process ... Go and live there: with one outside lavatory to serve thirty people, with the whole house sweating damp, with the only factory – the one *you* used to work at – shut down and dismantled: with families sleeping six in a room, and incest as common as keeping a whippet ... Try that life for a bit: and then come south again, and sleep soft and eat your fill four times a day, and tell the unemployed they're lucky to live in the richest country in the world."

I got up off the bed. "It's no good bawling me out," I said shortly. "I can't help it if there's not enough work to go round. And anyway, what about you? *You* live here, you get enough to eat all right!"

He put his hand on my arm. "Don't go," he said quietly. His lined face under the lamplight softened. "We don't need to quarrel about this ... It was from one of those valleys that I escaped: and I don't go back because I think I can do more good here."

"I thought you were a Londoner."

"I've lived in London for fifteen years, but my father was a South Wales miner: I was brought up in the sort of surroundings I've been telling you about."

"Good God!" I said involuntarily.

He smiled. "That's what I feel, sometimes." Then his face changed, rather horribly: he was looking back to that valley, to that house, to that poor childhood ... "I was to be a miner too, but I didn't want to, and I sweated blood – attending night school after I'd been working as a pit-boy all day – to get away from it. I *did* get away from it," he straightened up unconsciously, "I got a scholarship, I passed exams, I had a chance to be a teacher and I grabbed it. My father didn't understand – no one understood – they thought I was conceited, too good for my friends: even my mother thought I ought to stick to the pit instead of taking risks. Risks! The pit killed my father in the end, and my brother, and her too, I suppose. And I got what I wanted."

I said nothing.

"I got what I wanted," he repeated after a pause. "You see me now, triumphant – the high priest of learning, the keeper of the most sacred charge in the world." Swiftly his face changed again, to that old mocking bitterness. "Years ago when I asked the kids in my class what they wanted to be when they grew up, one of them said: 'A dustman'. Everyone laughed and made fun of him, but by God he was right. He's a corporation dustman at this very moment and he earns four pounds two and six a week to my four quid."

After a bit I said: "Come and have a drink."

The Alison Erroll affair went bad that month, finally and completely; and even though I had seen it coming, and could have forecast, to within a week, the moment of dissolution, yet it hurt damnably and went on hurting.

Our meetings had gradually got fewer and fewer: I could not really afford to take her out, and she didn't like the places I took her to when I did abandon thrift and proposed an evening together. That indeed was a lively subject for scrapping between us: it was almost impossible not to be sulky for the rest of the night when, in whatever restaurant we went for dinner, Alison would sweep in as if she were visiting a workhouse tea-party, flip disdainfully through the menu, and then say: "Oh God, this awful place! ... Can't you make some money, darling?" It gave the occasion a certain paltriness, from the outset ... She had never exhibited that insensibility before: I had not considered that she could be that sort of person; and it seemed to confirm the suspicion that she had fallen out of love and did not greatly care what sort of time she gave me.

In which circumstances I naturally lost my nerve and put on a very poor act indeed. And what an inferior performance the uncertain lover gives, by comparison with the confident favourite ... I ran through the whole miserable repertoire, from end to end: the hanging about for promised telephone calls: the breaking of engagements for some hardly won date which is itself cancelled at an hour's notice: the waiting for letters which *must* come by the evening's post, the self-persuasion that they have been held up and will arrive at breakfast time, the certainty that they will come by the second delivery, the fact that they never arrive at all and are explained by some negligent phrase with which one dare not quarrel – 'no time', 'forgot', 'couldn't see much point in writing' ... All, these things gave the affair a background of uncertainty: and besides these, the common currency of a one-sided relationship, there were other things – suspicion, jealousy, sudden conviction of hopelessness – which made of that November an unhappy declension into despair.

"If," said Dr Barrow at one point, "one may quote La Rochefoucauld without either straining or insulting your intelligence, '*Tous nos malheurs viennent de ne pouvoir être seul*.' I suggest that you would be better able to cope with adverse circumstances if you put this whole affair out of your mind, once and for all." He smiled dryly. "You will recognize that as the advice of an old man comfortably past all such conflicts."

It was advice which, in any case, I could not take until it was demonstrated without ambiguity that Alison was lost to me; and so I continued, all that month when I should have been job-hunting and saving my small store of capital, to pursue this wraith of desire which had less and less of reality as each day passed. Now it was more than a matter of forgotten letters and scamped phone calls: now I began to traverse successive hints and pointers which changed the old certainty of having the affair 'fixed' into a timid suspicious humility ... Now she often took meals with other young men, alone, in solid South Audley Street flats where I could not penetrate; and to deliver her there in a taxi which I could ill afford, to receive remote and automatic thanks as she glanced at her mouth in her mirror or set straight the little veil of her hat, and then to walk away with the absolute conviction, before I had gone twenty yards, that she was already in the other man's arms – of such shadowed misery, of such goading of the heart, was all that period made up.

Naturally I wasted money in the most foolish fashion, giving hardly any thought to finding a job and none at all to that other possibility – writing; naturally I was becoming less and less what she wanted.

The climax came at the beginning of December, when, sick of the frustration which a week of inconclusive meetings had brought me, I hired a car and drove Alison over to Oxford for a weekend which culminated, back in

London on Monday, in dinner at the Savoy and a fantastic session at the Old Florida ... The whole excursion cost me just under thirty pounds; and when I took her home at four on Tuesday morning it was all I could do not to burst out laughing at my own futility. Thirty pounds had been exactly a quarter of my remaining capital.

"Lovely evening, darling," she said absent-mindedly, up in the shiny cream sitting room with its smooth unusable furniture. "Lovely weekend too. Light the fire." She was sorting through her letters, her hair falling forward, her oval face pale: half of me thought "It's all right this time, thank God," the other half was still wondering where I got my genius for fatuity.

After I had lit the fire and poured a drink: "Anything in the post?" I asked. "If not, come over here and don't waste time."

She looked up with a half-smile. "There's a good old-fashioned ring about that ... Letters? Only one – Henry Skarington." She held up, with a certain air of pride, an oversize light blue envelope.

"Good God!" I said. "Why do you want to bother with that tyke?"

She stiffened. "Don't be silly. He's damned clever, and he runs one of the best weeklies in England."

"Waugh-and-water. And you've only got to look at the man, anyway – intellectual on the surface, lecher underneath."

"*You* can't talk."

"It's about all I can do ... What's he writing to you for? A subscription?"

She turned away. "He wants to have lunch with me."

"That'll be a classy session. Am I supposed to escort you to his flat?"

"You'll be doing very little escorting," she retorted, "if you go on like this. What's the matter? Why spoil a good weekend?"

"Oh, I don't know." I sighed: for some reason I was beginning to lose all my contentment. "Why *have* a good weekend? You know I can't afford it. Do you realize – "

"Marcus !" Her voice snapped out suddenly.

I said: "Yes, dear?" in a meek married manner. I knew exactly what was coming.

"For heaven's sake don't start that," she went on. "I've managed to keep you off it the whole weekend. This is a funny time to start whining about the money you haven't got."

I flared up. "It's all very well for you. You don't have to go back to that bloody boarding-house and wonder why you've been such a sap as to spend thirty quid on a weekend."

"You ought to think it was worth it."

"If I didn't have to fork out, I probably would."

"Oh lord, oh lord, oh LORD!" She jumped up off the sofa and stood confronting me, staring down in sudden spiteful anger. "What's the good of going on like this? It's always the same, every damned time we stir out of the house." There was such hate in her voice that I knew we had come to the crisis. "Why take me to Oxford, then?"

"Because I wanted you, and it was the only way I could get you to myself."

"And now you've had what you wanted, for a three-day stretch, you can start cursing me? Very nice ..." Her tone took on a clipped intensity. "It's a pity you didn't think of your thirty quid a little earlier – last night, for instance, when you swore that – Oh, I've had enough of this," she burst out suddenly. "You'd better clear out."

"All right." I stood up. "But I still think it's your fault. You insist on being taken out whenever we spend any time

151

together, and you know I can't afford it. If the only way I can see anything of you is by spending money, then the thing dies a natural death."

"A clear statement at last." With a queer smile, which somehow made me feel that she had manufactured the scene, she indicated the door; and as I hesitated, unwilling to put an end to something which had brought us both such a measure of exhilaration: "Don't go back on it," she said devilishly. "I *do* need money spending on me, and I can't get used to anything else."

Going up Church Street in the crisp biting cold of that December morning, sick with defeat and wanting a drink more than anything else on earth, I was accosted by a horrible woman in black. Her hat hid her eyes, but her face under the lamp was the colour of an unripe grape – livid with cold, channelled by wrinkles which the thick smudges of powder could not hide. She croaked at me, some words I couldn't distinguish. But I stopped.

"This is a hell of a time to be out," I said.

"Can't choose." With the birth of hope her voice became clearer. "How about it? I'm very French – you'll like it."

"I don't want it," I said. "I've had it already."

"OK, lucky boy." She turned away again, to the nearest shop doorway: the shadow of her slouching figure swayed against the wall like a huge drunken form. Then I had an idea.

"Have you a flat?" I called after her.

She turned: a caricature of a smile slit her face for an instant. "Changed your mind?"

"No. But I want a drink. Have you got any brandy?" She stared at me, pitifully angry. "What the hell? I *work* for my living."

"I'll give you a quid for an armchair and some brandy." She slopped towards me again, throwing back her head, peering up at me with red-rimmed, brown-pouched eyes. I looked at her in amazement, too tired and dispirited to feel any revulsion: she must have been at least sixty years old.

"Do you mean it?" The croaking voice had its own feeble menace. "If you cross me I'll cut your heart out … Let's see the quid, for a start."

I took it out, thinking as I did so: thirty-*one* quid for the weekend …

As she snatched at it I drew it back instinctively. "That's for the drink," I told her. "Where's your flat?"

" 's a hotel. Down here. And God help you if you welsh on me."

We set off side by side. I hoped we were what people called an ill-assorted couple.

The 'hotel' was a narrow-fronted slit of a place such as I would not have thought to find within five miles of Church Street: my companion had simply pushed the door open and walked in, and I had signed no register, nor indeed met anyone who questioned my presence there, though playing cards in the hall had been the prettiest pair of cut-throats I'd ever laid eyes on – dark, kink-haired, with tough bunchy little figures and skins like blotched yellow sandpaper. The crazy rope-lift jerked us upwards, the woman leaning in one corner of it with her eyes closed, looking as though she were going to die … On, as I judged, the fourth floor, we groaned to a standstill: at the end of a passage she kicked open a door and motioned me to enter. Then she peered inside, said "Sorry, dearie," and pulled it to, giving me the most revolting grimace I had ever encountered in my life.

"Careless, ain't they … Mind you, we don't always throw in a show for nothing."

In another room, tawdry, smelling of musty decay and of something else unanalysable and repellent, she said: "Here we are. Suit you?"

"It'll do". The impulse which had driven me to speak to her in the first place had long since spent itself, but to back out now would take too much argument and effort. "How about that drink? I need a good one."

"Sure. Brandy, wasn't it? Let's have the cash, and I'll get it for you."

I handed over the pound note, and she left me – alone in that truly horrible room with its smells and its begrimed bedclothes, in a great draughty house now silent as the grave, now shaken by a passing lorry, now resounding to footfalls or voices or strange thuddings which, for all I knew or cared, were the toppling bodies of young murdered men. And the rest of the session, with me sitting by the empty grate lowering my brandy in a gloomy haze of despair, and the woman sprawling on the bed under the single naked light bulb, overflowing out of her unlaced magenta corset, wolfing stew and cold potatoes in a series of horrible gulpings, and later croaking out in that death rattle voice the unsolicited story of her life – the rest of the night had the same measure of bleared subhuman inconsequence. When I went downstairs again, at seven o'clock, both men barred the way out and the toughest of them said:

"The room's fifteen bob."

He had the knob of a blackjack sticking out of his waistcoat pocket. I paid without a word: it was all of a piece with the rest of the weekend, anyway.

Of such contrasts were the last two months of that year made up: losing Alison, alternately hoarding and throwing away my money, interviewing unimpressed City men who promised to keep in touch, soberly discussing the universe with Dr Barrow; and all set against the impeccable background of Miss Fleming's Academy for Indigent Gentlefolk. I saw Armstrong the solicitor once, but nothing was settled in that quarter – they were still a long way from probate: I had a letter from Tania, honeymooning in Athens and Egypt; and finally I wrote an article for the *Yachting News*, which was returned within two days as neatly as by any slot-machine … And of course there was, all the time, Cummings to bear me company; Cummings explaining, Cummings raving, Cummings talking, talking the nights away; Cummings who wanted me to abandon everything I had been taught so far and turn to Socialism, and who would not relax his efforts at persuasion for a single moment.

Cummings who succeeded.

CHAPTER SIX

'Where there is such infinite and laborious
potency there is room for every hope.'

GEORGE SANTAYANA

❖

"Listen to me," Cummings said one night when, talking as
was our custom in his room after dinner, I had given a more
than usually decisive negative to something he had said;
"It's no use just saying 'Rot!' like that, when you don't
know the first thing about it. 'Sir,' said Dr Johnson, 'I have
found you an argument; I am not obliged to find you an
understanding.' ... Well, I'd like to find you one all the
same. How about giving me a chance?"

"Not a hope," I said. I was lounging in an armchair,
experiencing the novelty of counting my loose change to
see if I could postpone cashing a cheque for another day or
so. "You can quote what you like," I went on, "but you'll be
wasting your time – and well you know it."

"Why?"

"I tell you it's no good. I can't become a *Red*."

He shook his head. "Why say it like that? You don't even
know what Socialism means."

"Well, go ahead and tell me," I answered, meaning not to listen and ask fatuous questions at the end, as I used to do with Alastair. Then something – perhaps an infectious eagerness in his manner, perhaps the resolute attention of that tired face – made me change my mind. "I actually mean that," I told him. "Give me a couple of solid sentences – nothing about class-consciousness or bourgeoisie, but the basic idea behind it, if there is such a thing."

"Class-consciousness is the absolute essence – " he began forcefully. Then he broke off, and smiled. "I see what you mean," he said in his normal voice. "And I'll have a shot at it, though it's an idea which needs expanding, in every particular, to the length of an inaugural lecture at least." He threw his pencil down on the desk in front of him, and sat back. "The basic ideas of Socialism may be enumerated as: equality of opportunity, the nationalization of all essential goods and services, the elimination of the profit motive, and the putting into practice of the phrase: 'If a man will not work, neither shall he eat.' Nationalization doesn't mean the abolition of private property: it will simply make it impossible for a private individual so to gain control of the lives of his fellowmen that he can make them work for his own profit, or deny them the right to work except at his own price. The State controls the financial machine and is the universal employer, concerned with human welfare instead of dividends: it produces for use only, not for profit, and is far more efficient for that reason and also because it can plan production as an organized whole instead of leaving it to piecemeal competition."

"In fact," I interrupted, "they want to run the whole show on their own."

"It isn't *they*, it's *you*." He swung round to face me. "People talk about Socialists as if they were a gang of brigands who wanted to grab everything for themselves;

actually they want to liberate – to set free for everyone the enormous potentialities at present rationed and controlled, for their own advantage, by the few. Don't you see," he leant forward in earnest persuasion, "that there *is* something wrong with the present system? Something *must* be holding things up, if food is burnt and wheat ploughed in and fish thrown back into the sea, when all round there are people who don't get enough to eat. There's no answer and no excuse for that; the simple fact is that capitalism can't keep pace with scientific and industrial development, that production has outgrown the system of distribution."

I did not answer: there was logic in what he said, but it all seemed remote from myself – something which ought to be left to the experts. And then, for the first time, I found myself curious to learn more of what lay behind the rather bleak phrase 'nationalization of production', and what there was in Socialism which could fire the imagination and turn even insignificant men like Cummings into such passionate crusaders. You didn't find Conservatives talking till two in the morning about the innate divinity of the Primrose League …

As if he could read my thoughts, he went on: "How about giving me a chance? You've had twenty-one years of ignoring politics, and accepting your surroundings as incapable of improvement. That's a long start … Give me four weeks: read what I tell you and listen to me, really listen, as fairly as you can. And I'll try and show you in detail what's wrong in the world, and the plans we have to cure it. Will you do that?"

I laughed. "Well, it's a fair offer … All right, I will. Can I stop if I get bored?"

"You won't be … Mind you, I don't want to waste my time. You will treat this seriously, won't you?"

"Yes. In fact, I'm interested already. When do we begin?"

"Straight away." He got up and walked over to his bookcase. "I think I'll start you on Wells. He's not a Socialist, but he has some good ideas on the ultimate organization of the world, as well as on its present flaws." He took down and handed to me a book, of startling weight and thickness, called *The Work, Wealth, and Happiness of Mankind.* "Have a shot at that," he said. "It may start that handmade brain of yours working."

"Good lord!" I exclaimed. "Is everything going to be as solid as this? I thought '*facilis descensus*' would apply here."

"It's the beginning of your real education," he answered. "And seeing that it's you, that's liable to be a tough period … Take it away and get your teeth into it."

I found the book unusually stimulating, full of ideas – such as the *persona*-classification into peasant, nomad, and priestly-learned types, with their several derivatives – which opened up an immensely wide field of speculation. I wanted to know more, I wanted to cover the whole ground without shirking …

When I brought it back, three days later: "Well?" asked Cummings. "What did you think of it?"

"Grand," I answered. "I didn't know either that there was such a lot going on in the world, or that it could be set out so clearly. If the whole course is as entertaining as that, I'm not likely to be bored."

"It didn't take you long to finish it," he said suspiciously.

"I've had nothing else to do … What comes next?"

"A good solid armful of straight-cut Communism." Then he sighed. "But I wish, as a preliminary, that I could take you on a tour round England – not the show-places, but the bits of it that have had the life sucked out of them and haven't a chance in a million of ever being resurrected. It would be good for your conscience, I can tell you … Think of the Rhondda valley, with seventy-five per cent of the whole community dependent on the public funds: think of children – unwanted, most of them only born because some shady little pill fails to work – children consistently undernourished for years on end, growing up to a life of street-corner lounging in some little pigsty of a village in Durham – or, if they do get a job, learning to despise their fathers who have been out of work for six, seven, or eight years, and whom they have to support. I tell you," he emphasized his words with a darting forefinger, "you are stupid if you cannot see the logic of Socialism, you are wicked if you see it and don't act on it because you'd lose thereby. There's no middle way, Hendrycks – and I swear I'm going to make you understand it." He crossed to the bookcase once more – the faithful powder-monkey intent on keeping the guns served. I watched him as he moved up and down, his spare figure jerky even in deliberation, flicking a book here and there, half pulling one out and pushing it in again, selecting at length half a dozen assorted volumes. I realized that he was taking a great deal of trouble; and, curiously, this fact no longer seemed to stir up an opposing determination in my own mind. I wanted to learn. But what Alastair would have said ...

That was an astonishing month: it was as if there were no outside world at all, and no reality save the successive books which lay open on my knee, and on my pillow, and propped against the water-jug at meals, and balanced on the mantelpiece and the 'thing' which spanned the bath, and neighbouring the shaving mirror and seeming to fall open at the appointed page as soon as I unstuck my eyes in the morning: everything else was blotted out – there was no strange household or straitening of circumstance, no sighing for the old days or apprehension of the new, no Ruxton murder case or Sino-Japanese wrangle or curiously academic Naval Conference ... It was the most intensive effort of study I had ever made in my life, and yet it was as easy and natural as poker-playing and drinking had been a short time previously; I had set out with the resolve to give the thing all the concentration I could, and before three days had gone by I realized that such resolution was unnecessary – the immense range and novelty of the subject carried their own momentum. Of course I was talking with Cummings the whole time, and listening and commenting on what he said, on the wireless news-bulletins and the newspapers, on the Hyde Park speeches: and every point I raised was expounded with a candour and honesty which I had never encountered before and in which I could discern only an eagerness to assist and buttress my curiosity. And by any standard I read enormously, swallowing Cummings' library in great draughts that seemed sometimes cool and crystal clear, sometimes only torrential mysticism; it was a whole new world, a universe unsuspected and suddenly revealed; and since all my doubts and questionings I took to him, to hear them explained with profound attention to detail and an astonishing cynicism concerning what I had hitherto taken to be constant and enduring factors, it was natural that there came into our relationship a curious sort of hero-worshipping gratitude on my part, such as one might have laughed at in a ten-year-old schoolboy.

But certainly he was persuasive, certainly teaching was his job …

"Even if I hadn't had that childhood," he once said, "I should still feel and talk as I do. It isn't a matter of jealousy or personal discontent – at least, I don't think so: I like to believe it's a sense of social justice, which revolts at the idea of one helpless class of people being kicked around by another. I just can't bear to see certain men get away with murder – and be knighted and baroneted and swamped with money in the process. For it *is* murder by a new technique – smooth and above board and within the law: you make yourself richer and the poor poorer, till they haven't a nerve or a gasp left in them. And there are official things as well, things like the Means Test – really savage measures directed against the most miserable of all sections of the people: taking away not their self-respect – that went long ago – but their right to live lives that come within the human scale at all. And when you have, spread before people's eyes, and thrown at them on the cinema and the wireless and in the advertisements, the other side of the picture – unlimited wealth, senseless extravagance, ease and luxury – well, I don't know why the top hasn't blown off long ago."

To such an accompaniment did I complete my month's reading. I read all the relevant Wells, and two books of Strachey's; some Fabian Society and Labour Party pamphlets; Palme Dutt's *Fascism and Social Revolution*, Mitchison's *The First Workers' Government*, and Emile Burns' *Handbook of Marxism*, which contained the Manifesto of 1848 as well as various writings of Marx, Lenin, and Engels. Then back to the earlier prophets – Adam Smith, John Stuart Mill; then forward again to Shaw, and Brailsford's *Property or Peace*, and Stalin's *Leninism*. And lastly, the Webbs' *Soviet Communism – A New Civilization*, which had only just appeared.

And then I got it.

How can one describe that moment ? – the reverse of 'love to hatred turned', the trenchant conviction of knowledge, the 'light from Heaven' of Saul … That was the amazing thing about it, the immediate and absolute confidence that Socialism was *right* and that nothing else would do; it explained Cummings' passionate faith, and his driving force of persuasion, and his refusal ever to take no for an answer. I felt, now, that driving force taking command over my own imagination: I seemed to *know*, and to have the fact installed in my brain almost as a physical part of it, that this new idea was the only one which could resolve the complexities and problems of the world around me; that it might be thrice denied of men but must ultimately triumph; and that, those at present in power being of a certain cast of mind, the system would never be changed by consent and must be driven out by force directed to this one end.

On this last point, indeed, Cummings had been especially insistent.

"If you have these ideas," he said, "then logically you are a Communist. And if you are a Communist, you must *fight* against the opposition, not argue or pray for their souls. '*Ecrasez l'infâme*' – there is no middle way, these people being what they are."

"So I'm a Communist?"

"Yes." He laughed suddenly. "Don't look so scared – it's quite simple really."

I suppose I had been scared just at the beginning, when I realized the way I was going, but that feeling had not lasted long: it had been driven out by the same overwhelming conviction of rightness, and almost immediately I had come to the 'why-doesn't-everybody-see-it?' stage, when I gave absolute endorsement to Cummings' claim that everyone on the opposite side must be either a knave or a fool. And if neither my past life nor my vanished circle of friends seemed to confirm this – well, there were the books, there was Cummings, there was proof pressed down and running over that Socialism was the only complete answer to trade stagnation, to poverty and waste, to international maladjustment. And anyway, most of my friends had taken so little interest in politics that it was hardly fair to pass judgment on them in that way ...

But what had clinched the matter for me, what had been the final rivet for the brand-new shining encasement, was the Hoare-Laval proposal for the settlement of the Italo-Ethiopian War, and the partition of Abyssinia. That seemed to me then to be not merely a glimpse of the bad faith of the Government, but a full revelation of its temper and spirit; after the humiliation of seeing the League betrayed by one's own compatriots, by men who had won an election and taken office on a pledge to uphold the Covenant, one could only feel that any other body of legislators, and any other tradition of international dealing, was to be preferred. Cummings' books, and Cummings himself, might lack final authority: but Hoare-Laval was proof – proof of murder, with the carrion-stench rising from it as a damning cloud of witness.

"I've joined the faith," I told Dr Barrow a few days later. "Cummings' faith ... But I don't suppose you'll understand who, so I'll spare you the agonies."

"I see you have already acquired the fashionable truculence," he said mildly.

"Sorry ... But *do* you think it's a bad thing?"

"Not at all. Every young man should be a Socialist: it stimulates his conscience. And then he should grow out of it."

"Why grow out of it? Socialism is – "

He held up his hand. "You agreed to spare me." But a smile accompanied the words. "Will you deign to drink with anyone as old-fashioned as a Liberal?"

The small exchange had a depressing effect, a twinge of juvenility, though that could not last long: for naturally he would take that line, naturally he was bound to disparage Socialism, like all the old gang ... What was infinitely more depressing was waking up on Christmas morning, remembering fleetingly the snow piled up on the windowsill at Klosters the year before, and then returning to the crude present – to the fact that, when my current bill was paid, I would have exactly seventy pounds left in the world … 'God blast you, merry gentlemen' I thought as I heard the jangle of half a dozen competing chimes, 'there isn't a damned thing to rejoice about it.' Supposedly I must now do something definite about getting a job; and this place was clearly too expensive, as well as far too genteel, for the new regime. 'Time is the dog which barks us all to hell!' – I had to watch every cent now, I had to make that seventy pounds last at least nine months or even a year … In any case, was it worth trying to remain in such surroundings? And the answer, incontestably, was, No: better be *declassé* and have done with it.

That 'class' idea didn't matter a damn now – such was the thought with which I ended the year.

CHAPTER SEVEN

For this, be sure, tonight thou shalt have cramps.

SHAKESPEARE, *The Tempest*

❖

Since the two pubs opposite were still open, the Café Renegado – proprietor, B. Casliagari – was not full, or anything like it, besides Shep and Ted Accles and myself, there was only a drab woman sniffing thickly over her meat pie, and two mechanics who argued interminably about the merits of American cars. Behind the counter B. Casliagari ('Caz' to the *habitués*) lounged in his shirtsleeves, holding a newspaper in one hand and washing cups in a tin basin with the other: he was a huge man, a stage Italian with three chins and a gleaming moustache, collarless now and short of a shave, but still dominating the ten-by-twenty board-floor room, the half dozen chairs and tables, the urn and coke-stove which together comprised the Café Renegado. I would have called it a dirty little place – in fact, I did call it a dirty little place, but not out loud: since it was a favourite meeting place among the local Party members, Caz being a refugee from Florence with five years' political imprisonment waiting for him if he ever returned, and in any case one went there to meet and talk with people, not to criticize the appointments … Through a tinny crackling loudspeaker on a ledge overhead the wireless was blaring out the Luxembourg programme – mostly advertising of an aperient persuasion; and now and then the lone despairing woman would cock a moist eye at it, glimpsing another world where her hair had lustre, her skin a peach-like softness, her lovers impatience and virility, and meat pies no backlash. Then she would gulp and sniff. It was indeed another world.

The morose Shep was reading a newspaper, pecking his nose into it as though on a personal heresy hunt to sniff out deviations from the Party line: opposite me across the smeary marble-topped table Ted Accles cut a ham sandwich into eight small squares and popped them into his mouth one by one, like votive offerings to some quantitative god. Ted, who lived two doors away from me in Carter Street, was hardly the Communist of popular fancy – a little rolling tub of a man, about fifty, red face, plump hands, trousers loosely belted and sagging to a level far below the waistline. But he could argue well, with the North-countryman's wealth of coarse or homely simile to draw upon. I had met him at a meeting of Cummings', and was surprised and gratified that he had not mistrusted me on sight. I think I would have done so, had the roles been reversed.

Shep was a direct contrast, and pure Marx through and through: a long, thin, yellow edition of Cummings, with eyes which might once have been fierce but were now strained and weak from over-reading. I had not yet discovered whether 'Shep' was a contraction, and if so, of what: by trade he was a printer, and out of hours he worked with devilish energy at the whole range of Party campaigning – circularizing, paper selling, writing technical trade-union stuff for the *Daily Worker*, street-corner speaking, works-demonstrating, and hell-raising generally. (That was what had amazed me about all the Communists I had encountered so far – the extreme energy which they brought to a dozen various branches of their faith. All of them – Shep, Ted Accles, Hime, Jack Wentworth, the Hungarian Kreplan – did one man's work in the daytime and two men's at night.) I knew already that Shep disliked me: he suspected everything – clothes, accent, the fact that I did not work and yet had money – and he sometimes called me, with a peculiar emphasis, *Mister Hendrycks*; but where before I would have returned the dislike with the best will in the world, I now had only the dear wish to dispel that suspicion and convince him, as well as the others, that I was sincere.

And after all, I admitted as I glanced in the tarnished mirror behind the counter, after all, I really *didn't* look very convincing: the check Newmarket suit, the cream shirt, the sunburn which still survived from last summer, all were fancy dress in this world of scarves and grey creased faces and bulbous shoes. I supposed that sooner or later I would lose that self-consciousness; but so far it had been a potent source of embarrassment, and not only to myself.

Behind the counter Caz sighed, a draughty sigh coming fathoms deep from that immense chest: the hand which was dabbling about among the cups seemed to grow dispirited.

Ted Accles popped the last square of sandwich into his mouth. "What's the matter, lad?" he asked, munching. (He had a curious accent: Lancashire, but clipped and Cockneyfied by his twelve years' exile.) "What's in paper to upset you? Mussolini doing well all of a sudden?"

"Mussolini doing not so good, but still I don't like it. It say here," Caz tapped the newspaper with a thick olive thumb, "the new budget cannot balance, not by thirty-three million pounds. In *lire* that is – " be began to mutter under his breath, lost in calculation.

"You ought to be pleased, lad, you ought to give us a dance, like. If they have a fy-nancial collapse, that'll mean the end of Fascism."

Caz looked up mournfully. "I do not think of *Fascisimo* in this, I think of my countrymen who starve. And then you read of Starace and such assassins, who say they must all make new sacrifices for the glory of Italy. Sacrifices? I tell you they eat the dirt already."

"Don't take the short view, comrade," Shep joined in, his harsh voice so decisive that the two mechanics turned and stared. "The people may suffer for the moment, but it makes them hate the regime more, doesn't it? And the worse off the country is, the nearer the break-up. And we'll see something, then we'll see the workers really in command, instead of being duped by Fascist lies."

But Caz would not be comforted: his politics might take him on one road, but that wasn't to say that his heart shrivelled to nothing in the process. He returned to his paper and his dishes, with a slow inflexible shake of the head.

I looked at my watch. "I'll have to be moving soon," I said to Ted. "I wonder how long that queue is by now."

"Three times round the gasworks, I'd say. Mind you, 'e wasn't such a bad old buffer, even if 'e was king. But I'd sooner it was you than me, any road."

"It shouldn't be either of you, by rights." That was Shep, harsh and authoritative again, looking over his paper at me. "If you're thinking of joining the Party, what good is the lying-in-state to you? You don't want to get mixed up in that sort of thing, especially when the papers are plugging it for all they're worth."

"I know that: it's just – well, sentiment, I suppose." I wasn't very sure myself why I wanted to go down to

Westminster, but I knew that, whatever Shep and the others thought about it, I was going. "Also I want to write it up, if I can."

"Good God, what do you want to write about tripe like that for?" said Shep roughly. "There are *real* things, you know, that make the monarchy look like a dog's dinner. Think of those Red Cross bombings in Abyssinia – why don't you write about that, instead of shuffling along in a queue to stare at a lot of Life Guards?"

"Leave 'im alone, Shep," broke in Ted Accles. "What's it matter 'ow 'e spends the evening? – there's no meeting and 'e's not on selling yet."

Shep went back to his paper with a grunt, while Ted winked at me, a wink which reminded me of the old days when my father used to undermine my governess's authority in precisely the same way … Then the shop door opened suddenly, letting in a draught and a patter of raindrops. I looked up, and smiled at the new arrival, whom I had met the day before – a taxi driver called Hime, a young Jew of the lean sort with a mop of coal-black hair and a permanently drooping cigarette in one corner of his mouth.

"Evening, all." He took off his peaked cap with a flourish and shook the rain from it. "The old cab ain't exactly waterproof, I must say … Evening, Caz. What about a soak o' Rosie?"

"Tea – coming up!" Caz turned the urn tap and let the tea, stewed to a brackish-brown, trickle out. "How's the business, Himey?"

Hime made that odd sound with his lips which the French employ when they wish to disparage something. "Not so hot … An old tart just gave me tuppence tip on a four-bob fare: that's the sort of day it's been." He blew on his tea, and then sipped it. "Give us a pie, Caz."

"One pie."

Presently Ted began to talk about the next week's activities: a demand for Communist affiliation to the Labour Party had just been turned down, and headquarters were preparing to start a fresh drive directed to the same end. The discussion drifted on, now claiming my attention, now becoming too technical and allowing me to float away on an easy daydream. Shep had been right, in a way, about the lying-in-state: I was going to attend for reasons entirely sentimental, making it a sort of *fin-de-siècle* excursion before putting on the whole armour of the new god; but there certainly were affairs of far greater moment to claim one's attention. The new year had started off poorly, from our point of view – or indeed from any point of view which included humanity as part of its basis: besides Goebbels' depressing 'guns, not butter' speech, there had been Laval's victory in the French Chamber, a kick in the eye for Roosevelt's New Deal from the Supreme Court, and the Italian bombing of the Swedish Red Cross, whereby forty-two people were killed, fifty injured, and the whole equipment of the unit wiped out. Italian sentiment concerning this was summed up by the *Lavoro Fascista* in the words: 'The time has come to lay aside Italy's traditional chivalry and generosity towards her foe', and by the despatch through the Suez Canal of fifty-three tons of poison gas and a large number of flame-throwers. The epitaph on the old year had been fitly pronounced by General Goering: "If people ask, 'What has Germany done for world peace?' we should answer 'She has rearmed!' "

But: "All the same," I said to myself as I emerged into the Edgware Road and began my long walk southwards, "even if the Party don't like the lying-in-state idea and think it a propaganda ramp, I can't help feeling sincerely sorry that he's dead." It might be that that was the last time I would feel that way, about the monarchy or anything else in the same tradition; but whether that proved true or not, I had found the whole thing intensely moving – the first 'Confined to his bed with a cold' bulletin, the progress to bronchial catarrh, the fight for life and slow ebbing therefrom, the penultimate declaration which told the public everything in a phrase which could hardly have been bettered: 'The King's Life is moving peacefully towards its close.' I had taken a full part in that shadowed week, joining the huge silent crowd outside Buckingham Palace, watching the successive notices being posted: and whatever Shep thought about it, that feeling of personal loss, that 'father-of-a-family' relationship and consequent sense of bereavement which was widespread throughout the country, had been mine also.

The house in Carter Street in which I lived was one of a block of six, stuck (there is no other word) up a cul-de-sac among the black spider's web of streets round Paddington Station. The roadway which served it was rarely swept, indifferently drained, and full of children – many of them on roller-skates, all of them shouting with horrid energy from seven in the morning till ten at night: the houses were dilapidated inside and out, in a peculiarly forlorn way which suggested that the dirt which was everywhere apparent had actually eaten into their fabric. Certainly the process had reached my room on the first floor. It was a fairly large room, for which I paid six-and-six a week: it had a bed and a table and a chair, a gas ring, and a cupboard stacked to the scuppers with old copies of the *Sporting Times*; and a tap on the landing outside brought to a close an inventory of equipment which was, I suppose, sufficient to support life. (The precise species of life which it did support was only to appear later.)

One could have wished that the repetition of deplorable birds which supplied the motif of the wallpaper had had sufficient cunning or generosity to pin the latter to the wall

… But still it wasn't such a bad room, especially to one in search of certain romantic crudity; and though the surviving woodwork was grey and rotten with age, and some murderous stains on the ceiling gave promise of a lively future for those in search of newspaper copy, yet it would serve, it was the sort of thing I wanted. It had the advantage of facing south on to the street, the view including a lamp-post with a rope tied to the crossbar in general readiness, and a block of 'working-class' flats of particular gauntness and squalor. From one open window of this, directly opposite mine, an old woman with the whitest face I'd ever seen stared out all day long – never moving her head, never speaking or seeming to eat, just waiting with senile and stagnant patience. I had only just learned what she was waiting for. She was consumptive, the girls downstairs told me, and had about three months to go. She was in bed really, only you didn't notice it.

Having sold all my clothes except one suit and some flannels, I had found moving in a simple enough business. A clock and a few books were the only other things I had kept, together with a rug to supplement the exiguous bedclothes; and I had bought a dishcloth, a saucepan, and two each of everything in the crockery and cutlery line. That was really all … The sole thing which was out of character, the one exquisite object in a swamp of mundane and dirty inelegance, was something of my mother's from Nine Beeches – a Fabergé paperknife, of gold and pink enamel, finely and cunningly wrought, such as might by itself have justified that Tsarist regime. I used to play with it quite a lot. It certainly showed that room up.

And as for the rest of the house …

When I had first seen the 'Room to Let' notice in a window and had gone round to the address indicated, I had been met by a small, wispy, and slightly pathetic little man with virtually no chin at all – as far from my idea of a slum landlord as anyone could have been without incurring the suspicion of imposture. His name was Mr Tinker: and he proved almost embarrassingly communicative both about himself and what he called, inevitably, his bit of property. Some of the tenants were behind with the rent, and repairs cost money – so he dismissed, with a weak smile, the appalling state of filth into which the house had sunk; but despite this he was always trying to improve its tone and get 'the right type of lodger'. And apropos of this: "Excuse my asking," he had interjected suddenly, in the middle of our negotiations. He peered up at me in a childlike manner, as if it lay in my power to give him some kind of treat – a picnic, or a visit to the Zoo. "Excuse me, but you're Oxford and Cambridge, aren't you?"

To avoid a close analysis of current educational practice, I replied that this was so.

"Spotted it first time," cried Mr Tinker delightedly. He walked round me, eyes agleam. "You can't mistake it, and that's what I've always said. I'll be pleased for you to take the room, Mr Hendren: I want to get young university fellows if I can. That ought to make a difference, oughtn't it?"

"I dare say."

"I'm certain of it. And that's what I'm working towards, this very minute. Oxford and Cambridge, eh? Now if I could get one or two more students, you know …"

It had taken me very little time to discover just how far he had advanced towards his ideal.

The house was meanly narrow, of two storeys built round a bare and wavering staircase: the ground floor was a small general shop run by two girls, sisters called Jimpson, one rather pretty and one rather not, with a child of four to complete the *ménage*. Whose child? They had not volunteered the information, neither had anyone else: he was just young Reg, a very dirty little boy who left his toys in the hallway and other evidence in less public places. The girls were pleasant and gossipy, hanging about the shop door at all hours and clearly not knowing what to make of me: I used to talk to them, sitting on a packing-case and watching the stream of children who shuffled in, and mumbled, and shuffled out again with armfuls of things for which they made no effort to pay. The whole business indeed was run on those lines, the children giving no names and no money passing till the end of the week. The prettier of the two girls laughed when I first commented on this.

"Don't know much, do you? That's how the poor live – everything on the slate till Friday, and always a week behind with the cash. Haven't you met that before?"

"No."

She waited for confidences, but I postponed them. One day I'd spin her a good yarn, if I could think of one … Then the not-so-pretty Miss Jimpson came lumbering out of the back room: she was large, and about forty, and faintly terrifying.

"Seen Reg?" she asked. "Where's 'e got to now?" She raised her voice to a notable pitch. "*Reg!* Come and get your dinner, or I'll give it to the milkman."

And Reg came tumbling downstairs, inarticulate, staring up at me, and wiping his nose on one of my socks.

So much for the ground floor. The basement room was occupied by a one-armed Irish sailor called Malloy, a black square little man with a rather fine head and a ferocious vocabulary on which he placed no check at all. But his room was as clean and neat as the inside of a submarine (I'd put him to bed once already, late one Saturday night when he'd stood under my window bawling out a hair-raising version of 'The Harlot of Jerusalem'): nothing was an inch out of place, from the boots in one corner of the fender to the crucifix exactly centred over the head of the

175

bed; and on a long shelf at one end was a stack of about forty assorted tins – spaghetti, baked beans, Frankfurter sausage – which he had laid in against the next lean stretch.

"You nivver know, be Chroist," he had said, in answer to my query. (His brogue varied, sometimes as thick as cheese, sometimes forgotten entirely.) "If I lost me job, and no bloody cash coming in, thin where would I be? Right up the bull's – So I make a cache, see, and live on it when toimes are unaisy."

He had been at sea for twenty years, and then: "I thought I'd pack it up," he confided on another occasion. "Maybe 'tis a man's loife, but Chroist-on-a-raft! who'd be wishing to be cooped up on a bloody barge for a bloody month on end, with nivver the sight of a girl all that time? Onnatural – and don't tell me, young fellow, you've nivver gone thirty days without a … because it's a liar I'd call you, and a bloody rotten one at that."

On the first storey was my room, and another empty one, and a third tenanted by a depressed and mournfully pregnant woman who slopped around all day in a dirty chiffon dressing gown, and kept pushing pencilled notes under my door: 'Call doctor if I knock' – 'Tonight may be it, please be ready' – 'Tell Jimpsons feeling bad, will they warn doc and Mrs Blanker …' The phrase (rarely apt) 'living on the edge of a volcano' seemed to fit my circumstances here, although the ugly Miss Jimpson told me not to worry, with a remark of some indelicacy about wind-and-water; and the situation gave that section of the house an atmosphere of contingent discomfort which the people on the top floor did not go very far towards relieving.

They were two – a quite ordinary prostitute with yellow hair and stiltlike heels, and a tall man, a greasy sort of customer, who, when we passed on the stairs, gave me the sort of look one associated with stage detectives. He was not so ordinary.

"Him? Oh, he's a ponce," the girls in the shop told me when I asked about him. And answering my further query: "It's him and that girl, see? She does the work and he draws the cash."

"Oh," I said, "a pimp. Don't the police object?"

The ugly one sniffed. "It's no go – they've got two rooms, see? – so the police couldn't prove anything. And besides ..."

"What?" I asked as she paused.

But she only said: "There's some funny things. You don't want to open your mouth too wide." And with that I had to be content.

At all events that was the household – an Irish sailor, two shop girls, one expectant mother, one prostitute and attendant pimp, and me. University types? It seemed that Mr Tinker still had a fair way to go. But I'm not sure I wouldn't have preferred the present lot to, say, a house full of Jesus College men.

The bright spot of that month was the fact that I wrote up the lying-in-state in a 2000-word article, and had it accepted by the *New Weekly*. Three actual guineas – over nine weeks' rent. This was going to be easy ... But writing it (in a 'loyal subject', 'pattern of kingship and courtesy' tone which did actually accord with my thoughts at the time) brought a speedy reaction to the other side, prompted by talks with Hime and Ted Accles, by the flagrant militarization of everything to do with the funeral, and by the high-class futility which marked the Proclamation and the tributes to the new King in the newspapers. The latter, indeed, were the best antidote of all. The Services, and most public institutions, sent 'with their humble duty, assurances of loyalty and affection';

Parliament asserted its 'Loyal Devotion to his Royal Person' in swingeing terms; and of course the newspapers came out strong with coloured supplements, acres of photographs, and abstracts of the King's career as Prince of Wales, from which it appeared that a man more fitted by birth, training, instinct, and capacity to be King of England could not have been found in the length and breadth of the land. "We loved him as Prince of Wales," the common man was quoted as saying: "we will love him more, and serve him better, as King." "Rally round the young monarch": "Prince Charming now enthroned in our hearts": "The country acclaims its beloved leader" – such was the tenor of that treacly stream ... One could only applaud the refreshing simplicity of the Oxford University Labour Club's *Bulletin*, which headlined the accession as 'Magdalen Man Makes Good'. But whatever the quality of the chorus, it was obvious that Edward VIII was well started; and, politics apart, one could wish him well as a man with, quite possibly, a marked social conscience.

Selling the *New Weekly* article was some compensation for an extraordinarily foolish episode which took place at the beginning of February – a meeting with Helga Sangstrom which should have been marvellous and actually went to hell within half an hour. Helga was a Swedish girl I'd met the previous year, as lovely in a blonde glowing way as they usually make them up there: we had encountered each other on a May Week party, and both rather fallen, and spent together one of those superb nights when everything is so perfectly in tune – drinks, people, music, laughter – that one unconsciously chalks it up, to have something to aim at in the future. We had put in a couple of hours at First and Third Ball, after dining in College in the teeth of her regular escort, and then gone all over the town crashing the other parties and finishing up in Archie's rooms at about four in the morning, to find there laid out a breakfast consisting of a bowl of strawberries and cream, a mound of chilled asparagus, and a magnum of GH Mumm ready to hand in an ice bucket. Archie himself was asleep in his armchair, wearing a fixed and horrid leer. We did not wake him.

Instead we ate and drank like kids at a dormitory feast, and watched the sun get up behind the roofs of King's Parade; and then we took a punt and drifted down to Grantchester meadow under fresh nine o'clock sunlight, and had another breakfast there – not in the least tired, and still conspicuously pleased with each other, and Helga looking like a blonde lioness, smooth, provocative, vital under her cunning black and white frock with the jewelled shoulder-straps ... Though that was the limit of the excursion. She had a lover already whom she refused to *tromp* – yet somehow I did not mind. And when we parted she promised me first refusal, as soon as the wheel came round again: in fact we had, somewhere in the future, a dateless date, a sexual depth charge of which chance and impulse held the fuse ... Of course Alison had intervened, and we had lost sight of each other; but now and then the remembrance had returned in a small flash of exhilaration, as a small boy might say: "Some day I'm going to have a shiny motorbike like that one, *because Mummy promised ...*"

It thus happened that when, returning with Ted Accles from an FSU film show down near Victoria, I suddenly caught sight of Helga Sangstrom getting out of a taxi at the door of the Dorchester, I said "See you later, Ted," and fairly leapt across the road. I hadn't been so glad to see anybody for a long time.

Whatever date she had inside the Dorchester she agreed to cut, and we went down town and had supper at Monseigneur instead. (I felt I could be extravagant, just for this one occasion.) Helga was in sweet form – she had been given the lead in a show which opened in London in a few weeks' time – and though I didn't mention that promise for the future which she had given me eight months before, outside Trinity Great Gate, I knew that it was going to be all right: why else would she have broken her date for me, why else was she now holding my hand across the table, and making her eyes change in that funny way when she said, huskily soft: "Darling Marco, I thought I'd never see you again?"

Oh yes, it was going to be all right, just as we had both foreseen … About midnight I took her back to Carter Street, since she was inquisitive about it and charged me with living in sin with a female anarchist: she thought the room quaint, and sat on my bed laughing at the bird wallpaper and playing with my Fabergé paperknife, while I made tea on the little filth-encrusted gas ring and decided that life had its compensations after all.

(And by God how I wanted something of the sort! There'd been nothing for nearly three months, since the only women I had run across had been earnest Party members of peculiar intensity: the sort of women – their skins soaped to a dull adequacy, their eyes gleaming behind their spectacles – who were such a poor advertisement for free love that it was an embarrassment to hear them professing it.)

And then, suddenly, Helga was out of humour and everything went wrong. I don't know why: it may have been that the room was only 'quaint' for a moment and thereafter merely unpleasant, or the fact that presently the pimp from upstairs put his head round the door, said "Sorry, chum," and withdrew again, or simply that I took things too much for granted and asked a question of extreme particularity without any preamble whatsoever, but at all events she said, "No, of course not," with an air of finality which would have made Casanova blink, and a moment later added: "It's really about time I went home," and stood up straight as a wand.

An astonishingly crude wrangle ensued, on the lines of "It's a little late to back out now" from me, and "It's only your filthy mind" from Helga: a wrangle followed by – well, let's call it an attempt at masterful persuasion; and this in its turn withered away before the cold and malignant fury with which she countered it, and degenerated into the blackest sulk I had ever wrapped myself in. The 'starvation' of the last few months probably had made me a little uncouth, but damn it! I thought, she *had* promised, she *had* been prophetically sweet all the evening, she *had* seemed as willing as I had been counting on … Helga stood by the door, settling her wrap round her shoulders, no longer paying me the compliment of anger but looking down with an air of detachment exactly suited to the occasion and quite infuriating.

Finally she raised one cool eyebrow. "Anything to say?"

Thus challenged, I evolved a priggish and not very effective sentence. "I leave you," I said, "to derive what satisfaction you can from a lamentable exhibition. Good night."

She gave me a quick contemptuous glance, turned, and left the room. The crazy stairs creaked: a moment later I was listening to her step grow fainter as she passed up the street, and away from me.

I produced one of those black laughs one rarely hears on the stage nowadays. Really, I had been grossly misled … But tomorrow, I knew, I would recognize it as a salutary occasion, since anything of that sort was waste of time when judged by the new standard: I simply wasn't meant to be sleeping around nowadays, I had something better to do … And I took back what I had thought about girl Communists: whether they looked *soignée* and sensually attractive wasn't the point (it was only a question of pouring money over the neck and shoulders, in any case), for they were not concerned with unessentials, they were *working*, while the Helga Sangstrom brigade played at life, doing no more than paddle their toes in reality to the huge expense of their fellow creatures … I looked round the bleak room, and stretched, and thought: 'Damned good for me: what every wise man's son doth know – and doth not always experience – isn't up my street any longer, and it couldn't have been more neatly demonstrated.'

I then undressed and climbed into what seemed the narrowest and coldest bed this side of the grave.

That was the end of that, at all events: thenceforward I divided my time exclusively between Party meetings and long sessions in Carter Street: for there, surrounded by dirt and noise, by the woman who simply would *not* have her baby and be done with it, by Malloy roaring blasphemies and the pimp who kept dropping in to borrow things, by the staring consumptive over the way, I had started to write in real earnest. I still had sixty-three pounds left, and both clothes and shoes were holding out well.

But, of course, for some little time afterwards the insufferable sting remained.

CHAPTER EIGHT

Tell me where is Fancy bred,
Or in the heart, or in the head?

SHAKESPEARE, *The Merchant of Venice*

❖

Mounting the crazy staircase in that half-light which, it seemed, was all Mr Tinker could afford, I heard a growing chorus of voices out of which I could distinguish only one – the thin tone in which Shep refuted any unworthy argument. These evening meetings – to no special purpose, but simply for general discussion – had lately become our habit, and since mine was the only room large enough and unencumbered by wives and children, it was there that they took place. And certainly I was very glad to have it so, both as a mark of confidence and from the purely utilitarian viewpoint of learning as much as I could about the movement. A varied selection of people used to drop in – a journalist called Jack Wentworth who, a convinced Communist, worked on the most dogmatic of the right-wing papers, Kreplan the Hungarian who had known Bela Kun and was now a political refugee, a number of German Jews, a compatriot of Casliagari's who had escaped from

Lipari in a sixteen-foot open boat – as well as less romantic Party members; and to listen to their argument and question them freely was, for me, an education in the widest sense. The conspiratorial atmosphere which pervaded all those meetings was an additional stimulant naturally very much to my taste …

The noise of voices grew: Ted Accles' rich Lancashire laugh wheezed out, topping the blurred notes of conversation; and then as I turned the corner of the stairs and came level with the landing I saw a man standing outside my door, his head bent, obviously listening. At the sound of my step he whipped round and disclosed himself as Blake, the reputed pimp from upstairs.

He came forward with the friendliest smile in the world, a smile which did not look at its best under the sickly landing light.

" 'Allo, chum," he said jauntily. "Some of the boys waiting for you again."

"I know," I answered, without much enthusiasm in my voice. Of course his curiosity did not matter much, but once or twice lately he had shown himself inquisitive in this same off hand manner, and I didn't relish a closer communion with him than was absolutely necessary.

"Bit of a meeting, like?"

"Yes." I moved to get past him, and realized that he was staying where he was in order to see into the room when the door opened.

"Sort of club, eh?"

I did not answer, but slipped adroitly into the room, hoping that the furtive air would intrigue him. He probably heard Kreplan say: "Goot eefning, comrade," before the door closed behind me. I wished him joy of the rest of his eavesdropping, which was solid Marxism of an academic brand.

The meaning sequel to this encounter occurred about a week later, when Mr Tinker called on me at half past nine in the morning in a state of civil disaffection. I was washing, as well as I could, in the chipped enamel basin which also served for the cups and plates, and he waited while I dried myself and started to dress. He then informed me that the police had been round at his house that morning inquiring about his new lodger.

"What's it mean, Mr Hendren?" he asked with unexpected determination. "I've a right to know – I've had nothing of that sort since I came into the property.' This, I thought, was a matter for astonishment. "It isn't like a young chap of your class to be mixed up in anything. Is it some trouble? – because in that case – "

I cut him short. "I don't know anything about it," I told him halfway into my shirt. "What did the police say?"

"Oh, they wanted your name and suchlike. And a lot of questions – what sort of visitors you had, how long you'd been here – all sorts of things. I tell you straight, Mr Hendren – "

"Well, what's the harm in that? Just natural curiosity." But secretly I was perturbed, remembering various things which Hime and the others had told me. "They didn't make any complaint, did they?"

"No, that they didn't," he admitted, in a more quiet tone. "But still, it's a bit disturbing, you'll agree. Have you been doing anything, Mr Hendren? – a young chap like you shouldn't be on the run. I let this room in good faith, I'd have you know …" and so on, in a string of protests about the good name of his property which did him more credit as a citizen than as a realist. But finally, putting on an injured air, I was able to persuade him that no action of mine would jeopardize that reputation, and he took his leave.

I went down to the shop straight away, and found the ugly Miss Jimpson on duty, busy loading a small child with groceries till it looked like a pauper's Christmas tree. When it had tottered away: "What's Blake?" I asked her point-blank.

She stared. "You know what he is, well enough."

"No, I mean apart from that?"

"Why, what's up? Has he been talking to you?"

"*About* me, I think." And as she nodded: "What's his line?" I asked. "Informer?"

She nodded again. "Yes – PI. I said not to open your mouth too wide, didn't I? They all know about him round here. He's been slashed once, right outside this door."

"Slashed?"

"With a razor." There was a certain relish in her voice. "Haven't you seen the cut, just above his eye? Nearly blinded him … That's his game, see? – tipping 'em off at five bob a time. And when the chaps come out o' prison they're likely to have a bit of a grudge."

The prettier Miss Jimpson appeared in the kitchen doorway, eyeing me curiously. "What've you been up to, anyway?" she asked. "What's Blake got on you?"

"Nothing at all." There seemed no point in spreading the affair any further. "I expect he thinks I've gone to ground after robbing a till. I've a damned good mind to – " Then I broke off, and smiled. "Oh well, life's too short. Let him have his fun."

"That's a pity," remarked Shep when I told him about it. "Not that it matters much, you not being a Party member, but it means they'll keep an eye on the house, and if you *do* join they'll have you taped from the beginning."

"But what's the system?" I asked in some surprise. "Do you mean to say they really take the trouble to list everybody who has anything to do with the Party?"

Shep nodded. "Something of the sort, yes. I could tell you some funny yarns ... There's a lot more to the Communist Party than just paper selling and speaking – well, you know that already: so we do try to keep the membership as quiet as possible. There was a chap joined not so long ago, name of Robinson, who got in touch originally by filling up the form in the *Worker*. Day after he joined, someone rang up his office. 'Does Mr Robinson work there?' 'Yes. Do you want to speak to him?' 'No thanks – that's all.' And the caller rang off. Robinson tried to trace it, but the exchange shut up like a clam. That's the sort of thing you get if you're not careful."

"Good lord!" I said. "I didn't know it was as bad as that."

"That's nothing. Any Communist MP will tell you that all his letters are opened – he keeps getting them with little slips of paper left in by mistake – 'Passed by So-and-so'; 'OK, such-and-such a department' – that sort of thing. And all their telephones are tapped too – it takes them ages to get through, because the Post Office have to connect Scotland Yard as well." Shep laughed at some recollection. "There was one chap – I won't tell you his name – who was talking to a friend on the phone, and in the middle he broke off and said straight out: 'I wish the chap listening in wouldn't breathe so hard – he must have adenoids.' Next day a man came round from the Post Office and said he wanted to test the phone. My friend went out of the room, but left the door open so as to hear what was going on. All that happened was, the Post Office man dialled a number, waited a moment, and then said: 'OK, Bill – *breathe!*' ... So you see it's fairly systematic. Only work that doesn't matter goes through the post or over the phone: the real stuff has to be by word of mouth, all of it."

"Well, well ... Who'd have thought that in good old England – "

"Good old England has the most efficient police-spy system in Europe. You hear a lot about the *Gestapo*, but what you don't hear is how they manage things, in just the same way but tighter, over here."

The woman across the landing started to have her baby, in good earnest, at eight o'clock one evening, just when I had settled down to the final draft of a very funny article about door-to-door salesmen. The house was silent save for the creak of woodwork and the mice behind the wainscot, the sluttish room seemed almost friendly in the glow cast by the table lamp; and I was reassured by the litter of sheets spread over the table and the clatter of the typewriter into thinking that genuine progress was being made as far as earning a living was concerned. Earlier in the week the *Yachting News* had taken an article for the first time: true, they were going to cut it from 2,000 words to 750 and hold it over till the early summer, but it did at least give me a leg in, it broke new ground which I was well equipped to cover ... I made a typing error, lifted the carriage in order to rub it out, and then stopped dead, my hand poised, as a blood-chilling yell rang out at a range, it seemed, of about ten feet from my ear.

When I got out on the landing and had listened for a moment, it was quite obvious what was happening.

Childbirth had always been one of the unknown terrors for me: beyond the fact that it was a brutal and messy business liable to make me feel sick I was deeply ignorant of its details: and the temptation, standing there on the grim and rickety half-landing, to run from the house and escape, among other things, the horrible succession of moans which now made themselves heard behind the opposite door, was so strong that my foot was already reaching for the first step before reason and humanity overcame instinct … I knocked on the door, took a sudden silence for consent, and stepped inside.

There was little to be said about that room save that it was as dirty, disordered, and squalid as anything I had ever seen; that it smelt like a hen-coop; and that directly under the single bulb the woman lay on a bed whose grey and rumpled sheets seemed a positive guarantee of puerperal fever to come. At the moment she was easier and lay still, her hands grasping the iron sides of the bed; when she heard my step she turned to wards me a face white and drained under the harsh light. Then she spoke weakly: "It's come …" That had been my own guess. "You're no good …" Another bull's eye. "Get somebody else – tell the Jimpsons."

"All right." I didn't wait for any more but stepped out of the room and shut the door behind me, with a deep breath of relief; even this small dose of nature's essential gaucherie had been rather more than I could cope with. The Jimpsons could now take over.

The Jimpsons were out.

After a moment of confusion I started to go upstairs again, slowly, with a sick reluctance which did more credit to my delicacy than my nerve. There was something about the affair, a sudden revelation of intrinsic beastliness, which had destroyed confidence from the beginning. It was out of my line, to the extent of being physically revolting, and if that reaction seemed childish, then giving birth was one of the things I was still childish about, and no more could be said.

And then I had an idea. Passing the half-landing I went on up to the second storey – new unexplored territory whose principal attributes seemed to be dirt, crumbling plaster, and a smell which ran the backyard very close. I hesitated before the two doors – I didn't want to rouse Blake, in case I should later find myself haled before the authorities on some anti-social charge; but getting no answer to my first knock, I stepped across and hammered on the other door. It was opened, with a promptitude which I took to be professional, by the blonde young woman, in a state of lush informality which included a greyish brassiere which did not include anything very efficiently.

She said: "Hallo!" in a non-committal gum-chewing way – she might not have recognized me, since we had never spoken before.

"The woman downstairs is having her baby," I told her. "What do I do about it?"

Her face, which still had traces of a pert prettiness beneath its shell of powder, exhibited a sulky frown.

"Get a doctor," she answered briefly, and made as if to shut the door.

I put my foot in the way. "Well, can you go down and give her a hand? She oughtn't to be left by herself at this stage."

The girl shook her head. "Not much I can do, sonny. Out of my line, that is." She touched the wooden lintel, which I thought a not very potent charm in the circumstances. And then, seeing me helpless: "Oh, all right," she said, with a resigned toss of her hair. "I'll come. But don't blame me if the kid's back-to-front at the finish."

I led the way downstairs, feeling the braver for my ally: tart she might be, but she *was* the right sex, she did know what was what ... The woman was sagging on the bed like a weighted sack, in such a strange way that the thought immediately struck me that she had died in the interval; but as I tiptoed forward – the nearest I had yet been to that hated centre of crisis – she opened her eyes and stared at me, as if viewing some far-away object almost out of range.

"The Jimpsons are out," I told her. "Is there anyone else? Where do I go for a doctor?"

"Get Mrs Blanker – number twelve, down the street," she said in a high cracked voice. "The doctor's from Charlotte's – they know all about it."

Behind me the tart leant against the door-jamb, staring at the bed as if she were visiting the Zoo. Presently she said: "You'd better hurry, by the look of it. I'll stay here and see no one tries a smash-and-grab."

Mrs Blanker was out on a case, so I was informed by a yellow-faced girl with a yellow-faced child in her arms, and I could only leave a message for her; but at the hospital they told me, in an amused way, to keep my hair on, and promised a doctor almost immediately. Coming out into Marylebone Road I very nearly decided not to go back to Carter Street, but duty triumphed again and I retraced my steps, thinking: 'In the ideal state the whole thing would be done by machinery …'

The yellow-haired girl was still at her post, silhouetted against the light in a competent fashion for which I had no time and little inclination; when she heard my step she turned, took a wedge of gum out of her mouth, and said vaguely: "It's started again."

"The doctor's coming," I told her as I reached her side.

"That'll make quite a race."

We stood watching for a few moments: there was nothing else to do. I wished that the woman wouldn't make such a noise, though that was the least detail of a scene of exceptional crudity. Then I became aware of a stir round my feet, and Reg, the little boy from downstairs, suddenly crawled between my legs on his hands and knees. He stood up, in pyjamas, about two feet high, and joined the assembled audience.

"I reckon I've had enough of this," said the tart presently. "That doctor's taking his time."

The spasms, or whatever they were called, were now well under way, and I could almost feel, in my own intestines, that rhythmic grinding pain which was in every line and movement of the woman's body. Instinct told me that pretty soon I would have to take a hand myself. What I wanted was a good stiff drink before starting.

The little boy stared and stared, out of round unsleepy eyes. "Funny woman," he said presently, glancing up at me. Then he lost interest, and went down on his hands and knees again, and crawled away downstairs. I wished I were a little boy just like that.

The tart also said: "So long," tightened her greasy kimono round the waist, and slopped away upstairs. I was considering giving myself leave-of-absence as well, when the woman on the bed caught her breath on a rising note and said, very calmly and clearly: "Help me."

I helped her. She told me what to do. She was damned good. Halfway through, a young man strolled in and said: "I'm the doctor. Who are you?"

"The merest amateur." I got up with a certain alacrity. "It's all yours," I said, and left him to it.

He came across to my room a good deal later, after a lengthy session at the corner pub had restored me, and Mrs Blanker – a prizefighting sort of woman, plumed like a circus horse – had been and gone, and the child had cried once, very thinly, and then shut up. He was a pleasant young man of about my own age, tough and square and dependable-looking, with a precision of manner and speech such as one might have looked for in a much older man. When he had introduced himself – his name was Markham: "I just thought I'd thank you for helping," he said, standing in the doorway. It was clear that he was pleased – in no complacent sense, but as if conscious that he had done a worthwhile job with neatness and competence. "There was nothing for her to panic about, of course, but things certainly were a little quicker than I expected."

I laughed. "I was glad to see you, anyway: that sort of thing is rather off my beat. Come and sit down: there's nothing to drink, I'm afraid – how about some tea?"

"It's very good of you." He sat down on the other, least dependable chair, and stretched his legs. "Tea would be just the thing."

"You look pretty contented," I remarked as I got things ready. "I suppose there must be a special sort of satisfaction in that part of your job – bringing new life into the world – however inferior and unpromising the life is."

"Very true." He nodded with rather charming dignity. "This was only my second confinement on my own, and the 'miracle of life' idea still seems to cling to the process, in spite of its crudity."

"I thought you were rather young, for a doctor."

"Oh, I'm still a medical student."

"Really? I didn't know you could be sent out on this sort of job before you were qualified."

He laughed. "Unless we could practise on the poor, we never *would* be qualified." But seeing me frown: "No, it's not really as bad as that," he continued. "They don't just turn us loose with a pair of forceps and a medical encyclopaedia. We have a hospital course at Charlotte's, watching first and then working under direction: you take part in scores of confinements before you go out on your own. I've just started that: I'm what's called 'on district' – there are four or five of us on regular duty, waiting for calls."

I handed him his cup of tea. "That must be rather trying, the first time at any rate."

He shook his head. "Not really – you're pretty well used to it, as I've said. And also, if anything does go wrong, there's the district nurse, or a midwife, working with you who knows ten times as much about it as you do. She can always put things right again."

"Well, I can't say I enjoyed my first case."

"You'd think nothing of it after your twenty-first." He broke off, and looked curiously round the room. "I wouldn't say you were too squeamish yourself. This is a funny sort of place."

I smiled. "I'm getting used to it."

"Broke?"

"Yes. And a new idea as well." His competent and solid charm invited confidence. I sketched the last few months for him, and found him interested.

"Living in this sort of surroundings would turn anyone Red," he remarked presently, as he busied himself with a pipe. "At my job you go into houses, and see things and people, that are enough to sicken you of this system for life. Take overcrowding, for example. There's a girl who's been coming to our antenatal clinic, in such a wretched state that we got the local Court Missionary to make inquiries. It seems that she had her first child at fifteen, but it died, as well as the man, so she came back to live at home. Home consists of two basement rooms you'd be prosecuted for keeping cattle in. She sleeps regularly with the father, but she's expecting her next child by a Negro she goes to see twice a week, down in Whitechapel. The mother sleeps with the lodger upstairs and is also pregnant either by him or by another man who comes to the house occasionally. There are four younger children, all verminous, two with rickets, who will grow up in those surroundings, and probably die in them. That's the sort of material we have to work on."

"And prosperity is just round the corner ... There's only one cure for that sort of thing – a basic change of system. Don't you agree?"

"Well, I don't know." He looked at me in such an unmoved way that I felt about eight years old. "I've never gone in for politics at all, so I can't say what I think about Socialism, or any other brand. All I have to do is get on with the job."

Which was, I recollected, exactly what Dr Barrow had said in much the same circumstances. But somehow I didn't feel like arguing the point: Markham had done work that evening beside which speech-making and discussion were puerile. I even felt slightly envious of his whole mode of life, for an occupation which gave him such conviction of responsibility, which set him a path and turned him into his own type of dependable human being, made anything like freelancing seem of very small stature. But when I mentioned this point: "I don't agree with that," he answered. "Medicine is only a tiny section of the whole business of making things run smoother. I mean, I'm damned glad I brought that kid into the world without crippling it, but I can't help remembering the sort of life it's going to have. If you can improve things by Socialism, then more power to you, because it's God's truth that they want improving, and doctoring won't take them very far." He stood up, stretching. "I must go, I'm afraid – while I've been here, plague has probably broken out in a dozen places."

"Will you be looking in again? – for the child, I mean?"

"Sure." He smiled, and held his hand. "Thank you for tea. I'll probably see you again."

I walked with him to the end of the street, gleaming cold under a full moon. I had enjoyed the meeting. Indeed, the only misfortune about the whole episode was the fact that from then onwards the Jimpsons called me, with a giggle, 'Mr Blankers'.

"We're meetin' old David at Caz' place," remarked Ted Accles on the way down the Edgware Road. " 'E's goin' to open. Are you nervous, lad?"

"Just a bit." I was going to speak for the first time, at an open-air meeting down at Fulham, and though I had prepared a rough speech I was acutely unhappy at the prospect. It was going to be rather different from the swaying after-dinner orations which had been the limit of my public career so far. "What sort of crowd do you get down there?"

"Oh, they're all right. You won't 'ave to mind a bit o' hecklin' now and again – gives a meetin' spirit, I reckon. Just open your pipes and let 'em 'ave it – that's the only way."

At Caz' café we had a cup of tea, and were presently joined by a very old man with a neckerchief and a snuffle, who croaked "Red front, comrade!" at me as if we were together making a heroic stand at the barricades. I looked at him with some satisfaction: he shouldn't be a very difficult man to follow.

Nor was he. We set the platform on a busy corner with a good open space in front of it, and while Ted and I stood one on each side of the street ready to hand out 'Communist Affiliation' leaflets, old David mounted the rostrum and proceeded to make a speech about the Boer War. Passers-by stopped and gathered in groups almost immediately, it being the leisurely after-supper hour, and having listened for a few minutes I felt ready to share their surprise at a speech, fighting in character but delivered in a throaty mumble, which condemned Asquith lock-stock-and-barrel and demanded a peaceful settlement to avert the threatened conflict ... I crossed over to Ted.

"What on earth's this?" I asked. "Has he gone crazy?"

" 'Oo? Old David? Naa – safe as 'ouses, 'e is."

"But listen to what he's saying."

"Oh, you don't 'ave to bother your 'ead about that, lad. 'E's up there to collect a crowd, like – we don't want to waste our stuff before anyone's listenin', do we?" He glanced round him at the gathering, which now numbered a dozen or so. "Give 'im a couple more minutes, and then you get up there and let 'em 'ave it 'ot and strong."

And so it happened. Old David mumbled to a finish, to the accompaniment of a few claps and a shout of "Warrer abou' ther Crystal Palace?" from a man who rocketed out of the pub on the corner and almost immediately rocketed in again. I got up and on the platform, feeling like hell, and found straight away that the added height brought a sense of authority: the street lamp was directly behind me, shining on bare heads, upturned faces, a rocklike policeman with his cape folded under his arm. Just a nice little audience, I thought, and ready-made for me ... Ted and old David clapped hard, and I began.

It certainly wasn't much of a speech – an ill-linked dissertation on oil-sanctions and the Franco-Soviet pact – but making it was so much easier than I had expected that I was able to take it at a run, without faltering. The only attempt at heckling came from a rather smart young man with a rolled umbrella, who had the habit – the nervous tick, almost – of bawling "Sanctions mean war!" at thirty-second intervals. Finally the policeman was good enough to give him the lightest possible tap on the shoulder, whereupon he swung his umbrella and strode away down the Fulham Road. I was grateful for the rescue, which I had had no notion how to effect for myself ... I finished with the usual plea for Socialism, and when there were sounds of unrest at the back of the crowd.

"If you think," I said, raising my voice, "that everything's for the best in this world and this country, then just let me tell you something which happened in my street this morning – and then say, if you still want to, that there is justice for the workers under the present system … There's a man – or rather, there *was* a man, until eleven o'clock this morning – a window cleaner, forty-seven years old, who had been out of work for three years. Living on the dole for three years, my friends – bread-and-marge, and meat once a month … And then he got a job – weak, and undernourished, and nearly hopeless he got a job at last. He hadn't been up a ladder for three years, but he climbed one at eleven o'clock this morning. And at one minute past eleven he turned giddy, and lost his balance, and fell twenty feet on to the spiked railings below. Dead? – he was dead all right – you can't get an iron spike through your stomach and out at the back, and expect to pick yourself up and walk away whistling … And I say that the capitalist system KILLED THAT MAN – just as if it had put him up against a wall and shot him. It denied him work for three years, turned him into an old man, a physical wreck, at forty-seven: it took away his skill and his balance, and then sent him up a ladder to his death. It KICKED him off that ladder … And I say that a system which can have that sort of result wants changing, and changing in double-quick time, no matter by what methods. And if you think so too – well, join our Party and let's get some results, before the whole body of the unemployed, and half the working-class as well, become like that window cleaner – starved to death by the capitalist system."

Deafening cheers … Actually a thin trickle of clapping which may or may not have been genuine. But Ted, who followed me, really got them going. He was first-rate.

CHAPTER NINE

Ho hum! Spring is here.

OLD SONG

❖

One afternoon I had a most welcome encounter. It was the very beginning of April, the day that Italy suddenly intensified the use of poison gas in Abyssinia, and just after the terrific air-raid which wiped out the whole town of Harar at one stroke. (Harar, an open town of 80,000 inhabitants and no military importance, was subjected to a raid by a massed flight of thirty-seven Italian aeroplanes for two hours on end: fifty bombs were dropped on the Egyptian Red Cross, three on the Swedish, fourteen on the French, and the rest of the town reduced by means of incendiary and explosive bombs to one vast furnace, with an accompanying appalling loss of life.) In London the sun still shone: and I had the good fortune to run across a man whom I'd been wanting to meet for a long time – Julian Wingate, the Socialist undergraduate I had known slightly up at Cambridge. I was turning into Oxford Street when I caught sight of a figure vaguely familiar just ahead of me, clad in a raincoat, tall and stooping, crowned by a shock of black hair which could hardly belong to anyone else ...

When I caught up with him, the arresting face and arched eyebrows completed the picture. He was walking very fast, looking neither right nor left and cleaving a path through the shopping crowds like an ice-breaker dealing with an easy section of mush: I had to call his name twice before he checked his step and swung round.

"Marcus Hendrycks!" He held out his hand. "And now would you mind walking along very fast with me? – I'm late already. How are you?"

"Fine," I answered as I fell into step. And added, a trifle foolishly: "I'm a Communist."

He turned and looked at me with an amused expression. "Are you sure," he began dryly, "that you haven't got the name wrong? I can remember some conflicting declarations when you came over to Whewell's."

"No, it's genuine," I smiled back. "One of the major conversions of the age."

"Well, that's good news, anyway." I could see that he didn't believe a word of it. "Where are you living nowadays?"

"In a slum at the back of Paddington Station."

"So ..." We separated for a moment as a knot of people blocked the pavement. "And what have you done in the Communist line so far?"

"Oh, a good deal of speaking. And a couple of pamphlets. But I'm still learning really, as you can probably guess."

He asked me more questions, some highly technical, and then: "You know," he said suddenly, "I really believe you *have* come over to our side. I'm very glad ..." We were level with Bond Street already. "What are you doing tonight? I'd like to talk to you again."

"Nothing," I answered. "Can we meet?"

"Yes. Meet me about seven. I've got a girl. You'll hate her. Meet us at the Brasserie."

"I'm broke."

"I know. Dinner's on me – I sold some doggerel this morning." He was in a hurry to be off, shifting from one foot to the other. "Is that a date, then?"

"It's good of you," I said. "I'd like to see you again."

"Very well." He smiled suddenly, his deep-set eyes wrinkling up at the corners. "You've changed, Marcus. An odd humility. Seven o'clock. Don't be late – she's easily depressed." And he strode away through the thick of the traffic, which came to an obedient standstill. I stood watching, smiling at his energy. He hadn't changed, anyway.

It was very nice to meet Julian again, but dear me, I thought as we sat over our drinks, what an unlikely young woman he had equipped himself with. One might have described her as the sort of high-powered model I used to adore, and left it at that: and how on earth Julian – the adult and competent Julian – was able to endure her company for more than two minutes on end, I could not begin to imagine. Of course she was extremely pretty – a blonde with a mass of irreligious curls, a hell of a figure (unconsciously one reverted to the old phraseology), gay legs, and huge roving eyes: but pretty or not, she and Julian made the oddest pair in the world, the only women I had ever seen him with having been sternly clever creatures who hardly knew which end of a high heel was which. To watch him sitting there, holding her hand as it lay on the sofa and drinking in the flow of twittering nonsense which issued from that satanic mouth, was one of the most laughable puzzles which the last few months had brought me.

She was half an hour late: and Julian and I were at our third Bronx and deep in Party prospects when this superb figure presented itself – tall and arrestingly shaped, hung with furs, and made up as to the eyebrows, eyelids, eyelashes, lips, cheeks, and fingernails.

"My dear Julian," I muttered as she approached, "what have you been doing?"

He said: "Darling!" in a lost voice, and then introduced us sketchily as Denise and Marco. She gave me one of those smiles, arched one shoulder forward to bring her bosom into prominence (a work of supererogation), and sat down. Show girl, I thought, or perhaps a few cuts above.

"I'm mis," she volunteered immediately, in a muted babyish voice and with a pout that one wanted to get one's teeth into. "I saw such a lovely bracelet ..." She looked up at Julian, her eyelashes like feather-dusters. "Hallo, darling. Time for drinkies?"

"What would you like?" he asked.

"Cockatail – sidecar. I'm so thirst."

Good heavens! I thought, trying not to look at her legs: she really talks like that ... And she continued to talk like that, in a maddening series of pet phrases, clipped words, childish elaborations. "I was foxed," she would say, time and time again; "it foxed me completely"; or "he looked at me in such a *foxing* way." Young children were 'the smalls' – "We had a party for the smalls," she said, with a twist of her shoulders which took my mind some distance from the nursery. She said "Needling" instead of sewing, not once but four or five times: she said "Rightyho," she said "You're a presh" (precious?), she said "He was nicely-thank-you" instead of "He was drunk." And all the time Julian, who was a poet and a Socialist and liable to get a first in his History tripos, gazed at her as if she were the incarnation of ideal womanhood. It was easy to see that they were lovers, and proportionately inconceivable to understand what they found to do in between times.

"Are you up at Cambridge?" she asked me presently, with a loving smile. "Are you Julian's best friend?"

"No, I'm down now." I answered. "I live in London."

"So do I." She gave me a powerful look, which I might have taken as an avowal of availability had I not known it to be entirely automatic. "London's swell, isn't it? We saw a rav film last night – 'The Shape of something' "

I tried not to react too obviously to the word 'shape'. Sitting opposite her, there only seemed to be one, or perhaps two, shapes in the world.

" *'The Shape of Things to Come'*," explained Julian with a fond and fatuous smile. "Have you seen it yet?"

"No. I've only read the book. Is it worth seeing?"

"Very much so. A good piece of Utopianism. What you'll probably notice most of all is how small the National Anthem sounds at the end. Like singing 'For he's a jolly good fellow' after a speech by Lenin."

"I think politics are silly," remarked Denise with a certain quickness. It was clear that she had cured Julian of talking about them to her, and didn't want the old wound opened. "Anyway, I knew an MP once and he said, 'Why not go to Russia?' "

"To you?" I asked politely.

"You don't understand." A lovely peevish pout, like a bed glimpsed through penetrable curtains. "He was Conserv, and he said the others ought to go to Russia if they wanted a revolution. He said it was all very well to talk, and think you're superior, but everybody wants the same thing really." She gave me the first half of a smile, inviting me to misunderstand her: but she was beginning to induce the correct Communist boredom, and I let it slide. "So you see," she finished in triumph, "it's silly to talk. Drinkies, Julian. And then I must skip along. I've got a lovely din with some actors."

"But, darling," said Julian in anguish, "I thought you were having dinner with me."

"I made a mistake." She drooped – infinitely sad, infinitely regretful, and hard as nails. "Shall I give you a tinkle later? Then we can fix something up."

Presently she began to collect her things, with ultra-feminine inefficiency; then she whipped out a mirror and scrutinized her lips and the skin at the side of her nostrils, and thereafter put her hat crooked, looking at me out of the corner of one swimmy eye in a fashion such as, had I been six months younger, would have occasioned the liveliest anticipation.

"Perhaps see you again?" she said as she got up. "Julian can bring you along, if you'd care."

"I should love to," I answered, giving her (just to keep my hand in) a genuine line in gleams. Julian hung in the background, looked harassed to the point of hysteria, making it quite clear that he had started more than he could finish.

" 'Byes, then. Lovely meet." And she swam out of the bar, followed by my focused glance. I sat back, wanting to roar with laughter. Poor Julian …

It seemed that, in some measure, he shared my view.

"I know exactly what you're going to say," he remarked with a grin as soon as he returned. "And it's perfectly true – she is too damned stupid to live. But the shape, lad, the look and feel of it. I never thought I could get a girl like that …" There was something inordinately pathetic about the remark. "She is lovely, isn't she?"

"Yes," I agreed, in all sincerity: "she's one of the prettiest girls, just to look at, that I've ever clapped eyes on. But – "

He grinned again. "I suppose you're wondering what we do when we're off duty. To tell you the truth, I really don't know." He frowned and sighed. "The whole affair is slightly fantastic. I met her at a silly sort of party in Cambridge, the kind you used to stage. She came out to dinner with me, and I gave her a terrific line – intellectual, ascetic, but vulnerable – because I'd decided quite coolly that I was going to have her. And so it was."

"Good heavens!" I said, startled. "I didn't know you went in for that sort of *cochonnerie*."

"Nor did I." He sighed again. "What's the attraction about that type of bone-headed blonde goddess? I suppose one only wants it because one knows one shouldn't."

The remark had a trivial profundity which I found attractive. "Well, it's done now," I answered. "And going rather well, by the look of it. How are things otherwise? How's Cambridge?"

"Pretty good. Actually I must confess to being a little tired of it: at times it seems to be so much out of the world, so well insulated from reality. And I may say that I miss you, Marcus – although I have the Rowlandson drawings to recall you to mind."

"And the little engraving too? – the one of Anthea Lorensen's? I hope you've still got that: it's one of the things I miss."

"It's there, just over the mantelpiece of my room, whenever you want to see it. But you don't ever come up, do you?"

I shook my head. "No. I'm trying to concentrate here, on politics and the stuff I'm writing."

"I envy you … let's eat."

We had dinner at Bertorelli's, and it was the first meal worth eating that I'd had for nearly six months. Accounting, between us, for three carafes of *vin rosé*, we slipped a perceptible distance away from reality as expressed by our shared convictions: and I could not help feeling, as I dealt with the thinnest imaginable *entrecôte minute*, that it was disloyalty and evasion to sit there eating what would amount to three days' food for many of the people among whom I was now making my life. Was it fair to avail myself of a tonic of this sort, when people in far greater need went without, from one end of their life to the other? But when I mentioned the doubt to Julian:

"My dear Marcus," he answered with spirit, "you can't extend the Party line to cover vicarious hospitality. You might as well say that you ought never to walk across Hampstead Heath because the air there is marginally fresher than it is down at Paddington. You eat your steak and don't bother – I'll give you absolution at the end – you can stand on your head and recite the first paragraph of 'Anti-Duhring'. If the Capitalist system – that's me, for the moment – chooses to declare a dividend, you shouldn't scruple to skim off all you can. So plunder the bosses! – have some more asparagus."

"You're missing the point," I said. "But I never argue with my mouth full."

Of course we couldn't keep off the Abyssinian War for very long: it was filling the papers just about then, together with the German plebiscite about Hitler's Rhineland plunge.

"Abyssinia's going to cave in, I'm afraid," said Julian at one point. "It's the most miserable prospect one could envisage, but there it is. We, and the League, promised not to let her down: we stiffened her resistance, when she might otherwise have surrendered without fighting at all: and now she's going to suffer for that confidence. By God!" he broke out suddenly; "how can people stand by and watch a whole nation being crucified like that? This last month they've been gassed and bombed, and had liquid fire poured on them, and been mown down by tanks and machine-guns: they've tried to fight back with pitiful equipment – pre-war rifles, spears even; and now they're going to go down, while we look on and pass resolutions about the sanctity of international law. People in Italy must have been drugged and brutalized out of humanity altogether, to support such a war and cheer when they win it."

I nodded agreement. "I suppose so. My God, what a world! … And our turn next, obviously: all we can talk about is rearming – 'filling in the gaps' – 'we've cut our arms expenditure to the bone in the hope that others will follow suit' … Paralytic nonsense! We've spent a thousand million pounds on the Navy alone since the War: even before the present drive started we were spending nearly twice the 1914 figure. What sort of an example is that? One might forgive the Government taking precautions after making a thoroughgoing hash of foreign affairs, if they weren't so bloody sanctimonious about it."

Julian nodded, frowning into his coffee. "It's a pity they can't spare some of the enthusiasm for something worthwhile. If they gave a quarter of the energy into rearming to some thing less spectacular, they might make this country worth living in, for everybody. Three hundred millions for new armaments … Let's go for a walk," he finished suddenly, "a good long walk, and stop thinking about all this futility. No one else does – least of all the people who can do something about it. That circular which Malcolm Stewart sent out to nearly six thousand heads of business, asking them if they could consider establishing new industries in the Distressed Areas – only seventeen hundred bothered to answer at all, and out of those thirteen hundred gave a blank negative straight away. That's what unemployment means to your keen businessman – he'd rather keep the three-halfpenny stamp and let the Distressed Areas go to hell. Come on, Marcus – I want a change of air."

CHAPTER TEN

A mother is a mother still,
The holiest thing alive.

COLERIDGE, *The Three Graves*

❖

The woman and child had left at the beginning of March, with a lack of formality which woke me up at three a.m. and cost Mr Tinker six weeks' arrears of rent. But there was now another lodger in the room adjoining mine – a fearsome little man of about fifty, a near-Turk or Greek, with a pitted olive skin and a face seamed and cleft like a relief map of the Caucasus; as ugly as sin, he was, and (it turned out) appropriately so, for he had a Nansen passport which showed to the discerning observer that he had been kicked out of half a dozen countries. The night after he moved in I heard him, through the locked door which connected our two rooms, hammering away at the walls: 'he must have a great many pictures', I thought, as I tried to concentrate on what I was typing; but the precise quality of his murals I did not discover until next day, when a burst of giggling on the landing outside my room made me get up and open my door.

Malloy and the ugly Miss Jimpson were peering into the man's room, and laughing at whatever it was they had found.

"What's the matter?" I asked.

·They both jumped. "Creepin' Jesus!" said Malloy. "You give us the divvil's own start ..."

"Take a peep at these," said Miss Jimpson. "It's downright disgustin' "

I looked inside the room, which was smaller and even more drab than my own, with the regulation bed, table, and chair. A basin full of dirty water was on the floor by the window, and a heap of soiled clothes almost filled one corner. The broken sash-cord, the flapping jungle-scene wallpaper, the flaked ceiling – all these were the twins of mine. And then I noticed the pictures he had put up.

Actually they weren't pictures, but cuttings and half-pages of newspapers, loosely tacked. The subject was womanhood. There were photographs of women, of heads and shoulders and breasts and legs: there were advertisements for corsets and underclothes, for stockings, for reducing girdles and fattening tonics: any sketch or drawing or snapshot which included any part of the female anatomy (with, of course, a zonal partiality) had been brought into service, eked out by coloured covers of *La Vie Parisienne*, *Esquire*, and *Ballyhoo*. Many of them had been chalked here and there in red, to emphasize some detail or other: they covered two entire walls, and at the head of the bed was a particularly keen frieze of cut-out advertisements depicting with a fine abandon the female torso at play.

"Did you ever see such things?" exclaimed Miss Jimpson, in what might have been a shocked tone. "What would old Tinker say?"

"Faith, it's entirely crazed the man must be." Malloy fingered the nearest exhibit, which was of a mammillary tendency. "We'll none of us be safe in our beds – and as for you foine girls downstairs, 'tis murder that waitin' for you if you resist."

Miss Jimpson tossed her head. "I'd like to see the likes o' him try anything of *that* sort. Forrin little 'orror! ... What do you think of it, eh?" she asked, turning to me.

"Well ..." I fingered my chin in some perplexity: I had been pro-sex for twenty-two years, but if this were how I was liable to end up, it was high time I handed in my resignation. "I suppose one really shouldn't be surprised," I remarked at length. "It's exactly what he looks like."

Malloy roared with sudden laughter. "He doesn't look like that one," he said, pointing. "If he did, it 'ld take the Pope o' Rome himself to kape me from moving in ..."

"Ach, you men!" cried Miss Jimpson. "You're all alike."

Malloy looked from her to the photographs, and back again, with a great grin. "It's sorry I am I can't return the compliment," he answered wickedly. "It takes arll sarts, I reckon."

I retreated before the battle which this precipitated, and settled down in my own room again. It did indeed take all sorts, and supposedly the rather dog-eared Casanova (his name was Sievvitch) who was now my neighbour was entitled to his own taste in decoration, however repellent this might be to the casual trespasser. It could not be helped that one man's emetic was another's *Ris de Veau Angoulême* ... And the room I need never see again, nor the owner either, save in chance encounter.

The reflection was premature. He knocked at my door a few nights later and came in without more ado – squat, almost green-complexioned, with a spurious briskness like an old tortoise feeling the spring.

"Gootnight," he croaked, with a lackey's smile.

I answered: "Good night" too, hopefully.

He came further into the room. "I hurt your typer."

I looked down at the typewriter, which was intact. "Did you? When? How?"

"At this minute." And as I still frowned: "No, no – I hurt it, I *heardt* it …" He waggled his fingers. "Tip, tap, so … I sounded it through the wall."

"Oh …" I still couldn't make out whether it was a boast or a complaint. "Of course the door's not very thick."

"I ask if you do some vork for me." He was standing just by the table, looking down at the scattered papers brilliant under the lamp: one stubby wrinkled finger came within the circle of light, a scaly intruder in a comparative Eden. "I haf no typer, I haf a letter that must be written so, tip tap. You can help?"

"Yes, I suppose so." Not that I cared much for the idea. "How long is the letter?"

"One page, ten page …"

"Well, which?"

"Oh, too short." He produced a bundle of papers from his inside pocket and handed them over: they were scrawled with pencil and scarcely legible. "It is an apply. I apply to the Medical Coonsil. But bad, my English. You can make good, please?"

I read a few sentences. It was an application to be placed on the Medical Registry, on the ground of 'a diplome at the University of Bucuresti and some honoured service to well-kenned governments'. It was addressed to 'The Captain, The General Medical Council of England'.

"Good heavens!" I said involuntarily.

"That's fine …" Sievvitch gave me a creased smile, which made his face look like a Child's Guide to Gargoyles. "You make it good, you make it smoot?"

"Well, I don't know." I glanced up at him, in perplexity and some disgust: if he were a doctor, it was pretty clear what he specialized in, and I had no great wish to turn him loose on London. "What medical qualifications have you?"

"Please?"

"Are you a doctor?"

"Oh yes!" Another dreadful smile, and he produced a second sheaf of papers, tattered and not overclean. "I have the diplome, and testaments besides."

I looked at the diplome. It was highly ornate, stiff with seals, and made out in the name of 'Gustav Tulisch'.

"I thought your name was Sievvitch?" I remarked.

He spread his hands. "I have two names. Custom of family. You write it out for me, in good looks?"

"Is this all you have to send up?"

"Oh no – there are many others. You wish not to write?"

I shrugged my shoulders. "It's jake with me, if you can get past the committee." Presumably there would be references, which the Council would check. "I'll work out something and let you have it tomorrow."

"I thank you." He held out a packet of Gold Flake. "Take a cigar from me."

"I've got a pipe, thanks."

But he took a cigarette out and put it on the table. "Smoke it in the night, please. I come for my letter tomorrow." Then he took a formal farewell, and left me to it.

I had a lot of fun with that application, making it as flowery as I knew how: if they didn't smell a rat when they compared him with it, that wasn't going to be my fault … Sievvitch at any rate thought highly of it when I handed it over: in fact, he came in and put another cigarette on the table.

That might well have been the end of a beautiful relationship, but it wasn't. He had early formed the habit of knocking on the communicating door and asking for matches or pennies for the gasmeter: and now he took to dropping in about the time I made myself tea in the evening, and settling down, in spite of the cool silence with which he was greeted, to a neighbourly chat. In actual fact I did not mind this as much as might have been expected, for although he stopped me working, and really was the most horrible customer I had ever had contact with, yet he *was* interesting, and not only as a specimen of the sub-human. For he used to tell me stories, one after another, unflaggingly, in that thick accent which made one think of dirty treacle dripping on to a dirtier cloth; and they were stories of a world as remote and unimaginable as the pit: brothel stories, slavery and torture stories, cheating and clawing stories, set in places with names like jewels and a stench of iniquity like a garbage-tip in the sun. I would listen in fascination to these recitals, with the sensation of peering under the lid of a cauldron in which bubbled all the filth and scum and secret devilry which went to make up that Eastern corner ... It was clear, too, that he had had his share in these twisted histories, that he had thought and said and done things which blackened the sky for roguery, that blood was the very least that he had on his hands. I would sit watching him as he crouched in his chair like a dwarf image of sin, and think: "You want to call yourself Dr Sievvitch, and feel people's pulses and look at their tongues ..." And then I would say: "Have some more tea"; and off he would go on another story, about torturing Jews or selling little boys or getting a rake-off on some filthy deal, until it was hard to believe that outside there was only Carter Street and the Edgware Road, and policemen trying shop doors as they walked their beat ... One might have thought that he was making the whole thing up, save for the way the piggy eyes in that creased olive face darted or gleamed or shifted as he relived this corrupt and hateful past.

Some time afterwards I became aware that Sievvitch was keeping a girl in his room.

At a rough guess, I would have said that he might have got on very well with just the wall photographs; this, however, was evidently not the case. As if afraid of questions, he no longer came into my room, nor even shouted through the door to know the time in the morning: but though it was some days before I actually saw the girl, I could hear them talking the whole time – or rather I could hear Sievvitch talking and an occasional mumbled answer in which the feminine pitch of voice could be recognized. And there were other things too, faintly disquieting things: it sounded as though he were treating her abominably; there were scuffles, and the scrape of furniture, and once a cry, as well as the inevitable shuffling and creaking which went on half the night and made me restive. But I wasn't restive any more, after I'd seen the girl.

I came up the stairs one day, and saw her standing on the landing trying to turn the tap of the sink. She had on a shapeless blue dress, and one wrinkled stocking, and black strap shoes twisted over at the heels; she seemed quite young, but her figure was slouched and spiritless, like a drab old woman poking inside a dustbin for fag-ends of bread. When she heard my step she turned round and half put up her hand, like an ill-treated child. And in a way that was exactly what she was: for she had one of those vacant faces – the mouth slightly open, the tongue too big, the eyes empty – which excite to pity or disgust the moment one catches sight of them … For a second I was too shocked to move: then I stepped forward and said: "What's the matter? Can I help you?"

She had a kettle in one hand, and with it she motioned vaguely towards the tap. "Won't turn," she muttered, in a dead voice, and began trying to twist it again. She was twisting it the wrong way, of course. I wondered how long she had stood on that landing in the half darkness, wrestling feebly with the tap and not thinking of turning it in the opposite direction: an idiot girl with a thick ugly body and an untenanted mind.

I filled the kettle for her, and she took it without a word and went back into Sievvitch's room. The door banged after her, clamping down a silence like the journeying-on of death.

"But we ought to *do* something," I said to the Jimpsons. "Good God, the girl's mentally defective. He probably picked her up somewhere, and she doesn't know how to get away. Why doesn't Blake inform on this sort of thing, instead of snooping round my keyhole? Even if he only passed the word to Tinker, that would be enough."

Malloy, who formed the fourth of the indignation meeting, lounging as I did on a packing-case by the shop counter, shook his head.

" 'Tisn't ould Tinker who'd be asking him to leave," he said scornfully. "Too keen on his cash, be Chroist, that's what he is. 'Tis all one to him what the lodgers do, as long as they pay up and don't expose themselves indacent at the windows."

"You don't want to interfere," said the elder Miss Jimpson sagely. "First thing you know, he's been married to this girl for twenty years, and he'll have you up for libel."

"And besides," put in the pretty one, "there's no law against it, is there?"

"Bit of bad luck for us arll if there was," said Malloy, with a particularly base leer at them both. "There's some of us as'ld nivver be out of the bloody jail from one year's end to another."

"Speak for yourself, Dannyboy." The ugly Miss Jimpson took up the challenge with spirit, and, probably, justice.

"We all know about you, with your bits o' fluff and your blarneyin' – strikes me you do more with one arm than the rest of us put together with two. But that doesn't mean we're all alike, not by a long chalk."

"What about Sievvitch?" I said, still sticking to my point. "It's all very well for you – you don't have to live next door to them and listen to the girl crying all night."

"You're too romantic, that's your trouble," declared the pretty Jimpson. "She's not *asked* for your help, has she?"

"No."

"Then it's better to wait till she does ..."

I got up, feeling deflated. It might be that they were right, and that the fault was mine for importing standards from a different world into surroundings that had no use for them. Perhaps the girl wasn't mentally defective, anyway ... I sighed.

"Cheer up, young feller," cried Malloy loudly. "We'll find you a foine girl arll to y'self, and then there'll be no call for you to be castin' your eyes anywhere else."

"Oh, I'm all right," I said. "It's just ..." But I left it at that. Why continue to make a fuss about something which was, in this corner of the world, nothing at all?

But that retreat did not solve the problem for me, and through the days that followed it continued to be a potent source of unrest. Sievvitch still did not show himself, though I caught sight of the girl once or twice on the stairs, and she had been down to the shop to buy some groceries. ("Bit of a screw loose," said the Jimpsons. "That's all. Don't worry your head – there's plenty like that round these parts.") It is difficult to describe the effect, cumulative from day to day, of having those two people within earshot and almost within reach the whole time: of imagining happenings in the next room, possibly brutal, certainly unpleasant, and then having them confirmed and accented by chance-heard sounds – a whisper, a cracked laugh, a falling plate or chair … Several times I went out on to the landing, having made up my mind to intervene or at least to find out what was really going on: but each time I hesitated, listening to the curious expectant silence which supervened whenever I opened my door, and then went back to the typewriter and tried to concentrate until the next cry or creaking made me start up again. Once, when I went out, there was Blake already listening to them, on the half-landing … I wondered, as I slammed my door and sat down again, what he was making of this new element: and for once I wished him well if, in his official capacity, he should decide to pass the word along.

Impossible to work nowadays, with the street noises, the roller-skates, the occasional brawls on one side; and on the other, within a few feet of my table, this secret devilry which betrayed itself by slight sounds which the straining ear could interpret in half a dozen ways, each more dreadful than the last.

Then, one day, came the climax. Sievvitch had gone out in the early afternoon – I met him on the stairs, though he brushed past me without a word: and I had listened to the girl whimpering for more than an hour before she fell silent, and the creak of the bedsprings told me that she had lain down. Uneasy, I went out on to the landing and listened. There was nothing. On an impulse I tried the door, but it was locked, and when I called to her she returned no answer. Possibly she was asleep. I gave it up and went back to my room.

It happened that I had to go out that evening to meet some people at Caz' café; and since Cummings, whom I had not seen for some time, was there, I stayed talking and did not get back to Carter Street till midnight. As I mounted the stairs, voices told me that Sievvitch was back again. I passed his door, and shut my own, as quickly as I could: that corner of the house was getting on my nerves … Then I worked till one o'clock, on something for the *Yachting News* which was meant to be light and frisky, but which became more abysmally turgid the more I sweated at it: all the time, from next door, there were the usual whispers, the usual movements. And then, as I ripped the last sheet out of the typewriter and put it on the pile with the others, there was something more: there was a curious scuffling noise, as if a weight – a living protesting weight – were being thrown about, there were moans, there was a frightened gasping, there was a long mounting shriek that trailed off into a gurgle and a choke. And then there was silence, which was worst of all.

Dead silence. Silence which went on and on, getting deeper, more marked, more in-pressing. I stood up, suddenly hot and sweating in spite of the coldness of the room, and with my eyes staring at the keyhole of the connecting door I waited. The clock ticked, the watch on my wrist supplied a hurrying background. But there was no other sound: not even when I tiptoed across the room and pressed my ear to the thin door panel could I distinguish a single noise or movement which might render that silence less horrible, less terrifying … Surely one of them must speak – or were they both standing stock-still a few feet from me, waiting for my first move, my first reaction to those few vile seconds? Should I call out? Should I rouse the rest of the house? That shriek had had something about it which called for clear-cut action.

I went outside on to the landing, and knocked on his door. There was no answer save the drag of a foot across the bare boards; but at my second knock Sievvitch called out: "Who's that? What you want?"

His voice was sharp, and higher-pitched than usual, with an element in it I had never heard before – a sort of cruciality. I tried to imagine what he was doing. Sitting on the bed, preventing the girl from speaking? Or had she fainted, and he was standing there not knowing what to do next? What had that shriek and that spitting gurgle meant? ... I knocked again, and called to him: "What's happening there? Open the door."

After a moment: "It's nothing. There is no alarm." Again that sharp vigilance in his voice. "Go away, please. Goot night."

"Don't be a fool," I shouted. "Let me in." I rattled on the door, which was locked: and at this sound the bed creaked and there was a quick step on the floor.

Sievvitch unlocked the door and put his head round it. "Go away," he said. "There is nothing for you. This is a private room."

There was sweat on his forehead, and his eyelids were blinking and twitching as though he were going to have a fit. When I tried to see past him he began to push the door to again; and as I put pressure on it, and the gap widened, he suddenly lifted his free hand and snapped the light off. I had caught a glimpse of the foot of the bed and the dreary wall decoration: nothing more.

Then he came out into the passage, and shut the door after him. "What do you mean?" he asked in a cut-throat voice. "I do not wish interference. This is my own matter." He was in a silk dressing-gown, blue, with scarlet lapels: there was something about the olive throat, chicken-skinned and scraggy, rising out of it which made me feel sick. Suddenly I found him looking up at me with the most venomous expression I had ever encountered. "I told you stories, no? Stories about people who interfered." With dreadful neatness he pulled a knife out of his sleeve and held the point towards me – a sliver of light in a clenched hairy fist. "Watch this," he croaked, deep, in his throat. "Watch it careful."

"Don't be a fool," I called out. "What are you trying to do?"

"I try to be private." The knife was trembling, but it was as clean and sharp as a chisel. "I want not people knocking on my door in the night. You understand?"

I gave way a pace, scared. He looked crazy, standing there under the dull electric bulb, twitching all over and shaking his knife as if a single word or movement on my part would make him strike out. I knew he had used that knife before, I knew it meant as much to him as snapping my fingers meant to me ... I looked only a moment ahead, and saw the blade thrust six inches into my guts and the blood running down over my stomach. I took another pace backwards, and came up against the wall.

"Don't be a fool," I said again. "You can't use a knife here. I heard a scream, I wondered if anything was the matter."

"There is nothing. See?"

"All right."

"My girl fell and hurt her."

"All right."

"Now you go to bed, yes?"

The eyes glittered, the evil mouth curled, the knife-point gave little darts forward as if clearing a pathway to my flesh.

"All right," I said a third time. It was a rotten performance, but there wasn't anything else to be done: he'd built up his background too surely, he was too obviously on the very edge of using that knife and chancing the result.

He nodded: "So ..." with a smile like a wound suddenly laid open. In his eyes I could see: 'Bloody English coward! ...' Then he turned away and opened the door, and passed inside, his feet dragging on the floor like nails on sandpaper. I was left alone on the drab little landing, my heart thumping as if I had run a long way.

Something made me put out my hand and clasp, very gently, the handle of his bedroom door. Then I brought it away again, and held it up to the light.

It was sticky, and wet, and dark red.

For two days there had been absolute silence from the next room. No voice, no movement: neither Sievvitch nor the girl went out, or down to the shop, or fetched water from the landing tap. I worked as well as I could, conscious all the time of that oppressive *beating* silence, and trying to fit a story to it: there was something almost laughable in sitting at the table and tapping out the draft of an article on walking in the Pyrenees, while within a few feet of me were those two, both as quiet as death, and the girl in God-knew-what state ... Once or twice I thought I heard a creaking, once a moan – but it might have been my imagination, for there was nothing else, no shuffling as there used to be. They might no longer be there, I decided at the end of twenty-four hours, when their door had not opened once and there had not been even the sound of cooking: perhaps they had both left the same night, while I slept behind a locked and bolted door ...

I mentioned the affair to no one, beyond asking the Jimpsons if Sievvitch had left. "If he has," said the ugly one briskly, "then he's done me out of five-and-six ..." But he had been away for a couple of days before, so that didn't signify much. Gradually I found the silence getting on my nerves, to the extent of my being unable to work for more than a few minutes at a time: what had that shriek meant, and the blood on the doorknob, and the twitching terror which had been in his face when he first opened the door? ... It wasn't so bad in the daytime, when I could look out of the window at the April sun warming the pavement, and the old woman opposite (lower on her pillow now, and greyer than the curtains which framed her), and hear the kids shouting and the clatter of scooter wheels on the cracked flagstones: but at night it was with something like terror that I sat there, or lay in bed trying to go to sleep, aware with every second and every beat of my blood that behind that thin panelled door, outlined in the reflected moonlight, there was going on some dreadful activity which I ought at that moment to be trying to stem, if it were not already too late. I kept remembering the girl's face as I had first caught sight of it on the landing – vacant, puffy with weeping, the pale eyes seeming to take it for granted that I was an enemy who would strike her. What did it all mean? Murder? But how could that be, when the room was now untenanted? And the knife had been quite clean.

Or were they both there now, both silent in fear of whatever move I myself might make? Sievvitch might have been drunk that night, and have now woken up to the fact that he had pulled a knife in a country that didn't like that sort of thing.

So, during those two days, I strove to work or to sleep, in a prickling silence which seemed to take no account of time, which stretched into infinity, which made me an accomplice in something over the borderline of human activity. On the second night I found myself staring at the doorway in a dull panic, knowing that within twelve hours I must risk that knife and try to get into the room again.

Blake, the informer from upstairs, saved me the trouble – Blake, who rushed in at breakfast time next morning, his mean face a dirty grey, his hands plucking at the scarf twisted round his neck: Blake who said, in a cracked whisper: "Christ, mister, come and take a look next door ..."

I jumped up. "What do you mean? What's the matter?"

"Keyhole – I happened to look in." He was trembling all over now, every ounce of perky self-confidence knocked out of him. "It's bloody murder – I'm going for the police."

"Wait a minute." I followed him out on to the landing. "What have you seen? Pull yourself together, man."

"Christ, take a look."

I tried the door, which was locked. Then I bent down, and put my eye to the keyhole. I found that I could only see half the bed, though that was quite enough … When I had straightened up again: "We'd better break it in," I said, turning to Blake. I hoped my face was a better colour than his, but it seemed unlikely.

"The police," he muttered.

"You can go for them in a minute. Come on – we might be able to do something."

I put my shoulder to the door. One heave was enough: the rotten lock cracked and splintered straightaway, and the door sprang open. A waft of close and foul air hit me in the face, a smell indescribably nauseating.

There was only one person in the room. Not Sievvitch. It was the girl, the idiot girl, who lay on the bed, her face set in the most dreadful grin of agony I had ever seen on man or beast. She could hardly have been alive … The bed looked like a knacker's yard, the whole bottom half of it drenched and stiff and black with blood.

Round her, and overhead, a few flies wove their quicksilver pattern. Round her, and overhead, was the absurd frieze of chalked breasts and torsos, a death-watch planned by a satyr. Even as I looked, one of the cut-out advertisements – a pair of silk-stockinged legs – flapped in the draught from the door and then fluttered to rest on the pillow.

"It's illegal," said Blake. "I'm off." And he was.

The house was full of police, the ambulance down below hedged in by a stupid staring crowd which chattered and questioned and gaped. My room was full of police, talking, noting down, glancing sideways at me whenever I hesitated for an answer. I gave them what help I could, without much enthusiasm, the only relevant fact being that Sievvitch had at least forty-eight hours' start and must by now be out of the country. And though at the inquest they did their best to piece together the story, it was of little value: the girl apparently had been out of a mental home for about a year, and must (they thought) have been picked up in the Park and brought back to Carter Street. She had been about four months pregnant. An abortion at four months without anaesthetics – as pretty a piece of butchery as anyone could devise … For the next few weeks there was hardly any reality for me except the whispers that followed me in the street, the blank face of that door opposite me as I sat at table, and the remembrance of the girl's face on the landing and the scream which had destroyed the stillness. I couldn't have prevented any of it, but that didn't make any difference.

Sievvitch they did not overtake.

CHAPTER ELEVEN

We are the far-off future
Of the distant past,
We are the noble race for whom they dreamed
and died.

RICHARD ALDINGTON, *Life Quest*

❖

But then, as a tonic and an antidote, came May Day, and I was marching with Shep and Kreplan in the procession to Hyde Park, holding one end of the local division's banner. We were one of nine contingents converging from all quarters of London on to the Embankment, and thence marching in one pouring stream to Hyde Park: we ourselves, the West London brigade, had assembled at Shepherd's Bush soon after eleven in the morning and marched thence in a zigzag sweep, stopping now and then to let others join us and increase the winding length of our column. It was fine to be moving along under cheerful sunlight, to hear the drum-and-fife band marking out a brave rhythm, to see, far behind and far ahead, line upon line of gold-and-red banners swaying and tossing and pointing sturdily upwards: it was fine to move forward with purpose and strength, to have the ranks gradually swollen, to gather momentum and become a marching power through mean streets and aimless lookers-on. Fine – and yet somehow disappointing. For there was no doubt that we were respectable, shepherded as we were by mounted and foot police who gave us a self-conscious air of being out with our governesses: it was one thing to march to victory with streaming standards, saluting with clenched fist the people watching at their windows, and shouting slogans in a concerted roar of triumph, and quite another to go through all these motions under the aegis of the Hired Cossacks themselves, with the police-horse at your elbow turning a mild inquiring eye whenever you let out a shout of 'Nationalize the Banks!' ... I was reminded of a René Clair revolution, with the gendarmes decked with flowers and every single person turning out to be the hero in disguise. And even Shep gave me a sardonic grin when, at one halt, the nearest police horse was found to have picked up a stone and it was I with my little jigger who abstracted it.

But it was these halts which gave the occasion an increasing significance. To come to a standstill at a road junction, to wait perhaps ten minutes until another solid body of marchers appeared and joined the column, to exchange greetings and smiles with them, to harangue the onlookers or sell them pamphlets or buy an ice from the stop-me-and-buy-one man who had somehow got involved, to feel an almost tangible solidarity which grew stronger from moment to moment: and then to hear the band start again, and hoist up the top-heavy banner, and *get going* with still greater impetus and authority – all this had a force which no amount of directive control could diminish. And it was especially noticeable down at the main rallying point, the Embankment, where we waited nearly an hour – thousands strong by now, an army whose ranks packed and lined the river bank till the curve of the road hid them from sight. This was genuine, this *was* a demonstration … Of course there were weak spots, things one quarrelled with, people who made one self-conscious: the tall woman in the odd Chelsea cloak; the high-voiced youth, pale as Bloomsbury tea, who might have been a male impersonator just out of hospital; the young man with the Foreign Office hat and slick rolled umbrella, who spoke no word to anyone and may well have mistaken the procession for something else. But the rest was solid, dependable, and as far from parlour bolshevism as the Red Army itself. (Whether I could absolve myself from this charge was still uncertain: but I was broke – one ear-mark of authenticity.) And among the strong patches could be counted our own contingent – twenty-eight men in khaki shirts and red ties, a tough and disciplined body who marched well and looked alert and businesslike. It was a pity that Corporal Hendrycks' Lewis-gun section in the OTC never exhibited a fraction of this efficiency.

"Goot crowdt," said Kreplan presently, as we waited, leaning back against the parapet. "A fine May Day – that make me ver' happy. It show the Blackshirts how strong we are, hey?"

"Mosley couldn't raise half this number," said Shep decisively. "*Or* make the public look at it. Talking bunk about the Jews is all he's good for. Constipation of the mind and diarrhoea of the tongue – that's *his* trouble."

Near by, and down the whole length of the packed Embankment, was a bustle and clamour which grew in intensity as fresh groups joined up – young men laughing or arguing, stolid middle-aged workmen with something of purpose and determination in their step, an occasional bent old figure with a fighting eye. Beside me a tall young man in corduroys was mending an NUWM banner which had come adrift: marshals moved up and down the lines with directions and advice: sitting on the parapet a shabby wasted man was trying to keep the sole of his boot together by whipping it round with string.

Presently Cummings and the journalist Jack Wentworth put in an appearance – I had watched them walking down the long line looking for our banner. Jack was an expert on these occasions: before he got his present job he had taken part in two hunger-marches, one from South Wales and the other from Glasgow, and when I had listened to his account of these I wished that I myself could have joined that ragged army which set a course down the very centre of England, and after nearly four hundred miles had contrived to arrive, worn and footsore, on the appointed day in Hyde Park. That was an effort supremely worthwhile, no matter how quickly it had been frittered away to nothing.

When they greeted us: "Hallo, Jack," I said. "Have you come to write us up?"

"I did it last night," he answered with a grin. "I described the day as overcast, the procession as a handful of troublemakers, and the whole thing as a flop. Very comforting for my class of reader. And it leaves me free to march, so everyone's satisfied."

"Why waste your time?" asked Shep with a growl. "Where's it going to get you, writing bilge for that Tory rag? What's the good of us preaching solidarity if chaps like you let us down?"

"I'm not letting you down, son, I'm staying alive the best way I can. And it doesn't matter what I send in: the people who read it just *know* that a May Day march is the biggest fiasco of the year, and if you put anything else they'd think it was a misprint."

"It's truckling to the borjwa element," Shep contended, "and you ought to keep right away from it."

"Ah, what's it matter?" said Cummings. "We've all got to make a living somehow: it's what you do with your spare time that matters. I have to teach a lot of kids that the British Empire is the kingdom of Christ on earth, and that there was a good deal in the divine right of kings after all, but that doesn't make me a worse Socialist – it keeps me alive so that I can be a Socialist. That's all that matters."

"Nothing of the sort," grumbled Shep. "Let me tell you – " but whatever argument was coming was cut short by the order to move off, and the first beats of the drum ahead of us.

That last section was by far the best of the march, for by now we had real strength, the line of our banners stretching a mile or more in a brave red-and-gold sweep, and an audience, by no means apathetic, which lined each side of the streets and contrived to make the whole thing finally worthwhile. The air now seemed warmer and the banner light as a child's windmill, even though at every corner the wind caught it like an old squaresail, so that the pole was sometimes nearly wrenched out of my hands. At first we talked and shouted to each other: then we concentrated on carefully timed slogans: and then as we neared the Park we fell silent and gave all our attention to marching in line and step. The crowds round us were thicker now, and for the most part friendly, though an occasional catcall and a shout such as the 'Bloody wasters!' which greeted us at the Park gates showed that not the whole of London was accustomed to vote the right way … Presently we were marching over grass, between packed lines of people who stared or saluted or sneered, and making for our numbered platform where Harry Pollitt was going to speak: and when the banner had been folded carefully so as not to crease the lettering, I was free to listen, to draw strength, and to forget my tiredness in a flaying speech from Pollitt, who had his audience on their toes from the very beginning … A great May Day, I decided, as I walked back with Cummings when it was all over; and a pity that we couldn't have a demonstration like that twice a week, just to remind people that there *was* an opposition.

Ten o'clock of a July night, still intolerably close and heated: I sat in my little furnace of a room making up my accounts, wishing that the sour smell of cooking and dirt which overhung the whole house did not invade the room at such strength, wishing that I could get rid of the idea that Sievvitch's room next door was haunted, doing sums on a torn scrap of paper and trying to calculate how I could bring the weekly budget down from twenty-five shillings to a pound.

I had lived for six months at the rate of five pounds a month – an achievement of which I felt inordinately proud; and having earned so far twelve pounds by writing, I now had just over thirty left of my original capital. But even at this modest rate the money was going too fast: evidently six-and-six for rent, fourteen shillings for food, three shillings for tobacco, and a daily pint of beer, was too princely a style; and as it took no account of various things – shoes, clothes, and the like – with which I was well supplied but which would not last for ever, nor of various intermittent necessities such as haircutting, shaving, toothpaste, typing paper and ribbons, which occasionally cropped up to throw the budget out of gear, it was clear that if I didn't soon begin to sell stuff more quickly I should have to confess to failure and start crawling for a regular job again. (I worked an average of ten hours a day, quite apart from whatever I did for the Party, but apparently this did not rate as work in the commercial sense.) It did not seem possible to spend less than two shillings a day on food – an egg for breakfast, bread and cheese for lunch, tea for tea, and one square meal at Caz' café in the evening. Tobacco might be cut down, from three ounces a week to two; and the pint of beer was not a necessity except in so far as it enlivened, to a minute extent, the dreary uniformity of life on this scale.

And how dreary it was, whenever I stopped working and looked about me ... Writing and politics were the only things which made it tolerable: had I been unemployed in those surroundings and with the same lack of money, I could not have borne it with a fraction of the patience of the people living round me. I walked to the open window now, and leant out, feeling the sour heat rising from the pavements, aware of the garbage smells and the filth which turned that corner of London into a little hell-hole. The old woman across the way was no longer there – I had subscribed half a crown to her funeral a few weeks back – and the blank window which had been her setting for nearly two years now looked like a robbed picture frame; but at least she was free of pain, she had conquered a life which had shrivelled her face and body like bleached seaweed, given her at its close an extended agony, and taught her nothing save how to fit human existence to bestial circumstances.

I glanced down the mean street, with its two yellow lamps and littered pavements. I knew by heart its appearance at this hour: the dirty children evading the summons to bed, the misted windows of the corner pub, the still copulating dogs and already prowling cats, and their human counterparts – young fellows in thin flashy suits who chi-iked the girls, the girls themselves, fifteen or sixteen years old, who giggled or patted their hair, or powdered noses already chalk-white, collecting in groups round a bicycle or a lamp, jostling each other suddenly, screaming and looking over their shoulders ... Here and there were single, more quiet figures: a pair of lovers staring at each other in an alleyway, or an old man sitting at his doorstep in shirtsleeves, trying to escape the heat which clung to those little rooms through half the night. (Sometimes I would have given my soul for a refrigerator: the milk I bought in the morning was always sour by six o'clock, the butter lukewarm, the only drink the water from the landing tap, which never came any cooler no matter how long one ran it.) And there was noise always: shouts, laughter, quarrelling curses, a tinny loudspeaker blaring out inane dance music; and through it all came the roar of the main road traffic at the far end of the street, dying to a murmur near one o'clock, but interrupted, night after night at three am precisely, by two huge six-wheel milk lorries which thundered and jangled over a rough stretch of roadway.

I turned away from the window and sat down at the table again, pulling the damp shirt away from my chest, scratching the livid mark which disfigured one side of my neck. It was one of a dozen spread over my body: the hot weather had stirred to life what lay dormant behind the wallpaper and the dust-laden picture-rail; and for every specimen I caught, a battalion scuttled away, gorged on my blood, to sleep off the jag in safety.

When I showed one of the corpses to Malloy:

"Steamers,* be Chroist!" he had exclaimed, with extreme satisfaction. He squeezed it between his finger and thumb, unloosing a truly sickening smell. "We had 'em a year back, but I thought we were shut of the bastards."

"Well, we're not," I told him. "I get a couple of fresh bites every night. What do I do about it?"

"Tell Tinker – and kape this to show him." He put the body carefully on the mantelpiece. "Otherwise he'll not believe you."

"And what does he do?"

*Steamers = Steam-tugs – Bugs.

"That's his lookout, not the poor bloody lodger's. If he don't put 'em down, you can get the officer to come along and he'll make an order. Of course," added Malloy as an afterthought, "if you like to put up with them you might get your rent reduced, if you've a mind to do a bit of bargaining. God save us all, what's a bloody steamer or two if you can get a couple o' bob knocked off the rent?"

I scratched my chin. "No, I think I'd rather pay the luxury price and be rid of them ... I'll get Tinker in the morning."

Which I did. He had promised action, while deprecating anything hasty in the way of remedies. They *were* the local wear, at all events: only a couple of days before, I had stood behind a man at the nearby coffee stall and watched a wrinkled grey insect climb out from under his collar and scuttle up into his hair. With that as the ruling standard, Hendrycks was being too damned choosy.

It was a standard which was going to obtain for a good long time to come. I had had a final interview with Armstrong, the solicitor, that morning, and had signed the last of his interminable forms and papers: probate had now been obtained, and the estate wound up. Not very satisfactorily.

"You will observe from the figures," he had said, leaning back in his armchair in the drab Cheapside office where we had met, "that the estate was insolvent. It was, in fact, some two thousand pounds in debt – a sum," he added, bringing careful fingertips together, "which includes my total charges to date. But Mr Demetriades, who is at present in Paris, has already taken upon himself to adjust that deficit – a generous action with which I do not think you will quarrel."

Nothing would have pleased me more than to denounce the action as damned impertinence, but the whole affair was now too remote for me to give a curse either way; all

I could manage was to hope that Tania was not too unhappy in her choice. I hadn't heard from her since Christmas, when she had sent a long cable from Alexandria.

"I am naturally distressed," Mr Armstrong went on, "that the final clearing up of the estate will not afford you an income, however small." I felt him glancing down at my shoes, which were indifferently clean and rather loose as to the sole. "May I ask if you have obtained employment of any kind?"

"I'm writing," I told him. "I don't make a living out of it, but I think I may do, fairly soon. And I've still got some money left, enough to last for about six months."

He frowned, looking worried. "I do not feel easy on your account, by any means. I could wish that you had some regular work, or that the estate – " He spread his hands. "I assure you that you have my sympathy in what must be a harassing situation."

"Oh, it's not as bad as that," I answered, wanting to reassure him: strictly speaking, his anxieties should now be at an end. "In fact, I'm enjoying it." I scratched my neck with slow surreptitious fingers, wondering how Armstrong's tidy mind would react to a louse crawling out of my sleeve … "So please don't worry about me," I concluded: "I'm doing far better than I expected, and I didn't think there would be anything left out of the estate, in any case."

But the interview was certainly not calculated to cheer me up. Only thirty pounds left: and London so dry and close, and my room such a focus of frowsy discomfort … And though I was beginning to have toothache, I couldn't afford to go to the dentist: two-pennyworth of oil-of-cloves from the Jimpsons' dispensing counter was the limit of medical attention available.

All through those heat-baked months there were a great many meetings: we spoke in many different parts of London, sometimes in the 'easy' places like Bermondsey or Whitechapel, sometimes attacking the fenced jungles of Kensington, and now and then in Hyde Park itself. I grew to hate the latter corner, under the trees facing Marble Arch ... Not only because of the heckling, which was insignificant compared with the organized Fascist brand but because of the aimless crowds and the silly laughter of people who, pleasure-bent, seemed to look on any speaker as a Zoo specimen to be gaped at or poked through the rails. There was no merit in that crowd, with its many flash Jews, its urban smart-alecs, and its soldiers – hop-poles draped in red, staring with round sweat-stupid faces, their girls pendant and worshipping on their arms. The things we talked about meant nothing to them: they rang no bell, they slipped down into the hum and chatter and mindless giggling, and were lost. Of course it was good for the soul to be treated like a clown or a ticking clock: but the knowledge that what one was saying (on a subject of agreed importance) had not a quarter of the significance conveyed by the all-singing, all-prancing, all-bloody-awful film which they would shortly be watching, meant the draining away of every atom of enthusiasm which one had brought to bear at the beginning.

I would stand there, having spoken for a lively but fruitless half hour, and listen to Ted Accles continuing where I had left off: I would stand there, watching the face nearest to me, wondering what Ted's words meant to that popeyed mask of inanity, and sometimes turning away in a sudden rage to give attention to another nearby meeting. But they were all of the same quality – earnest, uncomprehended, manifestly futile: and for me they were typified by the religious gatherings – the circle of drab-clothed hymn-singers, the drip-nosed speaker with his eggshell thunderbolts, the accomplices with their sudden tired interjections – "Hallelujah!" – "Praise the Lord, brother!" – and round about them the crowd which listened or heckled because the religious guys were funnier than the Reds, and the Park wasn't yet dark enough for necking.

To listen for more than a moment was to hate one's fellow men ... The mild and hesitating speaker, clutching a tattered Bible: "And what, my friends, did Jesus say on the road to Calvary?"

"Come and 'ave one," from a thick voice in the crowd.

Laughter. Praise the Lord! Glory be! Stop shoving.

"And although Christ prayed that the cup of bitterness might pass from Him – "

"Pass it this way, mate. Mine's a bitter, too."

Laughter. Hallelujah! God, look at the blonde.

Better to listen to something else: even to the Shorthand Professor, with his bedlamite surroundings, his suitcase which might at any moment be set on fire, his persistent tormentors passing up cigarette cards or empty tobacco tins.

"Pitman's is the best, Professor."

"Yer shirt's frayed at the cuffs, Professor."

"How do you do a P in shorthand, Professor?"

Better not to listen at all ... I would go back to my own meeting, and Ted would say: "Up yer get, lad, and give it 'em strong. There's a gradely crowd tonight." And I would jump up again and start to spout, mouthing preposterous phrases, switching to seriousness, knowing that I was beating the air all the time: looking across the sea of heads at the lamps which were beginning to beckon over the roadway. It was no good: the idea and the ideal we stood for would not make a foot of headway in a thousand years. Better to leave it be, better to gape than to be gaped at:

better to be with the drug-takers in the cinema, or the lovers kissing under the trees.

I had already encountered the obverse of this apathy when selling the paper down near Victoria: for on the second day a couple of Fascists selling *Action* had tried to hustle me away, saying that I was on their pitch; and later there had been clashes with various tough young men who made a bee-line for any *Daily Worker* poster and, standing behind the seller, muttered threats and tried to get a chance of jerking the papers out of his hand. I got into a real scrap one night: a thick-set young man in black shirt and laced gumboots moved over from the *Action* pitch and took up a stand just beside me. I looked at him – he had a cut-throat face and a neck thicker than the top of his head – and then at Ted Accles, who was on the other side of the road and deep in conversation with a passer-by. Not much help there … With a smooth smile I said: "*Daily Worker,* comrade?"

He stepped in front of me. "Don't poke that — at me," he roared out suddenly. "We don't want you Red scum here. It's our pitch."

"There's room for us all," I told him, not particularly mildly. "Even with your boots on the pavement. Move on, and peddle your trash in the proper place."

He drew his arm back. "This is the proper place."

"No, it isn't. It's the one marked 'Gentlemen' over there." Fifteen years back, the remark would have set the Lower Dormitory in a roar.

He came swinging at me like a windmill on stilts. But it wasn't a very good scrap, quite apart from the fact that the police put an end to it before long: the Fascist got an inch of his jaw laid open, and I succumbed to a knee-jab in the stomach, and that was all the paper selling either of us did that day. The policeman contented himself with saying:

"Can't you little birds agree?" – a not unreasonable contribution.

But selling did not always involve a dramatic climax of this sort, and after some initial self-consciousness I grew to like the job. There was something very satisfactory in feeling the wedge of newspapers grow thinner, in counting the takings, in making up the returns in Caz' café afterwards and being congratulated on them (or having one of his customers call out: " 'Ere, I'll take one if it'll put the account to rights ..."). And it brought me one or two interesting contacts: people would stop, not to protest or argue but to pass the time in sympathetic discussion, and I found their presence and their comradeship heartening. Between whiles, and unless anyone addressed me by name, the selling was automatic: simply the calling-out of the paper and handing it over when asked for; and I soon got into the habit of not looking at the buyer at all, but just taking the money and saying "Thanks, comrade," without bothering to find out what he looked like.

On one occasion, paper selling near Piccadilly Underground, I emerged from a daydream to find before me a trim echo of the past – Uncle Octavian's friend Mr Crisp, who, in tailcoat, formal evening cloak, and silk hat, was staring at me as though I were some exceptionally disgusting cripple. I looked away, not relishing the encounter, and flicked through my papers with brisk preoccupation, but when I glanced up again he was still there, his jaw a trifle lower, his whole neat little figure on the alert, like a spaniel at a gunshot. To put an end to the tension I called out "Dyly Wurker!" in a loud and atrocious accent, and gave him a full-lipped smile.

He jumped, peered round him, and stepped up to me.

"Young man," be said, "are you not Edmondsbury's nephew?"

"Yes," I answered, as reasonably as I could. "Mr Crisp?"

"Certainly I am Mr Crisp!" he said tartly. "But what are you doing in these – these astonishing circumstances?" He glanced over my clothes, which were informal. "Upon my soul," he cried, quite loudly, "I can hardly believe what I see. Do you know the purport of that – that publication you are selling?"

"Oh, this?" I waved my poster, whose simple inscription was 'BALDWIN'S NEW TREACHERY'. "Well, yes, I do know what it's about. Er – my views have undergone a certain modification since I last saw you."

He flushed, and drew his cloak about him. "Modification? You must have taken leave of your senses! Does your uncle know of this?"

"No: I haven't seen him since that lunch." I was trying to think of a way of ending the meeting without too barbarous a jolt to his ego: by all the rules, Mr Crisp was a socially useless individual, but he was a poor target for either invective or bad manners, quite apart from the 'elders-and-betters' standard, which died hard and covered a good deal more than *Das Kapital* allowed for.

However, Mr Crisp got his blow in first. "Then I shall make it my duty to inform him," he declared on a rising note. "I cannot believe that he will acquiesce in such a course of conduct."

"My dear sir," I said, beginning to wake up, "do you really suppose that it matters to me whether Lord Edmondsbury agrees with my brand of politics?" A number of passers-by, who had been affecting not to listen, now dropped the mask and formed a close circle. I raised my voice, unfairly, being a good deal less shy of publicity than he was. "Why should I be molested like this, just because you don't like Communists? I don't like Conservatives, but that doesn't mean that I picket the Aquascutum and heckle them as they come out."

"Bloody Red!" said a man at the back of the crowd – to be countered by a taxi driver stuck in a block, who called out "Give 'em hell, comrade!" and blew his horn. Policemen began to look in our direction. Mr Crisp glanced about him, and wavered, being a good way out of his social depth. Then: "My dear Mr Hendrycks," he began, almost in a whisper, "I beg you not to excite yourself. My surprise is surely excusable, remembering the circumstances of our last meeting." He waited while the crowd, disappointed, began to drift over to a promising street-walker scrap farther down New Coventry Street; then he continued: "I have no desire to dictate your political interests to you, but Communism – upon my word, it is hardly fitting for a young man of your upbringing. Are you sure you have considered its full implications?"

"Of course," I nodded. "I know it must look queer to you, but it's the way I feel, and I've no inclination to excuse it."

"Then I can only say that I am shocked at such a development: shocked, and – deeply shocked. Yes." He patted his silk hat with a neatly gloved hand. "And I am quite certain that when your uncle hears of it he will share my view. Quite certain."

It was clear that he wished to elaborate the theme but feared to draw the crowd again; and that might have been the end of the interview had not Shep then chanced to come up with a fresh bundle of papers.

"You'd better take these," he said. And then he nodded to Mr Crisp. "Good evening, comrade," he remarked cheerfully. "Interested in the movement?"

It was an unlikely opening, and it drew sparks.

"My good man," said Mr Crisp in a fury, "don't address me in that disgusting manner. I am *not* interested in your subversive activities, and if I had my way you would both be arrested as dangerous agitators."

"Oh …" Shep laughed. "Sorry, chum. My mistake."

"Bah!" And this time Mr Crisp really did take himself off, stalking away at an extreme pace as a man who must write to *The Times* or else blow up altogether. For some reason I felt rather ashamed of myself. But presently Shep laughed again.

"Funny little cuss," he observed judiciously. "Queer how it takes 'em, isn't it?"

But a few days later I had a far more satisfactory encounter. Near midnight, when the bulk of selling was over and I was thinking of packing up, someone held out a penny, and as usual I handed over a copy without looking at the buyer. The transaction being completed: "Thanks, comrade," I said automatically.

"Thank *you*, Marcus," came the answer. I looked up quickly. It was Max Brennan.

And how good it was to see Max, after so long: we had not met, except for an hour or so at his wedding, since that holiday down at Antibes when he and Tania were nearly engaged. And now here he was, with a huge grin on his face, taking everything for granted as usual and apparently seeing no difference between beachcombing at Golfe Juan and selling the *Daily Worker* in Piccadilly Circus. I went back with him to his hotel, and we talked till nearly four in the morning – one of those hugely refreshing sessions that quarter the ground as if on a magic carpet and weave the past into a laughing coherent whole. Max had always been one of my heroes, and seeing him again made up for some of the heat and worry which had hedged about the last few months.

"We often wondered what had become of you," he said at one point. "Marcus Hendrycks goes Communist. Well, well ... Not a bad thing either, as a basis for action. But I wouldn't have thought it a very good bet, five years ago."

I swilled the brandy round my glass – the first brandy for months. "They've been a queer five years, one way and another. My father's death broke everything up, of course: I had to come down from Cambridge. And Tania ..." I hesitated.

Max stared across at me. "Yes, Tania," he said, after a pause which I did not know how to interpret. "How is she, Marco? Happy?"

"Average ..." And I added, on an impulse: "I wish you'd married her, Max."

He nodded. "It did seem indicated, didn't it? But you know what happened – your mother dying, and Tania refusing to leave home. She was being angelic, of course, but that wouldn't do for me. And so it petered out. And then I met Margaret, and the whole affair suddenly became impersonal and out of range. It's been like that ever since."

Later he said: "You know, you don't look very well ... I suppose you're living on nothing at all?"

"Oh, less than that ... It's the heat, I think: this town's getting unbearable. Otherwise I'm fine."

He shook his head. "You used to revel in the heat. Look here," he went on, after considering a moment, "why not take a holiday and come and stay with us? You can get some fresh air, and do all the writing you want."

"Down in Gloucester?"

"Yes."

The temptation was extreme: nearly seven months of Carter Street made a country house seem like a fore-glimpse of heaven. But I shook my head. "I can't," I told him. "I know I could write just as well there as five fathoms deep in the slums – better, probably: but I've such a lot of work to do here. I speak at three meetings a week, as well as paper selling and all the rest of it."

"Give it a rest." He leant forward. "Take another drink, and listen. You know a holiday would do you a world of good: you can't live this sort of sub-existence the whole time without a break."

"Other people do."

He shrugged. "I know – poor devils. Call it running away if you like, but that doesn't alter the fact that it'll make you properly fit – which you certainly aren't at the moment. There's so much I'd like to discuss with you, too: we live in the backwoods down there. And Margaret would love to meet you: she's always been intrigued."

I laughed. "Whatever intrigued her isn't there any longer."

"You can start from scratch, then … She's just had another baby, by the way, but we're getting into the swing of it now." He sat back again, and smiled at me. "You'll come, Marcus: you'll come at the end of next week. And you can do all the crusading you like down there: we have a deaf butler – and a stockman who's just become a raging convert to the Douglas Credit System. I can hardly get a coherent word out of him. Oh yes, you're coming down all right. It's fixed. Have a drink, and let's hear some more about the revolution."

"You know I ought to stick it out in London."

"Sure … We all ought to crucify ourselves, just to qualify for eternal life. But death can take a holiday, particularly during a June as hot as this."

CHAPTER TWELVE

He has his summer, when luxuriously
Spring's honey'd cud of youthful thought he loves
To ruminate, and by such dreaming high
Is nearest unto Heaven.

KEATS, *The Human Seasons*

❖

I thumbed my way across England in a day-and-a-bit, spending a total of four-and-sixpence and walking about thirty miles out of the hundred and fifty. The rest was lifts: as far as Maidenhead on a petrol lorry, manned by a tough crew who turned friendly as soon as I mentioned the Party, and thereafter by various private cars which zigzagged as far south as Marlborough but gradually worked me westward. My one night on the road I spent in a police cell, being arrested in circumstances not entirely heroic.

I had dropped off the lorry just before dusk and started to walk again, intending to get another lift and, if possible, keep going throughout the night. But with the coming of darkness no driver seemed disposed to stop: even though I must have looked a bona fide traveller, complete with rucksack (Max had taken the rest of my clothes with him when he left London), yet no sooner did I step into the oncoming headlights and raise that thumb than the chosen car accelerated and sped past as if fearing a mass attack. It may be that my parting curses confirmed the fear, and there was a certain amount of amusement to be drawn from this evidence of widespread prudence; but the thing paled before a very few miles and I was left with the alternative of looking for some sort of lodging or walking the night out. Since the former meant that whatever I was saving on the railway fare would be frittered away and the whole point of the effort destroyed, I got off the main road and started walking in good earnest.

I stuck it till one a.m. It was an eerie sort of progress, not particularly easy on the nerves: I did not encounter a single car, and only two people – a girl cycling and a tramp snoring under the lee of a haystack; and to strike a path down the road centre, to walk under trees which rustled as if in secret conspiracy, to listen to one's own footsteps and imagine others following, and to turn round and see only an empty moonlit path flanked by hedges which might so easily harbour an enemy – all this gave the excursion a ghostly quality progressively harassing. It was quite impossible, seeing those close-set hedges and the arch of trees which made a pit of shadow in the roadway, not to remember half a dozen stories of escaped maniacs amuck with axes, of men with glaring eyes who would rather garrotte a traveller than anything else in the world ... My footsteps clinked on the rough surface, my eyes flicked from side to side as they distinguished successive danger spots; and when I came at one o'clock upon a fairly large town, unlit but friendly with its clean-cut streets, I fixed it as the limit of the night's journeying.

The decision was easier to take than to put into practice, since not a dog was stirring and the only hotel I could discover was in darkness and its night-bell, ornate and labelled 'Pull', came away soundlessly in my hand. Startled,

I laid the remains on the doorstep and crept down the street in search of something more dependable: half an hour later I was still searching, in a slightly bemused fashion, this city of the dead; and finally, when I had worked round for the third time to the single lamp main square, whose shops were shuttered and barred as if in anticipation of this very occasion, I sat down on the Town Hall steps, put my pack behind my head, and prepared thus to spend the rest of the night. A cat slid by, alert under the revealing moonlight: in the distance another cat squealed its reproaches; flanked by the civic pillars, I slept.

But, naturally enough, not for long. I was awakened some twenty minutes later by a virile poke in the ribs, to find myself surrounded by police. There was a trio of them, incontestably solid, seven-feet-square against the pale sky; defensively I blinked, and sat up, and then, still at odds with my last dream, I muttered: "Officer, do your duty."

Unimpressed, the broadest one said: "What's the game?"

I stood up. They were all still taller than me. "I couldn't wake the hotel up," I told them, "and I got sick of walking."

"Where are you making for?"

"Beyond Gloucester."

"Where from?"

"London."

"When did you leave London?"

"About five. I got a lift part of the way."

They considered this, staring at me in efficient disbelief. Finally the one on the left said: "Are you out of work?"

"No," I answered. "I'm going on a holiday."

"Is your family in Gloucester?"

"No. Friends," I yawned, of necessity, though in actual fact I was getting rather bored with the interview. "I'm not escaping from anything," I went on. "I'm just walking instead of going by train."

"What's your job in London?" asked the one who hadn't spoken yet.

"Journalist."

"Are you broke?"

"Yes." And added, unwisely: "Otherwise I'd be telling you to go to hell, and you'd be touching your hats to me."

"That's enough," said the middle one, the sergeant. "If you're on a walking tour you'd better get on with it."

There then ensued one of those conversations which go on and on, settle nothing, and a decade or so earlier might have ended in tears.

"I don't want to get on with it. I want to go to sleep."

"Well, you can't sleep here."

"I've been doing so."

"And you've got to stop. Sleeping out's against the law."

"What can I do, then?"

"That's your lookout. You should have stopped walking earlier."

"I can start any time I like. And I can stop any time I like."

"Well, you can't sleep anywhere you like."

"But the whole town's locked up. Why can't I settle down here?"

"It's against the law."

"Then can I sleep in the police station?"

"No, of course you can't. Get along to the hotel."

"It's shut. And I'm broke. Hell, I'm a vagrant. Lock me up."

"We can't do that."

"What would you do if I lay down on these steps again?"

"Move you on, double quick."

"But if I kept lying down?"

" 'Ere, stop arguing and get a lift on."

"I can't. I'm tired."

And so on. And as it turned out, I *did* keep lying down and in the end they rounded me up and haled me to the station – though it took another ten minutes to bring them to the point of arrest. But once the thing was in train, it went as smoothly as a kiss-cannon.

The charge room had a roaring fire and the fattest, sweatiest sergeant I had ever seen: the cell in which I was presently locked was freezingly cold, and its outside wall glistened with moisture even more than did the sergeant. The bed was a stone ledge, the mattress an exiguous straw-filled affair, the sole blanket designed apparently against the day when a recalcitrant dwarf should happen into custody: and a single guarded bulb and an obtrusive khaki-coloured lavatory bowl completed a set of appointments which I personally rated immeasurably below the Town Hall steps. But I was hardly in a position to complain: and as it happened, neither the cold nor the mattress kept me awake for more than a few minutes. It is perhaps worth remarking that one of the policemen watched me undressing through the grille: how far this interest was official is a matter fruitful of conjecture.

I woke at six, cold to the bone: dressed, rattled on the bars, and was presently admitted to the charge room, where the same banked-up fire and a different sergeant were now to be found. This one had a kind and fatherly face, and was reading William Gerhardi's *The Polyglots* with a certain air of concern.

He looked up, and nodded, as the policeman led me in.

"So you're the young gent as was 'aving a game," he began amiably. "Don't you know it's against the law to sleep out?"

"I know," I told him. "But there wasn't anywhere for me to go."

"Down on your luck?"

"Not specially, no. I just thought I'd walk it."

"Gives us a bit o' trouble, you know. Spoils our record, too – we 'aven't 'ad an arrest 'ere for a matter o' five months or more."

"I'm sorry ... But there's something to be said for keeping your hand in, isn't there?"

He laughed at that, caught his subordinate's eye, and sobered up again. "That's neither 'ere nor there. We don't reckon to waste time with young gents like you, you know. You're down on the charge sheet, and I've got to take notice of it."

"I wasn't doing much harm, was I?"

"You were breakin' the law, that's what the 'arm was."

However, he presently slackened off again, and gave me some tea in a mug you could have brained a gorilla with; and after we had talked about Gerhardi for a little, with a side glance at Dreiser and Hemingway, he crossed me off the charge sheet, and that was that. I left the police station at about eight: just as I was preparing to tip him, he slipped me half a crown with the words: "Get yourself a bit o' grub before you start walking again ..."

Tramping a little, getting lifts for the most part, I completed the journey that day, through as fine a section of England as could be found on the map. There is something about that corner of the Cotswolds which gives it an unchallengeable beauty; and so I found it, as I progressed under a high sun past rolling green hills marked (it seemed) with exactly the right amount of woodland, and neatly laid-out farms built of that stone whose colour alone – a weathered yellow-grey – must place it among the loveliest mediums that man has ever worked in. I took no rigidly straight course, but one which showed me the best of the country, through towns and little villages which seemed by the cadence of their naming – Lambourne, Faringdon, Lechlade, Fairford – to make sure of an immortal beauty: the sun shone hot, the road set forth with each passing mile a more intriguing, more spacious vista for the eye; and when at last I dropped, by way of Birdlip Hill, to the plain in which Gloucester itself lay, it was with a sense of fulfilment such as only a pilgrimage through a fair and kindly countryside could bring.

By contrast with what I had left behind, the journey was like a release from care after long-continued harassing.

Max and Margaret Brennan lived in one of the finest houses, set in *the* finest position, I had yet encountered: facing due south on a thickly wooded slope, it could not be overlooked by any other house, the fields and woods as far as the eye could reach all being part of the estate; and the view from its terrace included a hillside covered with bracken and, about three miles away down a gentle incline, a wide gleaming streak which was the Severn Estuary. As I made my way up the long drive I found myself blessing my chance meeting with Max: and the fact that my holiday was going to be spent in these royal surroundings seemed to offset completely that latent idea that it was a break to which I was not entitled. For work, good work, could be done here – that was an immediate conviction: and if it were really a deception or a compromise with circumstance, yet it could be turned to good account.

While I was still a hundred yards or so from the house, and skirting the first of the spinneys which protected it, a dog leapt over the fence and came towards me, barking urgently, followed by another, a Welsh corgi which fell head-over-heels through the bars in its haste; and presently Max himself appeared, in wellingtons and a suit which even I would have discarded long ago, trundling a coiled hosepipe down one of the side drives. He saw me, and waved.

"Well met!" he called out, as soon as we were in earshot. "You look the complete wayfarer, Marco. How long has it taken you?"

"Twenty-five hours." I glanced round me. "And what a place to finish up in: I didn't know there *were* views like this left in England."

He nodded. "It still affects me like that, even after thirty odd years ... I've been washing the car in your honour," he went on, "and Margaret is even now bathing and polishing the baby, for the same reason. Sherry is replenished, a chicken killed, and the slightly haunted room laid out with tripwires. Your socks have even been darned – just in time, Margaret says. Come along in and meet her."

Margaret Brennan I remembered from the wedding as tall, well-featured, and rather pale, with dark hair and a graceful walk: as I saw her now, standing before a small pedestal bath and watching, with eyes lit up, the nurse manipulating her child, it was clear that marriage had worked every possible improvement on her. Her figure no longer had that fine-drawn look which earlier had threatened a decline to mere thinness: sex possibly, contentment certainly, had made of her a woman physically assured and fully alive. She looked up as I came in, and smiled – a wide warm smile which sprang from an assured peace of mind as well as a welcoming kindness: then she held out her hand.

"So you managed it in a day," she said. "I'm so glad. Max seemed to think that walking wasn't your strong point."

"There was a fair amount of cheating," I told her. "I started late yesterday instead of this morning, and I got about a dozen lifts."

"Before you go any further," said Max from the doorway, "will you kindly do your duty by the baby?"

I bent over the bath, and looked at it. It was ugly, and out of proportion, and the wrong colour: it was a girl. I caught the nurse's eye, stern and unhelpful. Then I looked across at Margaret.

"What a baby!" I exclaimed.

She laughed. "I can see you've had practice at this sort of thing … Don't you think she's the least bit like me?"

"Good heavens!" I said involuntarily. "I mean, now I come to think of it – "

"That'll do," said Max. "We'll let you off the rest."

"Where's the other one?" I asked.

"Wandering about somewhere." He raised his voice. "Tim! Come and see a new uncle."

Presently a small boy, in blue jersey and shorts, crawled in from the other room – I suppose the night nursery: he looked at me with the blackest frown, and then turned to his father.

"Uncle what?" he asked.

"Uncle Marcus."

"Marc'ss – Marc'ss …" The child smiled suddenly at me. "We've got a pig called Marc'ss."

"We have nothing of the sort," said Max.

"Well, very *like*."

"We have a pig called Blackberry, and that's the nearest we get to it."

The child laughed. "Uncle Blackberry, Uncle Blackberry. How funny! … Where do you live?"

"London," I answered. "A long way away."

"I'm going to school there."

"That's the first I've heard of it," said his mother.

"It's your bedtime, Master Tim," said the nurse, coming down on the side of the realists. "Say good night like a good boy."

"Don't want to."

"There's no such answer," said Max. "Not till you're fifty years old. So let's hear some good good nights."

We dined by candlelight, waited upon by a venerable old manservant who looked the part so triumphantly that he really had no need to be efficient. There was such comfort to be drawn from sitting down, bathed and changed, to a properly served meal on a table polished till it rivalled the cutlery, that I found myself surrendering to the occasion completely, without thought of the world I had left behind me and the gross reality which confined it. This was indeed a holiday, accorded to me out of the blue and correspondingly appreciated; and for a little while I was going to take account of nothing save these surroundings, these people, this sort of existence. It was part of what I had lost, the least worthless part, and its calm magic could no more be denied than could that mass of new ideas which were as strong as ever, if temporarily in the background.

Margaret, still under doctor's orders, went to bed early. "Don't keep each other up too late," she said on bidding me good night. "You are far too thin and pale as it is." But we soon forgot the warning and talked till after midnight, the dogs yawning at our feet, the whisky decanter ebbing steadily, the old shabby furniture creaking in the occasional silences. And later, while Max was putting one of the dogs to bed (the corgi slept upstairs), I wandered out, glass in hand, to the terrace and the sweet-smelling night. There was a full moon, which outlined the whole slope of the valley: and in the far distance its track on the Severn gleamed like a pointing sword, sharp and unwavering in the hand of darkness. Round me the banks of trees and the formal, just distinguishable garden were the focus of this universal beauty: here was peace, and a sheltered profusion of loveliness from which even the passer-by could draw inexhaustible delight ... The little dog pattered out of the front door, its claws clipping like knitting-needles the stone step: standing beside me it sniffed the air with a gourmet leisureliness, occasionally glancing up at me as if there might be the chance, however remote, of a walk. And then the silence round me resumed its interrupted flow, and this house, set royally at the head of the valley, its sway and command of the night.

Presently Max called from within, and followed by the dog I turned and went inside.

Exploring the estate next day I was struck by its compactness: there was no unwieldiness as in the case of Nine Beeches, but a well-knit square of some nine hundred acres, a good deal of it let for grazing, with a sizeable wood, a big orchard and kitchen garden, and a set of modern pigsties such as I would not have minded living in myself.

"I've concentrated on pigs," said Max when he was showing me round. "I can't go in for farming proper because I don't know enough about it, but I wanted to turn the land to the best account otherwise. We grow all our fruit and vegetables, and keep a cow or two, so at a pinch we could be self-supporting. Anyway, it's an improvement on my father's time, when the place was just a glorified shooting box."

"You've certainly got a pig or so around the place," I agreed. Before me was a field in which a whole herd of them were rooting up the ground. "What's the system? Do you fatten them for market?"

"That's one possibility: actually I work on another, which has always seemed to me slightly immoral. You buy a sow – an *interesting* sow – for about ten pounds: wait a little while, and then sell the litter – say, ten piglets at a pound each, which equals ten pounds: and you have a free sow left over. Then you have a boar – there he is over there. Whiteoaks Wonder – to repeat the process for you, and after that it's all sheer profit, except for bagatelles like foodstuffs and labour, which is liable to cost more than you get back at auction. But it's a lot of fun, and we've been doing pretty well lately: I'll show you the statistics some time – they're like a Board of Trade review ... By the time

Tim comes of age there may be something worth while waiting for him."

"I should say that child has a pretty lively imagination," I remarked as we moved on to the next field.

Max laughed. "I can't quite decide where imagination breaks off and downright lying begins. Sometimes he says the most extraordinary things – things he knows aren't true, and knows *I* know aren't true. I suppose it's a kind of showing off, but it can be rather disconcerting. The last time the vicar came to lunch Tim climbed up on his knee and said, very sweetly: 'Daddy says you're as poor as a church mouse.' ... Of course Daddy hadn't said anything of the sort – it was just something the kid remembered out of a book, and automatically connected with the vicar: but it happened to be true in this case, and I came nowhere near to explaining it away. And when Tim, at the end of the meal, volunteered to say grace and piped up with: 'My God, my dinner – can I get down?' that about put the lid on it."

In the afternoon I went for a walk with Margaret, up the hill behind the house and along the top of the ridge, keeping the Severn in view all the way but opening up a new vista of slopes and rolling farmland, and of the sea far away to the west: the first country walk I had had for nearly a year ... Afterwards I helped her to pick some plums, standing on the top rung of an uncertain ladder and throwing them down to her: and then I milked a cow, under the eye of the reputed Douglasite stockman, who said not a word but paid me the compliment of not taking a hand after I had finished: and then I walked down to the lower pasture with Max, where he was completing a pipe-laying system from the stream higher up: and then it was dinnertime, and afterwards I did some work, not very much, and yawned, and went to bed at ten, astonishingly sleepy … That was the record of that day, and of the succeeding ones: quickly I slipped into the country rhythm, hardly pausing, to wonder how life in London could ever have been tolerable. It was not only the pleasure of having a rest, of escaping the whips and scorns of time and finding this idyllic harbourage: the essence of its magic was to be close to the land again instead of shut in a dry and dirty box, to recapture those easy Nine Beeches years and realize once more the well-spring of life and movement and regeneration. The work, the hours, the days flowed smoothly, bound into a whole which *meant* something, which was no pale drudgery but an effort having kinship with the most eternal of all the verities.

The little boy, Tim, interested me: and once I had persuaded both Margaret and the nurse that I was fit to have charge of a three-year-old child, we shared a good many excursions. He was easy to entertain, since he liked make-believe games, and storytelling, and being read to: although in the matter of stories there was the initial difficulty that none of my versions agreed with Margaret's, and I was constantly being interrupted by "He killed the giant with a club, not a knife," or "He didn't say that, he said, 'Wake up, dear Sleepin' Beauty' " I found it easier to make up original ones, according to the good old model … Playing bears was another game in which nothing ever flagged except my strength: and it was amusing to see Max's surprise when he came into the nursery one day and surprised me in mid-canter.

"I didn't know this was in your line," he remarked, after he had joined in the game to the extent of biting me in the calf of the leg. "Where did you learn to entertain children?"

"Oh, I'm not always a soft-voiced strategist," I told him. "A lot of new interests have been developed since I saw you last. Tim's an amusing kid, too: in fact he does most of the entertaining."

Intently Max watched his son, who was now at the other end of the room absorbed in a pack of cards. Presently: "Yes, he *is* a success so far," he said. "It's depressing to think that he'll grow up to be rude to his mother, and rate me as a damned old stick-in-the-mud. I wish I'd been twenty-one instead of thirty-one when he arrived: I think the younger the parent, the more chance there is of a relationship between them that means something, instead of being fortuitous."

"I don't think that ten years will make much difference. By the time he's twenty, you still won't really be middle-aged."

Max shivered suddenly. "Middle-aged – what a horrible sound that has when you look at the kid playing over there."

Tim looked up from his scattered cards, and stared at us unwinkingly. Finally he said: "I saw the king playing cards."

"Where?" I asked.

"London."

"Tim," said Max warningly, "you haven't been to London. And you haven't seen the king, either. Have you?"

No answer.

"Tim …"

"I seen the king," He held out a card – a Jack. "Playing on a card. So it wasn't a fib, Daddy," he added after a pause.

Max smiled at me. "What is one to make of that?"

"A legal career indicated, I think. Only the most brilliant lawyers can have started to quibble at three years old."

Max seemed to think that this near-lying habit was important enough to be checked, but to me it indicated no more than that the child was highly imaginative and could invent, and retreat into, his own world, which was quite apart from the one which surrounded him. And no bad thing either, the place being what it was ... It made him, at any rate, a lively companion, and all those weeks during which I was led by the nose and expected to produce as well as listen to fantastic elaborations on reality had a novelty which never lost its charm.

Margaret still did not get up before midday, and sometimes I would go up and talk to her during the morning, as she lay propped up in the huge bed, her dark hair loosely bound with a ribbon and her wrap lying tumbled on the pillow. These occasions, too, had their own quality of refreshment. We would talk, sometimes idly, sometimes with point and purpose: myself lying across the end of the bed or wandering about the room playing with the odds and ends on her dressing table; and I came to recognize her strength and spirit, and appreciate the sort of life which she and Max were building together, and secretly to envy it. For they made a strong team, because they had a plan and shared a vital ambition – to make it work in all its aspects; and though that prejudice against marriage which dated from my parents' divorce was still as instinctive as ever, yet, watching these two, I could not dismiss marriage as an ideal doomed to failure through the simple imperfection of human nature.

"It's nice having you here," she volunteered one day early in my visit, and shortly after Max and I had had a rousing argument about the League. "Tim has fallen for you, of course. And I think you have a good effect on Max. He used to meet lots of different people before we were married – before Tim was born, anyway – but now we're both absorbed in this life down here, and liable to get buried in it altogether. It's good for him to be woken up."

I smiled at her as she lay there, a shaft of morning sunlight falling across her hands busy knitting some inconsiderable garment. "I wouldn't say," I answered, "that he showed any signs of stagnation, however sheltered this place is."

"Perhaps not. But I think that subconsciously he misses the parties and arguments and things, as well as theatres and music, that he had all the time in London. *I* don't, because there's so much to do and a whole lot of new interests. But they're not really men's interests, and if he is that sort of person – alive and interested in affairs – it's hard to have to drop it altogether."

I shook my head. "He's putting something else in its place, just as you are. And the thing's such a success anyway that it really isn't worth considering whether it is, or is not, absolute perfection."

Now it was her turn to smile. "Oh, do you think so?" she exclaimed. "I mean, do we really look a happily married couple?"

"It's so obvious that I think I ought to try it myself."

"Well, why don't you? We could find you a nice girl down here."

I shuddered. "I'm sure you could: the whole country must be overrun with girls whose niceness is of pedigree distinction. But I'm aiming higher than an aristocratic nose and a *châtelaine* manner. At least, I would be if I weren't in line for the workhouse instead. And, actually, I've no real desire to shoulder the responsibility yet awhile."

She looked across at me. "Any other desire?"

"Not really, no," I laughed. "You mustn't go by what I was like three or four years ago." I paused, on the point of recounting the Sievvitch affair, and then abandoned the idea for its patent unsuitability to her present circumstances. But it was true that that filthy little thumbnail of lechery-in-action had made a profound difference to the way in which I looked at sex, even to the extent of inducing disgust at its least manifestation. Instead I went on: "I've got out of the habit altogether, and put something else in its place. And considering that I don't shave and hardly wash, and scowl and swear and spit, it's just as well."

"M'm ..." She dropped her knitting, and settled back against the pillow. "You know, Marcus, I can't help thinking that there's something slightly priggish about your generation."

"Good heavens!" I said. "What more do you want us to do?"

"Oh, I don't mean you personally – and it wouldn't be much use if I did. But looking at people in their early twenties nowadays, and remembering what I was like then, it does seem that there's been a swing-over to something like Puritanism during the last few years. You see, I came out in nineteen-twenty-four, and that year, and the two following it, were really the peak of the post-War raffish period. We used to do absolutely senseless things – they sound pretty futile now, but they were exciting and *alive* then. Nowadays there seems to be a reaction to the other extreme."

"And not a bad thing either. It's all very well to call that an exciting period, but what was it really? – just a lot of idle people with too much money making a general nuisance of themselves."

She clapped her hands. "Spoken like a true old gentleman in a club armchair ... And that's exactly what I mean: if you'd been eighteen or so in nineteen-twenty-four, you couldn't conceivably have made a remark like that – you'd have been too busy digging a hole in Piccadilly or climbing Lincoln's statue in fancy dress. Or perhaps dancing to 'My Blue Heaven' and 'Yes, sir, that's my baby' " She sighed. "Ah, my lost youth – what has become of England, peopled by moralists wearing the only true shirt?..."

And then Max marched in with our twelve o'clock glasses of milk – to be dutifully drunk without any excuses. "Lazy swine, Marco," he grumbled: "just when I want someone to swing the tractor you go to ground here."

"Let him rest," said Margaret, licking the rim of milk from her upper lip. "He's a visitor."

"He's a Communist. He's meant to volunteer for anything."

"When I've finished this," I said, "I'm perfectly ready to start your tractor for you."

"If we couldn't both hear the tractor already at work," Max answered, "I should take that as a generous offer."

Late one night, when Margaret had gone to bed and the two of us were sitting by the open French window watching the long valley and that thin silver streak which cleft the Severn, I returned to a subject which had been worrying me all evening. Earlier we had had visitors to tea – the vicar and his wife; and, in spite of resolutions to the contrary, I had got involved in an argument about the unemployed which had ended in stiff-lipped silence on both sides and the vicar's departure at least an hour earlier than usual.

"I've been thinking about this afternoon," I now said, turning to him, "and, though I'm sorry for the crisis, I still don't see how the thing could have gone differently. You know yourself that the man was talking nonsense – and if one lets it go by without protesting, that's one to the enemy. It's by acquiescing in that sort of outlook that it gains ground and becomes general."

Max left the window and the night, and glanced at me with a half-smile. After a moment he said: "I don't think one need look at the thing quite so searchingly. It isn't a matter of principle or intense feeling, but simply of social convenience. This *is* a community, Marcus, and we want to run it as smoothly as possible. I suppose the rule is: if in doubt, make allowances. I know that both those people at tea must have sounded stupid and prejudiced, but the point is that we have to live with them. You know I've always voted Labour, ever since Cambridge – I can never forget that though this corner of the world is absolute perfection, yet just over the hedge in South Wales is one of the most hopeless areas in the whole British Empire; but I've toned down a lot of my views, simply so that I can fit in here."

"You mean, you sacrifice truth to politeness?"

"I believe one does that every day of one's life. Start writing a book on the evolution of the social lie, and you'd be staggered by the material available ... If you're introduced to a man with some kind of disfigurement, you don't immediately say what is uppermost in your mind – i.e. 'I don't like talking to you because of that wart on your nose.' You accept the wart as an unavoidable evil, you look at his chin instead and try to find some common ground for discussion. And so on, right through the whole range of human activity: you put up with minor idiosyncrasies, or even essential differences of outlook, for the sake of general harmony. Believe me, it is a gain in the long run, simply because co-operation is more productive than warfare."

"It's more productive of stupidity," I insisted. "Don't you see, if I hadn't said anything, that woman would have gone on to the end of her life preaching that it's disgraceful of the unemployed to marry, to want wives and families. Now there's a faint chance that she might reconsider that view – or at least not bring it out so complacently."

"You drag in such a lot of irrelevancies," said Max with an approach to irritability. "You can label her complacent if you like, but have you some divine roving commission to go about the world combating complacency? She's part of the scheme of things, our scheme of things down here, and it's senseless to bring her up sharply for some quite trivial difference of opinion."

"I didn't think it was trivial."

"When set beside that community idea, it was. And that goes for the vicar even more than for his wife: he has an official position, and," Max smiled suddenly, "you see, we *are* Christians."

"But is he?"

Max laughed again. "That opens up a larger question which I'm in no mood to analyse. But this is a formal society on an agreed pattern, and he has a special place in that pattern. And however priggish the idea sounds, we profess his religion and stand up for it – and him."

"But Christianity ..." I stared out at the moon and the long silvered valley. "That makes the thing so elaborate, and so far from reality. It seems to me that you can find all the truly Christian feeling you are looking for, outside organized religion. In the final analysis, Christianity is only a set of rules of conduct, as nearly perfect as man can devise: abstract its principles, and the principles of Socialism, and I defy you to tell the difference."

"Why not be a Christian, then?"

"No, it works the other way about. Why not be a Socialist?"

He laughed. "We got there first, you know."

"And we are the modern edition. Why wrap the thing up in magic, why give it a supernatural trimming? Who was Christ, after all? – a travelling preacher, literally an agitator of Socialist views, whose arrival in a cathedral town today would cause profound social embarrassment. Why try to look further than the man? The rest is sheer myth-making, borrowed from the conventional idea of religion which was current at that time. Religions twice as old as Christianity had the Saviour figure – and a virgin birth – and precisely similar miracles – and a resurrection at the end of it. These were borrowed wholesale to fit the man himself, because without them his teaching wouldn't have been accepted as a religion at all. But they were irrelevancies, highly stylized, and to look on them as the important part of Christianity is like smoking the cigarette card and pasting the cigarette in a book."

There was no reply from Max for some moments: the moon went behind a cloud, and both dogs got up suddenly and stood sniffing at the open French window, curious at its disappearance. For some reason I was reminded of a little play I had seen years ago – Maeterlinck's *The Intruder* – in which an old blind man surrounded by his family waits for death to strike in another room: there had been the same rustlings from the garden, the same discomforting moonlight … Then Max spoke, almost casually, as in an attempt at lightness.

"My dear Marcus, if you think that at eleven o'clock on a summer night I am going to start explaining why I believe in God in general, and the Christian revelation in particular, you may quickly get rid of the idea. I can only give you the simple fact that I do … I said just now that I voted Labour: you can call my brand Christian Socialism if you like. But I wouldn't say that it lost authority by being propounded by someone whom you call an agitator, and myself the Messiah."

"But it's such dope, the whole supernatural idea," I insisted. "Its sole modern application is to keep the poor quiet while the rich get away with ten times their fair share … I remember a phrase of Upton Sinclair's which said exactly what I mean: 'The workingman is told to fix his hopes on a future life, while his pockets are picked in this one.' That – "

"To be quite frank," interrupted Max, "I'll take Jesus Christ against Upton Sinclair."

"But it's true: it describes it precisely. They are taught humility for the good of their souls: they are taught to put up with lying and trickery, because the next world will be all right and they'll come into their own there. Poor devils! Why not apply Christianity to this world, instead of excusing yourself by plugging the blinding joys of eternity? In fact, why don't you come all the way with us?"

"Because you're too bloody truculent," he snapped out suddenly. "Because you want to reduce everything to a formula, in which anything spiritual is shoved into a corner under a label – 'C3: Dope for the Masses'. Because I've got my own idea of what is dope and what isn't. Because you want strife instead of tolerance." He drew a deep breath, and his voice lost its tension. "There are a lot of things which want curing, I know, but the cure isn't a gutter running with blood. You chaps are always shouting that war settles nothing: why not apply the idea to your own politics? Leave out force and substitute reason."

"The men in power aren't open to reason." Max's denunciation should have roused me, but it had actually had a rather depressing effect. "You know that yourself, Max: you can't reason a burglar out of his swag. Only by force can the bad elements in any society be coerced. The dictatorship of the proletariat will – " I caught his eye, and smiled in spite of myself. "Oh, I know it's a cliché, but it does mean something, something vital. You must have compulsion, to keep order."

"Your order?"

"Yes, of course."

He shook his head. "To put it in its lowest terms, you want more than one idea to run a nation. Marx – " Then he looked at his watch, and back at me, with a smile. "You're teaching me extremely bad habits, Marco, as well as sedition and blasphemy: I'll soon be getting curtain lectures from Margaret. I haven't analysed the ethics of

Communism after eleven o'clock at night for close on ten years, and I'm not going to start now."

"All right," I answered, "we'll leave it over till next time." I got to my feet and stepped out on to the terrace: there was a ring around the moon, and a curious circle of little silver-gilt clouds like courtiers reflecting the royal brilliance. Truth to tell, I was not sorry to postpone the discussion: the facts needed careful marshalling. And it was such a lovely night. And I wanted to do some writing, of a sort which accorded more with the night than did the elucidation of Marxism by Socratic *elenchus*.

A stream which ran through woodland bordered one side of the estate, and following this up one day while playing explorers with Tim, I came at one point upon a widening of the bed which had a curiously artificial look. It was overhung with trees through which the sun filtered sparsely, and banked on each side by a sunk wall: the stones of this had fallen in many places and been overgrown by tree roots and long grass in others, but their plan could be traced after a little searching, and it seemed to me that besides the two side walls there must have been at one time a third, across the lower end of the stream – the whole thing forming a horseshoe trap for the water, the depth of which would then be something over five feet ... The idea intrigued me: I imagined an Ancient British dam or a Roman bath; and standing on top of the wall I called to Tim, who was splashing manfully through the stream in his minute wellington boots, singing a tune peculiarly his own. When he was near:

"This is a funny place," I said. "Have you been here before?"

Legs sturdily apart in the stream, he looked up at me with grave consideration. "Oh, yes," he answered after a moment. "Daddy brought me often. I like it." He glanced vaguely round him, and up at the trees. Then: "There are fiss here," he added, with authority.

"Fish?"

"Yes. And monkeys."

I gave back stare for stare. "Monkeys are fine things," I said after a moment. "It would be nice to see one."

· "P'raps we will. Sh'h!"

We waited, silent against the tinkle and run of the water.

"I think I see one already," I told him. "In boots and a jersey."

His eyes opened wide. "Do you really? Is it big?"

"Not very."

"Speak to it."

I cupped my hands. "Hallo, monkey!"

We listened. Then: "He's gone home," said Tim with a sigh. "P'raps he'll be here tomorrow. Daddy says the monkeys come and catch fiss. I should like to see that."

"So should I. What else did Daddy say?"

"He said the monkeys only come once a week, and then they go to church."

"Daddy was evidently in good form … Listen! Isn't that Nanny calling?"

It was. The tyranny of milk-and-biscuits intervened, and I was left to myself and the monkeys. The little sheltered corner under the arching trees was attractive, and I stayed there nearly an hour, tracing the exact contours of the wall and sometimes replacing, tentatively, one of the smaller fallen stones. (Most of them were fully two feet square, and carefully trimmed: far too big for me to handle by myself.) When finally, near lunch time, I traced my steps through the wood and back to the house, I had cleared the site sufficiently of bush and derelict branches to see its complete shape – a neat oval, about thirty feet by twenty, a quarter of which was still squarely and strongly buttressed by the wall.

"Oh yes," said Max at lunch, in answer to my query: "I've often thought of doing something about that place. Attractive, isn't it? It was a fishing-pool, I suppose about four hundred years ago: the monks from Tintern used to come over when their own place was dry."

"Monks!" I laughed suddenly. "Tim's monkeys … I wondered where he got them from."

"Has he been spinning a yarn again?"

"Only one of yours … How about repairing it, Max? It would be a lovely place if we could make it watertight."

It took very little to persuade him of the idea's possibilities, and we started on the preliminary clearing work that afternoon, with a saw and a couple of billhooks. Next day we began the reconstruction proper. Cleaning, rebuilding, and refacing that fishing-pool kept us occupied fox the best part of a fortnight, and I have seldom enjoyed a piece of work more. We attacked the two side walls first, where less labour was needed, and then turned to the lower end of the horseshoe – ruined, tumbledown, covered with ivy – past one end of which the stream ran unchecked. It was immensely hard work: building up a dam backed by cartloads of rubble, hunting for the appropriate fallen stone (which might lie twenty yards off and be overgrown by long grass), bringing into alignment, refacing the finished product: scooping out from the bed of the stream the silt of hundreds of years … We scored our hands lifting blocks of stone, we broke spades and picks digging into clay and hacking at old tree stumps: once we worked for a whole day prising out a tremendous block (like a Stonehenge sarsen), only to find that it could not be lifted even by four men and would have to remain where it was in the centre of the pool.

It was good to be working there under the trees, stripped to the waist, standing perhaps knee-deep in the stream with the water gurgling past our waders, or staggering under the weight of a block of stone which was to be lifted chest-high on to the slowly growing wall. Through the woven arch overhead the sunlight fell speckled on to our shoulders, and turned the little waterfall at the head of the pool into a diamond-sparkling cascade. Sometimes Margaret would come down to watch us, sitting on the bank in her summer dress, cool and white against the living green which framed her: sometimes the pigs would come rooting through the wood, their grunts sounding nearer and nearer until they broke through the undergrowth and stood blinking at us on the edge of the clearing: wild boars surveying the forest pioneers ... And slowly, by our planning and effort, our hardening blisters and tanned skins, the pool took shape and emerged as its first builders had long ago intended: a sentimentalist might have been forgiven for hoping that its restoration brought comfort to the monks, wherever they were. We still kept uncovering bits of their work: one day a stone conduit beautifully contrived from three curved blocks, a little later a low flight of steps, overgrown with tree roots and grass but preserved unharmed. They built well in those days, even though it was only to ensure that Friday's carp should be caught in comfort.

Late one evening we finished the retaining wall at the lower end of the pool, except for the small gap through which the water now flowed at a quickened pace; and on the morrow we set to work, with due ceremony, to close the gap and crown our labour. It was an oddly exciting moment, as we first checked the stream with an enormous square-cut stone and then began, at high speed, to build on that foundation and to back it with the pile of rubble which we had ready. The water, held for the first time, swirled round in a muddy half-circle, seeking an outlet; and then its movement gradually slowed to nothing, and inch by inch its level rose ... Tim, standing on the big stone in the middle, played king-of-the-castle till his nerve failed and Max rescued him from the rising tide. In an hour's time the depth was over three feet, and the wall held at all points.

Of course it did not continue to do so; and seeing that we had cemented the stones with a mixture of shingle and clay, this was not surprising. But the pool was five feet deep before a leak developed, and when we came back after tea to examine it that level was still maintained. Grouped on the bank, we contemplated the finished product with some satisfaction. We had a POOL, a five-foot pool faced with stone, where before there had been six inches of running water.

To celebrate we went that night to the cinema in Chepstow, though the lamentable film which was the best we could find hardly came under the heading of 'Entertainment'. It was one of those backstage 'musicals' in which the stuff is thrown at you in waves, in long lines, in beds and mirrors and baths and 'fashion parades': we clung to our seats, watching bosoms swooping at us like fairground swings, and mouths gaping twelve feet across, and legs astride like the Colossus of Rhodes seeking what it might devour. The picture smote us with hip and thigh: one shut one's eyes, and saw only love on a *cache-sexe* basis … Beside me I heard Max yawning tremendously, and I followed suit, nearly dislocating my jaw.

"Good, isn't it?" he said softly. "How can one go back to one single girl after seeing acres of it under active cultivation?" But I noticed that he was holding Margaret's hand. "Wake me up," he said, "when the next hundred honours are in jeopardy."

Such story as there was wound its treacly course. At one point the hero and his mate found themselves in a mountain cabin under six feet of snow: a four-course meal was eaten (in twenty seconds) and then the shot dissolved to a ticking clock and a pile of clothes on the floor.

"Good heavens!" said Max, startled. And, a moment later: "No, it's all right – there's a fire."

That was the only time I laughed during the performance.

"The sex side of it isn't its worst aspect," said Max on the way home, when the three of us were crammed into the front of his car. "At least, it isn't the most dangerous. I think the pure commercialism it plugs the whole time does twice as much harm as a row of lush thighs on a cushion the size of Trafalgar Square. All those films drum in the one ambition – to make enough money to enjoy life on those terms. And all the women want to get married for money, or hook a man and blackmail him for money, or become front-page news for money, or inspire a man to get on in the world – i.e. to grab enormous sums and spend them on penthouses and staggeringly tasteless bunches of flowers. That idea's run away with the cinema altogether."

I nodded, staring ahead at the ribbon of road startling under the headlights. "Quite true ... What sort of citizens do they think they're going to turn out, if the greatest educational force of the present day concerns itself solely with that ambition?"

"But what a force it might have become," said Max regretfully. "If only it had got into different hands at the beginning: if it weren't run by the king money-grubbers themselves, with their gutter standards ... Think of the films you could turn out, Marco, if you really wanted to use the cinema for the best possible ends, to teach people what they can make of their lives, to tell them the truth, to educate them in beauty and honesty and unselfishness. But now it's money all the time: that, and nightclubs and dance bands and peeping-tom columnists – the apotheosis of the vulgar and the trivial."

We were near home now: the main road gave way to a narrow lane walled in by trees, and presently to Max's ill-surfaced drive.

"Damn!" he said suddenly, as we began to climb to the house, "we've forgotten the whisky."

"Never mind," said Margaret. "That'll give you both a chance to get to bed early. This new regime of Marcus' is all very well for London's night birds, but it's rather hard on the little woman who waits and waits, staring at the ceiling ..."

"Snoring like a walrus, you mean," Max corrected her. "It's all I can do to get to sleep."

How securely happy they were, I thought as I followed them into the house. How well they had planned, and with what confidence could they depend on each other's mood ... It was easy to be envious, easier still to recognize that their state was no accident but the outcome of self-control and consideration and compromise endlessly applied, in a fashion by no means the universal mode.

At any rate, their happiness was infectious: I had never spent such a holiday, nor been so carelessly content. I did a great deal of work down there, as I had expected, and succeeded in selling about a quarter of it and (what was more important) breaking new ground. More stuff for the *Yachting News*; a country sketch for one of the weeklies; and a set of four articles on working-class types for an evening paper: the acceptance of all these was heartening in the extreme, as well as earning me about fifteen pounds and setting bankruptcy that much further back. And meanwhile I had slipped into the country round and become familiar with its rhythm: I began to fit in – working with the men, attending market, fetching pigfood and stores from the chandlers', on nodding terms with a good many of the village as well as the occasional visitors to the house. Those were great days, full of a patterned variety: and some of them so hot that we were able to fulfil a particular ambition by bathing in the fishing-pool.

There were times when Max seemed to be in sympathy with my political slant, and other times when he would scoff at the idea of preoccupying oneself with what he called 'a minor section of human activity'.

"It simply isn't enough," he said on one occasion. We were having tea, with Margaret, on the lawn, after a strenuous afternoon spent in taking down the power-plant. "I know that one can get absolutely immersed in politics, but what's the good, if you just become the political animal and nothing more?"

I shrugged my shoulders. "Putting it at its washiest," I answered, "one can give one's whole life to a cause: one can dedicate it to an ideal. I know that sounds slop," I added defensively, "but it's a very real ambition with a lot of people."

"Including you?" asked Margaret, without malice.

"Well – yes."

"But it must be worth dedicating," broke in Max. "What can you bring to politics, Marcus? You're twenty-two; it's sheer cheek for someone of that age to go about telling people what to think."

By this time I was getting used to not taking offence. "That might be true," I answered equably, "if they were my own ideas that I was trying to force down people's throats. But you know they're not. The theory of Communism is a synthesis of the thoughts and ideals of innumerable intelligent and farseeing people, composed in the light of history as well as that of the immediate need. If I can grasp that idea at twenty-two, that shouldn't disqualify me. Rather the reverse."

"But you still don't know enough," he insisted. "Even if you're a political expert, that doesn't make you a complete human being. Think of all the other sides of life that you're leaving out of account. Until you stop swamping yourself in political theory and sample the rest of living, you're not worth the paper you're sitting on."

"Politics want energy and vigour. Those I can supply."

"They want intelligent energy, selective and educated vigour. And that means that you cannot concentrate exclusively on politics. Even for someone very politically minded, his life should be one-third politics, one-third personal and domestic and emotional, including love in all its aspects – "

"Steady, boys!" from Margaret.

"And one-third recreative and artistic – music, pictures, the stage, etc. I think it's vital for a movement, and therefore for an individual, to have the widest possible cultural background. Without it the movement atrophies, and wastes its inheritance: without it the individual is not complete – he is immature and ignorant. He ought to take everything that life and civilization offer, and then, and then only, translate that into intelligent political action."

"At the age of ninety-three?"

"If necessary ... One informed man is worth a hundred of the half baked."

"But numbers are essential. They can be used. They mean power."

"All they can do, *per se*, is to multiply a stupid or destructive blunder by one hundred."

"Or lend force to an admirable ideal."

Max laughed. "Now that we've each begged the question, we're back at the beginning again ... Still, I should give the idea a thought, Marco: there's more in life besides Communism. Oh, I know," he added as I made to interrupt, "that you're getting past dance music, and leg shows, and you can tell the Laughing Cavalier from Popeye the Sailor. But you only give these things a thin slice of your attention, and at your age that's wrong. You haven't heard enough music, have you? or seen enough pictures, or read enough books?"

"That's play," I interjected, "not work."

"It's equipment," he corrected briskly. "And one of these days you'll find you need it."

"Damn this!" I said suddenly. "You're putting me in the wrong and it isn't fair. The 'Points from Speeches' isn't the only column I read, and I *don't* think of everything from the political angle. If I did I wouldn't be down here, to begin with."

Margaret caught something in my voice. "Why not?" she asked gravely.

"Because it isn't consistent." I hesitated, and then decided to give them the whole thing quite frankly. "Because you're extremely nice people, but you're the enemy, for all that ..." They were both looking at me with attention, and I suddenly thought: they've been expecting this. "You've got nine hundred acres, Max," I went on, "and it's more than your fair share. I don't say that you're not doing a lot with it, but that doesn't mean that the land is put to its greatest possible use. Not by a long chalk. If it were properly developed it could produce twenty times what it does now."

I had expected a silence to fall when I stopped speaking, but Max took up the point immediately, without any trace of antagonism.

"That's perfectly true," he agreed. 'I told you at the beginning I was no farmer, and I know very well that, even counting in the pigs and the fruit and the grazing, a great deal of this place goes to waste. But I still do my best." He smiled. "There's another kind of landlord, you know, who either takes money out of the land and spends it somewhere else, or turns whole counties into glorified playgrounds for himself and his deer and pheasants. You can at least rate me above that: at the back of my mind *is* the idea that I hold the land in trust, and it isn't mine to plunder or waste."

"A realist might call that goodwill without application," I said after a pause.

Max shrugged his shoulders. "Let's say then that, like you, I'm not consistent. You can stay here without cutting our throats: I can enjoy the place without turning it over to the State."

"I stay here because I can't get away," I told him. I looked round the velvet-sloping lawn, with its great trees recalling those of Nine Beeches, its warm and sleepy air under the after noon sun; I drank in the garden sounds, the drowsy murmur of bees, the rustle of grasses and flower heads. Who indeed would leave this peace until he must? ... "It suits me too well – I wouldn't exchange it for anywhere else on earth, and I wouldn't be *doing* anything else, either."

But that was the last day that this was true. For on the morrow news came of civil war in Spain.

History will describe the contributory causes of this struggle, and apportion the praise and blame; but we could not wait for history, and to us there were only these three facts – that there had been an election at which a democratic Government had come to power: that an armed rebellion against this Government had been fomented by the Army, a rebellion which could only end in some sort of Fascist régime: and that here at last was a chance to fight for something worthwhile, here was a frontier worth defending ... No matter what the complications or the side issues were, for us the grapple was crystal clear – democracy against Fascism, freedom against tyranny, the proletarian against the officer class, the black beetles, the hated landlord. It was enough to know that official Germany and Italy supported the rising, for the whole weight of leftwing opinion in this country to come down on the Government side.

"I ought to go," I said after a few days. "This is the sort of thing to fight for."

"It isn't your quarrel," they both answered. "Let them settle it themselves."

The news got worse: though the revolt in Madrid itself was quickly broken – by men, inhumanly brave, who attacked machine-gun nests with no other weapons than clubs and knives – yet the full extent and organization of the rebellion were becoming clear. There was sporadic fighting in many parts of the country, and especially in Barcelona, where five hundred people were killed in a series of murderous street battles. From us and from the French came appeals for strict neutrality in the struggle, although there were rumours (and more than rumours) of German aid for the rebels. I hoped that the Russians, who were quieter about it, would be able to take care of that ...

"My dear Max," I said once, "what's the use of saying that it isn't our concern? It's just like Abyssinia: we lounge about in armchairs talking of the disgust of the whole civilized world, we switch off the news bulletin and listen to Mozart instead: we say, with a comfortable smile, 'Let us only conquer the best worlds' ... And all the time democracy goes down before the thugs and the people who can't tell Mozart from a tin whistle but are the best gut-slitters of the century." I looked down the valley, and the garden which was so peaceful and secure. "I said I'd stay another month, and it's hell to leave: but I know damned well where I ought to be."

"Stay," he said again. "It may be over fairly soon."

But it wasn't. It got worse. And I had a letter from Shep, a short letter which ended: "Some of the boys are getting ready to go out. If you're thinking of doing so, you'd better hurry, because there's a lot of talk about neutrality and the

Foreign Enlistment Act." That was persuasive. And when news came of Franco bringing native troops from Morocco, I decided that I'd shirked long enough, and said goodbye to them. Lotus-eating must wait: here was the need for action.

That was the middle of August, and the fact that I did not start for Spain till nearly a month later was due, I suppose, to pure funk. It was all very well to talk, down in Gloucestershire, of enlisting straight away and jumping into the firing line, but enlistment wore a different aspect when one read more about conditions there, and heard the talk of blood and wounds and slaughter. To exchange the spacious days spent down at Max's house for Carter Street's cramped sluttishness was bad enough: but what of Madrid and Barcelona, what of the scenes attending the capture of Badajos by Colonel Yague's force of insurgents, when fifteen hundred of the defenders were turned into the bullring and machine-gunned, while in the town every house was cleared and the pavements and gutters ran with blood. ('A filthy Red rabble,' the dead were called by our pro-Franco newspapers, dismissing the affair as if it had been part of Rat Week. But what was the 'rabble's' choice? Many of them were Civil Guards and militiamen, who had taken an oath of loyalty to the Republic: were they to betray that oath because the Army set them an example of disloyalty?)

And besides (I fooled myself) there was an immense amount to do in London: an average of two meetings a day for three weeks was surely worth more than my enlistment as a footslogger …

The taxi driver Hime had already gone out by the time I returned to London: Ted Accles followed him a fortnight later; but still I postponed the step, writing and talking and poring over maps, while non-intervention raised its ugly head and it became clearer than ever which side the bulk of the Conservative Party favoured. And then I chanced to meet Denise, Julian's girl, swimming up Bond Street like an elaborate and none too reliable metronome. She gave me a smile that stopped me dead in my tracks.

"Why, hallo, Marcus!" An observer might have supposed that we had between us a history of fiercely sensual encounters. "I haven't seen you for ages. Tell me some news."

"I've been away," I answered. "You tell me some. How's Julian?"

"Haven't you heard?" Saucer-eyed, she gazed up at me in huge surprise. "He's gone abroad."

"Oh, really?"

"Yes, a few days ago. I'm so *mis*." She was nothing of the sort: she was looking at me as if I were the missing heir. "Can't we do something?"

"Well," I said, decent-like.

"Oh, come on – what can we lose?"

Nothing, I thought, that hadn't gone years back. But I temporized. "Let's go and have a drink, then."

"Goody!" She crooked her arm in mine adhesively. "He's being so silly and political – I want to have fun."

"Why, where is he?" I asked, suddenly on the alert.

"Oh, some silly place – Spain, I think he said. Why, what's the matter?"

"Good God; he's gone already, then." I unhooked my arm, and turned. "Sorry, Denise – you're marvellous, and it'd be the screw of the century, but I've got to get moving too."

"Come back," she called after me. "I mean, don't be so rude."

But I was way up the street, delaying no longer.

Of such goodbyes as I thought it necessary to make, that exchanged with Dr Barrow was the only one of any significance. Sitting on the bed in his neat, grimly furnished room at Miss Fleming's, he questioned me closely about the project: I could see that he was distressed by it, and unwilling to admit either that the issue in Spain was as clear-cut as I made out, or that it was necessary for me to take a personal part in it. He advocated restraint, as I had expected; and seemed more ready to put the whole thing down to youthful exuberance than seemed flattering.

"It isn't just a joke," I told him at one point. "I don't really want to go, because I'm afraid of being killed. But I must. Spain is now one of the places where one can fight against Fascism instead of just talking about it. That's what we've all been waiting for – a chance to hit back, and do a little beating up on our own account."

He shook his head slowly: the eyes in the pale wrinkled face seemed to hold an infinitely wise reproof, a Christ-like rejecting of force.

"What dispute was ever settled in such a fashion?" he asked. "Strife, attrition, exhaustion – these are not settlement, nor a conceivable basis for it." And then, more urgently: "It is madness for you to fight, perhaps to throw your life away, in such a partisan struggle. Have you no close relatives? – no one to advise you?"

"To stop me, you mean?" I laughed. "No, I'm beyond control in that respect. 'When the brisk Minor pants for twenty-one' – that stage is past. I'm free to fight for whatever I think worth fighting for."

"It has a brave sound," he murmured, almost to himself.

"And *that's* not why I'm doing it," I told him decisively. "It isn't a Byronic gesture for liberty, and there's nothing heroic about it. Or if there is, no hero was ever in such a sweat when he was eight hundred miles from the front …

It's just something I've got to do, because of the way I look at politics."

He spread his hands in a despairing gesture. "But do you imagine that this 'way you look at politics' is a permanent viewpoint? Surely you must see that your opinions are still in a state of flux – you may modify them within the year, within the week even. Why commit yourself in this irrevocable fashion, over something which may be – I say it without wish to offend – a passing phase?"

I turned from the window, from which I had been staring out at the sooty trees, mournful even under the late afternoon sun.

"I know it may be a passing phase," I answered. "But it's what I feel now, more strongly than anything else, and so I'm going out to Spain now."

"Exactly. It is what you feel now, it is the body of opinion which your reading and your circumstance have given you. You are prepared to join the Republican side, but you might easily be doing the opposite. You can appreciate that? A year ago, by your own confession, you would have denounced the bolshevization of Spain and joined General Franco – a course of equal error with the one you now propose. You have become a young man of a certain viewpoint and certain strong convictions: a slight rearrangement of the last few months, and the young man you are now would be your natural and hated enemy."

"Perhaps – but can't you see how unreal that sort of supposition is?" He seemed to be treating the thing as an academic question, a weighing of biological pros and cons which had no regard for the realistic present. "It isn't a matter of what I might have become: it's what I *am*, and what that leads me to do."

He nodded. "Which shows the uncertain nature of an emotional conversion as compared with one based on reason. But I see you have made up your mind," he went on, in a brisker tone, "and that is at once your privilege and my capitulation. What are your immediate plans? You are going straight out to Spain?"

"Via Paris," I answered. "There's some kind of recruiting agency there, and they'll tell me what to do. Of course you *can* just land in Spain and present yourself: but you may present yourself to the wrong man and get shot in the back as you turn away. I want to make certain of going to the right street."

"Surely by going, say, to Barcelona, you would find yourself among friends?"

"I don't think they're unanimous, even there: in fact, they're catching and shooting spies every day."

"Spies!" he exclaimed, suddenly roused again. "What an example of abstraction, of giving a man your own label and hating him for it! Men who disagree with you on questions of policy, men of liberal instincts who are revolted by faction and strife – are these spies?"

"There's a war on," I answered stubbornly, "and anyone who is pro-Franco in Republican territory must take his chance."

He laughed, almost wildly, as if he had reached the limit of reasoned discussion. "And you hope to build a peaceful and united Spain on such a foundation? I tell you, no good can come from this conflict: you will lay up a store of bitterness and malice, you will engender a hatred which will last for generations after you are dead. You will not live to see the horrors which you, as well as your opponents, are letting loose in the name of liberty and peace. But they will be there: others will suffer, because you want to impress by force instead of by reason and co-operation."

"But, good God!" I exclaimed, stung by the contempt in his voice. "Are we to stand by and let Franco and his thugs get away with it? When the rebellion has been put down and order restored, then there'll be liberty, then it'll be time to talk of reason and co-operation."

"Or, alternatively, then the chance may have been lost for ever. As you trace and lay the foundations, so will the building take its shape. If you begin with coercion and bloodshed, your product when completed will be a monument to them." But he was quieter now, as if seeing beyond argument to resignation. "And you feel you must join in that building? I suppose it is not your fault."

"There's no fault. It's something I've decided on."

"It was decided for you," he corrected, "by the times you have been born into. These are your surroundings: war, and political passion, and social injustice, and the loudest shouting for the basest cause." His voice, low-pitched and tired, came out of the silence like a Delphic commentary. "This is the schoolroom: hatred, mistrust, and greed are its furnishings. Is it any wonder that you have become – what you have become, and that millions of other young men take their colour and habit from what that schoolroom teaches them is a high order of civilization?"

He got to his feet, and crossed to the window, and with me looked out on the drably urban garden. Then: "I admire your consistency and determination," he said slowly. "The rest is lamentable."

CHAPTER THIRTEEN

Il n'y a plus de Pyrénées.

LOUIS XIV

❖

"D'you know a way into Spain?" asked Comrade Spiers as the train rocked and clanked over the points running into the suburbs of Amiens. We sat on suitcases in the corridor of a crowded yellow-benched third-class coach, which smelt of stale air and staler humanity: Spiers, recovering from seasickness, was half reclined against the jolting outer wall. He was a young man of my own age, with the poor skin and imperfect teeth of habitual undernourishment, and a drooping lock of hair like that species of seaweed which turns dank at the approach of rain; and I had found him a trying travelling companion, since he had never been out of England and was under the delusion that every Frenchman had designs on his wallet and every Frenchwoman on his chastity. Getting him through the customs had been like playing courier to a bad-tempered suit of armour ... He had some kind of clerking job, but had thrown it up to make this journey; and I had the feeling that were it not for our political sympathy (he was a Party member I had met once or twice before), he would have disliked me with peculiar fervour, as the incarnate class-oppressor, the capitalist system made man.

"Exceptin' round by sea," he added as I was preparing to answer. " 'Ave you been over the mountains?"

"Only once," I answered, "and the wrong end of them, the northern end. I've been through on the coast too, when I was a kid: staying at Biarritz and San Sebastian." I took a map out of my rucksack and showed him, and traced also the path over the Pyrenees which I had taken later. "We'll have to go right down the other end," I went on. "Somewhere near Andorra or Prats de Mollo is more like our mark."

Spiers examined the map carefully, tracing the route with a forefinger nicotined to a brilliant yellow. Then he looked up.

"Travelled a bit, ain't you?" he remarked enviously. "Where else've you bin?"

"Down there," I flicked a finger at the Riviera. "And there, there, and there." I indicated, in turn, Sweden, Switzerland, and Germany. "It used to be a hobby of mine, when I could afford it. Spain I enjoyed as much as anywhere."

He looked at me curiously. "When were you in Spain? A good time ago?"

"Nineteen-thirty-four," I answered. "Just before there was all that political trouble."

And what a holiday that had been, I thought as we settled down to a jolting silence again: I had begun it as an experiment, a dose of fresh air after the languors and liquor of my stay in Germany, and it had quickly resolved itself into the best trip I had ever made. It was the middle of September, and I was due back at Cambridge in about three weeks: I had shipped on a tramp-steamer out of Southampton, carrying scrap metal and an evil smell to Lisbon, but this had palled after a couple of days, and I had dropped off at Bordeaux instead of completing the journey. Bordeaux I had found a place of extreme and lasting attraction: my arrival coincided with the grape harvest (or else with the actual wine-pressing – I wasn't sure which), and every cart and car and wagon had its barrel or vat or jar, rumbling through the cobbled streets in search of a purchaser. A wide river splits the town in two, and on the quays the biggest ships can moor, towering above the buildings (mostly dusky little cafés where yellow cider, of an unbelievable acidity, costs five centimes a cup): I used to wander down the quays, talking to the sailors ("Are you beaching, chum?" an American sailor had once asked me. "Have a drink on the old US"), watching the cargoes being unloaded, and listening to earth-shaking arguments about mooring berths and scraped paint. And inland were joints and dives and quite gentlemanly restaurants where one could drink conspicuously good claret for a quarter of what it cost in London ... Oh yes, Bordeaux had been a great city, and a great starting point for the next stage – a walk due south over the Pyrenees.

Spiers now slept, grey and unlovely in the fading sunlight, snoring jerkily with the train's jolting, as I stared back into the past and relived the hot perfection of that walk. Arriving one evening at St Jean-Pied-de-Port – lovely name, lovely miniature village hidden in the foothills, where they spoke French with an accent so much worse than my own: '*von*', they would say, instead of '*vin*', and something like '*le rowee*' instead of '*le roi*' – arriving there, I had looked up at the great range of mountains cleft with shadow by the evening sun, and thought: 'Tomorrow I take Charlemagne's path'. And what a path it had been: up and up by a road winding through thickly standing trees, past waterfalls, past the two customs houses, French *douane* and Spanish *aduana*, which stood at either end of the bridge at Arnéguy, past Valcarlos and the Col de Ibañeta: up and up, a baking twenty miles wherein the only people I met were two staring children returning from school, a priest leading a goat, and a young *Guardia Civil* with a bulging holster: up and up, till I stood at the top of that very pass of Roncesvalles where the brave Archbishop Turpin was slain by the host of pagans, and Oliver with him, and Roland, who wound his horn to summon help from Charlemagne far down the valley in France, and who died while the deliverer was no nearer than the Valcarlos, named after him, through which I had passed.

I could find no inn at Roncesvalles, and had to walk another three kilometres to the next village, Burguete. And there (I smiled as I recalled it) I had indeed found an inn, a noisy laughing Spanish *méson*, where, when I arrived at half past three, they were just sitting down to lunch: they had made me welcome, and after my seven hours' fast I had eaten the best meal of my life so far – onion soup, chicken cooked with rice and sliced bananas, three rosy swimming peaches, and a litre and a half of *vino tinto corriente* ... The rest of the day I had spent in trying to make myself understood, in watching a purple, gold, and black sunset which had its softer reflection in the fleecy clouds over the mountains behind me, and in sitting under a walnut tree in the patio and wondering what on earth was happening in the inn.

For it was a strange place: immensely crowded, not with visitors, but with what looked like every cousin and aunt and female relative which the village could provide. They rushed about screaming: they bore plates of food backwards and forwards: they rounded up goats, chickens, children, and dogs, and then let them go again while they argued with a second set of women hanging out of an upper window. I was asked to fill in a registration form containing seventeen items in Spanish, not one of which I could understand: three girls, one remarkably pretty, helped me to go through it, bursting out laughing at my stupidity, rushing out to other rooms to report our joint progress, repeating words which were meaningless to me in voices rising higher and higher and becoming a shriek, a cascade of laughter in which I joined till I was myself helpless and shaking ... We got through that registration form somehow, by signs and drawings and gestures: though the last word, '*estado*', seemed likely to kill us all off from sheer exhaustion. "*Estado, estado!*" they repeated, while I shook my head hopelessly. It wasn't 'profession', because we'd had that: it wasn't 'age' or 'home town' or 'destination' or 'nationality' ... But we got it in the end: the shapeliest girl, more daring than her companions, demonstrated it to me by a piece of dumb-show into which I wished I could enter more fully. '*Estado*', it seemed, meant 'Married or Single?'

Dinner, twice as long as lunch and starting at a quarter to ten, I shared with a greedy puppy and with the same pretty girl, Carlotta, who sat at my table in a brilliant green dress and taught me Spanish words: *muchas gracias, comida, tortilla, baños*, as well as 'I love you', 'lips', and 'kiss', the recollection of which had not lasted the intervening years ... She was sweet: and sitting out of doors on the verandah, which gave on to the main street, was sweet also: the darkness grew, while I sat at ease and remembered with deep content the day's walk and its variety of scene and colour – the friendly dog which had accompanied me for more than five miles, the view down the valley as I looked back (I had kept choosing sites on which to build a house, and then abandoning them in favour of others yet more superbly placed), the crisscross of streams and water falls, the towering mountains and thick larch-wooded slopes. I sat there, easing my blistered heels, watching the cows and goats and pigs and donkeys and mules which wandered as they willed: watching a tiny olive-skinned Basque child which bowled a hoop down the road centre, and hit the wall with it, and started to cry, until a black goat even smaller than itself trotted up and started licking it on the forehead ... The hotel was quieter now, but from the village came occasional stray sounds – a cow-bell, a child's laughter, a woman quarrelling on her doorstep. Past me a late wagon rumbled, loaded with tree trunks: the driver smiled, giving me a grave salute with his whip: and whenever I turned towards Carlotta, or touched her hand, I found her looking at me with a kind of brilliant readiness, her brown oval face soft in the twilight, her eyes deep and starry. I had never discovered who or what she was: she was chance-met, chance-loved (stealing into my room in the warm Spanish darkness, stealing out again, wordless, while I was still drowsy), and chance-lost when I wandered on to Pamplona and the plains next morning.

That had been Spain ... Now my train jangled over a long succession of points: Comrade Spiers awoke, bleary-eyed, and stared out of the corridor window as if the outskirts of Paris had been an ash heap with a bad smell; and I began to fasten my collar again and collect my luggage. That had been Spain, 1934; what sort of difference would two years have made, to me as well as to it?

Upstairs, in the dingy little hotel room which I was sharing with Spiers, I said:

"I think I'm going out to get a drink. Coming?"

"I've got the 'ell of an 'ead," he answered weakly. "Reckon I'll 'ave a lay down instead."

He was stretched on his bed, still pale from seasickness, his bony face relaxed and hollow, the dank lock of hair falling back on the pillow like a shop-soiled aureole. My comrade-in-arms, I thought as I surveyed him: shoulder to shoulder we march against the foe ... But it was impossible not to admire his courage in throwing up an assured job and going off into the blue. He did not know how long the war would last, he had no idea what he would do when he came back: like Hime and Ted Accles, he was giving up security and risking his whole future for that spark of idealism which could not be quenched ...

I gave him some aspirin, and drew down the slatted blind. "We ought to make contact with the French comrades," he said as I was moving about the room. "No sense in wastin' time."

"Tomorrow will do," I answered. "I want to enjoy myself tonight."

"Goin' to 'ave a woman?"

I laughed. "Present plans do not include that. All I'm looking for is a drink and some fresh air."

"Well, keep a watch out, then," he observed morosely. "This town's a fair sink, from what I've 'eard."

The hotel was in one of those little streets off the Rue de Rome which, being Paris VIII, ought to be solid and prosperous and are actually as dingy as any Montparnasse alleyway. But it was good to be in Paris again, on a summer evening of such cool splendour: and as I wandered into the Boulevard Haussmann, looking at its civilized shops and mingling with its talkative crowd, I found myself regretting infinitely that I must move on to Spain within a few days. There came back to me a whole host of memories: of times spent here with my parents, of drives to Chantilly or Fontainebleau, of trips up the Seine to Corbeil: life had seemed immensely exciting then, and Paris, with its lively elegance, the only possible place to live in and though there was work to be done now, yet it was difficult, standing there at the western end of the Place de l'Opéra, to make up one's mind that all this, all its tradition and habit, was alien to a real purpose in life and must be abandoned.

I bought some *caporals*, and turned to the nearest and biggest café for a bock. The first person I saw, lounging with an air of well-cut informality at a table just under the awning, was Peter Tresham.

I was very glad to meet Peter again, and the celebration was a full-scale one: but better still was to hear from him that Tania was actually in Paris, staying at the Meurice, and it was there that I called next morning, having fixed up my journey to Spain at a shady little recruiting place off the Boulevard Raspail. And how good to see Tania, even in the sumptuous gaudery of the Meurice ... She was still in bed when I arrived at eleven, and as I plodded into an enormous Byzantine suite, all colonnades and spongy carpets (having been conducted there by a graded series of servants – hall porter, reception clerk, page boy, liftman, and floor waiter – which would have cost any non-Marxist about a hundred francs), her voice came eagerly from the bedroom within: "Marcus? Come straight in here."

On the threshold I drew a long breath. "My God!" I said; "you do yourself pretty well, don't you?" Tania lay in a bed approximately the size of my room at Carter Street – a fourposter with a canopy like the nave of a cathedral; and the room itself was furnished with a richness which fairly punished the eye ... But she was looking lovely, I saw as I drew nearer: paler than usual, perhaps, and her face a little drawn round the eyes, but still Tania, who could hold any floor and stop any party ... She raised herself on one elbow, with a vivid smile.

"Marcus, darling, what a lovely surprise to find you in Paris!" We kissed each other, and her arms went tight round my neck. "But you look half starved – haven't you been eating anything?"

"Well, not up to this scale." I glanced round the room again. "The royal suite, I suppose?"

She smiled. "Something of the sort." I could see that she was quite unselfconscious about it, and that already, in less than a year, she had forgotten the straitened days at Nine Beeches and took places like the Meurice for granted. "But tell me what you're doing in Paris. Are you working here?"

"No. It's a long story, Tania, and you may not be too pleased with it ... Where is the master of the house, by the way?"

"Out, somewhere. He's frightfully busy nowadays: all the money-makers are." But there was no sneer in her voice. "You'll meet him at lunch, if you'll stay. In fact, you must stay." She caught my eye, and then taking my hand added impulsively: "He's not so bad, Marco, though I know you hate the whole thing. I'm really very happy, and he," she searched for a phrase, "he's a miracle of kindness. He gives me everything." There was a brittle determination in her tone: clearly she had convinced herself that only a certain frame of mind, never relaxed, would make her present circumstances tolerable. "In fact," she concluded, as if daring me to pursue the subject, "he's a model husband in every way."

Husband ... I stared down at her, lying young and fresh on the fantastically draped bed: and then I thought of Hugo Demetriades as I had last seen him down at Antibes – tight-suited, olive-skinned, thick and Levantine to his blunted fingertips. It was better not to dwell on that aspect of the affair: it was better not to think of Sievvitch ... Tania read my thoughts as easily as if I had spoken them aloud, but for the first time in her life she refused to meet them: instead, she took a cigarette from a shagreen-and-ivory box on the side table, settled back among the pillows, and said: "Tell me what you've been doing. And why are you in Paris?"

I told her of the last few months, and about Spain, and why I was going out. She listened attentively, never trying to interrupt except at the very beginning when she exclaimed: "Spain! Oh, Marcus ..." and her hand went quickly to her throat: thereafter she watched me all the time with wide-eyed attention, and with something else which was like a shadow across her loveliness. When I had finished she shook her hair away from her eyes, and said: "You mustn't go, Marcus."

"I've got to," I told her. "And I want to go: it's something worth fighting for. It'll be all right, anyway."

"It isn't that." There was a constraint in her voice. "I've been in Spain with Hugo: we were in Madrid all through April and June. He had business there." She paused. "Do you understand?

"No."

"He had business there," she repeated, "and I've only realized lately what it was. I didn't pay much attention in Madrid: but I knew a little of what was going on, from the kind of people who came to see him. And there was an officer who stayed talking one night ... Don't you see," she burst out suddenly, "if you fight for the Republic and are killed, it may be with a gun paid for by him."

A silence fell between us at her words. But after an initial twinge of dismay I found that I was not really surprised: it was natural that men like Demetriades, who made their money by fishing in such waters, should interest themselves in the Spanish conflict, and inevitable that they should therein lend their support to the Fascists. International capital was swift to look after its own.

"That can't be helped," I answered, as casually as possible. "That's his job, and if Spain looks like paying a dividend he's bound to have a finger in it. And it doesn't make any difference to whether I fight or not."

"But you can't win," she said, almost in a whisper: her eyes sought mine as if she could make of them an ally against my determination. "Hugo says you can't." And as I was about to interrupt: "I tell you it's no good," she went on vehemently: "however long it goes on, they'll crush you in the end. It isn't only private capital: Germany has been getting ready for this since the beginning of the year – she can't run the risk of a Socialist Spain as well as a Socialist France: the balance would be too heavy against her."

"I know that," I said quietly, trying to calm her. "That's why it's worth fighting, that's why it's a clear-cut issue – democracy against Fascism. And democracy will win."

"You fool, Marcus, you fool!" she burst out. "You treat this like a game of toy soldiers ... What do the men at the top care about democracy? – to them the people are so many units of work, so many cogs; if the cogs run smoothly, a line on a graph will rise by so much, and that means" – she swept her arms round the room with a gesture of hatred – "more of this for women like me, more yachts, more horses, more power." She shivered suddenly. "And that's why Franco has unlimited money. I *know*. I've met these people. They don't back the losing side."

She was shaking with emotion, and deeply moved: and though presently I was able to calm her, I knew that I could no more resolve her distress than I could put the clock back to her childhood. What hours of introspection, what agonies of self-loathing lay behind that phrase 'women like me', I could only guess: I had thought that she had succeeded in deluding herself as to her position, but it was clear that the reality lived with her every minute of her life ...

Presently, infinitely subdued, she said: "If you lunch with us, Hugo will want to lend you money. I wish you'd take it Marcus: even five hundred pounds would make a difference, wouldn't it?"

At that moment a roar of laughter would have been a luxury: five hundred *would* make a certain difference to my twenty-seven ... But instead I answered: "He'd better give his spare cash to Franco: the need is greater … And I don't think I'll lunch with you, Tania: Spain might come up, and I've an idea it would bring lunch with it."

"Oh, Marcus," she said piteously, "are we on different sides?"

I kissed her, as lovingly as I could. "We are *not*. But you'll admit that he isn't exactly arm-in-arm with me at the moment."

Tania knit her brows. "I'll put him off," she said finally, "and we'll lunch together. How about that?"

"Well …"

"I'll stand it you."

"Where?"

She smiled. "Voisin's?"

"A good bribe," I answered. "I'll take it."

And I did. We had a lunch which I remembered for many days afterwards: Tania, looking ravishing in black and wearing a fairly reasonable Schiaparelli hat, was waited on as though she were a princess; and we forgot Spain, and her marriage, and my imminent departure, in a mood of reminiscence and laughter which nothing could overshadow. For that single hour, snatched out of hurrying time, we were in partnership again, brother and sister who had never grown apart. Naturally it could not last: naturally Demetriades on the one hand and Spain on the other must sunder us at its end; but its joy and sweetness I carried with me like a charm, into a country which needed the most potent magic to make it humanly tolerable.

Barcelona …

"That town," said Cervantes, "for beauty unique, that register of courtesy, asylum of strangers, hospital of the poor": and the description did not date as much as a cynic might have expected. Beauty it certainly had, under a September sun which set the whole waterfront a-sparkle and played over its landmarks – the Columbus monument, the Montjuich, the odd and partly destroyed Iglesia de la Sagrada Familia – like a fountain over its ring of ornamentation. Its courtesy was intermittent: hotel waiters displayed revolvers and a certain intransigence, and if one did not return, mighty quickly, the clenched fist salute, and skip out of the way of the chalkscrawled 'FAI' and 'CNT' cars which roared down the streets a-bristle with arms, one was liable to a swift demonstration of native prejudice. But 'asylum of strangers' and 'hospital of the poor' were uncomfortably apt: already the refugees streaming in from the outlying districts threatened to disorganize food and sanitary services, and all through the day and half the night such meeting places as the Plaza Cataluña and the Ramblas, with its flower stalls and its long line of plane trees, were besieged by an aimless milling crowd which strolled and argued interminably, and on which the only effect of the war seemed to be to double its coffee-drinking and halve its industry. Whole days were passed like that: idling in the sun with a glass of cognac, reading the newspapers and speculating on the latest bulletins, listening to the loudspeakers and standing up fiercely for the national anthems; let the women struggle in the milk and bread queues – the man's job was to settle the universe under a café awning ... But if the days were easy, the nights atoned for the lapse with a grim savagery: there would be sudden shouts and cries, sporadic outbursts of shooting, the scream of a car's tyres and a single revolver shot – little vignettes of hatred and treachery and revenge; and when one ventured out in the morning, and perhaps took a walk towards San Cugat on the road called La Rabassada, one found the answer: a stiffening body with a battered skull or a neatly drilled hole through the forehead, a clump of corpses half hidden in a rubbish tip, a blood-splashed wall at the foot of which lay a staring sightless figure in dungarees … 'Executions', 'reprisals', 'political activity', 'spy round-ups', *'medidas de precaucion'* – there were plenty of words, but only one translation.

Almost as soon as I arrived in Barcelona I got, as it were, a whiff of this bestiality, and I told Spiers: "I'm not going to fight in this war – at least, not at the front. I'll get a job driving a lorry or an ambulance."

Spiers betrayed neither surprise nor resentment at the decision, which, I imagine, confirmed his view of me as a dude playing at Communism for the sake of something to do; and when he went off, after a ludicrously short period of training, to the Saragossa sector (at that time under the idolized Durruti), I was left to myself. And what a grand place was Barcelona during those weeks … One can hardly convey in words the tremendous upsurge of enthusiasm which permeated the whole city: the atmosphere, everywhere apparent, of a young emergent nation just finding its feet, marching not only to war but to emancipation, freedom, and justice. It was something independent of the chalked lorries rushing up and down the streets, of the long processions, the extremely good posters, the overdone saluting: hope and liberation were in every face, in the quietest street-corner conversation, in the very air itself. The war then was at an almost amateurish stage: organization was *ad hoc* and no more, troops were sketchily trained and rushed up to the front, often without any arms at all – "You're sure to pick up a rifle when you get there" was the current grim comment on this; and the city was at times reduced to queueing up for the commonest household necessities. But enthusiasm over-topped all this, made a joke of it: "Franco's worse off" – so ran the contemporary saying: "he's got to find sausages, spaghetti, and goats' milk as well." … Nothing really mattered, except that the young republic was winning the war, and the new Utopia would follow therefrom.

Naturally there were murderous excesses within the city as well as at the seat of war; naturally discipline failed at times to control young men driven by a pent-up lust for vengeance, young men who experienced at one and the same time a sudden access of power and a constant fear of treachery from behind. There were rooftop snipers and Fascist *pacos* who let slip no chance of creating confusion; and it was inevitable that reprisals, and even acts of private vengeance, should follow each fresh disturbance. But to say that such outbreaks were part of an official policy or a 'Red terror' is to go beyond common sense as well as the weight of evidence. Wars are not won on a race gang basis.

I was in Barcelona for about a fortnight: wasting time, it was true, from a utilitarian standpoint, but trying all the while to penetrate beneath the skin of the place and miss nothing of its force. And then, with no more trouble than was entailed by marching in at one door, signing two grey forms, and marching out at another, I got fixed up in my lorry-driving job, as one of a convoy which collected food and farm produce from round about Cuenza, and drove it into Madrid every three or four days. It sounded the sort of thing I wanted to do: neither wholly treacherous nor yet wholly secure …

My orders, given me in Barcelona by an overworked People's Commissar, were to report to whoever was in charge at Cuenza, halfway between Madrid and the coast, where I would pick up my lorry and join the next convoy. By way of an excursion I trained down the coast to Valencia, from where it was easy to get lifts, the roads westward being crowded with traffic ranging from motorcycle dispatch-riders to six-horse teams hauling logs: and at Minglanilla, where the road begins to climb steadily by a series of ridges to the high tableland round Almodóvar and Talayuelo, I fell in with a pale green Rolls-Royce, the rear half of its body cut away and a platform for milk-cans substituted, driven by a fierce man in a UGT forage cap and a blazing red shirt. Even the silver-nymph mascot on the radiator had a little skirt fashioned from a Caballero flag ... Our conversation was limited to curt nods and four words: *"Salud!" "Cuenza?" "Muchas gracias!"* and he had loosened his revolver in its holster as I climbed in beside him; but he proved a brilliant driver, putting the heavy car along as if the rough mountain road were the Watford bypass, and we were over the last rise and in Cuenza by three o'clock. There the Rolls disappeared in a minor duststorm up the Tarancón road, and I was left to myself in front of a supremely untidy garage labelled 'José Martinez, by a wavering hand, hoping that the car assigned to me would be of the same calibre as the one I had just left. 'Lorry' could mean a good deal in this war.

José Martinez' garage was, as it turned out, the place I wanted, though I did not find this out until I had been given conflicting directions, first by a young militiaman who had no notion of what he was talking about, and then by a genuine official so harassed that he had already described the full details of the convoy system before he turned suspicious and asked to see my papers ... In answer to my shout at the garage, José Martinez crawled out from beneath a huge old Renault *camion*, of that model which I did not think had survived the Great War, with a Cape-cart hood secured by straps to the front wings and a starting-handle placed at about the height of my shoulder; and I knew, even before he broke the news, that this was my assignment ... José was a grave young man, broad shouldered under his filthy overalls, with a high forehead and a sweep of thick black hair; and as a taxi driver in Biarritz he had learnt enough French for us to understand each other freely. He showed me the controls of the lorry – the driver's cabin was at least six feet from the ground, the steering wheel a massive affair with ten inches' play on either side of dead central – and when our united efforts had brought the engine to life I took it for a practice run of a couple of miles, during which the concerted uproar of its gears, motor, and bodywork brought the villagers out of their houses in dismay and set every dog within earshot barking as if beset by devils. With exceptionally heavy steering, and a clutch-travel of more than a foot, I could see that it was never going to be easy to drive: but still, it was something to have the old hulk moving at all, and it would certainly carry an imposing load.

"For ten years it has stood in that field behind the garage," said José when we got back. "The hens, they grow very fond of it … Now the war will bring it on the road again. C'est rigolo, n'est-ce pas?"

"Very funny," I agreed. I raised my head from inside the bonnet, where I had been reinforcing various bits of the carburettor with twisted wire. "But why don't you drive it yourself? Or are you doing something else?"

"I have another lorry, a fine *Americano*, only two years old. You must understand that formerly I conducted a bus service from here through Tarancón to Madrid: twice a week, with my brother Jesus Christi collecting the money and giving tickets. But who would wish to move about the country at such a time? So I have a bus, free for the service of the Republic … But the Republic does not need a bus, it needs a lorry, to keep up the food supplies for Madrid: so I take the seats out of the bus, and the back door, and a little piece of the roof, and there is a lorry, ready to spit in the eye of Franco." He grinned enormously. "You see it is easy, if one applies the mind."

How exactly alike all these young men were, I thought, with their brave enthusiasm, their carelessness of the future, their new singleness of purpose. In Barcelona there had been thousands like José Martinez, abandoning security and mortgaging their whole future in order that the measure of democracy which had lately been granted them might not perish from their earth; and already, out of the synthesis of muddle, courage, and squalor which had characterized the early days of the war, a distinct and distinguished nation was emerging.

"What's our route?" I asked José presently. "And how long does it take?"

He pointed vaguely north-west. "We go over the mountains – a poor road, but the best. To Madrid is perhaps two hundred kilometres: if one goes by the other road, south through Tarancón, it is forty kilometres less."

"Why don't you use the shorter way, then? The mountain road must take us through Guadalajara – almost to the front."

José nodded. "That is so. And later there will be times when we do not know who holds the country through which we travel." This was perfectly true, as I had heard already: there were still huge tracts of no-man's-land, where neither side had either the men or the energy to advance, and one might run into a patrol and give them – once only – the wrong salute ... "But there is an order," José continued, "that if possible we should not use the road between Tarancón and Madrid, which is part of the main Valencia road and already has too much traffic. Besides, the convoy is sometimes led by a lorry full of militiamen, and also," he patted the elaborate holster strapped to his waist, "one has this, and the speed of one's own lorry."

I looked up at the Renault, and back to José, with a smile not wholly sincere. Running the gauntlet in this ten-mile-an hour thunderer would have its ludicrous side, more apparent to the gauntlet than to the driver.

"Will I be driving by myself?"

"No." His voice changed suddenly, losing its carelessness, and taking on a subdued intensity. "My brother – that Jesus Christi of whom I have spoken – will go with you as mechanic: he is clever at such things. He wished to start driving the lorry himself without anyone else, but – " José stopped, and caught my eye with a grave stare, and then continued: "He is young, not yet sixteen: one would wish to keep him out of danger, if that is possible."

"Why doesn't he go with you? Then you could look after him yourself."

"He will not agree to that: he says I – I will keep him too well guarded, so that he sees nothing of the war ..." The words, and the look which accompanied them, were enough to reveal the whole relationship between the brothers. "He will go with you, unless you wish otherwise," José continued, "and then I shall be able to think of him as safe. Sixteen is not a great age."

I met Jesus Christi Martinez later that evening, when José took me home to have a meal with his parents. The latter were peasants, *campesinos*, living in a shockingly neglected cottage on the outskirts of the next village, La Melgosa: and both of them, though not much over forty, were prematurely aged by the harshness of their life, the man having a dried yellow face with the skin drawn tight across it like a parchment wrapping, and a back bent and twisted in an ugly bow, while the mother, gaunt and ungainly, stared at her life, her children, her surroundings, with eyes set so deep that they seemed no more than dull jewels within a skull. But it was clear that both of them were immensely proud of José, the eldest son who had lifted himself out of their own plane: they waited on him with a loving and pathetic eagerness, they gave him (and, through courtesy, me) what meat there was in the wretched stew, and contented themselves with the remaining scraps of potato and onion ... The younger son, who came in late, was a lively youngster with grey eyes, untidy hair, and the most compelling smile I had seen for a long time. He chattered continuously throughout the meal, turning to each person for corroboration on one point or another, and though José tried to keep him in order it was without any real insistence – Jesus Christi obviously had all the world eating out of his hand … When he spoke to me he used only the simpler words, helped out by some uncertain French: but he seemed extremely interested in England, inquired the price of everything I wore, and borrowed my revolver to compare it with his own.

"I meet English soldiers in Madrid," he told me at one point. "There is one in the convoy, too. They all call me Christ," he pronounced it in the English fashion, "and then they laugh. Do you know why is that?"

I had to confess that I didn't, while determining privately to call him Christ myself.

We sat round a table in the single room which comprised the whole ground floor of the cottage: from its walls great stretches of plaster had flaked away, leaving bare the rough unfinished stone through which daylight peeped here and there; strips of meat, and onions in long golden strings, hung down from the raftered ceiling, and through the wooden partition which made up one wall, cattle could be heard blowing and stamping their feet and rattling headstalls. The whole place bespoke a wretched poverty, a history of succeeding generations who had toiled their whole lives for an existence higher than the beasts they tended, and had never yet won the struggle. (When we had first drawn near the cottage we had seen, down the road, the mother hobbling home under a yoke supporting two buckets of water – water which had to be fetched three hundred yards from the village well.) And it was about this pitiful standard of life which José talked later, when the old people had gone to bed and he and I were walking back to the garage where we were to sleep.

"Can you wonder that we fight hard to keep our land?"
he said. Our two shadows, cast by the moon, strode ahead
of us down the road, formidable bodyguards in a perilous
countryside. "You have seen how it is with my parents ? –
it is the same all over Spain: the great landlords and the
Church draw huge sums of money from the land, money
which they spend in the cities while the *campesinos* live
like pigs and die as quickly. And the priests, too, who keep
the people in ignorance all their lives, and who tell them,
when they complain of hunger and misery, that it is God's
will. God's will!" José brought the words out with
immeasurable contempt. "Everything is God's will, they
say, if to set it right might give the people dangerous
knowledge and bring the landlords less money to squander
on their pleasures. But we will change all that – you will
see."

"I hope you will," I answered. "And I certainly agree
about resisting the landowners, and the priests, when they
come back with arms and Moorish troops to seize the land
again. But they tried it in Russia, and they'll fail as they
failed then."

José nodded. "Russia must be a fine country. I would like
to build a country like that."

The line of twelve lorries, headed by a small truck with a
machine-gun mounted behind the driver's cabin, waited in
the midday sun for the signal to move off.

I was number eight, behind a converted Hispano with a
long maroon bonnet: behind me was José's smart bus,
stacked to the roof with assorted vegetables. Indeed, we
were a haphazard and rather disreputable collection: the
Hispano was probably the most lordly, though somewhere
ahead was a Delage with a Paris numberplate, and the
convoy ranged from these elegant conveyances down to
my Renault, the most disreputable and (I had no doubt)

unreliable of the lot. The journey might take anything up to twelve hours for the hundred and twenty-five miles, and it was so timed that over the most dangerous part, from where we struck the Madrid–Saragossa road, we would be running in darkness. I supposed that it was a good rather than a bad point that the Renault had no lights of any description: the fact at least gave me an even chance as between bomb, gunfire, and ditch.

By my side in the cabin, young Christ, fidgeting to be off, wolfed a long piece of *salchichón* clapped between two slabs of bread. I was keeping mine till later.

"You let me drive?" he said presently, turning on me the full battery of his smile. "I can drive this one easily."

"I'll see," I told him. "I don't see why you shouldn't, if José doesn't mind. But the – " I tried to think of a word, in French or Spanish, for 'steering', and failed. I waggled the wheel, which creaked abominably. "This isn't very easy, you know," I continued. "You'll find it heavy."

I also found it heavy, and immensely tiring, before we had gone ten miles along the rough winding road leading into the hills. The lorry, of course, had solid tyres and its rudimentary springs did nothing to insulate the steering gear from the vile surface: every pothole, every dip and uneven patch, meant a jarring thud which came straight up the column and hit one's forearms like a blow from a mallet. Ten miles of that, added to the force needed to wrench the wheel round every corner, made me ache from fingers to shoulder-blades, and when I raised a hand to wipe the sweat from my forehead it shook uncontrollably.

But it was grand to be one of that moving column, spread out now over a mile or more of road, which thundered its way north-westward under the still-high sun: it was grand to be dropping from the heights round Cuenza to the sheltered and sleeping plains below. We ran through strange country, sometimes thickly wooded, sometimes so bare that it might have been long ago deserted by man; and this added to the excitement and tension which driving in the convoy necessarily brought, so that, handling that tough intractable lorry under a foreign sky, I was aware all the time that I was doing something with a special quality of exhilaration.

Here and there we saw signs, not of the war itself but of private or localized strife: perhaps a church with its windows broken, or a blackened patch of ground with the ruins of a cottage left derelict upon it. "Bad priest – try to fight," Christ would say, or "Family quarrel – two brothers for the Republic, one for Franco ..." Once, running slowly over a crossroads just past the village of Sacerdón, some fifty miles on our journey, I saw two figures pendant, one on either arm of the signpost: they did not swing or revolve, they just hung there, their clothes loose, their necks at that ugly angle which announces death from afar off.

I turned to young Christ, but he was already preparing to do the honours.

"Militiaman," he said, pointing to the one on the right: and "Priest," indicating the other. "There for five weeks now: everyone afraid to take them down."

"What happened?"

"A fight – two fights." He shrugged his shoulders. "Who can judge now? The militiaman came here to get food or recruits, and a man shot him and hung him there: they say the priest gave him money to do it, but perhaps it was a quarrel. Anyway, some more militiamen came and shot the priest, and hung him up there as well, *pour rendre la pareille.*"

The road began to climb, and the spaced-out column of lorries ground its way upwards, while the Renault swayed and shuddered and my arms braced themselves for the road's successive shocks. Presently the climb steepened sharply, approaching Alhondiga, and here, as the hairpin bends multiplied and the stress of effort grew, the engine began for the first time to falter. I listened to that break in the rhythm slowly developing: first an occasional splutter, then a fit of jerks which set the whole lorry rocking from stem to stern, then a gradual dying away of the engine altogether. I changed down, and we made a few more yards at an uncertain crawl; thereafter we failed at the next corner, and rolled to a standstill.

I sounded my horn four times – the agreed signal – which was repeated in front and brought the cavalcade ahead to a halt, while those behind closed up. Christ got out and raised the bonnet, leaving me resting my hands on my knees, glad of the respite; and headed by José a knot of other drivers – some eating, or puffing at cigarettes – walked up to see if they could help. I looked at my watch, and then at the rough map I had bought in Barcelona, to find that we had made about sixty miles in five and three-quarter hours. Poor time, but it was over the slowest section of the route.

The drivers started talking among themselves, using technicalities which I could not follow: presently Christ straightened up, holding in one hand a length of what I took to be the petrol pipe.

"Dirt inside," he called out.

"Blow through it," I answered, glad that I needn't do it myself.

The men round him all looked in my direction. "*Inglés?*" one of them asked politely. I nodded and smiled, whereupon he gave an imposing Communist salute. The others did the same, and so did I. It was neither so ridiculous nor so meaningless as it sounds.

Another driver strolled up to the group, a little rolling man in a khaki shirt and gumboots.

"Wot cheer, Christ!" he said surprisingly. "Can't you get the old bit o' wreckage outer the wye? Or 'as someone 'alf inched yer engine?"

I leaned out of my cabin, a flask in one hand and a hunk of bread in the other. "Less of it!" I called out. "How about giving us a hand yourself?"

"Blimey, 'e's got an English shuvver!" The little man came up, beaming. "Evenin', comrade. Pleased ter meetcher. Cupper's the name."

"Mine's Hendrycks." I held out the flask. "Have a swig?"

"Much obliged." He took a long pull, and smacked his lips. All the other drivers were watching us with grave attention, as if we were performing animals who might well show themselves almost human. "Ain't I met you before?" asked Cupper after a moment. "I don't forget a face so easy."

"I was just going to say the same thing. I think we've both spoken at a meeting down at Hoxton. Aren't you a friend of Hime's?"

"Was, yer mean," he answered, suddenly subdued. And as I looked at him uncomprehendingly: "Ain't you 'eard? 'E copped 'is, second day out at Saragosser."

"Good God!" I said, shocked. Poor old Hime, who got such immense amusement out of his taxi-driving job, whose arguments with Shep had always ended with laughter on both sides ... "How did it happen?"

He shrugged. "Gawd knows. Bit o' shell splinter, I 'eard. 'E's out, whatever it was." Then he seemed to throw the thought away, and smiled again. "Smart bus yer've got 'ere – I didn't know they was rafflin' 'em."

I laughed. "Oh, she's all right. Gets in a bad mood now and then, that's all."

"Like women, ain't they?"

"Too like."

Christ raised his head from the bonnet, and shut it again with a clang. As the drivers dispersed, he climbed up beside me, wiping filthy hands on his overalls. "Now we go fine," he said. "Just a little dirt, that's all."

I sounded my horn, and let in the clutch again. The convoy took up its interrupted rhythm, moving westward through the mountains towards the lowering sun.

By the time dusk fell we were almost on the main road, approaching Guadalajara itself: on our right there was intermittent gun-fire, and an occasional flash which seemed to light the sky from end to end. We moved now among a ceaseless flow of traffic: there were mules dead and alive – curious the way the legs of a dead mule always stuck out sideways, like an overturned table: sometimes we passed a small body of troops lounging by the roadside or looking important behind inadequate cover, and they would give us a cheer and a volley of salutes as we rolled by. And now it was suddenly intensely cold, as well as dark: draughts played in and out of the rocking rackety cabin, and between the hood and the top of the windscreen an icy wind blew steadily straight into my eyes. Even Christ, who had a coat with a strange sheepskin collar like a monk's cowl falling over his head, stamped his feet and rubbed his cheeks in the effort to keep warm. With stiff and frozen arms I wrestled with the deadweight of the wheel, taking turns so roughly that the overloaded body behind me rocked like a wallowing ship: the road and the hours of the journey stretched on and on, the traffic grew more difficult to negotiate, the skin of my face stiff and blue. "Memorandum," I said aloud, to give my scarcely felt lips something to do: "Buy in Madrid one overcoat, fur lined, one pair of goggles, one stout muffler." If we ever got to Madrid, that was: at the moment there didn't seem to be any end to the journey.

It was nearly midnight, eleven hours from the start, before we reached the outer suburbs.

I made that trip, and the return journey (sometimes empty, sometimes in ballast with a refugee family), thirteen times in seven weeks: and I spent in Madrid a total of a fortnight. They were days of general anxiety and personal revulsion: for though the insurgent advance was still a comfortable distance away from the city, yet it was subjected to air-raids, and I saw there, and up on the Guadalajara front, horrors which were horrors in any context, whether one pleaded the necessities of war or not ... Civil strife, of brother against brother, unloosed a brutality so revolting that a faithful history of it (if such is ever made) will serve to convince posterity that, at this point of time, humanity stepped back into a raving lunacy which knew only that to claw in blood was satisfying. There were air-raids, wanton and aimless in their slaughter: there were buildings mined and blown up, packed with their sleeping occupants: there were shootings of 'Spies', of surrendering prisoners, of hostages who hardly comprehended what the struggle was about; the firing-squad ruled, and a lust to avenge, and a swift and terrible injustice.

And I took part in it all: I helped: like thousands of other young men, I added my quota to the bloodshed and the hatred. The day on the Guadalajara front was an accidental excursion, due to the Renault's breaking down in the village: it was always breaking down, or refusing to start, or turning nasty on a hill (the rest of the convoy called us '*El Ancla*' – the Anchor), but this time it was a matter of a stripped crown-wheel which would have to be made specially, and while young Christ went on to Madrid to find the necessary workshop, I chose to stay where I was. But of course I didn't stay: in a café I got talking with a trio of young militiamen who were moving up to the front in an hour or so, and after a couple of drinks they said: "*Vente con nosotros*" (the war was like that in those days, and with my beard, Party cap and badge, dungarees, and filthy sheepskin overcoat, I must have looked the part), and I forgot my resolutions and went with them. We saw Caballero on the way up, solid and reassuring with his jutting face, dark blue overalls, silver-buckled belt, and forage-cap over one ear: he was surrounded by a quartet of far smarter staff officers, all of them staring at a map spread over the bonnet of their car.

It was bitterly cold as soon as the sun went down: the wind from the Sierras cut through one's clothes, defeating every effort to keep warm, and leaving a rime of frozen breath round one's mouth. But that night I went out on patrol, up among the foothills of the Somosierra, with a flaskful of brandy inside me, and a cocked revolver in one hand and a home-made hand grenade in the other; and I did find something magnificently exciting in lying there among the rocks, fearing to breathe, dreading to cough, staring at a black star-pricked sky glimpsed between two stripped trees, and listening to the *other* patrol which blundered through the scrub down in the valley, intent on the same brand of murder as ourselves ... We got that patrol: I got part of it myself, as my share in that hideously treacherous excursion; and something – probably the brandy – made me glad that I had killed two men who wanted to bring Fascism to yet another country. But at dawn, in the cold and candid light which succeeded that Night in the Gardens of Spain, there were too many corpses, there was too much blood on one's hands ...

Then Madrid again, for my third and worst air-raid. A little earlier, Madrid had been comparatively normal: though curfew was at eleven, and one was always being asked for one's papers by four men with fixed bayonets, yet the city's life moved as busily as ever, with no sign of serious dislocation; and the lovers in the parks, eking out their affections with *churros* fried in oil, the young good-looking *Madrileños* strolling with their coats thrown loosely across their shoulders and the sleeves swinging – all seemed unaffected by the proximity of the war. Food supplies were ample (with the exception of butter, which one missed inordinately): the Madrid Philharmonic played Beethoven, the cinemas were open and showed, among other things, some good Soviet films and a vintage Fred Astaire. Even the air-raids were still a diversion rather than an agency of terror: people laughed and pointed at the 'little birds', disdaining even the rooftop snipers (Madrid's vaunted 'Fifth Column') who busied themselves in trying to promote panic. Of course bombs fell and fires started: but they were always somewhere else.

And then, suddenly, all this seemed to change: the pot came to a boil, and nothing could disguise its hideous brew. To the westward the great crescent of Franco's forces made a spectacular advance: "Madrid will fall by next Thursday," said the insurgent High Command – next Thursday being October 29th, 1936 – and in the succeeding weeks it seemed that the fulfilment of the prophecy would only be a little delayed. Aranjuez was lost, and Navalcarnero, and Getafe: the enemy were in the outer suburbs, in the University City, in the Casa del Campo itself; they were over the Segovia Bridge ... And there they were held – it was the time of backs-to-the-wall, of hand-to-hand fighting at the very gates of the city, the time of NO PASARAN!: five thousand troops arrived from Barcelona under Durruti (who was killed three days later), in addition to the International Column under General Kleber, which played a matchless part in stemming the advance. But though it was stayed, the city, which knew that men and arms were daily pouring in to help the invaders as well, lay under a dreadful anxiety; and with each journey that Christ and I made, the number of black-labelled *'Evacuacion'* cars leaving the city increased steadily.

And then came the air-raids, the final brutal attempt to subdue the defenders. I was in Madrid for the last of three which had taken place in quick succession: in fact, I was in the Puerto del Sol, examining the bomb craters and the scarred buildings, when the sirens screamed their warning and people began to run. Standing under the huge 'Pedro Domecq' sign, already twisted and rent, I looked first at the hurrying figures round me, and then at the clear sky overhead, where in a minute the black shadows would appear. Civilization – scurrying to take refuge in holes in the ground before destruction was let loose ... the sirens screamed again, like the voice of God in anguish, and I began to run myself, wondering as I made for the Calle Arenal leading to the Opera House whether I was choosing right. Headed by two militiamen with rifles, and a fat man who jumped out of his motorcar and darted across the pavement like a lamb in spring, I turned down a side street and went to ground in a café cellar. A moment afterwards, the roar of the falling bombs began.

It was not dark in the cellar, which was really only a basement with the top of its window a couple of feet above street level; and besides the set faces of the two militiamen who with me were peering out into the deserted street I could see clearly the other occupants – in one corner a woman holding two young children, the café owner, a long morose man staring at the wall in front of him in brooding hatred of his circumstance, a couple of waiters still holding trays and napkins, and the fat citizen, who was mumbling what might have been prayers, with no great conviction. His voice, and the children's whispers, were the only sound within the cellar: the rest of us just stood there, listening without a word to the horrifying crescendo of noise which came from the outside world.

Bombs always *seem* to be coming nearer in an air-raid – perhaps because of the growing volume of sound which each explosion multiplies, perhaps through sheer increase of terror in the hearer; but on this occasion there was no doubt that streets were being hit, and houses shattered, within a few score yards of us. The planes of course we could not hear – with this wide and open target, where any mark would serve, they could fly as high as they liked: but what we did hear was the swift fury of explosion after explosion, which made the windows rattle and the deep ground under our feet shake like some rickety piece of framework, and thereafter – sometimes in the distance, sometimes so near that it might be the house over our heads beginning to topple – there would come the crash of falling masonry, the loose Niagara of brick and stone and wood from which all binding elements had been ripped, the high screaming, the prickling silence of death ... One began to hate even then – fury would come when one stepped out into the shattered chaos of the streets, but already that distant screaming (which might come, dreadfully, from a man's throat) was enough to swamp fear in dull hatred of the destroyer.

We waited in the cellar, wondering if it was to be our turn this time. Presently there was a much nearer explosion, and then two more in quick succession, which seemed to set the whole building rocking: the children whimpered, the café owner raised his head suddenly as if goaded beyond endurance; and peering out of the window I saw a wave of dust and smoke rolling across the entrance of our little street, and smelt faintly the bitter reek which at full strength threatened to make one cough up one's lungs in agony.

"Puerto del Sol," said one of the militiamen. He bit his lower lip. "*Que no se acerque más!*"

The fat man, now silent, stared and stared at the rectangle of light as if it were salvation itself. I stared also, out of the window, watching the smoke drifting round the street corner and then – almost by accident, it seemed – I was staring at something quite different, I was staring at a house thirty yards away at the head of the T where the streets met.

On the roof was a man with a rifle. He was astride the parapet, leaning over, and firing swiftly down the Calle Arenal in the direction of the Opera House. A sniper, a *paco*, trying to increase the panic and help the death-roll …

I found myself, suddenly, grinning with pleasure. He offered a perfect target against the skyline: he was one of the hated: it was his friends who, from the aeroplanes high overhead, were pouring death into the city with negligent hands.

I turned to the militiaman behind me. "*Dámelo!*" I said softly, and pointed. Without a word he passed his rifle over. I edged the barrel out of the window, and drew a bead on the single figure astride the parapet.

The others were watching me closely, in silence – there was less noise now from the bombs: but I could hardly bear to pull the trigger, so sweet and certain was that moment. The *paco* was sitting upright now, putting a fresh clip into his rifle, and I had his head, black-haired and clean against the smoky sky, balanced on the V of my backsight. For a moment longer I held it – a charmed second of the most blissful hatred I had ever experienced – and then I said: "To hell with *you*," and squeezed the trigger.

In the confined space of the cellar the single rifle shot was ear-cracking in its force. Deaf and grinning, I watched the man throw up his hands: I watched his weapon describe a wide arc and clatter on to the roadway below: and then I watched his body sag and topple sideways, catching momentarily on the lip of the parapet and then plunging down to the pavement forty feet below. The noise he made – almost an explosion – as he hit the flags had a sweetness and savour about it that I would have exchanged for nothing else in the world.

The militiaman winked at me. "*Muy bien!*" he said, with a wide smile. Then he took his rifle from me, and opened the breech, and blew a thin jet of smoke from the barrel – incense to speed the sacrifice. "*Muy bien!*" he said again. "One pig less for Spain."

The raid seemed to be over for the moment, and that meant that there was work to do. Leaving the others behind, I and the two militiamen climbed up to street level again, and walked out towards the Calle Arenal. The air was now thick with smoke, and presently we heard the fire and ambulance bells begin to ring, and saw people come out of their houses and collect in knots, surveying the damage or staring at the innocent sky. And over everything, sharp and bitter in one's nostrils, was that evil reek which we had come to fear for what it meant – in terms of death, in evidence of blood-letting. We spat, and kept on spitting, all through the next hour or so, but still the bitterness was in our throats and ears, to remind us of the penalties of being on the earth instead of in the sky.

Not that there was much need of a reminder ... In the Puerto del Sol was a huge new bomb crater, which went right through to the Underground line beneath: and spread over the square were five other new ones, including a jagged-rimmed hole where I had been standing a little time before. The car from which the fat man had jumped was overturned in the roadway, and blazing furiously: every inch of the pavements was littered with broken glass and stone dust, while up one side street was a row of wrecked houses, two of which were already pouring with smoke. Thermite, I thought, and stepped back on to the pavement as a clanging fire engine raced across the square towards them. They hardly looked worth salvaging. Then a man passed me, carrying a small, bloodstained, still twitching bundle: he was crying, and his face close to – blackened, streaked with tears, the lips touched with blood where he had kissed his child – had a quality of piteousness dreadfully moving. It was clear that he did not know where he was going, for he stopped at the pavement's edge, and peered first at the roadway, and then at the burden in his arms, as if between them they could both state and solve his problem. One of the militiamen went over to him, and touched him on the shoulder, pointing towards the ambulance which had followed the fire engine; but the man shook his head once, slowly, and then held up what he carried in his arms so that the other could see more closely … Round them, and us, was smoke in drifting clouds, and that nostril-gripping smell, and the hot desolation that Franco's bombs had left in their wake.

And there were cries – some of them far away, some nearer, some sounding almost within one's brain.

The second militiaman, the one whose rifle I had borrowed, plucked suddenly at my elbow. "I'm going to help," he said, pointing at the wrecked houses. "Come with me?"

I nodded, and together we ran towards that stricken corner.

Here the whole street was almost blocked by a mass of rubble, fallen masonry, and shattered glass, on which the dust had hardly settled. Besides the two burning houses, towards which the hoses were now coiling, another house had been practically split in two – the top two floors laid bare like an opened doll's house, the jagged ends of the beams sagging down, the stairway clinging to the remaining wall as a drowning man grasps the smooth side of a pool. From somewhere underneath cries were coming, pitifully constricted: and as we drew level a man staggered

317

out of the wreckage, dragging something which could hardly have been alive. Following with my eye the sagging staircase I saw another body, wedged in a doorway on the half-landing, and with the militiaman I scrambled over the heap of rubble and began to climb the staircase towards it, thinking it might still live. Halfway up, a fresh fall of brick work raised a cloud of dust which set us both coughing and groping for the inside wall, but finally we reached our objective – though we might have saved ourselves the trouble. There were two bodies, or rather bits of them smeared together in a still warm purplish mass: the only recognizable part was a woman's face – young, untouched, surprised – and a booted foot: the rest would have been unsaleable as slaughterhouse offal.

I turned my eyes away, and met those of the militiaman. His were grave and level, in a face which seemed suddenly to have been deprived of its youth. Perhaps it had been deprived of something else besides, for suddenly, without warning, he bent down, and then raised a dripping hand to his forehead. There he made a smudged cross of blood, and said, in a thick shaking voice:

"*Sangre por sangre juro venganza!*"

Blood for blood I swear revenge … It was odd to be thus embarrassed, twenty feet up on the edge of a wrecked staircase; but I found the gesture melodramatic, and unreal for another very good reason – surely he must have seen a score of split corpses like these, surely his age (which was a little under mine) meant that he had already assisted at dozens of cleanings-up after air-raids … I looked away from him, and down at the firemen and salvagemen clambering over the ruins beneath us, and then at the crowd which had collected round the ambulance, beside which a row of figures lay, some being tended, some ready for burial. Street scene – there was nothing to it – I'd seen it before, often, and smelt the smoke and reek, and pieced together bits of people who within the hour had themselves found life beautiful or terrifying or overrated. This was politics *in excelsis*, this was how we settled our wrangles ... Someone in the crowd called up to know if the treasure-trove were alive, and I made in return that gesture which signifies 'Washout' or 'Goal disallowed'. Then, with the militiaman – whose face now betrayed a sulky fury – I set to work to sweep up and carry down. Someone had to do it, and already I didn't really mind the job, except that baths in Madrid were sometimes hard to come by.

I managed to see a little more of the town before the next raid started – notably the Gran Via (London parallel, Regent Street or Piccadilly), which was literally a ruin from end to end. Great stretches of it seemed to have collapsed entirely, strewing the street itself with brick and stone and glass: there were corpses everywhere, and overturned cars, and children being carried out and added to the pile, and houses split in two like dirty cheeses, and screaming, screaming, screaming to prove a hidden agony as well. It was the same all over Madrid, though I didn't learn that till later: blocks of working-class flats had been smashed to bits by huge bombs and aerial torpedoes, great fires were started whose flames served as torches to light the work of loading shattered humans, or scraps of humanity, on to lorries. In that one day's raiding, hundreds of tons of bombs were dropped, scores of buildings wrecked by high-explosive or fired by thermite, and upwards of 400 people killed.

But while I was in the Gran Via, trying to soothe a man until he could be taken away to an asylum, the sirens went again. This time we saw the planes, black and silver against a lovely sky. Some of us shook our fists at them as we ran to ground – puny rats that still retained the power to hate and to resist.

Back in Cuenza, just before what proved to be the last trip to Madrid.

This time the Renault was *en panne* in good earnest – would not even fire; and the rest of the convoy had to leave without us. For hour after hour José and I sweated away at the engine under the hot windless sky: we took it down completely, we scraped and cleaned and adjusted, we tested and made sure of this and that; and still the lorry confronted us – stupid, *terco*, motionless as seaweed at low tide. Night fell, and we were still working, by the light of a spluttering acetylene flare which cast great shadows against the garage wall: and then, about two o'clock, the engine responded for no reason at all to a tentative swing and burst into a roar of such shattering force that instinctively I ducked the coming bomb ... In the harsh light José grinned at me.

"*Está bien!*" he exclaimed. "Though for what reason ..." He looked at his watch. "Too late to start: you wait till the morning, when my lorry is loaded, and we will go together."

I shook my head. "You forget – we're carrying milk: another six hours might make all the difference to whether it goes sour or not. I'll wake your brother, and we'll get off now."

I could see that he didn't like the idea: he started to argue, he said, again and again: "*Aguárdeme, aguárdeme –* what does the milk matter? You have eggs and bread besides ..." But I won my point in the end, after promising to go slowly so that he could catch up with us. As we pulled out he was standing in the roadway, staring at his brother, giving the two of us a grave salute as if it were a charm against evil.

The time was just after dawn, a blood-red dawn that spread from the hills round Valencia like the blush of God for mankind. It was bitterly cold: under the strapped Cape-cart hood that icy draught blew continuously, freezing the flesh round my goggles, turning my lips stiff and raw. Occasionally, as we lumbered over the devilish bit of road between Chillarón and Villar de Domingo (the wheel kicking like a dinghy's tiller, the back-springs shouting 'Any old iron' with every clanking yard of progress), I turned to look at young Christ: invariably his mild grey eyes met mine, and his face above the absurd sheepskin collar would pucker in doubt. Was this discomfort within human endurance? it seemed to ask: were we not fools to have set out before the sun had taken the edge off the wind's bleakness? And, finally, would this ludicrous old *camion* survive another journey, or would it die on us at last, a faithful servant overwhelmed by misuse?

This time it *did* die on us, beyond resurrection.

Between Alcocer and Alhondiga, a filthy little village whose street was no more than a gutter soiled and clogged with offal, there were over thirty hairpin bends; and on many of these I could not get the lorry round on one lock, but had to back and turn, wrenching at the tough wheel, lurching on to the bank, knocking here and there a stone from a crumbling wall on the other side of which was a sheer drop of two or three hundred feet ... Up and up we went, the lorry shaking and shuddering, the pressure of steam from the radiator cap mounting like an angry plume: up and up, while Christ fiddled with his rickety Mauser pistol or wiped from his nose that drip which threatened to turn into an icicle, looking at me in gentle concern whenever a more ferocious lurch than usual came near to tipping us over the precipice: up and up, past farms still asleep, past the dead priest and the militiaman – now old friends to us – who still swung from the signpost at Sacerdon. We climbed with immense labour, my hands in their stiff gloves already trembling and nerveless: occasionally a sleepy sentry would delay us, standing there in the middle of the road – sixteen or seventeen years old, in blue dungarees or a looted khaki uniform, perhaps with a bandage round his head, waving a rifle like a semaphore; but always, before we came to a stop, he would smile and wave us on, with a flash of white teeth as we ground into gear again and gathered speed. "*Salud!*" I would call, and salute him with grave Marxist precision: and "*Idiotas!*" Christ would say, with young contempt, as soon as we were past. "He sees us nearly every day – why waste our time?"

As usual, we somehow got to the top and began the lumbering descent towards the flat plain-land round Armuña; but before we were halfway down I realized that the engine was no longer firing, and that we could only freewheel. Luckily there were fewer hairpins, and those not so acute, so that I had no need to stop and manoeuvre; but it was clear that our momentum would not carry us very far and that sooner or later we would have to stop and investigate. And if the engine had packed up altogether – well, the road might still be ours, in which case we could get a tow, or Franco's spearhead might have broken through and cut it, in which case we would feel pretty silly – for just so long as we had the faculty of feeling … I smiled in pure terror. What a superb target we would be, sitting in the middle of that plain down there: even a Moorish outpost on the Majadillas (if they had got no nearer) could pick us off like a couple of clay pipes at a fair.

Above the rattle and clanging of the crazy bodywork I shouted the news to Christ, and he smiled too – a much more genuine smile, I thought, than my own stricken grin had been. Then he spread his hands.

"What matter?" he shouted back. "I fix it … Go at top speed now: that will take us into the open where they can't surprise us."

I gave the lorry its wild head … Down we plunged, rocking like a swingboat, the solid tyres clipping and flipping at the loose stone surface, the steering-wheel bucking in my hands as if that uncertain front axle were already severed. Down, swiftly down: the trees sped past, the road dropped away before us unendingly; near the bottom a detachment of soldiers waved to us to stop, and would have fired had not Christ put his head round the windscreen and screamed at them to get out of the way. As they scattered we both shouted "*Salud!*" in a frenzy of excitement, while the lorry lurched right across the road and halfway up the opposite bank missing a tree by inches … Now I stood up and took a mighty grip of the wheel, ready for the last corner: as we went bucketing at it I felt the top heavy back of the lorry heeling over, but the wall seemed to be coming straight at us and I had to pull the wheel ever further round: immediately the inside tyres left the ground, hung in the air, came down again with a sickening thud that must have broken every egg we carried; and then we were round, and facing a straight stretch of road, and Christ was roaring with laughter and clapping me on the back as if I had personally just won the war …

I wasn't far from feeling the same myself.

After that it was easy – a gentle slope down that took us nearly two miles into the level plain. The wind of our passing died slowly, the bumping potholes grew gentler in their attack, the clanking bodywork subsided to the merest protesting creak; and when we came to rest it was at the beginning of a mile straight of road running between deserted fields with no house near and no sort of movement anywhere. I put on the stiff handbrake, more as a matter of form than anything else. The lorry looked, and felt, as if it had chosen its graveyard and would there sink to rest.

Christ hopped out briskly. "I fix it," he called back over his shoulder. "It will be nothing at all." The bonnet-cover clanked open, and his head disappeared from view. I smiled, lit a *caporal*, and looked about me.

The place seemed innocent enough; and it was good to be at peace again, with no sound save a stray bird singing, and the tinkering under the bonnet and bubbling of the radiator, and some gun-fire miles and miles away – perhaps far ahead on the Guadalajara itself ... Lazily I stretched, pulling at my cigarette, staring at this strange peaceful world in which we had been set down. The sun was well up now, but a haze hung over the plain in front and around the foothills on our right – those foothills which might either be ours or Franco's, safe or perilous ... The bodywork creaked, Christ grunted a muffled oath into the lorry's innards: ahead of me and behind, the plain stretched out, a strange uneasy oasis in the midst of a vicious terror. I couldn't understand why there was no troop movement. Had things moved on in the five days since our last trip? Or was that very hedge on my right stiff with Falangists or Moors, creeping up to surround us ...?

Suddenly unnerved, I called out: "How's it going, Christ?" and at my voice he straightened up and lifted a face smeared with oil.

"I think no good," he answered. "There's no spark – it must be the battery this time." He shrugged. "I try again, but maybe we stay here and wait for José."

"We can't." I frowned, preparing to get out and take a hand myself. "We don't even know whose country this is. Look at the target we make."

Before diving into the bonnet again he smiled so gaily that I was ashamed of my fears ...

But he was right: at the end of half an hour, in which there was still no movement round us, and only a rattle of machine-gun fire from up above Brihuega to remind us that we were at war, the lorry was still immovable. We abandoned the job finally, and climbed back into the cabin.

"So we wait," Christ said cheerily. "José will be here soon. Have you a cigarette for me?"

I gave him one, and routing about in my pockets produced a hunk of bread and a piece of garlic *salchichón* which I began to eat. The wine in my flask was by now sour and undrinkable: I poured it into the road. Then I tried to relax, taking the goggles from my forehead, feeling the faint sun unfreezing my face gradually; but I still could not conquer that feeling of uneasiness, of isolation: I visualized the picture we must make to other eyes – straight road, bright sunlight, single stranded lorry in the middle of this wide plain under a sky in which, distantly, a pall of smoke mounted and spread and converged again, like a tall clouded wine-glass ... That was what we looked like, that was what the target was.

Christ was munching an apple contentedly: suddenly he stopped, and put his head on one side. I heard it too – the far-away note of an engine. We both sat there, alert, listening to it. It grew louder: it might well have come from behind us.

"José," I said.

"Maybe." Then: "No, not José." He pointed straight ahead. "Look there."

I followed his pointing arm. In the sky to the north-west was a single speck, an aeroplane.

I sat silent, leaning forward on the steering wheel with my chin in my hands, and watched that aeroplane grow larger and take shape. It was coming from the direction of the main Madrid road, and flying not very high – about a thousand feet, as far as I could judge; as it drew nearer I could hear the rifle fire with which it was greeted, and make out an occasional burst of smoke as the anti-aircraft boys got busy. They did not seem to be getting anywhere very near it ... Within a few minutes we could distinguish its shape, but it wasn't one that either of us knew – it was neither Heinkel nor Caproni nor Savoia, nor anything like our own Russian model. When it was about two miles away, and might have passed us, it changed direction. It was coming to take a look at this strange derelict.

The noise of its engine was now quite loud. It did not seem to have any markings. Its fabric was silver-grey. The sun gleamed on it, attractively.

"It may be one of ours," said Christ in a low voice. I could tell that he was afraid, the same as I was. "It's *rather* like a little Russian."

"Coming from over there?"

"Returning from a raid, perhaps ... We shall soon know."

We *did* soon know.

When it was level with us it dropped quickly, circled, and flew past quite close. It was a small and battered biplane, something like an old Avro with a rotary engine, carrying two people and a fixed machine gun, firing through the airscrew, in front of the forward cockpit. We could see both men, helmeted and goggled, staring at us. We were very much alone, and quite helpless, sitting there at the head of that long road. When they had seen enough they climbed again, till they were about a mile away and straight in front of us.

"They're going away again," said Christ, rather shakily. "It *was* one of ours after all." He let his breath out with a long sigh. "For a moment I thought – "

He never completed that sentence, or any other sentence.

The aeroplane turned, on a neat half roll, and started to power-dive at us. A sighting spatter of machine gun bullets, a sort of gentle tuning-up, hit the ground about a hundred yards ahead.

I stared at it, frozen. "We ought to get out," I said, almost to myself, like a man hypnotized. "We ought to get under the lorry. No, we won't have time. Perhaps they'll ..."

Then I stopped speaking. There was really no use. The line of bullets was travelling up the road towards us, in a track admirably straight. They – no, it was the engine, of course – made a truly hellish noise, so that instinctively I put my hands to my ears. It was the sort of noise that no human being could endure: it was shattering, it rang with terror, it was straight from the mouth of Hades.

Stiff with panic, I watched the bullets cutting a swathe down the grey strip of road straight at us. They made a jangle of dust and flying stones, but no noise above the fiendish roar of the engine. They were a few yards away, they were here, spraying the lorry before the instant of flattening out. The windscreen went, ripped to pieces: a streak of jagged light came through the hood; and as the noise rose to its final hideous crescendo something tugged at my shoulder, something searingly hot. I felt rather than saw the blood welling out of my numbed arm, through the oily overalls and the torn coat.

"Good lord!" I said foolishly, in the diminishing roar of the engine. I felt rather dramatic – a Wounded Soldier. "That got my arm."

Then I looked at Christ.

Christ was certainly dead. A bullet – several bullets – had gone clean through his mouth and throat. No, clean wasn't quite the word … The blood welled and dripped, while I stared at his surprised eyes and smooth brown forehead above that shattered chin with the bone-splinters sticking through. Without a chin or throat – with just a *gap* – his face was curiously characterless. He looked weak, and vaguely annoying, as chinless people do. I wished his eyes would close. He was so young and astonished. What would José say when I told him?

"Poor Christ!" I said aloud. I knew his parents – and his girl. We'd been drinking *vino tinto* twelve hours before. ("So you've got a girl?" I had asked him. "Sure, a fine girl," he

327

had answered; and he had offered to get me one as well, so that I could settle down and be happy in Spain.) Jesus Christi Martinez, fifteen-and-three-quarter years old, with bullets through his mouth, jaw, and throat. What cause was worth that?

We had called him Christ because it sounded rather funny.

I was sick, and then my arm began to hurt.

And then I heard the aeroplane – or rather, I didn't hear it; for suddenly its engine, which had reached a curious high note, almost a howl, cut out, and when I glanced out of the cabin I saw the machine circling in powerless silence, looking for a place to come down.

It made a good three-point landing on the bumpy field a hundred yards to my right.

Both crews waited, without a sound: all I could hear was blood dripping on to the floor beside me, and a bird, like a nightingale only sweeter, singing its heart out somewhere near by. The two men in the aeroplane were motionless, watching me for the first move; and when I had taken one more look at Christ I decided what that move was going to be. Easing my revolver from its holster I dropped it into my overcoat pocket, and then I opened the cabin door and jumped the six feet into the road. I saw that milk was running out of the back of the lorry and losing itself in the dusty road surface. Milk dripping, blood dripping, my shoulder dripping – a formal pattern of violence ... I began to walk towards the stranded plane.

When I was within twenty yards of it the man in the forward cockpit turned from his fixed gun and covered me with a revolver. I put my hands up, but kept on walking until I was just below it. There I stopped, and waited. I noticed that the airscrew had only one blade left – the other had been broken off short just by the boss, leaving a jagged stump.

Presently the man in the rear cockpit heaved himself out of his seat and stood leaning forward, elbows on the edge of the fuselage, looking down at me. He was a big man, with a tough brown face and wiry hair: his white overalls strained across his shoulders as he towered over me. The revolver was still covering me: the gunner – blond, and close-cropped in the German fashion – was also staring at me unwinkingly. He was in uniform, with a black helmet hanging low round his neck and goggles pushed up over his forehead.

After a moment the big man said, in an American accent: "Well you've got a nerve ..." And then: "*Habla Inglés?*"

"More than you," I answered. "Can I take my hands down – I haven't got a gun, and my arm's giving me hell."

"Christ, a limey!" He jerked upwards and laughed loudly, so that his companion looked at him in surprise. "A limey wanting a shave ... Sure, put 'em down – but don't start anything, because Fritz here is kind of nervous."

He signed to the gunner, who lowered his revolver.

"*Guten Tag,*" I said to the latter amiably. "*Haben Sie viel geschossen in der letzten Zeit?*"

He stuck out his chin. "*Halts Maul, rotes Schwein!*"

"He doesn't like your sort," said the American. "Nor do I, for that matter. How come you're fighting for those bums of Reds ... Oh well, that's your worry. What d'you think you're going to do now?"

"Well, what are you?"

"God knows. This antique's finished." He nodded towards the shattered airscrew. "The machine-gun did that – synchronizing-gear packed up – that last dive was no bromide. Say, I joined this war for the fun of it – and then I go and knock my own prop off ..."

"Why did you shoot at us?"

"I thought maybe you was explosives. What were you, anyway?"

"Eggs. Milk. And a boy. You got the lot."

"Sorry, pal …" He looked round him. "Mighty quiet here: we could get out of it, at that."

"You won't," I told him. "You're twenty miles behind our lines."

The German began to fidget, and then shouldered his way out of the cockpit. Side by side they stood there, in their useless machine: a hundred yards away was the derelict lorry, its chassis high off the ground, its khaki hood flapping, its young and tragic burden hidden.

"Well, I'm all right," said the American: "they wouldn't shoot me. But this guy's for the jump, I reckon: they don't like Hitler in these parts, do they?"

"No."

And then, quite suddenly, the German gave a grunt and crumpled up: a moment afterwards I heard a single shot, from somewhere to the north … He hung down over the side of the cockpit like a draped flag, blood oozing from a neat hole in the back of his neck and dripping into the suspended helmet – the tin cup under the inverted whisky bottle.

"Nice shooting," said the American calmly. He must have had magnificent nerves: he never moved, or tried to take cover. "But they won't get another natural like that one … What do I do next?"

"Don't ask me." I jerked my thumb over my shoulder. "You machine-gunned me, and you shot a kid through the throat." I noticed that he wasn't attending but was looking about him, drawn by the sound of another shot, which must have gone wide. I dropped my hand on to the revolver inside my coat pocket, and came a step nearer, till I was standing just beside the limply lolling German. "He was only sixteen," I said, trying to make my voice normal. "Don't ask me to help you."

"This is war, sap!" he answered roughly, turning back again. "Don't be a daisy – it was you against me, see? But that's over now: you're English, I'm American – that makes it so's you give me a hand."

"You're Fascist."

"Aw hell, what's the label mean? I'm flying this crate because the dough's good … Reckon I'll surrender," he went on after a pause. "Even these Red runts will respect an American citizen."

"Respect?"

"Sure, you know – safe conduct and all that mush. I've got my passport." He was beginning to clamber out of the cockpit, twisting sideways on to me: to get down he would have to turn his back completely. I watched him with a dry throat, my hand loosely round the revolver, the blood beating at the wound in my shoulder: he was broad, and his suit of grey-white overalls was close-fitting. With one leg hanging down he began to feel for the single rung outside the fuselage; and as he did so he called out over his shoulder: "Give me a hand to fire the plane. And then I'll go find a patrol."

"I'll save you the trouble," I said softly, and shot him twice in the back.

It must have severed something in his spine, because he didn't make a sound, except the single thud as he hit the ground, and the flop of his hands as he rolled over.

CHAPTER FOURTEEN

You do look, my son, in a moved sort,
As if you were dismay'd.

SHAKESPEARE, *The Tempest*

❖

"Don't be a fool," said Markham, shaking the thermometer down and feeling my pulse at the same time, the whole thing with a professional air which one hardly looked for in a medical student. "You can't go out for at least another week."

"But I feel all right," I told him, lying on the dirty pillows and starting to count the birds on the wallpaper again. "I'm only depressed, not ill."

He put the thermometer away in its little metal case. "Now listen to me," he began decisively. "That shoulder of yours is still in a mess, and wants resting. And you've just had flu, which might have been something a great deal worse, considering the state you were in when you made the journey back. Unless you want to crack up completely, you must give everything a rest. You can't go back to meetings and street corners as if you were normal."

"Good God! I don't want to start political work again: I feel as if I could never make another speech in my life, or even look at a newspaper. But I'm sick of lying here, scribbling away at nothing in particular: not *doing* anything."

"There's nothing for you to do except get properly well again. Are the Jimpsons looking after you all right?"

"Yes, they're angelic."

He began to gather up his things. "Well, you be angelic as well: stay here, don't use that arm, and drink the stuff I'm going to have made up for you."

"I'm damned if I pay you any sort of fee for this."

He laughed. "Did you imagine I expected one? Nowadays I can tell a bilker a mile away."

When he had gone I lay in the semi-darkness of the Carter Street room and tried to think, as I had been thinking during the past weeks, of the next step. Spain had done something to me, as far as politics were concerned. Remembering the hate and slaughter, remembering José's face as he came to a standstill behind the stranded Renault and I walked back with my blood-covered arm to deliver the news – with this as the background of political action, how could I start on the same road again? Cummings had come round, just after I got back, to commiserate with me on my illness and hear the latest reports from the front; and there had been something in his eager, almost gleeful air, as he listened to my account, that had caused a profound revulsion.

Jack Wentworth, the journalist, was another visitor, a rather more understanding one: he didn't press me for details of the fighting, and I think he realized perfectly well why I didn't want to talk about it. He came in one afternoon when I was sitting up in bed, doing, as a last resort, a crossword puzzle.

"God, you look ill!" he said at once. "How are you?"

"Ill, I suppose," I answered defensively. "You don't leave me much choice. Sit down."

But he ranged about the room, examining what appointments there were. "How was Spain?" he asked presently, toying with the little Fabergé paperknife.

"Awful," I said. "In fact, too awful to talk about. It made me do things, Jack – well, when I look at them now in cold blood I think I must have been entirely mad. It cured me of wanting to fight, for the rest of my life: it's too filthy a business to join in, whether you're defending democracy or trying to kick it down the drain."

"I know," he answered, suddenly depressed. "I spent all last week making up atrocity stories for the paper … I thought of a swell one when I was in the Café Royal one night – a nun with one leg tied to a lamp-post and the other to a motor lorry: the lorry is slowly driven off while the Red rabble cheers. It'll be headlined next week. Oh, I've got a grand job."

"Cheer up. What's the news otherwise?"

He brightened a little, and started to enlarge on current topics: his blighting cynicism, heritage of all good newspapermen, was just the sort of tonic I needed. He finished up with: "And there's a hell of a story coming pretty soon – about the end of the week, though we've had the type set up, with variations, for the last month or more. It's the King: he wants to marry Mrs Simpson before the Coronation."

"Good God!" I said instinctively. She had been journalistic gossip a long time before I went to Spain; and I had seen some cuttings from the American tabloids which emphasized their own mature version of the facts. And then: "Well, why not? Everyone says she's intelligent and attractive – it'll make a change. And what a kick in the eye for the Old Guard!"

"The Old Guard will win. Just you wait, Marco: they'll turn him out sooner than have a queen they don't approve of. And don't forget they've got a ready-made king and queen waiting to take his place if he cuts up rough."

"M'm," I said vaguely.

"Don't you believe it?"

"I don't give a damn either way. Nor should you. What difference does it make who's on the throne? The monarchy is surrounded by a great mass of privilege and snobbery and plutocratic insolence: change that, and I'll see if I can raise some interest."

He laughed. "You're pretty low, aren't you? I thought I was bringing you a nice fruity story."

"A story for morons and scandalmongers. Whether he goes or stays, the system is the same." I dropped my head on the pillow. "And I'm not sure whether I give a damn whether *that's* changed, either: it'll last out my time on earth, so I might as well make the best of it."

And that was, in truth, all the thought I gave to the Abdication, which left, for me, only two minor hangovers. First was a genuine doubt as to the strength and basis of royalist feeling in Great Britain, having regard to the fact that a man 'enthroned in our hearts' for over forty years could be swopped over the weekend, for someone entirely different. "Today," said Mr Buchanan, during the debate in the House of Commons, "I have listened to more cant and humbug than I have ever listened to before. Without doubt you will go on praising the next king as you have praised this one. But if he was a tenth as good as you say, why are you not keeping him?" It was one of the loudest why's I have ever heard unanswered. The second point concerned the part played by the Church. It seemed to me at the time that the outburst of anti-clericalism which followed the Abdication was a trifle unfair: both the Bishop who first called attention to the King's 'lack of grace', and the Archbishop who rounded off the matter by rebuking, with some measure of indignation, his circle of friends, were only doing their traditional job. The job, of course, need not be confused with Christianity in any form save the official one: charity and forgiveness may be in the book of words, but they are no part of the fabric of the Established Church; and given this cleavage, it was naturally a bishop who cast the first stone, and a very prince of the Church who administered the final kick to the fallen man ... Perhaps the Archbishop's words in his broadcast were a trifle exuberant: even the sternest ritualists were ready to concede that they were not the very accents of Christ; but in the main the Church fulfilled its historic role with skill and agility, and if it became unpopular in the process – well, the martyr's crown is as authentic a tribute as can be found anywhere.

One more visitor called on me before I got up for good – someone particularly welcome. I was lounging on my bed waiting for the kettle to boil, and wondering why the three sterling articles I had written during the past week had been returned with such promptitude, when there was a knock at the door. In answer to my shout there entered, with a smile, Dr Barrow.

"Cummings told me you weren't well," he said, "so I've come to form my own opinion." He shook my hand, and then held on to it for a moment. "I'm extremely glad to see you again, but what have you been doing with yourself?"

"Oh, I'm perfectly all right – just a bit run down. I got hit in the shoulder, and then I collected some sort of germ just afterwards. But don't worry yourself because I'm in the doctor's hands already."

He smiled. "I'm an amateur now, and I can be as unprofessional as I like. Is the arm painful?"

"On and off."

"Let me have a look at it."

He probed about a bit, asked questions, made me do a series of movements and exercises. Presently, when he was bandaging it again: "An inch or two to the right would have been a far more serious matter," he said. "As it is, you will escape with nothing more than a slight stiffness. Who dressed this, by the way?"

"A friend of mine, a medical student."

"It is well done. Has he prescribed you a tonic?"

"Yes. And if you'd prescribe a tastier one, I'd take it very kindly."

"I'm afraid that is outside my province altogether ... Shall I make tea?"

We talked idly and pleasantly, enjoying each other's company after the three months' separation. I saw that, without any special effort, he was keeping right away from the subject of Spain, and I suddenly realized that I did not mind whether he brought it up or not – he was the one person from whom I could stand any question and any judgment. So when presently a silence fell between us, I said: "You were right about Spain – they'll never reach any sort of balance or agreement in this way."

He nodded. "Then it was not only the bullet wound which brought you out? Did the fighting itself shock you? I imagined that your mind was sufficiently – robust to withstand a reaction from it."

"I shocked myself – I was getting a damned sight too robust. I was taking the horrors for granted, I was joining in and enjoying it. And there *were* horrors." I told him something of the air-raids, of the facility in murder to which I had attained, of Christ's death in the lorry. "I think that finished me," I said finally. "It didn't seem possible that with so much death and treachery and hatred we could be doing right. Socialists shouldn't hold life cheaply like that – it's a negation of the whole creed."

He nodded again. "That is perfectly true – I'm glad you've been able to see it so soon. I wish all your side had learned the lesson as quickly."

"But we can't allow Fascism to – " and then I stopped, suddenly aware that there were a great many things in which I no longer believed with anything like the previous enthusiasm. "I dare say you're right," I went on more quietly. "I'm in the hell of a muddle at the moment – half of me knows that we ought to take a crack at Fascism whenever the opportunity occurs, and the other half has learnt, in Spain, that to join in that sort of struggle simply extends the chaos by one more man, and puts a just settlement so much further away. And that must be true of any war, international as well as civil."

He smiled. "And so, pacifism?"

I dropped my head. "God knows – I don't ... Does Christianity cover it? We've been hanging priests where I've come from," I added irrelevantly. "But real Christianity – the *man's* teaching, without the officialdom and the myths and the conjuring tricks – that might be the answer."

"He taught a way of life which has never been surpassed," the doctor agreed gravely. "Separated from its elaborations and irrelevances, as you wish it to be, it supplies a model course of conduct, and one that has been continuously applicable, and as continuously ignored, for nearly two thousand years. I take it that you are agnostic?" And as I nodded: "That is of no account," he went on: "we are concerned with human perfectability, not extra-human survival ... The expectation of eternal life is a comforting doctrine, particularly to people of my age; but I have never had any conviction of it, except in moments of cowardice or despair, and so I have been denied its comfort. That has not stopped me from doing my best to love my neighbour – a rule of life which has always seemed of basic necessity in any working towards a balanced state."

He was sitting in the armchair by the fire, his head sunk deep in his chest, his tired face with the thin grey hair above it blurred by the increasing dusk of the room. He seemed to me to be some kind of saint … And, in confusion with my own thought, I could draw comfort from his determination and sanity: he had things settled in his mind, not because that mind was prejudiced or bigoted, but by the simple fact of its charity. He had the strength to be consistent, and a kind of selective genius as well, which ensured that he was consistent about the right things, as well as tolerant of the unright … I wondered what chances I myself had of attaining to his stature. And then, as if he read my thoughts: "You are young and confused," he said gently, turning towards the bed and meeting my eyes. "But despair at the age of twenty-three is premature." He smiled suddenly. "Wait till you are my age, and have really plumbed the depths."

I decided that I felt better already. And a lot more of the dark mood was presently blown away by Malloy, who rolled into the room, patently unsober, and invited us to have a drink on the old country. I had imagined, from the stage Irishmen I had seen, that he would call Dr Barrow "y'r honour" or even "y'r rivverence", but he confounded this view by addressing him as "me boyo" – which was a great deal more than I would have undertaken.

"Be cheery!" he cried, after greetings had been exchanged. "Sure, don't you know 'tis Christmas Eve, and a great day for the whole world? I'll go down and get a little bottle now, and we'll be making on occasion of it."

We made an occasion of it. The two of them got on famously: they even sang. Later Markham came in, to dress my shoulder, and made a good fourth and a generous contributor in the whisky line. The shabby little room expanded glowingly, leaving human goodwill and contentment in no doubt whatsoever. Spain, with its bloodshed and treachery, was far away – was hardly on the same earth at all. Safe among my friends, I drank and laughed and stopped thinking.

That was Christmas. New Year's Eve was different.

Sentimentally inclined, I determined to make for Westminster Bridge, as I had done the last few years; but I very nearly failed to get there, not because of the crowds but because of someone I met. For when I left the house, my arm in a tight sling, and was halfway down Praed Street – garish, noisy, flaring with liquor – I noticed something familiar in the small man just in front of me; and having caught him up, I found it was Dobson, the gatekeeper at Nine Beeches.

He was astonished, and delighted, but presently, in the pub where we went for a drink, I became aware of how much he had changed. It was not only that he was meanly dressed, and unshaven, and looked ill: there was something about his manner which made him seem furtive, and his face was shut-in and mistrustful. The merry little man of my childhood, with his kindnesses and shrewd good humour, had become, as it were, urbanized and second-rate. And when I asked for his story:

"I reckon you can see what's happened to me, Mr Marcus," he said bitterly, with a glance down at his loose-hanging suit and dirty scarf. "The old house was sold – ay, it's buildin' lots now, with a lot of little roads cuttin' up Wood End Spinney, and the foreman's hut where yer ma's rose garden used to be … Of course there was no job for me there – I've been on the parish for the best part of a year, until I couldn't stand it any longer." He sniffed and sipped his drink, sitting forlorn on one corner of the bench: a single glance told you that he was one of the defeated. "So I left the village and came here. I've had a bit of jobbing gardening, but that was in the summer, and you can't get that sort of work at this time of year."

"But what about the family?" I asked, struck by his hopeless air. "Isn't Mrs Dobson with you?"

For a moment he hesitated, his face seemed to hide itself in a cunning extension of the secrecy which I had noticed when I met him: and then suddenly it cleared, as if for the first time he had found someone he could trust.

"I'd better tell you, sir," he said: "your family was good to me in the old days ... I – I cut and run from Nine Beeches, Mr Marcus: there was a bit of trouble about a sack of coal, and I was bound over. Sir George was very kind, he gave me some money outside the court, but I couldn't stand the whisperin' and the gossip in the village. And of course there was nothin' comin' in: Mrs Dobson was wonderful, like she's always been, but she couldn't do miracles." He stared straight in front of him, reliving the crushed months. "I stood it as long as I could, and then I got sick of it, not seein' anything different in the future, not for the rest of my life, and I ran away. I reckon she and the kids are on the parish," he concluded: "I send them something now and then, when I've got a few shillin's to spare, but it's not easy, it's not easy." He looked at me suddenly. "It doesn't sound too good, does it, Mr Marcus? But perhaps if you'd been in my place – you don't know what it's like sir, to go on like that for weeks and months, and not see any change comin'. It makes you desperate, so that you'll do anything rather than stop still."

It was hard to find any answer which would comfort him, quite apart from the sense of futility brought home to me by the manner in which he had put a barrier between us. That barrier I had met so many times before, in dealing with all sorts of people both within the Party and outside: I was gentlyborn and brought up in luxury, I 'couldn't understand' what it meant to be poor, not for a romantic year or so but from one end of life to the other ... Sometimes it seemed to me that this clean-cut division between the proletarian and the 'intellectual' could never be resolved: there must always be mistrust on one side and embarrassment and a hint of patronage on the other. And if this were a self-conscious view which might disappear with the passage of time, yet at moments like these it came into prominence so sharply that the conviction seemed inescapable that a movement grounded in the masses could have no use for me.

I turned back from my thoughts to Dobson, still sitting downcast before his half empty glass.

"I'm very sorry indeed that this has happened," I began slowly. "It's our fault really – we should have been strong enough to take care of you, and we failed when the test came." But surely I oughtn't to be saying that: workers engaged in employment of a parasitic or feudal nature should renounce such tasks and join the revolutionary struggle ... "I wish you had got in touch with me earlier: I might have been able to help you, though I'm not exactly rich myself."

He looked at me curiously, with something of the old relationship in his manner – the kindly servant sympathizing with juvenile scrapes and difficulties.

"How are things with you, Mr Marcus?" he asked after a moment. "You're not at college any more, are you?"

"Oh no, I've been working for over a year now – writing for the newspapers."

"Newspapers, is it? You'll need a good head on you for that, I dare say. What sort of things would you be writin'? Stories?"

The talk drifted, far away from any point and bringing no sense of leisure or comfort: I should have said straight away that I was working for Socialism, that that was the only thing worth working for, and that he should join me; I should have thought of him as a natural ally, and of course I didn't think anything of the sort ... I gave him five pounds when we parted, and told him to come round to Carter Street whenever he liked: but afterwards, making my way through the cold clear night towards Westminster Bridge, I could not be pleased with anything about the encounter. In spite of all I had learnt and thought since I had last met Dobson, I had got nowhere near him, as a man, on this occasion: the relationship had been exactly the same as formerly, and I had accepted it as a natural one – as if there were no such idea as the level comradeship of man in the whole world. And of course, giving him five pounds solved no problems at all: rather did it point their patent insolubility, for as far as the master-and-man question went, five quid was ludicrously inadequate for a man who had been dependent on us for half his working life, while at the other end of the scale the giving of money in such a case was a degrading act which denied, in the most insolent fashion, the equality of mankind.

Five pounds ... I walked now along a cold Whitehall, leaving behind the gathering uproar of Trafalgar Square, packed with people who shouted and waved balloons, as if the last quarter hour of the old year had some especial quality of triumph which must be acclaimed at top pitch. Five pounds ... I had no wish to indulge a sense of romantic generosity, but I could not help remembering that the sum was exactly half my remaining capital: I had drawn it out of the bank that morning, and it had been meant to last me a month or more ... I had earned nothing since I came back from Spain, and the journey itself had entailed expense: my clothes were now in a wretched state, I hadn't been to the dentist for nearly a year (though a visit was obviously necessary), and on this last day of 1936 there seemed no prospect of any improvement in my circumstances – if I couldn't sell something by the end of January I should have to pass the hat round or try (dressed like a down-at-heels corner boy) to get some sort of job. It would mean a prodigious amount of crawling in either case – and the worst of it was, I felt quite ready for the exercise.

There were not many people on Westminster Bridge: half a dozen parked cars with people standing on the seats leaning out of the sliding roofs, an intent couple who, staring at each other, were out of the tide of time altogether, a party of assorted drunks with the precarious exaltation of their own balloons. It was bitingly cold: leaning over the parapet to glance at the black flow of water, one saw there mirrored only a conviction of frustration and futility. Better to watch the moonfaced clock, better to think of the hopeful future … Near me was an old man with a filthy grey beard, drooped against the balustrade, seeming to mourn the coming burden of days and the necessity of shielding the hated, unwanted spark. I felt sad about him, and Dobson, and politics, and my lost sister Tania, and Spain, and being broke: about my shoes with their wretched flapping soles, my suit with its seams and turn-ups held together by safety-pins, its shiny trousers, its frayed and spreading cuffs. The only difference between the old tramp and myself seemed that he had found there was no prize in the endurance test: living was its own reward, its own mean justification … Carter Street was so cold this weather. I would have to go to the bank again in the morning. And Alison had been married three days before – strictly speaking, I shouldn't have given a damn for the fact, for it oughtn't to matter whether she were married or in love or in the casual ward for young ladies at Gloucester; but it did matter, it seemed to be the final thrust … When you're alone and you hear that sort of news suddenly, when you have nothing to avenge yourself on, then it hurts.

Silent under the indifferent moon, we waited for midnight and the new year to strike.

PART THREE

❖

Personal

CHAPTER FIFTEEN

By our first strange and fatall interview,
By all desires which thereof did ensue.

JOHN DONNE, *Elegie XVI*

❖

When she drew back again, still looking at me with an intent self-possession, I thought she was going to speak; however, she kept silent, and I understood that she was waiting for the clock to finish striking. (Ever afterwards, we understood the reason for the smallest or strangest of each other's actions.) But when the new year was ninety seconds old, and she was still silent (wanting to find out by some word or action of mine the sort of person with whom she was dealing), I glanced away from her and towards the two people in the open car she had just left – a man and a fair girl, both laughing – and then said, in as level a tone as I could manage: "Thank you for that ... And the happiest New Year to you."

We were staring at each other again: I knew that she had noticed my shabby clothes, and was not exactly discounting them but viewing them in their true unessential perspective. She had lovely eyes, and as I felt

347

their compassionate directness meeting mine on an exact level, and then glanced without inquisitiveness over the rest of her – slim and fresh under the dreary bridge lamp – I could find no one within my memory with whom to compare her. It was not solely that she was lovelier than anyone with whom I had had the smallest contact before (with a *deep* loveliness, as unlike, for example, Helga Sangstrom's dazzling blondeness or the groomed showgirl slickness and *embarras de bichesse* of Denise as anything could be): but in addition, though she had done this very curious thing, she was now confronting me with honesty and candour, in command of the situation and yet somehow showing that she would put it into my hands, if these were gentle and competent …

"It was a bet, really," she said presently, while our eyes still held each other. Then she laughed. "But now I'm not so sure …"

That also I understood, and glowed suddenly at the honour she was doing me. But it still needed elaboration.

"What bet?" I asked. "To kiss the first man you saw after the clock struck? No, it wouldn't be that – not quite."

She smiled again. "No, it was a better bet than that. We were feeling happy tonight" – with a graceful movement of her head, like a dark curling wave, she indicated the other two occupants of the car – "but as we drove along we saw more and more people who weren't happy at all, looking as if they could hardly bear the idea of the New Year. And when we got here on the bridge, to wait for the clock to strike, we thought we ought to do something about it."

I understood now. "You were looking for the most depressed individual you could find?" And when she nodded: "Well, I'm glad I can win some sort of championship," I went on, lost in her eyes and the shape of her mouth. "But suppose the man had been – unsuitable, or if it had been a woman?"

"Money," she answered gently. "It's no more of a panacea than a kiss on the cheek," she brought the words out without change of inflection, "but it was the best we could think of. Money for people who looked as if they needed it: and for those who wanted – " and there she hesitated, searching my face with a sudden questioning intensity, "who wanted comfort, who might be glad of an odd surprise, we thought that kissing them gently would probably work."

"You were right … And you chose me?"

"Easily. Why was that?"

I shrugged. "Lots of things. I've been standing here in a swamp of self-pity for the last quarter of an hour."

"Does your arm hurt?" She had a lovely deep voice: it made one think of her heart.

"Yes. Not much though." I looked at her with more practical eyes. "Haven't I seen you somewhere before?"

She laughed. "Let's keep this out of the ordinary, shall we?"

"That wasn't the Brighton voice." But even the disavowal was cheapening to the occasion, and I broke away from it swiftly. "You've put me in such a different mood – there was a wretched old tramp here just before the clock struck, and I might have been his twin as far as high spirits went: but now – that cure of yours – " my voice petered out foolishly. How difficult it was not to impose on that enchanting moment when she had crossed the pavement towards me: how difficult to be grateful without exaggerating the moment's significance or taking the future for granted … But now, as so many times later, she took competent charge of the situation.

"The cure was – a cure," she said evenly. "When it's over it can be lost sight of." She gave her voice a questioning lift at the end.

I nodded. "Agreed."

"Very well. But if you like to make a fourth in the car, on those terms, you're very welcome."

"Well ..."

"Money?"

"Yes."

"We have some. Alternatively, we won't spend any." She turned away from me, and towards the car: the slight movement had a certain sadness about it, marking as it did the end of one intensely personal scene and the merging of it in the general flow of events. Perhaps she recognized this – in fact, certainly she did, for she laid her hand on my arm, and said gently: "It won't be any different. You'll like these people. You were their choice too."

Then she led me the few yards which separated us from the car.

It was close to the kerb under a lamp, and as I stood there and met in turn the eyes of the fair-haired girl and the solid young man who were its passengers, I was immediately conscious of my disreputable clothes and especially of my shoes, the soles of which seemed to gape like jaw-dropped fish in the revealing lamplight. But it was clear that they had not noticed, or perhaps that they took them for granted: they were looking only at my face, and that with an attention into which the idea of appraisement somehow did not enter at all. The girl resembled clearly the one who had crossed the pavement towards me, but her face had a fine-drawn intensity instead of the oval rounded strength of the other – she was pretty rather than lovely, and immature in some degree, and perhaps nervous. Her voice, when she said: "How nice to meet someone like that!" compared oddly with the low poised tones to which I had been listening during the last few minutes.

I heard them again, gratefully, as my companion introduced me.

"That is Tim Hannay," she said, her hand still lightly on my arm, "and this is my half sister Elisabeth. And my name's Anthea – Anthea Lorensen."

"I've seen a lot of your pictures," I answered. "In fact I used to have one myself."

She smiled. "So I actually have a public."

"It doesn't need me to prove that ... I'm very glad to have met you." And I was glad, independently of the circumstances of the meeting. Anthea Lorensen was much publicized and much written-up in the smoother weeklies – so much indeed that one might have supposed that her reputation owed everything to publicity and nothing at all to painting; but this was far from the truth, and one had only to come upon something of hers in a gallery – a Negro head against a flaming sky, a child playing with the buckle of its shoe, or that little steel engraving of wood nymph and shepherd which I had had to sell to Julian – to realize her quality. For her pictures *meant* something, they were not only technically flawless but cunning in their presentation of ideas: she could express emotion and invoke sympathy with more sheer economy of line than one would have thought possible, no matter what triumphs of techniques were accomplished.

And now here she was, standing by my side, exactly the same height as myself – far lovelier than her photographs, with immense grey eyes set wide apart, and masses of dark hair (long, but cunningly ordered at the nape of her neck), and a mouth of that shape which, formed as it were a little outward to display its frank vitality to the world, curves so easily to laughter or trembles, in childish unhappiness at the contemplation of cruelty. She was carelessly dressed (as all of them were), but it seemed neither a self-conscious nor an ill-kempt negligence: her loose Jaeger coat and red scarf completed a picture not of Bloomsbury rag-baggery but of an attractively conceived and brilliant freedom. I got

351

the impression, straight away, that she disdained to make a god of her clothes, but could have beaten, hands down, those who did, whenever she cared to make the effort.

"You paint admirable pictures," I said slowly, feeling humble. I looked round the trio, and guessed them to be alive, effective, and genuine: if this were true, I had much to envy them ... "There is nothing to commend me. My name is Marcus Hendrycks."

"Good evening, comrade," said the fair girl called Elisabeth.

I stared. "How did you know that?"

"I heard you speak once, in Hyde Park. And later in Trafalgar Square. You were talking about Spain. Did you go there?"

"Yes. I've just come back."

"The arm?" asked Tim Hannay.

"Yes."

"It was a lovely speech," said Elisabeth. "I put half a crown into the box afterwards."

"Thank you ... But I didn't get the collection myself: it went to the Scottish Ambulance. Are you – er – ?" I made the clenched-fist sign.

"No," said Anthea. "I used to be – and then somehow I seemed to get past politics altogether. Elisabeth doesn't know an anarchist from a municipal reformer – in fact, I can't imagine why she was listening to you – and Tim is true-blue."

"Oh ..."

"It's all right," he said, "you needn't like it. I paint pictures as well – better than Anthea's, but not so well advertised."

He didn't look in the least like a painter: in fact, he reminded me of Charles Terrington – the same mahogany toughness, the same six-foot-three of barrel-chest and sloping shoulder. He had thick wiry hair cut almost *en brosse*, and a prizefighter's chin: one could imagine him in a South Seas bar laying about him with a bottle, but hardly as wielding anything so delicate as a brush or painting anything less robust than the side of a hotel. Later, however, when I got to know his work, I was to discover in it, and in him, a delicacy and a fastidiousness which gave the lie to the whole outer man; and his strange relationship with the girl Elisabeth, with its almost unreal submission to her own hesitancy, was the sign-manual of this delicacy, which informed and ruled his whole nature.

"But you write, don't you?" he volunteered suddenly. "Haven't you had some stuff in the *Yachting News*?"

"A fair amount, yes. Do you sail?"

He nodded. "I've got a boat at Dover, a cutter – fifteen tons, rather clumsy and tough, but fit to go anywhere. We were across-Channel last week, as a matter of fact, and got the tail-end of the gale coming back, but she didn't turn a hair."

" 'She' is *not* me," interjected Anthea gravely.

I laughed. "Winter sailing? You must take the sport seriously."

"He certainly does," Elisabeth chimed in. "All we have to do is make rum-and-coffee, and take it up to the wheel every half-hour. Tim does everything else, including the brandy smuggling."

"Hannay!" I exclaimed suddenly, realizing why the name was familiar. "You were second in the Fastnet the year I was crewing on *Calliope*. Remember *Calliope*, the yawl? Remember cross-tacking up the Channel, five miles on each leg with us heading you every time?"

He smiled broadly. "Do I not? You'd have beaten us easily, barring that top-mast going. We heard it, you know, though we must have been a couple of miles to leeward: for a moment I thought – "

The dark-haired Anthea interrupted us with a smile. "You gentlemen," she said, "may be interesting each other, but you're deadly bores as far as we're concerned. This is New Year's Eve, you know – not guest-night at the Little Ship Club."

"Of course," said Tim Hannay to me, "we could go off somewhere by ourselves ..."

They knew each other extremely well, these three. Anthea turned immediately to Elisabeth. "Do we call that bluff?"

Charmingly worried: "Well, I hope not," Elisabeth answered. "I rather want Tim tonight."

Irresistibly, I found myself meeting Anthea's eye.

"In default of a parallel indication – " I began.

"After five minutes?" She laughed, deep in her throat, deep in her eyes. "That rate would burn us out in a week."

But that was the moment when the possibility was born.

I took it on myself to restore a surface normality: for though there had been something between us – a thread rather than a spark – ever since her lips touched my cheek on the bridge, yet the thread must still be fragile, and a single false touch (which she would be quick to recognize) would endanger it. So: "What are you going to do for the rest of the evening?" I asked, glancing up at Big Ben. "Or rather, morning. It's no good driving anywhere near Piccadilly – it's jammed tight and you'll never get through."

"Too hearty, anyway," said Tim. "I resent having balloons and trumpets and whistling ticklers – or whatever they're called – thrust down my neck by a dozen strangers standing on the running board."

"You know you love it really," broke in Elisabeth: "if we weren't there to watch, you'd be hanging on to Eros, covered with paper streamers."

"I like doing it *myself*: it's only when other people celebrate that one sees the true bestiality of it … We could take a trip," he went on after a pause, "if you're all still wide-awake, or we can go back to the flat and have a drink and let the evening die."

"Where do you live?"

"Warwick Square. Belgravia we call it, when boasting – the edge of the peke district."

"Of course," said Anthea suddenly, almost to herself, "we are on the Dover road, at this very moment."

"It's over seventy miles," Tim answered dubiously.

"A night's run – we could spin it out, and have breakfast on the boat in the morning. Think of the appetites we'll work up." She gave me a quick glance, and then, quite unembarrassed, touched with her own minute foot the loose sole of my shoe. "But that's part of a larger subject," she went on, in an altered voice. "Have you had dinner?"

"In a sense, yes." I smiled at her. "I'm not hungry at the moment, though I know there was room for the question."

"Writing is slow?"

I nodded. "Very."

Thus, without emphasis, was my position ascertained and acknowledged.

"Get in, then," said Tim, "and we'll start. But absolve me from responsibility, in the event of us all getting so bored or bad-tempered that the expedition falls to bits."

"Now, Timmy," Elisabeth took him in hand expertly, "you're going to love driving us. And if you want a rest, I'm sure this wild Communist will take over and drive beautifully too."

"Thanks – I don't want to throw my life away."

"Hey!" I said. "I had one of these cars when I was a kid."

He turned and smiled at me as I settled down with Anthea in the back seat. "Hush," he said softly, "I'm trying to stave off your life story till we're out of the limit. Then with luck I won't hear it."

"That rather leaves me in the lurch," Anthea remarked pensively.

"You've brought it on yourself," he answered, and set the car in motion.

We turned and smiled at each other as the car gathered speed and set a course for the Old Kent Road: sitting there with her dark hair blown by the wind, with her wide grey eyes, with her air of uninsistent readiness, she seemed a travelling companion of a divine order ... Tim Hannay drove swiftly, through streets almost bare of traffic, and when I lay back with my head against the hood the patchy sky overhead seemed to be racing past the housetops, like a revolving backcloth which has got out of control. But there was peace to be had, sitting by her side with my shoulder touching hers: it was as if I were sailing out of the already-hated life of Carter Street and Spanish death and political rancour into a harbour where she – with gentleness, consideration, and complete assurance – was ready to take care of me and guide my dazed footsteps ... It was easy, indeed, when I glanced sideways at her glowing loveliness and her cheeks whipped by the wind, to dream of her compliance and sweetness under some possible circumstance of intimacy: and, oddly, the quality of frankness which shone from every movement she made, and especially from her voice, did not seem to contradict what my dream of her promised – rather did it put it on a plane of exaltation as well as certainty ...

After five miles of silence: "We need distraction," remarked Tim suddenly. He settled his neck deeper in his coat collar. "Make a speech, Marcus Hendrycks," he called out: "I feel benevolent tonight."

"It wouldn't last," I told him.

Elisabeth smiled back at me. "The one I heard in Hyde Park would turn Tim inside out."

"An agreeable spectacle, hard to forgo ... Actually I want to give politics a rest, for quite a long while: Spain was so ferocious that it seems sheer insanity to add to the strife."

"I admire your guts for going out there," said Tim, "even though – " he broke off, and I saw him smiling. "Oh well, I'll let you off the next bit."

"I killed four men," I remarked, as matter-of-factly as I could. "And as for guts – there are too many people *thinking* with their guts nowadays, for that to be any satisfaction. We want a little clear reason, backed by tolerance. Four corpses down to my account, plus all the horrors which are piling up at this very moment, don't make politics very attractive to me."

By my side Anthea nodded. "That's easy to understand ... But what about your writing – wasn't that political as well?"

"A good deal of it, yes. That'll have to be dropped. But then I'm not sure about writing in any case – I'm not really good enough, I ought to get a proper office job and settle down to it."

"Don't you!" exclaimed Tim over his shoulder. "I was a solicitor once ... It damned nearly killed me, and the effect on the firm was very much the same. Clients used to come back from the dead to complain about the wills I'd made for them. And lots of times people would turn up at the office in a rage, having found that their houses didn't belong to them at all. After I'd been very funny in a letter to the Inland Revenue, I thought the time had come to move on ..."

Thus laughter and comradeship for thirty flowing miles under a cold sky: their partnership was flawlessly secure, and I had slipped into it with no hesitation on either side. But I felt all the time the absolute necessity of finding out more about this trio, and the circumstances which had bound them together so securely; it was obvious to me that they were people of significance and vitality, and Anthea Lorensen in particular was a public figure on that account, though I suspected that the public façade consisted largely of the unessentials and that the real person had ten times the quoted notability.

At one point on the journey she turned to me and asked: "Which picture of mine did you have?"

"You may not even remember it," I answered. "I bought it at one of your Cork Street shows – a little engraving called 'Pastoral' "

She nodded eagerly. "The shepherd with the Greek profile, and the nymph peering from behind the fountain … I remember it: it was one of my favourites."

"Mine too. I had to sell it, though – to a friend of mine who had another of yours already: I think that was called 'The Blue Smock' – a French porter with a huge moustache and a twinkle."

She nodded again, laughing. "I got him at a little wayside station in the Pyrenees, somewhere near Tarbes."

"*I* got him," corrected Tim over his shoulder, "but he wouldn't sit for me – he wanted to stare at Anthea. Who bought the picture, by the way?"

"Julian," said Anthea.

I turned to her, interested. "You know Julian Wingate, then?"

"Very well," she answered. "He lives quite close, and comes in a lot. He's clever, don't you think?"

"Yes." I laughed suddenly. "Have you met his girl?"

"Denise? Yes, she's been in once or twice. I wonder if that's over now: I'd like to see him get back to normal."

"He may not. When I saw him last he was even thinking of getting married."

Anthea shook her head, so that her hair in the swiftness of the car's passage spread like a wavering halo. "But they don't love each other," she said. "It's sex on his side, and a kind of intellectual snobbery on hers. It's as far from love as – well, it isn't enough for marriage, anyway."

"Give them twelve hundred a year and a lot of alcohol, and they won't know the difference."

She turned towards me in sudden attention. "Are you really like that?"

"No – that was just a flick of the wrist. But you can run a marriage on a lot of things besides love. You can even keep them separate: get married as a social convenience, or for the comfort it can bring you, and as for love – well, if you're damned lucky, if the laws of chance *do* overcome the odds, you'll have that as well. You see," I said largely, lying back and staring at the sky, "you need somebody to laugh with and win approval from, someone to kiss and rumple when you wake up in the morning: why wait for love, which is elusive to the point of infinity, when these other things – which are often essential to your peace of mind – are so ready to hand?"

"For the sole reason," she said, very slowly and carefully, "that if you wait you may be able to combine the two. Don't let go, don't squander, before you must; and in the end you may find that it's been a million times worthwhile to hang on."

"And if you don't find that?"

"You have the satisfaction – not to be despised – that you haven't compromised, or put up with second best, in the most important personal problem of your life."

Her voice was not sad, but subdued almost to a whisper: I had to turn and look closely at her, so compelling was the assurance of her words. She met my eyes squarely, exhibiting neither shyness nor hesitation over a matter which clearly affected her in the deepest degree – for I understood, beyond doubt, that she had been stating a personal case, and not generalizing, as I had been ... So she was waiting for love, I thought – and did not, for a wonder, find the idea either pathetic or novelettish. Hitherto that aspect of life had for me been so tied up with 'Write-to-Aunt-Hester' in the slush weeklies, with Mr Right, and don't-make-yourself-cheap, and my-boy-is-tongue-tied, and suchlike stale inanities, that I could hardly visualize it as a real problem which exercised the adult mind as well ... But as she had stated it, it was clear-cut, genuine, and immediately recognizable as having only one answer; and that was another moment when the thread between us made itself felt, like a gentle tug in a troutstream, and this time it came from my side, and could hardly have been shared with her – however blinding the clarity with which I suddenly realized that her problem directly concerned me.

It was my eyes which wavered first, and fell, and sought refuge in the trees and dark fields between which the car moved swiftly ... But it was necessary to answer her, or at least to dispose of the subject without an awkward jump to the next: and presently I said: "You've thought of it more than I have. Obviously you are right. The only danger is to wait too long: that 'non-compromising' idea is more of an academic satisfaction than a personal one."

"I'm twenty-eight," she observed – relevantly, and yet seeming to answer quite another question.

"Five years ahead of me."

"So much?" Could I say 'It doesn't matter?' ... "You look older. Have you been ill?"

"Yes. And short of money. And I've been to a war."

After a moment she said, almost to herself: "You could be taken care of."

And there, with no sense of frustration, we left it. We had all time to play with.

That was a curious night, even on the surface. Tim was no longer driving fast, but loitering, taking us down odd by-ways as fancy or an attractive signpost dictated, spinning out the night in the most inconsequent way he could devise; and to drive through the darkness of that Kentish countryside, now under thickly arched trees wherein our headlights made a glaring tunnel of brilliance, now through fields whose horizon was harsh against the sky, now past some deserted foreshore where the tide drained and sucked at the mud-flats – to drive thus, with the good-looking friendly couple in front, and beside me Anthea Lorensen, who was a dream of loveliness and whose grey eyes now met mine as readily as if we were already lovers, gave the whole journey an air of sympathetic unreality to which I surrendered with thankfulness. If I were indeed driving out of the squalid and violent past, I would have wished for no other quality of transport ...

A few miles short of Canterbury Tim suddenly headed south-west again, "Because," he explained, "we're very near the Pilgrim's Way here, and I'd like to find it." We did not find it: what we did discover was an old chalkpit, lying just off the road and sheltered from the wind, into which Tim drove the car as unhesitatingly as he would have parked it in St James's Square ... We got out. In the car's headlamps the white face of the pit rose high above us, seeming almost to overhang the perpendicular: installed there, behind a breastwork of rough chalk blocks which the pit-workers of long ago had abandoned, we might have used it as a base for foraging raids or held it against an army.

"What next?" I asked, after I had prowled round, on the lookout for tramps or escaped lions.

"A fire," answered Elisabeth. She was leaning against the car and staring up at the pit-face: in the reflected glow of the headlamps her slim coated body was extraordinarily childish, so that I found myself wondering how much younger she was than her half sister. "Light a fire, Tim," she called out. "Perhaps it'll make the birds sing. Anyway it'll cheer us up."

"How do I light a fire," asked Tim from the shadows, "when all I have to do it with is lumps of chalk?"

"Bustle about," Anthea told him briskly. "Collect bracken, find packing-cases, cut down a tree. Isn't there some methylated spirits in the car?"

"Even methylated spirits and chalk won't make the hell of a blaze, will they?" he observed dubiously. His voice trailed off as he went further into the darkness at the other end of the pit. "I'll see what else I can find."

I joined the search, and presently stumbled over a mass of rubbish which had been heaped in one corner. "Here's something," I called out, and struck a light. It was a rubbish-tip piled high with cinders, rags, tin cans, empty oil-drums: at the further side was a heap of what looked like wooden boxes. The match spluttered out before I could identify them, but I struck another as Anthea and Tim came up.

"What have you found?" she asked.

"Well, as a matter of fact," I answered, slightly taken aback, "they're beehives."

There were six of them – some broken, some lacking tops or sides, all derelict.

"Admirable!" exclaimed Tim, as he set to work to drag them out. "And highly symbolic, too – a ruined world, ripe for the burning. We'll pile them up and settle a few old scores."

Presently, when I had selected the driest, stuffed it with newspaper, and soaked the latter in methylated spirits, we got the fire going. It caught quickly, helped by the dried wax which lined all the hives, and the tiny desiccated bodies of dead bees which many of them still contained. Tim was right, I thought, as I watched the flames licking round these and heard the curious whining noise which some trick of the fire set up: it *was* highly symbolic, this consignment to the flames of the husk of a highly organized community which had come to ruin and now lay with its dead piled thick upon it. The flames took hold swiftly, leaping and crackling round the hives as we piled them on top, illuminating the polished coachwork of the car and the pitted surface of the chalk-slopes close about us. But my eyes were drawn more strongly to the ring of faces round the fire: looking from Tim Hannay's rugged thrusting air to Elisabeth's shy-nymph delicacy, and then turning to that wide-eyed and dependable loveliness which was Anthea's, I found myself marvelling at the good fortune which had placed me suddenly in their company. And then Anthea, feeling my gaze upon her, turned with infinite grace, and smiled at me, and laid her hand on my arm; and in that swift moment we were very close to each other, and something within both of us reached for an answer, and was drawn out irresistibly, and almost met: and then it was gone again, and we were left to acknowledge it privately and recognize beyond doubt what it meant.

The flames licked and leapt, up-surging to the freer air: from the ledge of the topmost hive little dead bees rolled off and were swallowed traceless, as in the heart of hell.

"Funeral pyre," observed Tim, leaning back and turning his head sideways to shield it from the heat. "We ought to compose epitaphs, or make up some of those fatuous Chinese proverbs that mean nothing – 'A dead lion is a temple of indifference' – 'Better the strength of princes than a roll in bed with honey' … Do you know any more?"

"I can't say I know those," I answered. "Wouldn't it be better to make up a proper funeral oration? Here's the dead earth burning: we set a light to it – we'd better say why."

Anthea nodded, her hair flickering and gleaming in the fierce light. "We'll each make one up," she said. "I'm not going to share my grudges with anyone."

"Oh, darling," said Elisabeth in dismay, "I can't make speeches."

"Then we'll let you off. But we don't really want a speech, except perhaps" – she touched my arm – "from the professional agitator here. We want a little piece of the truth from each of us. Who'll start?"

Tim stirred again. "I'm feeling quite vocal, if you want a lead."

"Very well." She leant back, and put her hand in front of her face. "How hot the world burns! ... Pray, silence for Tim Hannay, the first mourner."

"Mourner?" Tim began immediately, getting to his feet and throwing an immense shadow against the chalk-slope. "I'm no mourner at this party – I've come to gloat ... Oh world, oh vulgar, trivial, and spiteful world. I've helped to set you alight, and I'm damned glad. And for my reason I'll take one single thing – the way you've treated the artists, and the creators, ever since you began your job." His chin came out, threatening the flames. " 'Trivial and vulgar' I called you, and by God that's true! Whom have you glorified, for decade after decade, from one century to another? Silly people with catchphrases, rich men with the taste of hogs at a trough, charlatans, thugs, killers ... And what have you done with your *real* people – the people who wouldn't conform to your filthy little yardstick, the people who wanted to make one small *alive* corner in your stinking graveyard? I'll tell you: these people you have strangled, and stamped on, and their wings you have clipped, for age after age: one of the best of them you crucified, with a thief on each side to show what you thought of him ..." For a moment he paused. "And now – what's happened now? – what have you been doing these last few years?" His chin was out once more, his hands clenched: we watched him as if he were a certified messiah. "You've given us a new motto: '*Evil be to him who thinks.*' You've given us a new standard: '*Learning will be cast into the mire, and trodden down under the hoofs of a swinish multitude.*' Well, it's your swinish multitude that we're burning now, and even so we're being kind – we're giving you a quick end, but you left your victims to rot. And while they rotted, we were bidden to worship, as our natural gods, the hip-swingers, the daubers, the cinema-organists, the strip-tease harlots, the band leaders, the tenth-rate fakes ..." He brought his hand up sharply. "That's why we're destroying you, and that's why we're glad to have the chance."

On the last sentence his voice died away to a minor note more potent than any climactic outburst. All three of us, his hearers, drew deep breaths, almost glad of the relief of tension: his manner and his words had been rather more than we had bargained for ... He turned away from the fire and looked at us, his face breaking into a smile as he noticed our startled air; and so for a moment the four of us were still, grouped round the flames which were now at their fiercest, so that little rivulets of wax melted and fell from the topmost hive into the heart of the embers. And then: "That's my contribution," he said slowly. "I yield the floor."

"A difficult man to follow," I remarked.

"Well done, Tim," said Anthea: "you've got the damned world on the run. And we must keep it there. Who's next?"

I looked at Elisabeth, but she shook her head. And so, after a pause, but without prompting, I myself stood up, glanced once at the shadows behind me, and began: "My comrades, I shall not long detain you – "

"Hear, hear!" from Tim.

" – but I also have one particular aspect of this dying world's shortcoming to which I would draw your attention, and I speak now for the small and inarticulate people who have lacked a champion from the day of their birth till their deathbed." I felt Anthea's eyes on me, compelling and confusing, but resolutely I faced the fire, which no longer showed itself flaming but glowed with an intensity that I was determined to conquer. "Oh world, I've come to gloat, too: to return cruelty with cruelty isn't always a good answer, but in this case what choice have we? – it is the only answer you understand. Let me tell you what we, the silent, the obedient, the small – let me tell you what we wanted. We didn't ask much, we have never asked much: simply fair play, decency, a space to grow a little and sample the loveliness we only dream about, an opportunity to show that gentleness and kindness which we had ready for you whenever you chose to evoke it. You never chose thus: you had no use for anything but servility and silence ..." I stared and stared at the fire, seeing in its heart an image of long-continued evil. "You have had a full measure of these, you have made them the habitual currency of nine-tenths of your citizens; but the common people have not always been without spirit – sometimes we grow impatient and wish to rise a little, we murmur, we even shake our chains ... What happens when we try to break those chains?" The fire flared once and then began to crumble and cave in: round my feet the last sparks flew. "I have shovelled up and tipped into the back of a lorry the odd scraps of flesh of those who have tried to gain freedom: and topped the load off with what has been left of their children, in order to prove a complete job of work ... All through history it has been the same: the graves of our martyrs are as thick as corn, the ranks of the oppressed cannot be numbered. And when you cannot kill because we dare not give battle, you use more subtle weapons – the weapons of poverty, the laughter of rank and privilege. You see our state now: duped and betrayed by the power of money, disciplined by murderers, ordered to suffer all things meekly by the priests. We are the little men, who beg for freedom and are struck across the mouth ... Even if you had a voice left, you could not blame us for striking back – once, harshly, like this."

Then silence again, save for the settling fire which did indeed seem to have been dealt a mortal blow ... The others were watching me with that same startled air with which we had greeted Tim's speech, but of their three faces it was Anthea's which claimed my eye, so vivid was it and so intent upon my own. That thread which was between us tightened again, making itself felt with supreme insistence. It could not be long before we acknowledged it to each other openly.

Tim finally broke the silence.

"But whom are we entertaining?" he asked with a smile, "This man is an agitator indeed."

"Very true," said Anthea. "And what there is left for me to say, I really don't know. In fact, may I be excused?"

"You may not," I told her decisively. "The fire's still alive: take your chance while you've still got it."

"Very well." Charmingly acquiescent, she got to her feet and advanced a pace or two towards the fire: as she approached it her whole body glowed, and her dark hair shone as if she could shake from it another shaft of flame. "This is the last variation," she began, "and it will be the weakest, since I haven't really made up my mind." Then, like all of us, she stared suddenly right into the fire. "I'd like to have given you another chance, but perhaps, on balance, we did right to destroy. You've had so many chances, haven't you? – and all you can do is to repeat your mistakes and make people go through the same ordeals, the same terrors. You gave them no peace ..." Her voice became stronger on the phrase. "Yes, that's the real reason why we have lost patience and done this to you because while the majority only want peace and security, you give them hatred, and mistrust, and murder for sport or money or lust. Anyone who stands out against that, you call a crank or a traitor, and ultimately you crush him, and go on your way, your cruel way ... Of course we can resist that way, but the weapons we have – honesty and toleration and generosity – never seem to win: or if they do win for a space, they're somehow turned upside down and put to wicked uses, while we are still using them in good faith ... Goodbye, world," she said more lightly, shaking back her hair in a gesture of freedom, "and while you die once, quickly, think of the countless millions of people whom you condemned to kill each other, for the sake of giving power to men who could no more use it properly than could madmen or drunkards. If you were to have another chance, I would say: forget hatred, and cherish love instead – there's such a huge amount of it, ready to come to life. But as it is, you *haven't* another chance – for which I'm glad!"

And she did look glad, too, standing there before the dying fire whose flames seemed to have been translated to her face: at that moment one could only love her, for her strength and honesty of purpose and signal beauty. "You've killed it," I murmured, glancing back at the fire, which had caved in altogether and on which the dead ash encroached more quickly every moment. And from the fire I looked at her again, wondering what I would do if there were any flaw or check in our relationship; and then round about me, marking the shadows, the car whose outlines were now emerging from the gloom, the frost at the edge of the road. The dawn must have been near at hand, for when my eye followed the line of the chalk-slope upwards I found that above its rim was to be seen a sky already turning pale.

It was very cold, and my arm felt stiff and painful. But thinking of what I had gained that night, I cared nothing.

Anthea stirred with her foot the grey embers. "That's the end," she said slowly. "Now let's seek the sea – let's get off the earth altogether."

It was a strange night to the very last. We drove through Canterbury at about six o'clock, pausing for a few minutes under the grey lee of the cathedral; and then we set out on the last few miles of the road to Dover. It was much lighter now, though we still could not drive without headlights: on our left a bank of cloud which filled the whole eastern sky had an under-side faintly tinged with pink; the first day of the new year promised well … Tim drove in silence, while at his shoulder Elisabeth lolled asleep, her fair hair tracing a pattern of disorder against his coat collar; and Anthea's hand now rested lightly in mine, in a fashion natural and yet unlooked for. Indeed, I felt, for the moment, a certain hesitation in regard to her: she and I seemed to have fallen into step with an unanimity which I myself found astonishing, and now and then I wondered if this were really her wish, or if it had been largely dictated by circumstances.

"Who's who in this party?" I asked at one point. "Are those two engaged?"

She smiled. "In a way, yes. They live together, though the relationship is limited to that. You see?"

"Certainly. But why?"

"I don't really know. Elisabeth's only eighteen: she's in love with Tim, but she just isn't – isn't ready for sex, I suppose."

"And he?"

"They don't come any more patient, or kind, or generous." She spoke with deep feeling, as if this were something she had tested and found certain. "And I think

369

that he – " she broke off, and then raising her voice a trifle. "Can you hear, Tim?"

"Yes, my darling, I can." His voice came grave and level from the depth of his coat collar. "Don't believe all you hear, Marcus Hendrycks: it's probably just some more of this insufferable Red propaganda."

"Then I'll talk lower," answered Anthea. "I think he's satisfied," she went on, "and doesn't get impatient, because it's what Elisabeth wants and he's content to wait for her to make up her mind … Could you do that?" she asked suddenly.

I considered for a moment. "If there were a guarantee that I would get what I wanted in the end, yes. Otherwise I think I'd be too selfish. But of course it would depend on whether sex was a – a decisive element in the relationship, whether the girl was so obviously attractive in that way that I could never forget it."

"Wouldn't that mean too much emphasis on the physical side?"

"Not necessarily. If sex were only a quarter of it, and you had to do without it, that would make you discontented."

"Then sublimate."

"When you were living with the girl? – it wouldn't be possible. At least, I don't think I'm made that way."

After a moment: "Expert?"

"Used to be. There's been nothing for a year now, though – genuine sublimation." I smiled. "I usually work most of the night, anyway."

"And I most of the day." She laughed without the least affectation. "We'd never see each other."

That was make-believe, of course; but even at that stage the thing was already settled.

"Organization is a great thing," I said airily, wanting with all my will to tread softly. "Time is the invention of man –

let him juggle with it as he wishes … Is Elisabeth a painter as well?"

Her hand in mine was a cool comment on the switch of subject, with which she seemed to agree. "No, she plays the piano. Extremely well, too: you'll hear more of her. She's giving her first recital some time this year, if everything goes all right."

"What does she play?"

"Mozart, mostly – and some of the early Beethoven, which is real music in spite of the way these professors sneer at it. Is that sort of thing in your line?"

"It's beginning to be."

The car was over the heights above Dover now, and dropping down to the water's edge: the rim of the sun was just up, and thus the whole town lay before us, emerging out of the thin mist of night like a shy urban ghost. Elisabeth woke up, exclaiming "The sea!" as if she had just quitted some dream wherein every ocean had been dry these last ten years; and indeed it was worth an exclamation, that troubled and unquiet waste of water which was now our new horizon and on which the near-horizontal rays of the sun played their own sparkling fantasy. As we were moving down the approach road to the inner harbour: "There she is!" exclaimed Tim suddenly, pointing straight ahead. "Just astern of the white motor cruiser."

"Good tough lines," I said, after a glance which showed me a straight-stemmed cutter with an unusual amount of free board. "But what happens to that counter in a following sea?"

"It makes an angle of sixty degrees with sea level, but you don't have to mind that. *Marie Louise* could stand on her head, and you'd only break one or two plates."

"There's another boat rather like that," I remarked, "a converted smack, about twenty tons, lying at Falmouth.

I've had my eye on her for years, but I don't suppose I'll ever get her now."

Anthea laughed. "Why do sailors always have a boat that they've 'got their eye on'? Some of you people seem to trail boats all round the coast for years on end, waiting for a chance to spring."

"Anything so individual as sailing is bound to develop the predatory instincts."

"In every department?"

I met her eyes. "Socialists prefer co-operation to any other relationship."

"But even *they* won't wait indefinitely for it."

"Perhaps not."

"You're running away."

"*Pour mieux sauter* ... I wouldn't want to convert anybody who isn't ready for it. They can easily indicate their readiness."

Said Tim to Elisabeth, in a tense whisper: "What do you think of our performing animals?"

"I think they're sweet," she answered. "I think they're good for each other."

"How strong an indication?" asked Anthea, with a kind of gentle perseverance.

The car rolled to a standstill on the quayside.

"One uses subtlety when one wants to conceal one's meaning. In such a case one would want to admit it, in the clearest terms."

"And you would proceed only on that?"

"Agreed."

She sat up, and opened the car door. "I'll let you know," she said, without a trace of hesitation. Then she smiled, and stepped out, leaving me to follow her and knowing well that I would do so.

There was something essentially satisfying about treading a deck again. "If you want to explore, don't mind us," said Anthea, as soon as we were marshalled on board; and the next ten minutes were pleasantly spent in running over the points of Tim's tough little boat and touching on the Bermudian-versus-gaff argument, in which the owner was, as might have been expected, an unshakable conservative. But it was clear that *Marie Louise*, though she had no 'lines' in the aesthetic sense and though her standing-rigging might have served to stay a mast of at least double the height, was an immensely dependable boat in which one could have faced any weather.

The sun was well up. We made coffee, and fried eight eggs, and topped the meal off with three fingers of rum apiece: the atmosphere in the snug well-fitted saloon was a blend of liveliness, comradeship, and contentment which made an apt ending to our journey. Anthea's hand was again in mine, a warranty of the now-acknowledged thread between us; and as I sat there, lounging against the back of the berth, watching one cunning shaft of sunlight which had traversed a porthole to find Elisabeth's hair, and listening to the sustained lapping of water against the hull, it did not seem possible that the moment could be improved on or that I could wish to change places with anyone.

And then, suddenly, a swift change from general well-being to intensely personal significance. Elisabeth began to fall asleep, and was carried by Tim to one of the foc's'le bunks; and when presently he returned with the announcement that he also was tired and planned to sleep till lunchtime, I knew even before I met Anthea's eye that the loose ends of the night were now to be gathered up and resolved into a formal pattern at last. And as soon as we were alone, with both the cabin and the foc's'le doors shut, and the galley between us and any interruption, that pattern emerged as swiftly as if we were both trying with all our might to evoke it ... Anthea leant back, her coat lying open, her red scarf loosely round her neck – a vivid frame for a striking loveliness – and looking at me with that direct simplicity so much more compelling than any display of eagerness, she said: "This is a fine harbour to be in."

It was not only Dover that she meant ... I was standing before her under the ribbed skylight, the sun just reaching my forehead, with a glimpse through the portholes of the grey ruffled water and through the hatchway of a cold square of sky; but when I answered her slow smile she patted the edge of the berth beside her, and added: "It's your harbour, too."

As I sat down: "You're a realist, aren't you?" I remarked.

She nodded. "I like to acknowledge and deal with things, yes."

"Such as tonight."

"Such as tonight. A lot of odd things have happened, very quickly, tonight."

The boat rocked to a gentle lift of the harbour tide: the ray of sunlight on the opposite wall woke and trembled in sympathy.

"And what more do they need?"

"Not acknowledging – we've done that." She turned towards me, chin on elbow. "But dealing with ... Emotionally, we are level?"

"I hope so."

She laughed. "*Si vous saviez à quel point* ... And being level emotionally should mean that whatever either of us does, we cannot be shy or – or embarrassed by it."

"It means that we can't put a foot wrong, no matter what we do."

Her whole face brightened suddenly, becoming startlingly lovely: I looked into her grey eyes, and was lost … "There's something extraordinarily comforting about you," she said softly. "It's as if I knew that, if my own brain and feeling failed, I could use yours and not know the difference."

"Anthea …" I began.

"Again."

"Anthea."

She sighed. "I think I was christened just to hear it said like that. And I think also," she leant towards me, with a loving readiness, "that that's all you need to say."

On that we kissed each other, with a gentleness which delayed only for a few moments the ecstasy that lay beyond. So sweet were her lips, and so subtly and deeply rousing the feel of her body against mine, that when I drew back I found myself looking at her in a fashion quite undisguised and quite unmistakable to her.

She met my eyes with her own shining grey ones. Her face was lit with a sweeter expectancy than I had ever thought I would find in a human being.

She said, in that low and lovely voice: "Now?"

I hesitated, knowing quite well what I wanted but seeing beyond it the promise of an incomparably greater happiness, if only the moment could be fittingly handled. When she saw the look on my face her own glance seemed to falter, and she added, in a whisper which had in it a deep pathos: "A foot wrong, already?"

I shook my head vehemently.

"I said it wasn't possible. Do you think *you* could be shamed in that way? But there are rules – though I don't know if they're still valid …" I touched her hand. "*Connais-tu le pays?*"

"*Où fleurit –* " She laughed. "*Où défleurit* … No, I don't. It must be taught to me. That matters? – that's a rule?"

"It was."

"Let the past bury it."

"Willingly. But that does complicate the thing. Anthea: it can't be just – automatic."

"You mean, from the physical point of view?"

"Yes. And in any case …"

"Well?"

"May God, and you, forgive what must sound either insolent or priggish: but – " I glanced round the cabin, and listened for a moment to the slapping run of the water against the hull. "This is good, but it's haphazard, isn't it? We might regret, because the – the suddenness, the insecurity of it, would make it seem trivial. It isn't to be trivial."

"But it *is* to be?"

I nodded once, slowly. "Oh yes."

"And long-term?"

"Of course. It's the only thing that would make sense. And that's why I'd rather cut my heart out than run the risk of cheapening it … Am I taking too much for granted?"

"If you are, we're doing it together …" She was lying now against my shoulder, with an air of trust intensely satisfying. "Do you remember," she said slowly, "my saying that you could be taken care of?"

"Yes."

"Shall I do that very thing?" On the instant she seemed to gather herself to take us and the moment into her hands. "It's New Year's Day, Marcus Hendrycks. Shall we waste no time? Two white arms won't cure all your ills, I know, but there's more than that for you, if you want it. *Do* you want it?" And as, wordless with happiness, I waited, she lifted her head, showing me once again the beginning of that shining expectant look. "I think," she said, "that if you kissed me a good deal more, I could make it do until we get back to London tonight."

❖ ❖ ❖

CHAPTER SIXTEEN

Happiness was born a twin.

BYRON, *Don Juan*

❖

Anthea was not ordinary: and under her guidance no moment of the life which we now began to share was either dull, or automatic, or prescribed by the compulsion of habit.

The fact that she was twenty-eight to my twenty-three did not straitly determine the quality of our relationship: but it did ensure that she took command of certain phases, to a far greater degree than might otherwise have been the case. So clear was it that I could rely not only on her judgment, but on an unfailing level of generosity and a sort of competent loving kindness, that from the very beginning I left to her the determination of our day-to-day existence: it could be said that, by agreement, she took me in hand, planned the present and future, and herself made the most potent contributions to both.

Anthea was not ordinary. Both her childhood and her later experience had made of her an individual independent, self-sufficient, and extremely capable: she could take her own line and stick to it, she was a separate person with the ability – predominantly male – to control her surroundings and order their details, whether these concerned a newspaper interview or a dinner party, the leasing of a house or the painting of a portrait. She could *deal with* things and people, she could find the right word or phrase and (what was more) present it surely and expertly, so that it did not misfire or exert anything less than its full weight, no matter how curious or fugitive the situation. And throughout this varied and adaptable competence she managed to preserve an essential femininity – not because of her loveliness, though this was as difficult to overlook as the colour of the sky on a spring day, but because her relationship with the world was of that charming order in which laughter takes the place of inflexibility, and a grave dignity that of insistence … No, she was not ordinary: she was beautiful, sensuously alive, and proof against all hazards: she was a unit of strength.

What had turned her into such a person? "I really think my upbringing was a leftover from the Victorian Age," she told me once, when we were exploring each other's histories. "My mother died when I was two, and after that I don't think Daddy gave a damn what became of me. He married again fairly soon, but that didn't make any difference: I saw them both for an average of one hour a day, when I was sent down to the drawing room, either to be shown off to visitors like a little polished doll, or to sit in a corner with a book and not open my mouth. The rest of the time I spent with nursemaids who were always ignorant and often cruel – not on purpose, though there were one or two like that as well, but just because they didn't know any other way of handling children except telling them what to do and hitting them across the face if they didn't do it."

"Poor darling," I said, squeezing her hand: "it sounds pretty grim."

"It was grim ... I hadn't anyone to appeal to, because I was frightened of my father, and my stepmother couldn't be bothered with me: the nurses just had a free hand, and they certainly used it." She sighed. "I remember I used to be locked into the night nursery because I was afraid of being there alone, without a light, and tried to get out. And once, when I'd spilt some milk on the tablecloth, I was made to stand in the corner for an hour, holding a pair of walking-shoes above my head ... I was ten when Elisabeth was born, so I really *was* on my own for a long time."

"But couldn't your father see what was happening?"

"Oh, he was busy ... Luckily I used to read a terrific amount: otherwise I don't know what I would have become. But I could sneak into the library and hide there – between the curtain and the French window – with any book I wanted; and I liked drawing things, birds and trees and ugly faces, and I had lots of time to think ... And so here I am, with a will of my own, and pretty keen to know the why and wherefore of everything I'm told. And if ever I have children, I'll see that I'm available as often as they want me, so that they don't get their facts either from the gutter or the mouths of fools."

Such had been the small, the formative years ... But she seemed to have emerged from them with a credit balance; and her later progress had been in the direct line of this independent growth. For she had made a real success in her own world, quite apart from her quality as a person; if you heard the name 'Anthea Lorensen' you said: "The painter – I've seen a lot of her work," you did not say "Who's she?" or "One of these Elstree prodigies?" Not that public recognition, *per se*, is a test of merit; but in this case it only confirmed what was obviously *there* and obviously of supreme value and attraction.

At all events she was competent to command: and if, in my submission to her influence, there was a certain element of snobbery, if I gave her a readier attention because she was Anthea Lorensen the artist, that did not mean that she was not worthy of almost limitless deference. In surrendering, I could rely on her never misusing the ascendancy; and the relief to me, after the discomfort and the petty struggling of the past year, was so great that I would have borne a rule ten times more burdensome. And (another cause for relief) the position between us was clarified by the frankest discussion.

"This is a partnership," she said on another occasion. "You can be my equal, whenever you want to be – I know that already: I also know that you're tired, and would rather I took us in hand, at the moment. But I want the thing to grow on lines of equality: when two people are living together the idea of mutual service should be there, terrifically strongly, the whole time … One can do so much for a person if one sets one's mind to it: if we both keep that in sight, there can hardly be an upward limit to the thing."

"Darling," I said, "why are you so sweet to me?"

"Because I've fallen in love with you, and for the first time in my life I'm trying my hardest."

"Is it an effort?"

"Actually making love is an *effort* …"

I smiled in the darkness. "Confirmed … But still, why? What's it all about? Why am I here?" (We were in bed.) "What do you see in me? I'm not good-looking, and yet – 'In sleep a King, in waking no such manner' – you honour me like this, and yet it's all in a sort of vacuum: I'm not really worth it, when I'm away from you."

"Then stay."

"Try and lose me … But that isn't an explanation of anything: you're so lovely, and I'm just me."

"Let's call it 'Beauty lives with Kindness,' since we're quoting." She touched my shoulder. "I haven't made a mistake, Marco darling: we're a clear case, we're *right* together. Feel my heart: and when you take your hand away, do it gently, because my heart's in it."

That was after two months, when we were quite sure that the thing wasn't a sexual impulse (as I had feared at the beginning, with my eyes on that odd accelerated night), when we were quite sure that we were on the right lines, and beginning to find them so singularly sweet to be on …

We had the flat underneath Tim and Elisabeth's, in Warwick Square: three rooms and a kitchen, a little balcony, a view of some treetops – a secure and eminently defensible haven. She had furnished it out of the mass of furniture which they had in store (the father was dead now, it seemed, and the stepmother extending into its fifth year a trip to America originally planned to last six months); and there was for me an extreme pleasure in seeing emerge, almost at a stroke, this resting-place which was on the surface simply a collection of rooms and could yet be brought to life by our joint enthusiasm. The contrast with Carter Street, even physically speaking, was ludicrous; and when there was added to this the fact of Anthea's presence, the knowledge that she loved me, and the certainty that the security of our future lay in our own efforts, which had already proved themselves potent, it was no wonder that those first few months brought an unassailable contentment whose dreamlike quality seemed to guarantee its endurance into the far future.

'Mutual service', she had called it; but though I did my best to attain her level, it was difficult not to be left far behind, unable to match her spirit or return a comparable answer to her bounty. She looked after me, she solved each problem as if it were her own invention, she took the world in hand and made a formal pattern of it, with myself apparently enjoying a godlike immunity in the middle … We were happy, Anthea and I, because we shared a purpose and could rely on its continuity; and the day's timetable had its own subdued excitement, its own significance – with myself busy at a desk in one room, with Anthea painting in overalls in another: knocking off for meals, resuming work, calling to each other when the mood took us: raiding the flat above for drinks, entertaining the other two in the evening, talking at ease in the secure comfort of night, loving each other with laughter, deep feeling, and the assurance of concord. In such days and nights there was no flaw; and by comparison, the love affairs of the old days were revealed as jerky, inconsequent, and patently second-rate.

Of course, there was the money question.

"You go ahead and write," she had said at the beginning. "I'll keep us both alive until you get moving." And as I frowned: "That doesn't appeal? Marcus Hendrycks, you're just a damned old Tory at heart. If we're to be a partnership, you must stop thinking about the functioning of the separate parts. Jump on the machine and watch it turn over: I'll tell you when it's starting to creak." She laughed. "Have I sufficiently confused you with metaphor for you to drop the subject?"

"No. It's all in line, you see: you're too sweet, and I'm not sweet enough. What do I supply to this partnership?"

She put her mouth to my ear and started to whisper.

"Darling, you're tricking me," I protested. "Loving you isn't a contribution."

"I can't think of a better."

"Darling, don't stall."

"Darling, don't heckle." But then she took a grip, becoming grave and competent all of a sudden, the way she could. She leant away from me, slim and lovely, watching me with drowning grey eyes. "We'll have this out," she said, "and then forget it … You needed a clear space, didn't you? – you were getting in a mess, you wanted time to breathe? Well, I'm giving it you. I want to. I love doing it. Money is such shoddy stuff anyway – it doesn't count … You go on with your writing, and make a success of that; and then we'll talk about paying back, and debts of honour, and living on women. But not now, because that'll spoil it all."

"But it's something I'm not entitled to."

"Then it's a surprise, it's a dividend, it's Christmas." She kissed me. "Oh darling, I want you to take all this for granted. It's just something I'm doing for you, like sleeping with you or going on breathing. It isn't anything different from that. See?" Another kiss, deep and stirring. "It's like this," she said in that low voice. "It's all my love."

So I agreed, and said no more, and set to work. Writing went well, from the very beginning: I broke new ground, especially in the way of general articles, I sold three or four short stories, I got my teeth into a novel … Naturally, it meant that a lot of other things had to rest: I had no time for any political work, and paid virtually no attention either to home politics or to the happenings of the outside world; and where before I had read at least four daily papers and a couple of weeklies, I was now content to skim the *Telegraph* and perhaps listen in to a news summary. And even this minor interest was of a different order from the old: I felt myself to be outside it all, with no compulsion to be up and doing and taking a hand: I was listening with only half an ear to the affairs of the world, in a manner detached and strictly non-participant.

In this connection, as in so many others, Anthea had a plan.

"You want to change your ground completely," she said. "You've given politics a good run: now try something different. Try a year of completely personal life. I'll help you: there's so much I can show you – in music, in pictures, in all the things you've been missing."

"That was Max's idea," I remarked. I had told her about Max, and Dr Barrow, and the Carter Street house.

"Then Max was right. You're in danger of losing a whole stage of development – or you will be, unless you turn towards it now. But we can make it easy for you: you've seen the sort of crowd we live in, and they're not all exhibitionists. Elisabeth gets shoals of concert tickets, and Tim and I can do a good deal in the painting line."

And so it was. Wandering the galleries with Anthea, or exploring some out-of-the-way picture show of which she had said: "I want you to see this – there are two things of his really worth looking at"; going to recitals with Elisabeth, listening to her playing, picking out under her direction some symphony or concerto on the wireless which (as she phrased it) would fill in another square in the pattern; watching Tim at work on one or other of the strange models I was constantly passing on the stairs – all these combined with the alive and intelligent world in which they lived to promote in me a flowering of half a dozen fresh interests. Those were full months, fuller than anything I had experienced before: they were yet another cause for gratitude, yet another thing on which, in the future, I would look back and say: "I owed all that to Anthea."

"Elisabeth says you're a promising pupil," she remarked one night, when we were lying in the semi-darkness of the bedside lamp, she ready to go to sleep, myself smoking and correcting the proof of a short story which one of the richer monthlies had taken. We had been to a recital that afternoon, of some Ireland and Dohnanyi sonatas, and had argued most of the way back about our personal reactions to atonality. "And you are interested, aren't you? – genuinely?"

"Genuinely. Of course, I'm not exactly starting from scratch: I've been attracted to music ever since the days of Julian's gramophone."

"You're lucky," she said sleepily. "So many people never come in sight of it all. Same with pictures, too: they stay round the corner, they never come into view."

That of course was perfectly true; and must remain a matter of individual fortune. One might go a lifetime with no knowledge of what one was missing; often it was only chance which opened those portals and made one free of the enchanted country within. I remembered, for instance, the unorthodoxy of my own introduction to the realm of painting – a visit to the National Gallery, undertaken because (aged fifteen) I had been told by a schoolfellow that the Rokeby *Venus* was 'hot stuff'. And it *was* hot stuff – that I could fervently endorse: and what attracted me was not the depth of colour nor the charming mirrored face, nor the noble rhythm which was Velasquez' secret, but simply the rosy flesh and the curve of the waist, and (projecting myself into the canvas) the knowledge that my two hands could easily encircle that waist, and that if I laid one of them gently on its curve the girl would turn towards me, in trust and expectation, to reveal her glory.

Proceeding from this point, with an enthusiasm purely libidinous, I sought a like exhilaration in other pictures and other galleries: I would stand daydreaming in front of canvases, taking part in their revelries or withdrawing into their discreet shadows, looking at them all for the wrong reason. But I *did* look at them, at these royal creations of the world's Masters; and unconsciously I was absorbing all the time a sense of artistic values, an appreciation of line, an embryonic faculty of discernment. They might be nudes to my more immediate consciousness, but they were also works of art whose cunning enchantment my inner mind and memory could not withstand.

And the same with music. An early love of dancing (for the main reason that it gave me occasion to clasp to myself a succession of otherwise unapproachable young women) led me to study dance rhythms, to prefer this arrangement to that one and to analyse such preference, and finally to 'collect' favourite melodies and phrases and forms of harmony for their own sakes; and this enthusiasm, long continued, left in me an understanding of musical colour and pattern which, when chance threw in my way a visit to a concert hall, ensured that I neither yawned my head off nor sighed for the more specious subtleties of the Washboard Rhythm Kings. Hitherto I had not considered it possible that there would ever be a piece of music which could give me more pleasure than Ellington's 'Mood Indigo' or Armstrong's 'Mahogany Hall Stomp' – unless it were something from the same robust stable. Now I woke to the fact that I was actually finding in this highbrow stuff an entertainment worthy of repetition.

And lastly (because after a few weeks that was probably its position in the scale), lastly sex.

She began, as might have been expected, with a basic reorganization of everything I had settled in my mind so far.

"But it isn't wrong," she declared at the very beginning, when I had used some phrase which demonstrated that the idea of 'sin' was lurking in the background of my mind. "There's no more harm in it than there is in drinking when you're thirsty." She tapped my arm with a hand at once loving and cautionary. "Stop thinking that there's anything evil in sex: morality simply doesn't enter into it at all. It's the same thing, isn't it, whether you have a little piece of paper saying you can do it, or not … But when I put it like that, I don't mean that promiscuity's anything except a betrayal of the whole idea. One's an absolutely free agent in sex, but it should be kept as – as a special gift, one of the highest you can give to anyone; and you give it them because you love them and because you've nothing dearer that you can let them have."

"Then you think it can never be wrong?"

"It can be wrong for three reasons." Thus, grave and lovely in her capability, she taught me. "Firstly, if there's any idea of over-persuasion on one side or the other: it should go by agreement, not by conquest. Secondly, if you *think* it's wrong you shouldn't do it: if you sleep with someone in spite of your scruples, then you're playing yourself false. Conviction of sin is in the heart, not in the code of conduct."

I nodded. "Yes, I see that … And the third reason?"

"A minor one – you may not agree. Have you read any Stendhal?"

"*Chartreuse de Parme*. That's all."

"He once quoted, in another book, a sentence from a twelfth-century 'Code of Love', which has stuck in my memory ever since I read it. It was: 'It is not seemly to love a woman whom one would be ashamed to want in marriage' " She glanced up at me questioningly. "I don't know if that strikes any chord."

"I agree with it absolutely."

"So … In any case, one's conception of loyalty should be the same, whether the tie is marriage or simply that of lover and mistress. Love is a contract, as binding and as carefully to be honoured as anything you can sign on the dotted line. But Marco," she pressed my hand again, as if there were now some new element in me which she would cherish, "if these few conditions are fulfilled, it's never wrong. You see? When it's between two responsible people who know what they're doing, it isn't a sin, and there's no one in the world who's competent to give it that label."

It took me a week to realize that this was an exact truth; and the realization marked the last of four distinct stages through which I had gone, in sexual matters. And since they *were* so clear-cut, they may be thus tabulated: (1) idealistic: the idea of going virgin to one's wife: (2) the daring first experience, the reactions to which are (a) a sense of shame, and (b) a feeling that one is now a cut above one's fellows: (3) promiscuity: sex as a matter of course – that is how an evening should end, and anything else is a flat and juvenile anticlimax; but sex is still sweet by reason of its being deliberately stolen: and lastly, (4) the new idea, that there is nothing evil in it, but it is still something special, to be used on special occasions, and for the rest a suitable object of sublimation.

Through such a slough had I dragged my feet for a substantial term of years, to be now confirmed and set right by Anthea's candour and honesty ... It must be said that she managed it admirably: the period of experiment and adjustment was a period in which, even though I was supposedly the expert and she the pupil, she still seemed capable of taking command and inducing order. The help she gave me – because of her candour, her accommodation of mind as well as of body – marked a subtle difference between her and, say, Alison, whose animal frankness had not been much more than the surface manifestation of a purely physical appetite. Anthea treated the thing as a problem, to be solved by two adults who did not throw off common sense and understanding with their clothes: she was clearly aware, all the time, that it was not enough for her to make me free of her body – she had to help me to exploit that freedom with every artifice of intelligence and trick of instinct which her liberality made available to her.

And for this last reason, we were never a prey to self-consciousness. Sexual fervour must imply, in some degree, an abandonment of dignity; but from the very beginning we were too much in accord to take note of this or to use it, even subconsciously, as a lever for dominance or a weapon of ridicule. It was enough that the wildness and the surrender of control were mutually induced and shared.

"Thank God," I said once, rather early in the morning, "that we can be frank about it. Thank God I don't have to knock on any doors. Thank God for a double bed."

She smiled. The curtains were drawn back, and the dawn light showed her face softened and contented. "It would be awful," she answered slowly, "if either of us had to ask … How *would* we get on if we had separate rooms? Think how self-conscious both of us would be, if I had to listen for footsteps, and you had to tramp down the corridor, and poke your head inside the room, and cough and look shifty … People who go in for twin beds must have a bad enough time, as it is."

"But if they were like us – "

"I don't see how they could be. There'd be bound to be a cold-blooded look about it, a sort of 'Here-I-am, I've-moved-over, you-know-damned-well-what-for' idea. I think that would get on one's nerves. Darling," she said suddenly, "we don't laugh too much, do we?"

"Why anxious?"

"Because it can be dangerous, I think: too many things turned into a joke can make the whole relationship flippant. We might begin to rely on cross-talk, on laughing instead of feeling … There's something more important, isn't there? – a sort of communion."

"A sort of communion," I repeated. I turned towards her. "By God, do you think I'll ever lose sight of that? Do you think the ambition that I have is going to be wrecked on a laugh? I'd sooner never make a flippant remark again."

"The ambition?"

"To remain deeply in love with you." I answered her slowly, wanting her heart to take hold of that moment and cherish it. "Already there's nothing comparable to that, for me."

"And how I'll help you …" She put her arms round my neck, twisting them till I was softly bound. "Marcus Hendrycks," she said, on a low note, "this is your home, this is where you're going to stay, this is your locked prison, and the key – " she now whispered, in the tightening of her throat, in the constraint of love – "is buried as deep – as deep – "

"The key is lost," I said. "*Tu veux?*"

It was her eyes, as wild and clear as a flame, which answered for her, and for me.

CHAPTER SEVENTEEN

When man is at peace with man, how much lighter than a feather is the heaviest of metals in his hand! He pulls out his purse and, holding it airily and uncompressed, looks around him as if he sought for an object to share it with.

STERNE, *A Sentimental Journey*

❖

With such strong backing, that year went like the wind. With the love she lavished on me, the humblest activity became a royal progress: with so many problems settled I was free to set a course and keep to it. Among these snapshots of contentment – sex fixed, loved assured, a régime of co-operation, Tim's strength as a buttress for us all, Elisabeth saying "You can hear it in the background? – the clarinet?", drinks in the middle of the night, the circle of the bedside lamp, the cigarette glowing in the darkness, the comradeship and the fulfilling laughter – among these interlocking certainties, I was out of the reach of harm.

In February I joined Julian (back from Spain, unharmed but twice as lean) on a paper which he was starting – a small weekly review of all the branches of entertainment to be found in London. There were four of us, working an almost supernatural number of hours a day in a little office off Ludgate Hill; and every week the twenty-four hours before going to press were a period of chaos out of which it seemed scarcely credible that the paper could emerge. But emerge it did: somehow it was got down to the printers, in driblets and hacked strips and 'triple urgent' sections, half advertising matter and half pencilled suggestions: somehow, every Friday, it reached the hands of the wholesalers and of the lone lorn man who sold it at the corner of St Paul's Churchyard. I suppose that Julian was in one sense the editor, though all our jobs were interchangeable: a representative week's work for me would be to write the editorial – a page of shorts which had to average a joke every three lines: to tout for advertisements by lying about the circulation: to settle the layout with the printers: to answer queries addressed to the information bureau: to dine at a restaurant, pub, or road-house, and write it up (on a mutual back-scratching basis): to review a book, play, film, ballet, concert, ice-hockey match, all-in wrestle, night club opening, meeting of the Public Morality Council, or Civil Liberties Rally; and to supply, while the printers waited, four very funny lines of verse to fill the gap on page 16 ... Those were full weeks: if I'd been on space I would have made my fortune. But £15 a month seemed to be all the paper would stand.

Unbelievably, it prospered. The circulation crept up, and the advertising revenue with it: the number of typists increased, and began to be called secretaries ... It was fun to watch the paper grow, and realize that it had been created out of nothing, that our efforts had put into the world something which hadn't been there before; even if the work had been drudgery, instead of varied and interesting, there would still have been that creative satisfaction to compensate us. We all enjoyed every moment of the struggle; and a small additional interest, for me, was the weekly effort to circumvent Julian and introduce some political jab into the editorial.

At the same time I was getting ahead with the novel, which was in fact nearly finished. After spending two whole months in Spain, it had been difficult to resist the temptation (and the prevailing fashion) of writing a book analysing the political history of the country during the past hundred years, ascribing the causes of conflict, and giving a considered estimate of the future. But I had resisted.

"And in any case," Tim had said, when we were discussing it, "you'll be on the wrong side. If the Fascists win, there'll be a real future for a pro-Franco book; but there are too many of the others already. At the moment it looks as if they *will* win: in which case we'll all be breaking our slats rushing for concessions, and propaganda *sub specie* Rio Tinto will have a big market."

"I don't want to write about politics. I want to be funny."

"Can't they mix?"

"Not my brand. That's one of the things one can't help noticing about Communists: they won't stand for laughter. Of course I know that what they're interested in isn't a laughing matter, but I don't think any movement loses by having a leavening of that sort."

"Said Dr Johnson: 'A man should pass part of his time with the laughers.' Singlemindedness is all very well, but you've got to consider what sort of a man you become in the process." He pondered for a moment. "Humour? Can you be as funny as James Thurber?"

"No, I can't. Nor Leacock, nor Robert Benchley, nor Thorne Smith, nor any of the people who can turn me inside out with a twist of the pen. But I've got an idea – I'm not sure how to describe it – 'Four Horsemen of the Apocalypse' on a Marx Brothers basis."

He laughed. "You've given yourself plenty of scope."

And so it proved. But the book emerged, compact enough and reasonably plausible – a modern novel with a certain satiric grin about it – and I sent if off to Julian's agents without much diffidence. I had worked pretty hard at it, not escaping an occasional protest from Anthea, who had liked going to bed early even before she met me and was now liable to be woken up by my preoccupied entrance at three o'clock each morning.

"Darling," she said on one occasion, "do you have to work so late when you've been at it all day as well? I never reckoned to share my life with a night watchman."

"Got to be done," I answered, dopey and half asleep. "Not much longer, anyway."

"A girl likes regular hours ... And the stuff you write between midnight and three isn't worth very much, is it?"

"No." Which was perfectly true: what had the appearance of an exquisite prose-poem at three a.m. usually looked like Sunday's gossip column in the morning. "But it gives me something to rewrite: it gets one stage over and done with."

As soon as it was finished, and I was still in the thick of working for the paper, I had a stroke of luck. At a studio party in Bloomsbury I found myself wedged next to a fat and keen-looking Jew who proclaimed himself, between drinks, to be a director of the Thunderbolt Film Studios; the fact might have been deduced from the way he was appraising the women present, as if he were a talent scout who only recognized one talent. He seemed a curiously impressionable man, and his little black eyes, when they were not focused on a contour glimpsed through the crowd, would seek mine as if looking for approval of his activity; and something – the drinks or the protective uproar of the room – prompted me to give him a line in bluff which was ludicrously successful.

When he volunteered some statement about the time wasted on a film set: "Ah, you have the same trouble, do you?" I remarked affectedly. "It appears to be chronic in every department of the cinema."

"You worked in the motion-picture business?"

"Only in America."

"Hollywood?"

"Naturally."

His nose twitched – an impressive phenomenon. "Acting job?"

Between swallows: "Dialogue writing," I told him. "I am on holiday at the moment, though it wasn't easy to break my contract."

And I talked in much the same strain for ten minutes or so, throwing in names and places and technicalities, till my companion's sweaty olive face had taken on an absurd deference, and even the impact of a young woman with a figure of prodigious exaggeration, who swayed past us like a poppy on a stalk, made only a fleeting impression. Presently, when I paused for refreshment: "I didn't catch the name," he said hesitatingly.

"Hendrycks," I answered, with some misgiving.

"What say?"

"Hendren."

"Herbert, eh?"

He looked puzzled, as well he might, and I was forced to add: "You remember '*One Night of Love*', surely?"

"Say, did you write the scenario of that?"

But I had turned away to talk to someone else. In a little while he plucked at my arm.

"I suppose you don't want a job in England?" he began.

"I am extremely busy at the moment," I answered, very sternly, as if he had made an offensive suggestion. "I'm under contract, and I'm due back in Hollywood in the autumn."

"But still, you've a lot of time. Come down to the Thunderbolt and look around. Have you any scenarios we could see?"

"None of my scenarios remains unsold for more than six hours."

"I suppose not." He appeared dejected, but added after a moment: "We could do with a good dialogue writer, you know. And the money isn't bad, at that."

I took one more drink, feeling at the top of my form, and asked: "What do you call not bad?"

"Well," he looked at me sideways, "we might run to five quid a day."

"Good heavens!" I said involuntarily.

"Of course I know it isn't up to Hollywood, but it's something."

I looked disgusted. "I needn't tell you that it is very far from what I've been used to," I answered, speaking the absolute truth for the first time. "But perhaps it would do no harm to keep my hand in."

In the end he sent a studio car for me at eight next morning, before I even had time to consider whether I had a hangover, and I was presented with a six weeks' contract at £30 a week. As well as the size of the salary (which it seemed I earned by hanging about the set, volunteering jokes when I thought of them, and attending an occasional 'story conference' from which nothing emerged save our relative capacities for lowering whisky), the fact that I was called for at that ridiculous hour might be taken as a sample of the futility which ruled the Thunderbolt Studios. For I was given no work of any sort for the next three days, which were taken up with some cabaret scenes; and on the fourth day (after a phone call at midnight bidding me to be present without fail at nine in the morning) I was only given something to do at half past five in the afternoon. There was evidence everywhere of the same preposterous extravagance and time-wasting: there was a whole corps of 'executives' aping Hollywood with multiple telephones and violent calls for extras, for real flowers in the ballroom, for experts on Adam ceilings: there were people kept hanging about for days on end with nothing to do, there was money poured out on details so trivial that only a lunatic with delusions of grandeur would have considered them for a moment. I myself was always being rung up, or traced by special messenger, or (once) summoned to a cinema telephone by a notice flashed on the screen: I would rush down to the Thunderbolt in a car driven by a chauffeur with every attribute of a Cossack save spurs and an Astrakhan cap. I would draw up with a squeal of brakes and a shower of gravel, I would tumble out and dart down the corridor to one of the boardrooms – to find it empty, to wander about for a couple of hours, to be noticed finally and told to report next day *without fail* with four extra lines for the Scotland Yard scene ...

In all the time I was there, I never had the smallest inkling of what the film was about. But I drew my money with commendable precision; and the only difficult part was the director's habit of calling me suddenly on to the set, saying "Give me a joke here – a short one," and then waiting – as everyone waited, electricians, property men, carpenters, dressers, camera experts, and the curious fellow who limped about brushing people's hair – while I set my brain to work, sweating under the arc-lamps, to turn out something very funny ... No one seemed to find this an odd way of making a picture: and indeed, at £5 a day I found it increasingly hard to quarrel with it myself.

A final proof of the extraordinary amateurishness of British pictures was instanced by the strange gang of people I now found myself working with – that curious half world of dance band leaders, show-girls, wrestling promoters, Jewish music hall comedians and those preposterous young women who sing 'hot numbers' with every part of their anatomy except the voice: that affluent stratum of society which seems to devote its time to spending, in the loudest possible fashion, at least ten times as much money as it was originally educated to handle. Their connection with the film world was obscure but well-established: indeed, the majority of British pictures may be taken as a monument to their standard of taste; and to work alongside them was deeply instructive, affording as it did a chance to discover just what sort of gods democracy will raise up when left to itself ... Incidentally, no account of twentieth-century culture would be complete without reference to the impact of the dance-band world upon the public consciousness: as well as strange words and phrases like 'rendition' or 'So-and-so will take the vocal' or 'Gob-stick' (clarinet) or 'Gut-bucket' (sousaphone), it has given us a new pronunciation – 'bokay' for bouquet, 'rómance' thus accented – as well as dance lyrics whose sentiment has set a new low level in slush and slime. In addition, its use of the microphone is in process of so distorting the public ear that in another fifty years no one will know what the natural human voice or the normal tone of an instrument sounds like: conditioned to accept a treacly boom as the proper quality of all musical sound, they will judge the dry purity of an unrelayed violin or a lyric tenor to be itself unnatural and obviously second-rate ... Working among these people, as I did for nearly two months, and noting their prodigious success and the amount of public esteem they commanded, it was difficult not to look forward to an English culture in which speech, music, and sentiment had alike been debased to a gutter level.

But April brought to our house a triple success in a world which seemed, by comparison with the Thunderbolt environment, to be midway up the slopes of Parnassus. Firstly, my book was accepted by a firm of publishers – Duncannon's – far more reputable than I had ever hoped for: Elisabeth's recital at the Welmore Hall attracted the notice of more than one critic of standing: and Anthea gave a one-man show which was a resounding success commercially as well as from the assured standpoint of merit. Of course, there was no need to exaggerate the worth of such successes, which by any significant standard was of the slightest; but by these three efforts, which came within a week of each other, we did seem to have justified our existence in a manner of which the outside world could take note: it was as if the strength of the house, hitherto in doubt, had now been vindicated by a threefold blow the echoes of which would never quite be lost. And basically it was a matter not of complacency but of relief – relief that the household had productive as well as comforting capacity.

I don't think any of us really enjoyed Elisabeth's concert, being far too nervous on her account; but after a shaky start (with a Haydn Andante in F Minor) she gained confidence, and the final item, the Mozart Sonata K 457, was played with a fluent delicacy which showed both her technique and her power of interpretation at their best. That, I thought as I sat back watching her white flickering hands and listening to the curiously dark and tragic flow of the last movement, which seems to deny its *molto allegro* label, that was how Mozart should be played: with fire, with love, with profusion of spirit ... Afterwards, when we met a tired and exalted Elisabeth in the ante-room at the back of the stage:

"We're so proud of you, darling," said Anthea, putting her arms round Elisabeth and kissing her. "Did you hear how they were all clapping at the end? I bet you get lovely notices."

"Clever girl," said Tim, with immense pride in his voice. A little earlier he had been the most nervous of us all, staring up at Elisabeth and gripping my arm in a paralysing fashion. "Clever girl …"

Over their shoulders I caught her eye, and she smiled at me, her whole face alight with a sort of brilliant triumph. "Well, Marcus," she said softly. "How was it, really?"

"Well," I answered, smiling, "as soon as I was able to listen instead of sitting there sweating and holding thumbs for you, it was first rate. We *are* terribly proud of you. You made the Mozart sound like – well, like the splendid piece of music it is. By the way, what's the marking of the second movement, exactly?"

She laughed, still nervously tense. "I'll not give you a weapon: you must find out for yourself. But I know that was the worst part: it's meant to flow on and on like a stream, isn't it? – and I tried too hard and took it too firmly. Did it sound terrible?"

"It sounded – strong, that was all. But you could hardly be expected to be in a *legato* mood, at the end of an evening like this. And the rest was beautifully done."

"I'm glad." Then she drooped suddenly, as if at the limit of her command. "Take me home, darling," she said to Anthea. "I'm so tired. It's been such a lovely day."

May was the Coronation. You couldn't miss that, however hard you tried, however determinedly your eyes were turned from the world inwards towards your own progress. The first stands had gone up in the Mall the previous December, and from then onwards the transformation had crept over the town bit by bit, eating up the suburbs, boarding over the more vulnerable windows, erecting barriers as insurmountable as the class ones of which they were the symbol, covering Hyde Park with what must have been, in scope and variety, the finest vista of sanitation in

Europe. ("Evidently," remarked Dr Barrow to me with a dry delightful coarseness, "evidently they anticipate the populace in a high degree of excitement."...) But London really was a mess: no building without its Union Jack, no view of the sky without its intervening paper streamer: only its height prevented the Nelson Column from becoming a gigantic maypole; Bond Street hung out the coroneted washing, Selfridges decked itself as the biggest laugh in London. ("No, madam," said an apocryphal policeman, "I don't think Mr Selfridge will be appearing on the balcony this evening.") And of the commercial side of the festival, the less said the better: at times, noting the flagrant profiteering, it was difficult not to conclude that the whole thing was a money-making ramp whose sole design was the enrichment of tradesmen.

At any rate, the atmosphere of gush, the immense and stupid crowds which clogged the town, and the astute flunkeyism of those who a year previously had been cheering themselves (and us) sick at Edward's Proclamation, was too much for us, and we spent the period in a borrowed cottage in Hampshire, working, playing poker, and brewing on Coronation night a rum punch such as left us prostrate with loyalty ... But the service itself was worth listening to, no matter how Republican the ear on which it fell: there was much comfort, as well as much that was stirring, in the music, in the really splendid fanfares, in Handel's 'Zadok the Priest' anthem; and there was one phrase, uttered by the Archbishop of Canterbury as he handed over the Bible to the King, which could not fail to remain in the memory: 'Here is wisdom: this is the Royal Law: these are the lively oracles of God' ...

"I wish," I said, when the service was over and the return procession to Buckingham Palace was being described, "I wish it was anything else but religion that inspired words and music like these. They're so fine and exciting, and the ideas they glorify are so bogus."

"Can't you think of them standing by themselves?" asked Tim. "If you don't like the associations, ignore them and concentrate on what you hear from the purely artistic standpoint."

"I suppose that's possible. But it still rankles that religiously minded people can point to so many achievements – in music and painting and especially in architecture – and say: 'There – that's what belief in God can produce.'"

"It isn't always belief in God, though," put in Elisabeth. "Lots of church music was just written to order, and I suppose even cathedral architects were only doing a job of work which had been commissioned from them. One of the loveliest things in music, Bach's B Minor Mass, had no connection at all with the glorification of God – it was written to curry political favour with the King of Saxony."

"What sort of procession is this?" suddenly broke in Anthea, who had been listening intently to the wireless. "Representative of the nation? It's all fighting men and stuffed diplomats. How about a few doctors and engineers? – how about a few *people*? They do these things better in Russia …"

"That would be too dull," I answered. "The idea *is* a sort of circus, after all; and for that you want the brightest colours possible. Not that I agree with the thing, as a function: in fact I think it's a pretty good tribute to England's servility that there isn't a terrific counter-demonstration."

"We've plenty to be proud of," said Tim sharply.

"That may be. But there's even more that's deadly wrong, and that's what we should worry about, instead of wasting time on this bolstered-up back-scratching," I sighed. "Oh well, one can hardly grudge people a bit of variety, a holiday from their usual filthy surroundings. They'll pay for it later, though: they'll pay with their lives for an agreeable ten-second's glimpse of a golden coach."

"Don't you think any of it's worth fighting for?"

"At present? – no. There's too much inequality, Tim: too much privilege. You're told you're fighting for England and freedom, and actually the truth is so very different. 'Fight to keep the rich where they are and the poor in the gutter' – that's what they'd say if they were honest: 'Fight to keep the City rolling, fight to give the ship-owners eleven million pounds each while half their work-people are rotting on the streets.' ... How can you expect a loyal and undivided nation, when it's split by injustice in that way? It's simply childish to ask us to line up and fight, just to make sure that those who have cornered an immense slice of undeserved possessions should be confirmed in that position. Are we mice or men? – slaves or determinate beings? What sort of democracy is it that we're going to die for? Things will have to be levelled out a good deal more before the words 'National Unity' make any sense ... But they could be levelled out, you know. Think how strong our unity might be, if every human being in the country was convinced on that point: think of the will and the energy which people would bring to National Service, and, if necessary, to war, if they were all fighting for something approaching a level stake. You see, the stuff *is* there, but it isn't so stupid as some people seem to think: it won't back second-rate causes and it won't go to war for a slogan that sounds like a music-hall joke as soon as the war's over. But if you base your unity on social justice, and make *that* worth fighting for, then you won't need white feathers, or any filthy nonsense like that, when the time comes. Your division will disappear, and you'll be able to count on any support you like."

"And until then?"

"Until then, you'll get pacifists with every conceivable justification for their refusal to fight, and you'll get chaps like me sneering at patriotism." I smiled. "But if that's the worst you'll get, you won't be doing so badly."

"Good old Marcus," said Anthea after a pause. "You never miss a chance of a little tub-thumping, do you? But I think I agree with most of that; and certainly today has given this country rather an odd taste, as far as I'm concerned."

"We might take a look at Europe," I answered slowly. "We might do a little exploring, before the whole continent blows up."

Anthea bought a car, we ran it in, we crossed via Dover–Calais, we made a beeline for Cannes and the sun; all within a fortnight of that Coronation afternoon. For my suggestion had seemed doubly attractive, when we got back to London and found its amenities still being slaughtered to make a provincial holiday: when I heard from Duncannon's that they could not produce any proofs for at least a couple of months: when Anthea met me one night with a long face, and said: "Our mouse is pregnant."… Clearly it was necessary to seek relief elsewhere; and a long and planless trip, ranging as far as we could and seeing as many countries as possible, was the obvious antidote to England's current diet of complacency. So we set out, almost on the spur of the moment; and I had not yet found an exhilaration equal to that of landing at Calais, and standing there, as it were, at the top of France, and being free of the past and ready to roam the whole of Europe as we willed.

As usual, it took no more than two hundred yards to get the feel of driving on the right-hand side; and our introduction to France – long straight roads, poplars, villages still battlescarred, military cemeteries, place names such as St Omer, Hazebrouck, Béthune, and Arras – all these formed a subdued prelude to the varied excitements which we knew lay ahead. We were in no hurry that day, and slept the night at Arras – or part of the night, for we talked till two a.m. with an old French Army officer, tremendously upright, tremendously self-conscious as a defender of *la patrie*, who seemed almost to be looking forward to another knock at the Germans and who took us outside to examine, by moonlight, the bullet holes which still marked the face of the *Mairie*. "Is everyone getting to be like that?" Anthea asked me later, when I was putting cold cream on a blistered forehead: "so charming, so proud, and so mistrustful? Is everyone really getting ready for the explosion?" But the question was rather more serious than our true mood warranted; and it disappeared for good with next morning's breakfast, the worlds' most civilized breakfast – *café complet*, in bed, with the one you love ...

We were four days in Paris, and three more cutting a swathe through the Burgundy district, the warm heart of France, loitering in places whose names read like the more endearing pages of a wine list – Chambertin, Vougeot, Epergnay, Beaune, Mâcon – with a special session at Nuits St Georges; and then we set ourselves on the *Route Napoléon* and hurried to the sea. But Cannes was over-civilized, and St Tropez sub-tropic: we stayed on the coast not more than three days before heading north again, first to Geneva and then on to Lake Thun. Geneva was depressing – or perhaps it was the regret in our own minds that all that the place stood for was steadily sliding into the pit; on the Thun lakeside, however, we came upon a small village, Därligen, where we had a room with a balcony right over the water, and a view of a black-and-green mountain sloping into the sea, and our first bathe in a little *Strand-Bad* sheltered by trees. And when we drove round the lake, to a tiny village with a lovely name – Beatus

Hohle – we had another fine view, with deep green shadows falling across the lake like the brush-strokes of a firm and loving painter.

"We'll remember Därligen," we told each other as we drove away one morning under a blazing sun; but of course we didn't, of course it was lost in the infinite splendour of the mountains where presently we climbed. We filled up with petrol at Interlaken (and had a laughing two-minute encounter with an Englishman driving another Talbot – a coincidence which seemed to take him by the throat, with sheer stupefaction); and then suddenly we were among the hills, doing an ominous amount of second-gear work already, and with the warning notices about giving the inside berth to every *Post-Wagen* lending to our progress a sense of imminent danger, of 200-feet drops and hungry chasms, of wheels skidding within a few inches of death ... We crossed three noble passes that day, the Grimsel, Furka, and St Gotthard, climbing each time by a sustained effort which took us, in bottom gear, round innumerable hairpin bends, over steep shoulders which it seemed no car could surmount, beneath overhanging walls of rock, above the snowline where the road had been cut by steam-plough and its sides still gleamed and dripped – a reminder that, for all the warm sunlight, we were nearly 7,000 feet up and out of the embrace of the fat plains. Three times we made the slow and laboured ascent, three times we paused at the top to survey the view we had won – the line of rolling mountains, the crashing escarpments, and the ribbon of road below us, up which other pigmy cars were churning their way, like the animated figures of a model village; and three times we completed the descent with care and prudence, slipping down the falling route and past the banked corners like a fugitive who fears the hazards of the way more than the peril behind him. The car behaved all the time with an admirable dependability, jibbing neither at slope nor corner nor the vilest of surfaces, doing exactly what it was asked to do and above all steering round those wicked hairpin bends, as if it were running on rails.

We lunched at Gletsch, and looked, like good tourists, at the scarred outcrop of the glacier which overhung the village, dark blue, pitted, and dusty – "Just like a glacier," said Anthea disappointedly: "why, I *knew* it would look like that."... Indeed, the only thing to recall about Gletsch was the fact that, confused by lunch and the switch-over from French- to German-Swiss, I asked for ten litres of petrol with the immortal words: "*Zehn, s'il vous* please." After lunch, more climbing, more acute twists of the road, more cringing away from the dominant *Post-Wagens*, until finally we had reached the head of the last pass, the St Gotthard, and the way to Bellinzona and the plains lay open.

Comparatively open, that is to say. "I'd rather go down this side than climb it," said Anthea as we began the descent; but indeed, we had quite sufficient to cope with as it was. The southern side of the St Gotthard is distinguished by an exceptional number of hairpins, coming very close together and often ferociously acute; and to steer a smooth course, to control the speed of the car, and to give at the same time as easy a passage as possible to the ascending cars, who were in far worse case, meant that there could not be a second's relaxation of attention, even when the eye was tempted by a green opening valley and a range of hills of such splendour. Bottom gear was not enough to hold the car on the steepest parts; and I had to picture all the time, as I wrestled with the erratic camber, those overworked brakedrums getting hotter and hotter and perhaps burning out altogether ... Of course it could not last for ever: gradually the slope lost its menace and the road (after a last vicious bunch of hairpins like the curl of a whiplash) shed its quality of aggressive surprise: soon we were clear of the worst, and within sight of Airolo, the first village of the plain. Near the bottom we passed an enormous closed Rolls-Royce, toiling upwards with a mountain of luggage strapped on the roof: at the wheel a harassed and sweating chauffeur was dealing with an acute corner by reversing on to the grass verge, and in the back were two old ladies, very upright in grey silk, sitting like a pair of Queens Regnant in a glass-sided box. If they were aware either of the heat or the nobility of the country they were traversing, they gave no sign … However, they did at least acknowledge our presence: as the little windswept Talbot slid by, crossing to its wrong side to give the Rolls a better chance, they both turned and stared sideways at us – at Anthea with a gay red scarf over her hair, at my flaring check shirt and the goggles pushed up on my forehead, at the Swiss pennant, the hopeless tangle of suitcases and rucksacks in the back, the palpable unorthodoxy of the whole carload; but when, out of habit, we waved a greeting, their glances centred themselves again like foolproof gyroscopic compasses.

"Oh dear," said Anthea, when we were past and their dust was thick all around us, "are we really as disreputable as that?"

"Good grief, I should hope so! Would you like to be touring this country in that sort of conservatory-on-wheels?"

She turned to me with a lift of her eyebrows. "Angry, darling?"

"A little. Every single English car we've passed so far has waved back. It's just damned snobbery to cut us like that."

She laughed aloud. "You are a baby, really. This isn't Blackpool promenade. And they weren't wavers, anyway."

"String 'em up, then. The firing-squad for financiers, the lamp-post for snobs."

Anthea patted my hand. "We've got each other, darling," she answered, grotesquely sentimental. "I'll do all the waving you want, free."

"It isn't the same thing," I said, as I accelerated for the first straight stretch of road since the early morning. "It isn't the same thing at all."

We were making for the shores of Lago di Maggiore: we had chosen the village from the map, for its position and for the charm of its name – Vira-Magadino; and as it turned out, the choice could not have been bettered. "This is the place," said Anthea, with extreme confidence, as we left the main road and began to climb the hillside track which led to the Italian frontier; and "This *is* the place," she repeated, when the last corner was turned and the superb position of the hotel became apparent. It was about 300 feet above the lake surface, standing on an outcrop of rock in such a fashion that its wooded garden and small terraced restaurant seemed to hang over the water: its view included the whole northern half of the lake, the range of hills opposite, and the town of Locarno – "Very clear," said Anthea, "even though the Pact is fairly misty at the moment." The hotel could accommodate no more than a dozen people, and in fact we had it to ourselves, save for a French couple – middle-aged, talkatively charming, and still as patently in love with each other as Anthea and I must have been. It was they who gave us all the guidance we needed in the matter of walks, bathing places, and local history; and sometimes the four of us would drink together on that strange overhanging terrace, sharing a *carafe* of red wine, and the sun which filtered through the vine-clusters, and a deep satisfaction with our lives and loves and selves.

Indeed, these friendly sessions in the cool of the lakeside evening, might by themselves have been sufficient warrant for our intensity of contentment, had there not been much more that made Vira-Magadino a lasting delight. Our room was airy and pleasant, overlooking the lake and having the sun on its balcony from midday onwards: "Hurrah for civilization and *bidets!*" said Anthea, lapsing into utilitarianism, as soon as she walked into it – though that invaluable adjunct was possibly the least of its charms ... And here again, if there was one thing which might have been taken as the crystallization of all the happiness we found in this corner of the world, it was the simple act of breakfasting, each morning, on the small private balcony which no other eye could reach but which had as its outlook one of the finest lakes in Europe. We discovered its exhilaration the first morning, when the servant – an Italian-Swiss girl with dark eyes and an angelic smile – had entered with the tray at nine o'clock and, throwing us a good morning as she passed the bed, carried it out to the balcony: when I had put on a dressing-gown and myself wandered out to a world which seemed to hold only fresh warmth and the gleam of sun on water: when I had glanced down at the breakfast tray and then called out:

"Anthea! Peaches!"

She came out presently and stood by my side with her hand on my shoulder: the stone balcony was cool under our bare feet, the morning air like a friendly caress, free from languor; and together we drank in the superb view which seemed to be our exclusive privilege, to be enjoyed only from our secure haven – the glittering, dancing lake, the haze overhanging Locarno, the green-grey slopes beyond, the white steamer just setting out from Magadino landing stage towards Brissago, with the noise of its engines reaching us, and its wash spreading in a series of gentle ripples, twin arcs which widened to infinity. Such was our morning greeting, such the setting which made of our happiness almost a living substance, to be handled with the joy and pride of ownership ... Her eyes still held by

Maggiore's loveliness, Anthea began to eat a peach, in an ear-wetting fashion which she should have long grown out of: her face seemed at once fresh and fatigued, as if sleep had only just been able to make up her expense of vitality.

"This is the finest spot I've ever found," I said presently. But my eyes were still on her face, as if they knew better than my mind, where lay a beauty and an excitement which could challenge the lake even at this revealing hour of the morning. "We can call this a honeymoon, darling."

She smiled up at me. "Whether we call it that or not ..."

"Darling, you *were* sweet."

"Was I? You make it easy, easy and natural." Occasionally Anthea took over the initiative, made love to me, 'did everything' with a candour as lovely to watch as her moving face. "This is just the place I'd have chosen for a honeymoon," she went on, turning back to Locarno's hazy outlines and the dying ripples of the ferry-boat. "It is fine, of itself: and love clinches it." She took another bite out of her peach, hydraulically. "I love you more than peaches," she concluded, in an indistinct voice, as the juice ran down her chin on to her breast, "but peaches get a vote too."

"Sensual little pig."

"A girl likes a bit of everything ... Won't it be lovely when the sun comes round, and we can bathe down there!"

'Down there' was a little vineyard right on the lake's edge, fenced off from the other fields and reserved as a bathing place for the hotel: later in the morning we climbed down to it and spent an hour alternately lying in the dappled sunshine under its deep green canopy, or bathing in the warm water and swimming out to one of the curiously shaped fishing boats which had their nets spread on a framework over the stem, like the hood of an old-fashioned wagon. Later still we drove round to Locarno, and then on down the lakeside, passing at least two villages – Ascona and Brissago – which in their colour, setting, and aspect rivalled anything either of us had yet seen. They had the true loveliness of symmetry, those little water's edge hamlets; and exploring them on foot or pausing for a drink under a café awning which shadowed a few feet of the lake itself, we no longer doubted that this corner of Europe was, of all others, the one to which we had lost our hearts.

We drove back in the cool of the evening, making a slow pace through the dust, which we had endured since Calais and which had turned the green car into a grey-white ghost. We left the lake at one point, crossing the flat plain: we passed a road gang, of bronzed men stripped to the waist and spendidly muscled, who straightened up to watch us go by and smiled at Anthea with alarming attractiveness: we passed a village in which the women standing at their doorways waved to us, smiling also as if we were part of a gala procession which they were there expressly to welcome. Presently we turned to the lake again, running down its eastern side with the last of the sun setting the water on fire: presently we were home, home to a final bathe, to an *apéritif* with the French couple on the vine-hung terrace where the birds and insects chirped a muted chorus to our slow exchange of sentences: presently it was dark, and silent, and we were dining on the balcony under a string of fairy lamps, and Anthea was looking at me over the rim of her glass, looking at me with a love and confidence which made it impossible not to take her hand and press it to my cheek ... Before us was the lake, now a black sheet of water whereon the lights of Locarno, and of the stray houses on the hillside, were reflected with faithful clarity: behind us was the shadowed room and the wide cool bed, around us a night which embraced us, and all humanity, with tenderness, with the uncloying kisses of darkness; and in our hearts such a love and such expectation of delight as seemed almost unendurably sweet.

We had come sixteen hundred miles to find Maggiore, and Vira-Magadino, and it had been worth every mouthful of dust. But what we had found besides, in our own bodies and spirits, transcended even Maggiore's enchantment.

Thus, for a space, peace, rest, heat, clear water, love; and then, with three weeks' sun packed into our bodies, we turned ourselves into explorers again and drove on towards Austria. "Darling, you *are* looking well," Anthea called out to me suddenly, when we were filling up again at Bellinzona and I was flicking over the radiator with a wash-leather: "the difference from that first night on Westminster Bridge is absolutely amazing." "But you fell in love with me then," I answered – rather vaguely, because I was doing a sum in my head which involved the relative price of a litre of petrol in sterling, paid for in Swiss francs which had themselves been exchanged against French ones and would shortly become Austrian *schillings*. (It seemed to work out at half a guinea a gallon: possibly through an error in addition, though that may have been the actual price of Shell in this backward country.) "If it was love then," I went on, "I'd like to know just how tied up you are now."

Not very much later we were well up above the mountains again. That was a good day's drive, taking in three passes – the St Bernhardin, the Albula and the Ofed – crossing the Italian frontier at Münster, and finishing up at Merano, where we spent one night. We had hesitated about entering Italy even for this short stay – "Are they friends with us this afternoon?" asked Anthea as we slowed down for the frontier-post, "or is it one of these Days of Hate and Vengeance?" But things seemed normal, barring a lengthy delay over the stamping of our *carnet* – and barring also our scrutiny by an Italian officer, infinitely polite, infinitely haughty, superlatively cloaked, who strode round the car as if he were reviewing a defaulters' parade. When we had borne it for some moments: "This is disconcerting," Anthea whispered to me. "Should we say '*Viva* something'? Is he going to explode?"

"It's all right," I whispered back. "He's only doing it for your benefit, so that you can have a good look at him – and he at you. They don't get all the pretty girls they need, at six thousand feet. And I must say he's damned good-looking."

But if we found the examination uncomfortable, it was nothing to the ordeal at the Brenner next morning, when we left Italy and passed into Austria. Here was a frontier-post so martial that I was ashamed of presenting myself in civilian clothes: here were men and officers so sharp-eyed and so fiercely efficient that it seemed impossible that we were not breaking some regulation and would be led away in chains. Every piece of luggage was searched, every item of equipment checked against the list on the *carnet*: my camera excited a frenzy of inquisitiveness, and even the hub cover of the spare wheel was unscrewed and sniffed into – presumably for contraband mice. Inside the little office I had to answer question after question: what was my purpose in whipping in and out of Italy like that, had I taken any photographs that day, had I not exchanged more *lire* than I had declared on the form, how was it that the description on my passport had been altered from 'Student' to 'Writer'? And when, reluctantly released, I came out again into the pale cold sunshine, it was to find Anthea sitting in the car surrounded by a whole detachment of *carabinieri*, staring at her as if she were something in an auction room – something appetizing but probably illegal ... No, the Brenner Pass was not pleasant, in spite of the beauty of its setting and the nobility of its surroundings; and it was a relief to leave the little hotbed of fervent chauvinism behind us, and drop down to the plains, to the Tyrol and Innsbruck.

We were three days there, charmed by its peaceful and welcoming air, and three more at Klagenfurt in Carinthia; and then, in Carinthia also, we came upon another little village which we said again, with the same conviction: "This is the place ..." It was called Feld-am-See, a cluster of houses on the edge of a tiny lake to the north of Villach; and this time our hotel was right on the waterfront, and we took our meals on a sort of combined terrace and landing-stage round which the knowing fish loitered all day, as overfed and choosy as the pigeons in Trafalgar Square. The place had not the solitude of Vira-Magadino: in fact, the hotel was full, though the only foreigners besides ourselves were an engaging couple from Prague – Czech man, Russian girl – with whom as it happened we spent a good deal of time. The remainder were Austrians: solid, kindly folk who really sounded as though they meant '*Grüss Gott*' when they said it, who exclaimed "*Mahlzeit!*" to the general world when they entered the dining terrace, who drank beer and sang nobly and were unenviously proud of their countryside.

Naturally I invested in a pair of *Lederhosen* – those leather shorts which, besides being the delight of tourists, have at the same time a genuine native existence of their own, based on their exceptional comfort and simplicity; and Anthea bought the local 'peasant costume', complete with a flowered *Dirndl* which became her exceedingly well.

There was a honeymoon couple in the hotel, a sleepy-eyed pair of Austrians who started to yawn and stretch at 9.15 each night and slunk upstairs with expressionless faces at 9.30. But it could hardly be maintained that we were much better ourselves – as might be deduced from the face of the waiter who brought us our *Kaffee mit Schlag* each morning: his glance would flicker from Anthea's half-buried head to my bare chest, he would give me the widest conceivable grin as he turned from drawing the curtains, and his inquiring "*Gut geschlaffen?*" had a rich satiric quality at which it was impossible to take offence ... We were intensely happy by that little lakeside: the days flowed by under a warm sun and a sky whose feathered blueness turned the lake into a sapphire; and with the Czech pair – Leo, huge and slow-moving and deep of laughter, and Maria, the Russian girl who was tiny and had a kind of waspish beauty as potent as her tongue – we sampled everything that Feld-am-See had to offer, and found no flaw in it anywhere. We would bathe nearly all day, the four of us – or rather, settle down in one corner of the miniature *Strand-Bad*, Anthea sketching, myself scribbling an 'Englishman Abroad' column for Julian's paper, Leo splashing about on the log which served as a diving platform, Maria talking in a high incisive voice of the sacredness of Communism, of the god Lenin, of Russia's task in a cut-throat world. Then we might climb up to the tree-shaded waterfall above the village in search of coolness, or row across the lake to the tiny *Heuriger* and there drink a bottle of Niersteiner and enjoy the *lüstig* jollity of *Dorf-Musik*, the village carpenter playing the harmonica, the couples sweating at a *Schuhplattler-Tanz*. Or else we might wander through the woods picking wild strawberres for supper – holding hands, calling to each other through the sun-filtering trees, happy in the simplicity of sensual perception.

In the whole of Feld-am-See there was only one flaw – the breath of politics, of which we became aware for the first time. There was some kind of *Student-Haus* in the village; and many of the young men, exceedingly fierce in aspect, hardly bothered to conceal their Nazi tendencies: they answered a "*Grüss Gott*" with a level stare and an ejaculation of "*Heil!*", and it was clear that this was all you would get and you could take it or leave it.

"Yes, they're all Nazis," said Leo when I asked him about it: "it's very strong round here, as well as in the Tyrol."

"Do you think it will come to Austria?"

He shrugged. "Who knows? There is much discontent, there is much poverty: men look around them for a saviour, and they hear of one just over the border ..."

"Dope-fed swine!" interjected Maria, her eyes on the white stockinged group we had just passed. "I'd like to show them how we treat counter-revolutionaries in Russia."

So much hate, so much cruelty of man to man ... But Anthea and I, at any rate, could forgive them their Fascism on account of the other aspects of their studenthood – their corps hats with the tassels, their romantic duelling-scars, their splendid voices when they sang at night from boats which moved over the water bearing lanterns and torches, when they sang not *Horst Wessel* but *Augustin* and *'Burschen heraus!'* and those songs of Heine's which Schubert has glorified ... Those moments seemed to come straight from fairyland; and it was those that we chose to remember.

So much for Carinthia: next was Hungary and Budapest.

It had practically been decided beforehand that we would name Budapest the finest city we had ever seen; and it was agreeable to find that we could endorse this view with a clear conscience. We made the approach to it a slow one, loitering for two days in those wide plains, sometimes richly fertile farming land, sometimes dressed with vineyards, sometimes no more than flat grassland wherein we could see droves of horses – horses which would take fright at the noise of the car and stampede away, their uncut manes streaming like wild banners with the speed of their passage. That was Hungary – and here was Budapest, a city which seemed all Danube, all spiders of light following the curve of the river, all thronging cafés and open-coated strollers. We saw all the sights: we climbed the hill of Gellerthegy, from which we could look down on the whole magnificence of the city: we shopped in the Vaci Utca, we bathed on Margitsziget, we drank sleepy Hungarian wine and topped it off with Barack, and ate paprika chicken on the terrace of the Dunapalota ... The night life of Budapest – in its most simple form of café-lounging and strolling along the river front – must command the loveliest setting and be the most exhilarating in all Europe.

Nothing befell us there: we were free to soak ourselves in its colour and its profoundly moving spirit; and it was with regret that we made Budapest the peak of the journey and turned homewards again after ten days of it. But the road back was no monotonous retracing of our steps, for "Let's take in all the capitals we can," said Anthea the night before we started, and accordingly we planned a route through Vienna, Prague, Berlin, and Brussels. Vienna, by contrast with Budapest, was wretchedly depressing; and it was there that political affairs made themselves felt again, and the realities of a decayed Empire and a dying city were paraded for all to see.

I had never been there before, but my father had lived there before the Great War and had often told me about it; and what I carried in my memory contrasted pitifully with Vienna's poverty-stricken atmosphere and its air of nostalgic despair. One could hardly bear to sit in a café, so many were the beggars – neatly dressed, with young student faces or the laboured carriage of old age – who wandered among the tables with postcards or matches or pen-and-ink sketches: whose eyes stared from pinched and under-fed faces at the sleek opulence of the foreigners crowding the Bristol or the Imperial: who would watch a party leaving a restaurant table and seize on the scraps of food which remained uneaten ... And that other sign-manual of poverty – the number of young, good-looking and obviously gentlewomen who were on the streets was apparent every time we walked down the Kärntnerstrasse or explored the noble solemnity of the Schotten-Ring.

"And the worst of it is, it's our fault," said Anthea one night, when after a day at Schönbrunn we were dining at Sacher's, and had watched a wretched old man in tailored rags hawking some miserable daubs round the restaurant at fifty *pfennige* a time. "*We've* destroyed this country, and made this city what it is. I'm ashamed to be English and to live in a rich city like London, when Vienna – which is ten times more civilized – is in this state."

She said a good deal more in the same strain; and presently a young man who had been sitting at the next table edged over and joined in the conversation, at first in strained English and then in German. When he spoke his own tongue he whispered ... I noticed that he had the little striped ribbon of the Fatherland Front in his lapel, and when I questioned him about it: "You see we have only one party, Schuschnigg's," he answered in a low voice, "and it is best to belong to it." His eyes, which were grave as his thin face was grave, held mine for a moment before they turned away to survey the sparsely filled tables of Sacher's ground floor. "You know my sympathies are yours," he went on softly, without looking at me, "and there are many such in the *Vaterland-Front*, but our time is not yet. Since Dollfuss killed our comrades and destroyed their homes, in 1934, we have said nothing out loud. Even if that word '*Genosse*' (comrade) was overheard, I might find myself in prison."

"But Schuschnigg himself?" I answered in the same low tones. "Has he a following? Will he remain in power?"

"He makes the mistake of ignoring the workers. One day he may need their help. One day, the *Anschluss*, and Hitler marches. It is only the workers who can stop him, but they will not stop him just to keep Schuschnigg's spies and torturers in office." His pale eyes flashed. "But who knows? Perhaps we strike first, perhaps we will gain power before that."

"There are many Nazis here?"

"More in the West, in the Tyrol and at Linz," he answered. "But in Vienna too, many young men of my own age think that in Hitler lies Austria's greatest hope."

"Certainly there must be changes, before long."

He looked round at me, and nodded. "You have seen Vienna? It is all like that, all like the old man over there," he pointed, "trying to be neat, and even gay, when he has not enough to eat. I have just finished at the University, a law student, but there is no work for me. I do a little typing, that is all. Certainly there must be changes."

"And Hitler would bring prosperity?"

"To some. A few doorkeepers would be made factory managers, a few *Sturmabteilungen* who cannot write would be made sub-editors of the *Wiener Tageblatt*. And I suppose that all over Austria the painters would be busy changing 'Dollfuss-platz' into 'Adolf-Hitler-platz'. And ah yes! someone would get a job digging up Planetta and Holzweber, who murdered Dollfuss, and burying them in Stephans-Kirche – "

"They'd never do that," I interrupted: "they were simple gangsters, those two."

"Well, isn't that a reason? Wait till we hear the jackboots on Vienna's cobblestones ... But for me there would be nothing: it is known that I hate the Nazis, and I would probably be shot or imprisoned. It is saddest for the Jews in Vienna: they believe that the *Anschluss* must come, and they know what will happen to them then." He sighed, looking round the room as if he saw its inherent hopelessness for the first time. "It was the War, I suppose," he finished sadly. "Versailles has many victims."

"It seems to be agreed now that it was a bad peace, an impossible one, though in England only the Liberals and the Labour Party said so at the time. You know they did all they could to prevent Germany being crushed?"

He nodded. "So I have heard. But your financiers and your war-makers were too strong ... They were too strong for us, too: I was born during the War, and my mother died in the blockade: you can understand why I am thin," he smiled, with a ghastly jocularity, "and why there are so many cripples and beggars in the streets of Vienna, and so many pretty women too. And the worst of it is, many people remember 1919, and think of England as the enemy still, and want to join up with Germany and have their revenge."

"That would settle nothing."

"That would settle nothing," he repeated after me. "But it is an easy thought, when one is hungry, and remembers the War and the Peace, and wants something to hate." Then he turned to Anthea, with a charming smile – the signature of a natural courtesy. "We are boring you, *gnädige Frau?*" he asked formally. "You understand German?"

"Only a little," Anthea answered, "but I've been following what you've said."

Considerately, the young man slipped into his strained English again, and we talked of the film we had seen the previous night – *Dreigroschenoper*. After that, Anthea whispered to me, and a trifle belatedly I stood our companion a meal: his politely ravenous air as he disposed of trout and a *Wienerschnitzel* endorsed her intuition. We finished up the evening at *Femina*, which was obviously another treat for him ... As we said goodbye in the quiet street outside our hotel: "You have been most kind," he said gratefully. "I wish there were something I could do in return." He considered for a moment. "Have you been to Grinzing?"

"No, not yet. We were hoping to go."

"You shall come with me, as my guests."

"You shall come with us, as ours." Anthea corrected him. "We have a car – we'll call for you."

And so, after an amiable wrangle, it was arranged. But the "*Servus, Genosse!*" with which he saluted me on parting was in fact the last we heard of him. He was not at his address when we called next day, nor did he reappear at Sacher's before we left Vienna. "Perhaps he had no money, and was ashamed," said Anthea when we were speculating about it. Either that, or else he had for the first time talked a little too loudly. We never found out, and it cast a shadow over the rest of our stay, in a city which had its fill of shadows already.

On to Salzburg, where my *Lederhosen* came into their own, and three days of the Festival enabled us to attend *Don Giovanni* and *Die Meistersinger*, both conducted by Toscanini, and a concert under Bruno Walter which included the most stirring performance of Brahms' Second Symphony I had ever heard. But apart from the music, Salzburg was rather too much of a good thing – too many foreigners, too much fancy dress and self-conscious junketing, and above all too much snobbery about the Festival itself: the atmosphere in the *Festspielhaus* rivalled Covent Garden for bad manners and high-class gush. But that corner of the world was not all yawns and sophistication; and in the Salzkammergut, where presently journeyed, we found such simplicity of loveliness as would have balanced a dozen opera houses, with Ascot and the Horse Show thrown in. For there was peace, under an unrivalled sun and by water the colour of floodlit emerald; and whatever we were doing – bathing at Mondsee, climbing the Schaffberg, wandering round Bad Aussee and St Gilgen, sipping the first drink of the day on the terrace of the White Horse Inn at St Wolfgang, recoiling before the almost superhuman baroque of the nearby church – we were conscious always that the time could not have been better spent. I had picked up the proofs of my book in Salzburg; and correcting them in places of such charm seemed to inform Nature with exactly the right measure of intellectual activity. The book, in print, seemed very jerky and amateurish, but I hoped that was the fault of our flawless surroundings.

Prague approached Budapest in its liveliness and attraction: Berlin was drab, slouching, and sullenly militant – a city of darkness in which our gay little car with its triple pennants – Hungarian, Austrian, and Swiss – seemed a shamefully flippant intruder. "Hitler is in Munich, at another exhibition," our hotel proprietor told us, and when we had voiced a cautious surprise at the number of these gatherings, he, like the young student in Vienna, opened his heart and showed us its bitterness. Hitler was mad, he said with quiet conviction: mad, or drunk with power; he had ruined the tourist trade, he had brought the standard of living down to the gutter, he was heading straight for war. Goering was a drug-taker and a homosexual, Goebbels a blasphemous little ape. The Jews were always being beaten up – one had been stabbed in the Kurfürstendamm that very morning – but nothing was said about these blockheads of SA and *Schützstaffeln*, who marched about like drunken swine molesting decent people and turning Berlin into a dirty Nazi pigsty. No, he wasn't a Socialist: he took no interest in politics, never had and never would; but it was enough to turn any one into a Red, the way these jumped-up guttersnipes behaved …

A man prejudiced, with a grievance and a bias, we thought as we left him after dinner and strolled towards Unter den Linden; but whether or not we were affected by his denunciation, we certainly found Berlin a caricature of what it had been. My father had talked of this city also, and I had spent some time there in 1934; and even to my memory it was only a shadow of its former robust self. It was not the number of uniforms on the streets, or the obvious poverty of the majority of passers-by, or the truculent stupidity on the faces of the SA men slouching down the pavements: all these might have passed as natural evidence of a period of transition, if it had not been for the utter deadness of the whole town. Indeed, Unter den Linden, which I remembered as a lively thoroughfare crowded with traffic and window-shoppers, now seemed a very graveyard of civic aspiration.

"Isn't this queer, darling?" exclaimed Anthea, when we were sitting in a café near the *Tiergarten* end. "It's like my idea of the Island of the Dead ... And so far I've liked all the main streets. What was the name of the lovely one in Prague, running all the way up hill?"

" 'Vaclavske,' " I answered, "though I wouldn't guarantee the pronunciation. But we've certainly taken a good sample of them – Rue de Rivoli in Paris, Laupenstrasse in Bern, the *Kärntnerring*, the Corso in Budapest. And now this ..." I looked round me – at the stray couples under the trees in the centre, at the few passers-by, at the trio of uniformed SA men clumping up the street like conscripted plough-boys given, for one night, the freedom of the city. It was all dead, all sullen and vaguely dangerous. "No cream, no butter, not much meat: plenty of whale-oil and bullets. And you saw the clouds of dust rising from the only *Tischfrau* in the hotel ... Well, if they'll stand for it, it can only be because they're expecting to win something very different, in one way or another, before long."

"War?"

I nodded. "I suppose so. Or the threat of it, if that's enough. The main point is that they *deserve* something very different. And if we won't give it them when they're weak, why should I fight to keep it from them when they're strong?"

"There may be a settlement without fighting."

"With this spirit?" I swept my hand round. "It's too late. And that's our fault, as sure as we're going home tomorrow."

We left Berlin by *Avus*, the roadrace track, on which we gave the little car its head and did a speedometer eighty-two. And that might be called the only part of the homeward journey which we enjoyed. It rained from Berlin to Calais without respite: the windscreen-wiper jammed before we had gone ten miles; and though our route lay through noble country – Frankfurt, the Rhine, Bonn – yet the greater part of it was completely spoilt by the number of hateful little notices – Jews Keep Out, Jews Not Wanted, The Jews are Our Misfortune – which disfigured nearly every village we passed through. Nor was it possible to ignore the copies of the *Stürmer*, whose usual flaring and pornographic front page shouted at us from a dozen display boxes on our journey … That was the message we took out of Germany: we could not help doing so. And incidentally, though the famous *Autobahnen* were models of what main roads should be, yet they seemed to have been built at the expense of the rest of the trunk system, which was neglected to a degree we had only found rivalled in the remoter parts of Hungary. It was a relief to pass the last militant frontier-post, to *heil* Hitler with a last tongue-in-cheek formality, to fill in the *Grenzbescheinigung* form and smuggle two whole registered marks out of that rule-ridden country: to reach the *pavé* and the milkcarts of Belgium and know that the stress of Europe was behind us.

As we were waiting for the car to be loaded at Calais: "Seven thousand and two miles," I said, reading from the speedometer. "And we're three months older than when we last stood on this quay ... A comprehensive trip, darling. Enjoyed it?"

"M'm ..." Anthea was combing Europe's dust out of her hair in the traffic-mirror. "We found some lovely places, Marcus, didn't we? But whether they'll be able to stay lovely is another question. There's a little matter of *Sturm und Drang* ... What'll happen to that lake in Carinthia if the Nazi cross the border? What will Prague be like? What'll be left of Vira-Magadino if they start squabbling about it?"

In Calais harbour a tug hooted. It was, possibly, the most coherent answer which Europe could give, at the moment.

PART FOUR

❖

Tendency To A Design

CHAPTER EIGHTEEN

BOTTOM: *What beard were I best to play it in?*
QUINCE: *Why, what you will.*
BOTTOM: *I will discharge it in either your*
straw-colour beard, your orange-tawny beard,
your purple-in-grain beard, or your French-
crown-colour beard, your perfect yellow.

SHAKESPEARE, *A Midsummer Night's Dream*

You are horrified at our intending to do
away with private property. But in your
existing society, private property is already
done away with for nine-tenths of the
population; its existence for the few is solely
due to its non-existence in the hands of
those nine-tenths.

KARL MARX and FRIEDRICH ENGELS,
The Communist Manifesto of 1848

This Autarchy of Selfhood, which we blame
not at all in plants and scarcely in brutes,
is by Reason denounced heartless, and
outlawed from the noble temper of man, the
original sin and cause of half his woes and
shames.

ROBERT BRIDGES, *The Testament of Beauty*

429

*My dream expanded and moved forward. I
trod again the dust of Posilipo, soft as the
feathers in the wings of Sleep. I emerged on
Baia; I crossed her innumerable arches; I
loitered in the breezy sunshine of her mole; I
trusted the faithful seclusion of her caverns,
the keepers of so many secrets; and I
reposed on the buoyancy of her tepid sea.*

WALTER SAVAGE LANDOR, *The Pentameron*

Truth hath a quiet breast.
SHAKESPEARE, *King Richard the Second*

❖

My book burst on a resentful world like a cotton wool
bomb. Indeed, it did not explode at all: it landed with a
soggy thump, spread a little way outward, and there
hardened its arteries against further expansion.
Duncannon's talked of a moderate success, and asked for
another 'in a more straightforward style': I received six
unsolicited letters (four scurrilous, two matrimonial) and
an anonymous complimentary ticket for The Wind and the
Rain; and the book's reviews were evenly divided between
deploring its lecturing tone, damning its impertinence, and
rendering its contents harmless by negligent and almost
evasive praise – a process one might call gilding the lily.

To Max, who wrote asking how it was getting on:

It is not getting on, [I wrote in return] it is flopping,
and probably deserves to. Sure it was a masterpiece –

but what are they? – here we throw them off like heavy colds. Of course I'm a little depressed, but there must be more in life than scribbling about its unessentials. The dogs bark, and bite off the caravan wheels: only the old piebald horse goes plodding on, looking for a worthier vehicle. Can you suggest one?

Actually I was working hard enough, with sufficient success, at other writing, not to mind pronouncing an epitaph on this effort of the past. I supposed that I had been attempting too much, or going about it the wrong way; and that the critics were right – as instruction the book was an impertinence, as a joke it failed.

Collapse of vicar, who thought it was Thursday.

❖

2

I ran into Julian Wingate unexpectedly in Oxford Street – I hadn't seen him for some months, since he was no longer on the paper. Looking lean and grim, he was gutter-walking in a line of a dozen other people carrying a poster-board slung over his shoulders. 'BOYCOTT JAPANESE GOODS' it said on one side: and on the other, 'TO BUY FROM JAPAN IS TO BOMB CHINESE BABIES'; automatically he had thrust a leaflet into my hands, and so intent was he that not until I called his name did he look up … He refused to step out of line and have a drink with me, but I met him later, for tea in a nearby café.

"You ought to have been with us today," he said, when he had ordered a fairly substantial meal. "It was a good parade, and we had a grand meeting after it, too."

"I haven't been to a meeting for years," I told him.

"I know. Lots of people have been asking about you, down at headquarters. What's the trouble?"

"I don't know. It doesn't seem to do any good, somehow. I mean, that parade of yours was pretty futile, don't you think? How many converts do you think you made, among that crowd of people who only wanted to shop and gape and think of their own troubles?"

He ate in silence for some moments. I wondered how many meals he had missed lately, how happy he really was among the discomforts and the makeshifts of Party work ... Presently he looked up.

"So you've slid back as far as that, have you?" His voice had an edge of bitterness. "You used to carry posters yourself, you know, and think yourself lucky to be able to help the cause. Do you think the fight's over?" His tone changed, cracking out in sudden stridency. "Wake up, Marcus, for God's sake! The fight's only just beginning. You ought to be back in the Party, and damned well you know it."

"Fight, fight, fight – I'm sick of the word. I'm for co-operation, I want a quiet life, instead of all this snarling and scrapping. In fact, I want to be Left in peace."

"A pernicious deviation," said Julian roughly. "You won't get peace, or Left politics either, without fighting for them every minute of your life." He sighed, looking on the instant immensely weary. "But at least, you *are* still Socialist?"

"I'm not even sure of that. Can there be one cure for all our ills? Isn't there room for anonymous goodwill?"

"Inside the Party, yes."

"Inside the Party, you seem to see nothing but your own reflection. Did you notice the *Daily Worker* poster a few days ago, the night after Mosley was knocked senseless by a stone at Liverpool? It said, simply: 'MORE FASCIST VIOLENCE' ... I'll vote the right way, and I'll help men that

I think are on the right lines; but I won't take people by the scruff of the neck and rub their noses in the true faith. You don't convert people that way: you just make them sore."

Julian sat back, with a smile. "I've never heard a bigger concentration of wrong-headedness than there was in your last few sentences; but I don't suppose it's any good explaining it in detail. Apart from politics, what are you doing with yourself nowadays?"

Welcoming his change of mood: "Well, I go to about three concerts a week," I told him, "and I'm beginning to enjoy ballet, even though, not being one of the backstage Haskell clique or a gallery homosexual, I'm outside the pale and like it for all the wrong reasons. I've just sold a scenario to Thunderbolt for two hundred and fifty pounds, I'm writing a play about a lunatic asylum, I talk to a great many people every day, and I make about four quid a week, freelancing."

"Success story," he commented. "No wonder you look so prosperous. How's the paper going?"

"Pretty well, I gather: I don't do much for it nowadays – I'm writing more for the *English Survey*. Do you ever take it?"

"No, we buy ours in rolls," he answered inelegantly.

"Ha!" I said, on a snarl, "The *anal-erotik* amuses you? ... It isn't such a bad paper, Julian; and Rackham's a good man to work for."

"He's a Fascist."

"He is *not*!" I said, stung by the contemptuous dismissal. "He's a liberal who doesn't like having a whip cracked over him, by you or Mosley or Stalin or anyone else. And he's the sort of chap who'll keep cultural tradition alive, while your gang are blood-bathing the opposition. You, at least, should see his value as an ally. Can't you use a man who knows as much about writing and music as he does?"

433

"We can use him if he does what he's told. Otherwise – well, we can still use him – to mop himself up with."

"There speaks the good Marxist."

"What do you expect me to say?" He tapped the paper which was lying on the table between us. "Here you have people being slaughtered in Spain, here you have hundreds of men and women being killed in China at this very moment – and you talk to me of keeping culture alive … You're in a dream, Marcus, a selfish dream: you're leaving other people to stay awake and protect the place you're sleeping in. Well, don't blame them if, when the time comes, they kill you as unfit or let you rot in your sleep."

On which note he left me, on his way to yet another meeting, while I sat on, staring at the headlines of the paper and wondering which of us was right. It was sad that we should be so far apart … The headlines, certainly, made horrible reading: there had indeed been an unimaginable slaughter in at least two crowded Chinese towns the previous night. What did such figures mean? 'Five thousand killed in air-raids' – 'Four hundred children in an orphanage killed by a single bomb' – they conveyed nothing except that one was living in an obscene madhouse. And even in England – I turned the page – even in England there were ferocious and unrelenting struggles.

For yesterday, I read, had been 'the evening of the hat party, which you may have heard about, when a group of women (among them Princess — and Mrs — and Mrs —), angry at being refused admission on another occasion because one of them had worn a hat with her evening dress, plotted together and, all very much behatted, took a conspicuous table and flaunted their hats in company.'

This was more like it … Apparently, I learnt as I read on, they had not found it easy to screw up their courage to the sticking-point: nobody had wanted to go in first, and for a good part of the evening half the sisterhood was driving round and round Leicester Square waiting for somebody else to take the lead. And inside, one of them had actually lost her nerve and taken her hat off – 'a little net cap swirling with birds of paradise that more than once disconcerted her neighbour by striking him in the eye'. But at any rate the thing caused a tremendous sensation, 'providing a subject of conversation at every table on the most crowded evening of the week. Prince and Princess — found, indeed, that the topic was not yet half exhausted when people went to their house for cocktails yesterday'.

I threw the paper aside, seeking relief from the infantile, the melancholy, the parochial. But opposite me at the table there was now another man, with a face even more vilely depressed than my own, reading a morning paper. I could not escape its back page, eight inches away from my eyes, nor the photograph of a girl which filled one corner of it, nor the printed caption underneath:

'Miss — , the English dancer,' it read, 'who is going to show Hollywood how to swing its hips. "I originated the slow snake-hips dance," she said on leaving, "and I challenge any white girl to swing her hips as far as I can." '

Quem deus vult perdere, prius dementat.

❖

3

Tania died in childbirth, fifteen hundred miles away in Athens, before the year was out. From her letters she had been immensely looking forward to the birth of her child; and I knew why, though she had never enlarged on the subject. The child was to be her escape from the indignity of her position, her second chance: it was to give her marriage, not the lineaments of decency, but its only possible justification: it was to redeem the cheating and the falsity of her bargain with Demetriades.

But the escape was not allowed to her.

> *'Brightness falls from the air,*
> *Queens have died young and fair,*
> *Dust hath closed Helen's eye –'*

Dust closed Tania's, in some agony of body and a merciful dullness of mind, when she was on the verge of quitting the shadows. It was difficult to relate this to any pattern of a Divine Will, even when characterized as 'inscrutable'.

❖

4

In the environment and the society in which we lived, our ménage excited not the smallest comment: the fact that Anthea and I were living together was taken for granted, and was made the excuse neither for giggling, spite, gossip, or the leer of confederacy. Our flat was visited by a very large number of people, not one of whom gave the fact of our 'living in sin' a second thought, except perhaps to envy us our happiness if their own were in default; and we could, without smugness, be glad of our good fortune in moving among such a set of people – painters, writers, journalists, musicians, all of whom practised their art and trade with diligence and often with distinction: adult Bohemians, one might have called them, with a social as well as a creative responsibility, and akin to the French in giving the impression that they had lived a long time for their age ... And if a man's attitude to sex is one measure of civilization, then they were highly civilized: they did not deride marriage, though for the most part they proclaimed its idealism and doubted its realization; but sex was to them as natural a phenomenon as walking and sleeping, and to be taken as much for granted, while love, in their view, needed no ritual sanction to make it either respectable or trustworthy.

This acceptance and normality set the seal on the happiness of Anthea and myself. After two years, we were just beginning to be good lovers, in the sense of absolute physical sympathy and the full flowering of instinct; and beyond that we could both see and feel, all the time, a deep and settled understanding upon which we could draw in time of need, without stinting ourselves. It meant that we would never part on a quarrel, because we were past that tradition; it meant a sort of fusion, knowing that however much we gave ourselves away, we wouldn't be cheated or laughed at or left in the cold. It meant being able to trust, because what one was trusting was part of oneself. It meant not being ashamed of tenderness, or surrender, or nakedness of any sort ... And yet, in some way for which she was almost wholly accountable, the excitement and the taut exhilaration had not gone out of our relationship: there were moments when we felt ourselves still to be romantics, still able to play Manon and Des Grieux as well as Darby and Joan ... So much so, indeed, that sometimes I wondered whether these lapses into intoxication were entirely becoming.

"Shouldn't we be settling down?" I asked her once, when some *jeu d'esprit* or other had demonstrated once more that we were not yet past an almost indecent stage of mutual exhilaration. "Are we really respectable? Shouldn't I be less in love and you a little more dowagerlike – a shade less round the chest and more round the hips? I've heard so much about marriage dropping into the humdrum category – "

"If we were married," she interrupted, "that's what it might do."

I waved my arm round the bedroom. "This is indistinguishable from marriage. An extra tie of that sort wouldn't make any difference to the way we felt. And I'm ready to prove that, any time."

"I know you are, darling." She stared at the ceiling. "Of course, there's one method of settling down, for good ... A child."

"So soon?"

"I'm thirty, Marco. That's a long gap already between the generations ... We haven't talked of this often, but it's been in my mind a good deal. Children to love and work for, children to correct our mistakes and make a better job of living than we've been able to – they'll give us another chance, an extension of our spirit ..."

"That means we get married, sometime soon, then." I glanced sideways at her. "I know you'd say that there's no compulsion, but after all there *is* nothing standing in the way, except a prejudice that I think we've both grown out of, and it *will* make things so much easier. I don't give a damn for illegitimacy, but the kid may, and a lot of people in his future certainly will. And apart from all this – "

"Well?"

"Being married won't tie you any more strongly than you're tied already, but I'll be able to think it will, if ever I'm depressed about us. I want to stake a claim ... Forget everything I said about that book last night" (we had been reading Henri de Montherlant's *Pitié pour les Femmes* together, and I had rounded it off with an arrogant and wholly misconceived little lecture on masculine superiority). "It doesn't make any difference how many women I could get if I lost you: a compensation of that sort simply can't be weighed in the same balance. I want to marry you, with the purely selfish motive of making sure of you in as many ways as possible."

"And for love?"

"And for love, which – " I paused and smiled. "If I called you my heart's delight, would you think I was only quoting Léhar?"

"You're very affectionate tonight," she said, in that tone of voice which bridged, for her, the mocking and the potentially fervent mood. "We must have baked apples again …"

It was good not to be alone any more.

❖

5

Austria went. Spain also. Czecho disappeared, sunk under sheer weight of guarantees. Albania suddenly wasn't there any more. Memel turned a different colour in the night.

"What's the good," Cummings wrote to me, "of crippling ourselves over armaments, or bringing in conscription, when we lose a friend or an ally or a strategic position every other weekend? One gets the impression of a Government simply not knowing which way its boots are pointing. And there are some things you can't gloss over, no matter how much money you pour on top of them: and one of them is refusing to stir hand or foot except from pure self-interest. We'll pay a fearful price for it one day. And dare one hint that collective security was a better idea than the self-seeking, the baseness, the intolerable tension of these days? And what happens when the supply of small countries runs out? So many questions …"

So many questions, indeed: and one must be careful not to foul one's own nest by asking them out loud. For there he was in command – Chamberlain, 'J'aime Berlin', the amateur of foreign affairs, the promoted alderman, the reputed autocrat with the hard business head. Presumably we were to wait, to suspend judgment and see what sort of job he made of his policy. If he were successful, well and good: if not – well, we would not be there to pass sentence: only the death-pits and the mangled towns would bare witness to the last kick of individualism; and the names of Chamberlain and his colleagues would (in the *New Statesman*'s phrase) 'echo down the centuries to the hate of a ruined world.'

If that would be any compensation.

6

I had been extremely busy with writing, and yet somehow convinced that I was wasting my time; and a chance visit from Dr Barrow was like the finger of reality, laying itself on the core of all the conflicting impulses and the conviction of futility which was never far away.

"You're looking well," he said, when he had recovered his breath after the stairs and was at ease in the deepest armchair. "Marriage must suit you, in spite of your sturdy declarations in the past ... Is Anthea in?"

"No. She won't be long, though. You seem pretty lively yourself."

But that was hardly true, I realized as I looked at his thin slumped body and lined face; he was older, and obviously tired, and I gathered from a stray word here and there that his work had been going badly. But he cheered up after a cup of tea, and we talked of men and affairs with something of the old vigour of the days at Miss Fleming's.

I was not able to convince him, however (any more than I could convince myself), that the work I was doing had much significance.

"But what are you going to *do*?" he asked suddenly, when I was outlining my writing plans for the next year – they included a cloak-and-sword novel and a series of television sketches which the BBC had commissioned. "You are making a success of writing, and you must be earning a great deal of money, but surely you don't regard that as the end – what Disraeli called 'the sweet simplicity of the three-per-cents' makes no very strong appeal to you, does it?"

"Writing's a job," I answered defensively, "and I'm in it for a living. If I can get the play produced, as seems likely, I'll be in a pretty strong position."

"You will have a most superior bank balance, certainly," he agreed. "That, however, is what you are doing for yourself: what about the rest of the world? Or is it your intention to mould your life on such Hedonistic lines – 'the fattest hog in Epicurus' sty'? You can contribute a great deal more than that – as I suspect you know," he added, with an upward glance from under wispy grey eyebrows.

"Of course I know. But how much time have I got? I'm working like a black as it is –"

"And you wish your work had more significance?" he broke in.

"Yes, I certainly do."

"You must have narrowed your interests, to concentrate on writing."

"Only in politics," I answered. "I've given up there altogether – I'm just watching, like a lot of other people."

"You dislike their trend?"

"I don't like the friends we're making. We're a democracy, on paper: why we have to go cap-in-hand to every thug in Europe is beyond my comprehension.

Appeasement? They called it toadying to bullies in my day."

Dr Barrow nodded his agreement. "It is a sign of the times that we can no longer choose our friends by their quality."

And that was true, I realized: the hunt – for allies – was up, and strength and ferocity were their own credentials ... The world, or at least our corner of it, was slipping back, back to the rule of the louts and sergeant-majors, of the power-maniacs and the dirty lunatic children: fit leaders, indeed, for a western civilization compounded equally of force and fraud. Christianity might have stood out against the stream, but it was clear that in this country at least it would never rise above doing the Lambeth Walk with pious adroitness, and would end by backing the guns, blessing the flags, and preaching pie-in-the-sky-when-you-die ...

"It is indeed monstrous," the doctor broke in on my thoughts, "that we should be back again under the shadow of war. Europe is tiny – smaller than India: why must we perpetuate these miserable little tribal squabbles?" He sighed. "The new technique of thinking with the blood is sounding the defeat of reason. I do not wonder that you have turned from its contemplation. But politics from the internal standpoint no longer interest you? You would not work even for a modified form of Communism, or something akin to it?"

"I'm not sure – I don't think so." That was perhaps an answer dictated by the mood I was in; but among other elements of persuasion, André Gide's *Back from the USSR* had had a depressing effect – since the plea that the individual must not drown in uniformity was for me strongest of all, outweighing any argument concerned with expedience or immediate public security. "All those creeds seem to rely on compulsion; and what does a rule of force breed, except more force keyed to a pitch of brutality which has to be answered itself?"

He nodded vigorously. "There we are in complete agreement. No state of balance can be thus achieved. You had an inkling of that in Spain, did you not? – and a reading of history will tell you the same thing. You cannot regiment human beings with any hope of lasting order: it can only come by agreement, and this in turn must be the product of a change of heart. And even that –" he smiled dryly, "even that errs on the side of emotion. It will not come that way: it will come when men grasp with their brains how to arrive where they want to be."

"But a reading of history," I broke in, "is still uncertain. There is bias in the way it's presented, as well as in personal interpretation."

"It still lies with us to learn from the past," he answered slowly. "Search it, examine it, not with fervour but with reason and insight. And *then* to your teaching; and if you require a rule – 'Resist not evil, but overcome evil with good' can hardly be bettered."

"And my own part at this moment?" I asked, feeling ineffectual.

"That you must determine for yourself. But remember that you cannot contract out of society, and remember also that a small beginning is not to be disdained: a beginning, indeed, must be made with the individual, since it is from that individual, through the community, the state, and finally the human race, that progress towards the comity of mankind must be traced." He sat back, an old man at ease, but his voice came strong and unfaltering. "Achieve stability and balance, internally first: set your own house in order; for without this – without a social code which ensures justice and equality, and a nation united in the conviction that such is their possession – without this, you will not be equipped, *nor entitled*, to attack the larger problem of world co-operation."

❖

7

What was I going to *do*? Dr Barrow had posed a question which I could not answer. But three days afterwards it was answered for me, with persuasiveness, with precision, with complete authority, by a letter from Max Brennan.

I can remember that moment exactly. It was early evening, and I was tired: we had been to Glyndebourne the night before, for a performance of 'Die Zauberflöte' such as enriched the eye and ear with a cargo that was in truth magic. Anthea was out shopping, and I had a record on the gramophone, an oddly sympathetic little record, a movement from a concerto of Litolf, with Irene Scharrer producing its cascades of brilliant irrelevancies as if she had a concert-grand up either sleeve. Just as it finished, a letter slid through the flap of the front door and flopped on to the mat. Recognizing the writing, I opened it in pleasant anticipation: I had not seen Max for a considerable time, and then only for a hurried exchange of greetings.

It was a long letter. It read:

DEAR MARCUS, – That was a good wedding of yours, and we both enjoyed it. I hope the formal honeymoon was as good. But that isn't what I want to write to you about.

Do you remember, a very long time ago, talking to us here on the lawn about my land, and the best use to be made of it? I haven't said anything to you about it since, not even when you were staying here with

Anthea; but it's not too much to say that I've been thinking of that conversation ever since. And now I've evolved a plan. It's still vague, but here is the outline.

I know that the focus of attention is on foreign affairs at the moment, and is likely to be so for a very long time to come. But that hasn't altered affairs inside this country: there is still poverty and wretchedness, and over a million and a half unemployed, and a huge amount of preventable distress which, it seems, is being ignored. Let's make a start on that: let's try not to think of the possibility of war, and pay attention to something nearer home and more curable.

I want to start some kind of settlement down here, on a farming basis, allied possibly with a small bacon factory and a fruit-canning plant: a sort of trading estate on co-operative lines, with a complete social life of its own. (You see how vague the plan still is; but I have plenty of ideas, as I imagine you will have.) I intend to house the people in cottages, but create also a community life and a full one. I know it's a tiny beginning to a huge problem; but the example might spread, and at least it is a beginning.

I am building up a team to run it: already I have a doctor friend interested, and a woman-magistrate from one of the children's courts in London, and a man who has farmed in Russia. I want you and Anthea to join us – it will occur to you what contribution you can make; and I would also like Tim and Elisabeth – he's just the right kind of tough man to oversee what I might call the physical section, and she can concentrate on music, which will certainly not be forgotten. (And all our children can grow up together: the second generation of the community will be far more important than the first!) The rest – mechanics, labourers, clerks, engineers, experts of all kinds – we can get through the Labour Exchange (who have already been helpful with suggestions).

That's all I'll write about it, at the moment. Think it over – or better still, come down here and listen to us talking, and talk yourself, and let's see if we can't make a start. It's not to be cranky or priggish, it's no closed system, it's not living in the woods in a hand-woven smock; it's an attempt to relieve distress where distress has arisen, instead of telling people to work for the revolution and in the meantime leaving them to shiver. You are still pacifist, I suppose? Looking round me sometimes, I don't blame you. But pacifism isn't the last word. Come down here and make one corner of the world worth fighting for.

MAX

❖

8

That was it, I thought, folding the letter up again: that was at last something in the line of constructive sanity, that was Dr Barrow's 'small beginning,' exactly ... And as I waited for Anthea, I took hold of Max's idea at the point where he had left off, and made it my own, my thoughts racing through the possibilities, seeing a future opening up of almost limitless potentiality: stray words, stray ideas, stray elaborations presented themselves in quick succession, all co-ordinated to this one purpose of making a start in something I could really believe in.

A community. Communism in practice. A community bound together by the acknowledged need to help each other as well as themselves. And not only farming, not only work on the canning plant and the bacon factory (with the profits shared, and with wages perhaps partly paid with our own produce – butter, milk, fruit, vegetables, bread): but a complete social centre. Handicrafts, special training, equipment for various hobbies: cricket and football teams to play other villages. And lots more things: group discussions and listening to the wireless, our own theatre and cinema and concert hall. (Get good players down, and perform ourselves as well.) Our own school, even, if that were allowed by authority: that second generation would certainly be important ... *If only we could be left in peace* ... For here *was* the plan I had wanted, the one I had been shaping towards: to help the needy, the cramped, the futureless; to quicken and enlarge their interests: to take care of everything, of their physique as well as their minds, in the sense not of drilling things in but of opening up possibilities to people who knew nothing of how full life could be. Let them breathe again, let them begin to laugh: let them have a chance, where no chance was before ...

Yes, it might be called Communism. Or anarchy. Or brotherhood. But why give it a name, why assign a label or a colour or a shirt? The wisest of men had summed it up as 'cultivating one's garden'. It was a spirit of order: it was co-operation-plus: it was something in the heart, to be planted there by one man and nursed by his fellow.

Anthea came in, with some parcels and a bunch of white carnations: she stopped on the threshold and looked at me over the flowers, which her dark hair rendered dazzlingly bright. I had thought that I would find ugliness in her pregnancy, but this had never been so. And now she was smiling, she was lovely with a glowing loveliness, she was, by agreement, mine ...

"You've got a secret," she said after a moment. "You look as smug as I'm feeling at this moment. Tell me."

"Gladly … The secret," I said, kissing her, "is that your child will be born in Gloucestershire, in a rather strange community which I will now proceed to describe."

❖

9

The trouble with writing an *envoi* nowadays is that history promptly overtakes it and tips it, looking mighty silly, into history's own ditch. I had thought – we all thought – that we could now set to work on the task which Max had put in our path and which seemed to commend itself as necessary, urgent, and concerned with hope. But, as you know, history caught us up, before we were well started.

My story, then, ends as-it-were with its head in the air. It is the record of what many young men in England thought and experienced during the latter half of the vanished thirties. War stultified whatever point of decision or stage of endeavour they had reached; war suspended their further education. But they are not whining, because there is no cause to. At the end of the war – *through* the war – will emerge new ideals and new chances to implement them: there will be a brand new stage on which to build a brand-new ethic and a brand new system, on which to enthrone reason and justice. The young men know its essentials already: for many of them, that is why they are fighting.

I said 'head in the air'. Whatever happens, that will be the keynote, for both the near and far future.

NICHOLAS MONSARRAT

THE PILLOW FIGHT

Passion, conflict and infidelity are vividly depicted in this gripping tale of two people and their marriage. Set against the glittering background of glamorous high life in South Africa, New York and Barbados, an idealistic young writer tastes the corrupting fruits of success, while his beautiful, ambitious wife begins to doubt her former values. A complete reversal of their opposing beliefs forms the bedrock of unremitting conflict. Can their passion survive the coming storm ...?

'Immensely readable ... an eminently satisfying book'
Irish Times

'A professional who gives us our money's worth. The entertainment value is high'
Daily Telegraph

SMITH AND JONES

Within the precarious conditions of the Cold War, diplomats Smith and Jones are not to be trusted. But although their files demonstrate evidence of numerous indiscretions and drunkenness, they have friends in high places who ensure that this doesn't count against them, and they are sent across the Iron Curtain.

However, when they defect, the threat of absolute treachery means that immediate and effective action has to be taken. At all costs and by whatever means, Smith and Jones must be silenced.

'An exciting and intriguing story'
Daily Express

'In this fast-moving Secret Service story Nicholas Monsarrat has brought off a neat tour de force with a moral'
Yorkshire Post

Nicholas Monsarrat

The Time Before This

On the icy slopes of the great ice-mountain of Bylot Island, set against the metallic blue of the Canadian Arctic sky, Shepherd has a vision of the world as it used to be, before the human race was weakened by stupidity and greed.

Peter Benton, the young journalist to whom Shepherd tells his story, is dramatically snapped out of his cosy cynicism and indolent denial of responsibility, to face a dreadful reality. He discovers that he can no longer take a back-seat in the rapid self-destruction of the world, and is forced to make a momentous decision.

'In his wry and timely novel Monsarrat unfolds a tremendous theme with gripping excitement' Edna O'Brien
Daily Express

The White Rajah

The breathtaking island of Makassang, in the Java Sea, is the setting for this tremendous historical novel. It is a place both splendid and savage, where piracy, plundering and barbarism are rife.

The ageing Rajah, threatened by native rebellion, enlists the help of Richard Marriott – baronet's son-turned-buccaneer – promising him a fortune to save his throne. But when Richard falls in love with the Rajah's beautiful daughter, the island, and its people, he find himself drawn into a personal quest to restore peace and prosperity.

'A fine swashbuckler by an accomplished storyteller'
New York Post

Nicholas Monsarrat

The Tribe That Lost Its Head

Five hundred miles off the southwest coast of Africa lies the island of Pharamaul, a British Protectorate, governed from Whitehall through a handful of devoted British civilians. In the south of the island lies Port Victoria, dominated by the Governor's palatial mansion; in the north, a settlement of mud huts shelter a hundred thousand natives; and in dense jungle live the notorious Maula tribe, kept under surveillance by a solitary District Officer and his young wife. When Chief-designate, Dinamaula, returns from his studies in England with a spirited desire to speed the development of his people, political crisis erupts into a ferment of intrigue and violence.

'A splendidly exciting story'
Sunday Times

Richer Than All His Tribe

The sequel to *The Tribe That Lost Its Head* is a compelling story which charts the steady drift of a young African nation towards bankruptcy, chaos and barbarism.

On the island of Pharamaul, a former British Protectorate, newly installed Prime Minister, Chief Dinamaula, celebrates Independence Day with his people, full of high hopes for the future.

But the heady euphoria fades and Dinamaula's ambitions and ideals start to buckle as his new found wealth corrupts him, leaving his nation to spiral towards hellish upheaval and tribal warfare.

'Not so much a novel, more a slab of dynamite'
Sunday Mirror

OTHER TITLES BY NICHOLAS MONSARRAT AVAILABLE DIRECT FROM HOUSE OF STRATUS

Quantity		£	$(US)	$(CAN)	€
☐	A Fair Day's Work	6.99	11.50	15.99	11.50
☐	HMS Marlborough Will	6.99	11.50	15.99	11.50
	Enter Harbour	6.99	11.50	15.99	11.50
☐	Life is a Four-Letter Word	6.99	11.50	15.99	11.50
☐	The Master Mariner	6.99	11.50	15.99	11.50
☐	The Nylon Pirates	6.99	11.50	15.99	11.50
☐	The Pillow Fight	6.99	11.50	15.99	11.50
☐	Richer Than All His Tribe	6.99	11.50	15.99	11.50
☐	Smith and Jones	6.99	11.50	15.99	11.50
☐	Something to Hide	6.99	11.50	15.99	11.50
☐	The Story of Esther Costello	6.99	11.50	15.99	11.50
☐	The Time Before This	6.99	11.50	15.99	11.50
☐	The Tribe That Lost Its Head	6.99	11.50	15.99	11.50
☐	The White Rajah	6.99	11.50	15.99	11.50

ALL HOUSE OF STRATUS BOOKS ARE AVAILABLE FROM GOOD BOOKSHOPS OR DIRECT FROM THE PUBLISHER:

Internet: www.houseofstratus.com including author interviews, reviews, features.

Email: sales@houseofstratus.com please quote author, title, and credit card details.

Hotline: UK ONLY: 0800 169 1780, please quote author, title and credit card details.
INTERNATIONAL: +44 (0) 20 7494 6400, please quote author, title, and credit card details.

Send to: **House of Stratus**
24c Old Burlington Street
London
W1X 1RL
UK

Please allow following carriage costs per ORDER
(For goods up to free carriage limits shown)

	£(Sterling)	$(US)	$(CAN)	€(Euros)
UK	1.95	3.20	4.29	3.00
Europe	2.95	4.99	6.49	5.00
North America	2.95	4.99	6.49	5.00
Rest of World	2.95	5.99	7.75	6.00
Free carriage for goods value over:	50	75	100	75

PLEASE SEND CHEQUE, POSTAL ORDER (STERLING ONLY), EUROCHEQUE, OR
INTERNATIONAL MONEY ORDER (PLEASE CIRCLE METHOD OF PAYMENT YOU WISH TO USE)
MAKE PAYABLE TO: STRATUS HOLDINGS plc

Order total including postage:_____Please tick currency you wish to use and add total amount of order:

☐ £ (Sterling)   ☐ $ (US)   ☐ $ (CAN)   ☐ € (EUROS)

VISA, MASTERCARD, SWITCH, AMEX, SOLO, JCB:

☐☐☐☐☐☐☐☐☐☐☐☐☐☐☐☐☐☐☐

Issue number (Switch only):

☐☐☐

Start Date: ☐☐/☐☐   **Expiry Date:** ☐☐/☐☐

Signature: _____

NAME: _____

ADDRESS: _____

_____

POSTCODE: _____

Please allow 28 days for delivery.

Prices subject to change without notice.
Please tick box if you do not wish to receive any additional information. ☐

House of Stratus publishes many other titles in this genre; please check our website (**www.houseofstratus.com**) for more details